ROOM FOR HOPE

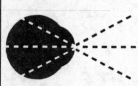

ROOM FOR HOPE

KIM VOGEL SAWYER

THORNDIKE PRESS
A part of Gale, Cengage Learning

GALE
CENGAGE Learning·

Farmington Hills, Mich • San Francisco • New York • Waterville, Maine
Meriden, Conn • Mason, Ohio • Chicago

GALE
CENGAGE Learning®

Copyright © 2016 by Kim Vogel Sawyer.
All Scripture quotations or paraphrases are taken from the King James Version.
Thorndike Press, a part of Gale, Cengage Learning.

LIBRARY OF CONGRESS CATALOGING-IN-PUBLICATION DATA

Names: Sawyer, Kim Vogel, author.
Title: Room for hope / by Kim Vogel Sawyer.
Description: Large print edition. | Waterville, Maine : Thorndike Press, 2016. | © 2016 | Series: Thorndike Press large print Christian romance
Identifiers: LCCN 2015048971| ISBN 9781410487025 (hardcover) | ISBN 1410487024 (hardcover)
Subjects: LCSH: Large type books. | GSAFD: Christian fiction.
Classification: LCC PS3619.A97 R66 2016b | DDC 813/.6—dc23
LC record available at http://lccn.loc.gov/2015048971

Published in 2016 by arrangement with WaterBrook Press, an imprint of the Crown Publishing Group, a division of Penguin Random House LLC

Printed in Mexico
1 2 3 4 5 6 7 20 19 18 17 16

For my quiverful of granddarlings —
Alana, Connor, Ethan, Logan,
Rylin, Jacob, Cole,
Adrianna, Kaisyn, and Kendall —
with prayers that you find
the strength to stand for right
by leaning on the Father

He giveth power to the faint; and to them that have no might he increaseth strength.

ISAIAH 40:29

CHAPTER 1

Buffalo Creek, Kansas
September 30, 1936

Neva Gaines Shilling

Aromatic steam wisped around Neva's chin as she spooned up a bit of broth from the savory vegetable stew simmering on the Magic Chef range. She blew on the spoonful — three careful puffs of breath — then poured the broth into her mouth and held the warm liquid on her tongue for a moment before she swallowed. She gave a nod. Perfect. The beef bone had flavored the soup so well Warren might not even notice the absence of meat.

A light *clack-clack* carried from the adjoining dining room. Silverware meeting the walnut tabletop. She settled the lid on the kettle, turned down the flame under the pot to a wavering rim of blue, and called through the kitchen doorway to the dining room, "Belle, remember to set four places. Your father's due home tonight."

Neva's heart gave a joyful skip even as melancholy threatened. The days stretched so long and lonely during Warren's away weeks and seemed to race by when he was home. But weren't they blessed to own a successful business given the country's economic troubles? She shouldn't complain.

"Oh, goodie!" Belle's exclamation, accompanied by a girlish giggle, made her sound much younger than her fourteen years. "Will he bring presents, do you think?"

Neva released a short chuckle. "Doesn't he always bring presents?" Elaborate gifts — gifts that made the women in town look at her with longing and envy. But she always told them she'd be satisfied just to have her husband home every night, under her roof, instead of traipsing across Mitchell County in his gaily painted sales wagon. She meant it, too.

Belle peeked around the corner. "Should I set out the good plates then?"

They only used the good plates — a matching set of French Haviland china with delicate clovers of freshest green painted around the edges of the pure white dishware — for special occasions. But Warren's return after a month on the road was reason enough for celebration.

"Yes," Neva said, then frowned. "Mind you don't chip the plates."

"Of course not, Momma." The girl slipped away.

Neva crossed to the Frigidaire in the corner, the soles of her brown oxfords squeaking on the sparkling clean linoleum, and peeked into the glazed ceramic pitcher shaped like a little Dutch girl. Still half-full of milk, more than enough for their supper. Thank goodness Bud hadn't drained the pitcher dry the way he'd been doing lately.

She shook her head in indulgence as she thought about her son's voracious appetite. He must be entering a growth spurt. Would he be as tall as his father someday? Everyone said the twins resembled their mother, with slender builds, wavy nutmeg hair, hazel eyes, and narrow faces. Having Belle resemble her was fine, but she wouldn't mind if Bud grew to be as tall and broad-shouldered as Warren. Such a handsome man, her Warren.

Hurry home, dear. I miss you . . .

She plucked out a bowl of butter and a fat jar of raspberry preserves from the icebox and glanced at the green-and-cream enamel clock ticking on the kitchen's floral-papered

11

wall. Almost seven. Bud would finish sweeping and straightening the store soon, and then — her pulse gave a flutter — Warren's wagon would rattle up the alley. She hoped he wouldn't be late.

The biscuits were done and waiting in the stove's warming oven. As much as she loved the luxury of her six-burner, double-oven range — a Christmas gift from Warren last year — she'd learned the warming oven sometimes browned bread beyond recognition. Warren liked his biscuits feather light, not as firm as charcoal briquettes. And Neva always strove to please her husband in the little things. It was the least she could do, considering how she'd failed him in the biggest thing of all.

Belle breezed into the kitchen. "Momma —"

Bud, with a match caught in the corner of his mouth and wearing one of Warren's castoff straw hats shadowing his eyes, thumped in on his sister's heels. "Ma —"

Neva burst out laughing. "You two . . ." They'd come into the world nearly on top of each other and fourteen years later still operated in synchronization. As she always did, Neva turned to Belle. "Ladies first."

Bud scowled and folded his arms over his chest but kept his lips pressed together.

12

"The table's all set with the good dishes and linen napkins. Should I use the candlesticks, too?" Her green-gray eyes sparkled. "It would be . . ." Belle hunched her shoulders and giggled. "Romantic."

Bud rolled his eyes. " 'Romantic,' she says. Been spending too many nickels at the picture show."

Neva frowned at her son, but inwardly she agreed. Belle did tend to squander her weekly allowance at the movie theater. The picture shows, while entertaining, rarely depicted life as it was in reality. Belle was so naive, so trusting. The bigger-than-life images on the screen might be detrimental to her. Neva intended to discuss the issue with Warren. She answered Belle. "The candles will let us save on the gaslights. So go ahead and set them out."

Belle scurried off, her patent slippers pattering against the gleaming floorboards and her thick braid flopping against her spine.

"My turn now?"

Bud's wry question pulled Neva's attention to her son. "Yes." She moved to the stove and picked up the wooden spoon, ready to give the thick stew another stir. If the bottom scorched, it would ruin the whole pot.

He pushed the hat to the back of his head,

stuffed his hands into the pockets of his trousers, and scuffed across the floor toward her, his sauntering gait similar to Hopalong Cassidy's. Neva swallowed a smile. Bud enjoyed the picture shows, too. "Just wanted you to know I found the place where that mouse's been gettin' in. Plugged it with a wad of steel wool. He won't be chewing through any more cornmeal sacks."

Neva clapped the lid into place and beamed at Bud. "What a relief!" Thanks to the little pest's intrusion, they'd had to discard three twenty-pound sacks of finely ground meal — a sizable loss. "Your father will be so pleased."

Pink splashed Bud's face. "Think so?"

Smiling at him, Neva wiped her hands on her apron and then gripped his upper arms. "Of course! He's always proud when you take care of things in the store."

He shrugged. "Figuring out where a mouse came in isn't so much."

She removed the match from his mouth and gave his chin a bump with her knuckles. "Such a thing to say. It's a big thing, Bud — something a shopkeeper does to protect his goods. Just wait. Your father will tell you how important it was when he gets home."

A rare, slow grin climbed Bud's cheek.

"Now go get washed up. We'll eat as soon

as —" The clatter of a wagon's wheels carried from the alley through the open kitchen window. A smile captured Neva's face, bringing a light laugh of pure joy with it. She dropped the match into the little metal holder on the windowsill and waved her hands at Bud. "That must be your father now. Get Belle, and we'll go welcome him home."

Neva followed Belle, Bud close behind, down the enclosed staircase to the store level and then up the hallway leading to the back door. Belle came to a sudden halt, and Neva had to grab the wall to keep from plowing into her daughter's back. "Belle!"

Belle whirled, disappointment tingeing her features. "It's not Poppa."

Frowning, Neva peered through the square glass window. An unfamiliar wagon piled high with various furniture pieces and crates sat in the yard.

Bud stared out and released a soft snort. "Looks like another drifter wanting to trade for supplies." He straightened his shoulders and puffed out his chest. "Want me to handle it, Ma?"

"No, no." The ruddy, big-boned man sitting on the wagon seat probably wouldn't respond well to a smooth-faced youth telling him they weren't interested in a trade.

15

She gave Belle a little nudge toward Bud. "You two go up. Wash your hands, Bud — and Belle, keep the stew from scorching. I'll take care of the customer."

The pair trooped toward the staircase, and Neva stepped into the yard. The early-evening sun hovered above the horizon, casting long shadows over the wagon and its driver, but two lanterns hung from hooks at the front corners of the high-sided bed and sent a soft glow over the contents. Neva had been a shopkeeper long enough to recognize quality when she saw it. This man must have had a flourishing business at some time to afford such nice things. But no matter. Warren insisted on cash only for strangers to Buffalo Creek — no credit and no trades. Even when Warren was away, she honored her husband's preference.

She steeled herself to deny the man's request as she crossed to the edge of the wagon. "Good evening. May I help you?"

The man whipped off his cowboy-style hat and ran his hand through his thick, dark hair. "I hope so, ma'am. My name's Jesse Caudel. I'm looking for Neva Gaines."

She hadn't been called Neva Gaines since she said "I do" to Warren more than fifteen years ago. But she wove her fingers together and nodded. "You've found her then."

16

Mr. Caudel blew out a breath that held both relief and resignation. He left his hat on the wagon seat and slowly climbed down. Then he stood before her, feet widespread and hands resting at his waist. A silver star glinted on his left patch pocket. Not a drifter, but a law official. Worry began a wild dance in her stomach.

"Ma'am, I'm sorry to be the bearer of bad news, but I have to tell you your brother and his missus passed away last week."

Neva drew back. Brother? She didn't have a brother. Or did she? She'd been told by the orphanage directors — a warm, wonderful couple she called Pa and Ma Jonnson — that she was an only child. But maybe they hadn't known she had a brother. Or maybe she was the wrong Neva Gaines.

She sought a way to ask for more information without sounding as befuddled as she felt. "I . . . um . . ." Heat rose in her face.

Apparently the officer took pity on her, because his lips curved into a sad smile. "I know you're probably plenty shocked."

Bewilderment rather than shock plagued her, but she nodded anyway.

"They succumbed to botulism. It went pretty quick, so they didn't suffer overmuch."

Neva shuddered. Even though she didn't

know the people, she wouldn't wish such an unpleasant passing on anyone. If they couldn't be cured, she thanked God they hadn't lingered.

Mr. Caudel went on, his tone low and compassionate. "His missus went first. When your brother knew he'd be joining her soon, he gave instruction for word to be sent to you, along with all his worldly possessions. Well . . ." He lowered his head, scuffing the toe of his boot in the dirt. "At least the possessions that weren't sold to cover his debt. Sheriff's officials auctioned his store building in Beloit, his stock, and some of the furniture from his house. Even so, there was quite a bit left." He gestured to the wagon.

Neva glanced across the wagon's contents again. So the man wasn't trading, he was delivering. From a deceased brother she didn't even know she had. She turned a puzzled look on him. "Are you sure this is meant to come to me?"

He pulled a folded sheet of paper from his shirt pocket and held it out. "This says 'Deliver to Neva Gaines at Main Street Mercantile, Buffalo Creek, Kansas.' Is there another Main Street Mercantile in Buffalo Creek run by Neva Gaines?"

"N-no. Then . . . it's true." She needed to

18

learn more about her brother who knew about her but had never made himself known to her. That could come later, when Warren was home. In the meantime where would she put everything? Their apartment above the store was already well furnished thanks to Warren's extravagance, their barn barely accommodated Warren's merchant wagon and horse, and they didn't have room in the store for big items like bureaus and bedsteads. She stood speechless.

The man jammed the paper back into his pocket. "I'm sorry you didn't know about your brother and sister-in-law's service. For some reason he didn't want you notified about the burial. But I can tell you most of the town showed up. The headstone carver even donated the stones for their graves. That's how much everybody liked the Shillings."

She shot him a startled look. "His name wasn't Gaines?"

"No, ma'am. Shilling — Warren Shilling and his wife, Violet."

"Warren and his . . ." Neva's knees buckled.

"Whoa there!" Mr. Caudel caught her before she crumpled to the ground. He slipped his arm around her waist and guided her toward the back stoop. His hold on her could be considered brazen, but his firm, strong arm was too needed for her to protest the familiarity.

He eased her onto the little bench sitting next to the water pump and then hunkered in front of her. "Guess the meaning of it all finally caught up to you, huh? Do you need a drink?"

Their sweet well water couldn't wash away the terrible pictures forming in her mind. "You said . . . Warren. Warren and . . ." She closed her eyes. *Dear Lord, this is a nightmare.* Warren — her Warren! — had another wife? And now he was dead? Bile rose in her throat. How would she tell Bud and Belle? What would she tell them? She couldn't divulge the awful truth!

She gulped. "My b-brother — Warren — he had a store in Beloit?"

The man remained crouched in front of her knees, his hands braced on either side of her hips as if ready to grab her if she toppled. "A nice one, right on the main street. And he also did some traveling in a merchant wagon." He grimaced. "I kinda forgot. The merchant wagon and horse got sold, too. That wagon over yonder belongs to a liveryman from Beloit."

She shifted her gaze to the wagon. Dusk had fallen, and from this angle the large

20

wooden conveyance resembled a slumbering beast with yellow glowing eyes. She shivered.

Very slowly the man pushed to his feet but stayed close. He flicked a look left and right. "I'm not meaning to be unkind, but could you fetch your husband? I need to get this wagon unloaded and back to Beloit tonight if possible. I won't be able to empty it by myself."

Fetch her husband? Neva swallowed a hysterical laugh. She formed a sentence that pained her worse than anything ever had, even childbirth or having her womb removed from her body. "I'm a widow."

"Oh." Great consternation filled the simple utterance. He scratched his chin, eyeing the wagon. "Then you probably can't . . ."

She tipped her head to look at him. Her head might have been filled with sand. Such effort it took to force her gaze upward. "No, I can't unload the wagon." Wild sobs pressed for release, but she pushed them down. She didn't want any of the things Warren and his wife had left behind.

Mr. Caudel turned a frown on her. "Ma'am, how well did you know this brother of yours?"

Anguish twined through her. "Not well." She clutched her stomach, nausea attacking. "Not well at all."

He nodded, the movement slow, as if his head were weighted, too. For several seconds he stared at her, unblinking, his full lips set in a solemn line. Then he crooked a finger at her. "Can you c'mere? There's something . . . important . . . in the wagon you need to see."

The hesitant way Mr. Caudel said "important" stirred Neva's numb brain to life. She rose on quivering legs and scuffed across the yard beside him. He plucked one of the lanterns free of its hook and carried it to the rear of the wagon. Then he paused with one hand braced on the high gate, his expression grim.

"Ma'am, your brother gave instructions to send you his belongings, but also his —" He clamped his lips tight and grimaced. "Well, let's just let you see, huh?"

Neva stood unmoving while he set the lantern on the ground, unhooked the iron pins holding the gate in place, and eased the thick, unpainted wood gate downward. Heavy shadows turned everything in the wagon's bed to gray lumps. He lifted the lantern. Its golden light illuminated the lumps, and Neva clapped her hands over her mouth to muffle her gasp. There, nestled together on a folded feather mattress like puppies in a litter, three children — a boy and two little pigtailed girls — sat staring with wide, uncertain eyes.

Mr. Caudel spoke softly, almost singsong, the way someone might try to calm a frightened animal. "This is Charley, Cassie, and Adeline Shilling — Warren and Violet's youngsters. Warren said to take them to Aunt Neva. I guess that's you."

CHAPTER 2

Neva

The children stayed so still and quiet, Neva thought they might be carved from stone. But statues didn't blink. Or shed tears. The littlest girl's cheeks shone with fresh silver trails, but she didn't make a sound. Despite the shock and revulsion rolling through her, Neva couldn't deny a twinge of compassion. They looked so lost. The way she felt. She turned away from their sad, seeking eyes.

Mr. Caudel set the lantern on the ground again, sending the children back into shadows. "Your brother must not've known you were a widow woman."

Like a prairie fire stirred by the Kansas wind, anger blazed through her. Of course he'd known! What had Warren been thinking to send these children to her? As quickly as it rose, her rage fizzled beneath the cold splash of guilt. If she'd been able to give

him what he wanted most — a big family
— he wouldn't have lain with another
woman.

She glanced at Mr. Caudel — did he sense
her deep shame? — but he was staring up
at the apartment over the store. Neva lifted
her gaze, too. Bud and Belle stood framed
behind the square glass window above the
kitchen sink, their curious faces peering
down at her.

Pain threatened to collapse her chest. *Oh,
my dear son and daughter, how I wish I could
protect you from your mother's failure.*

Mr. Caudel continued, his face still aimed
at the kitchen window. "If he'd known, he
wouldn't have expected you to take these
children in. Three youngsters, all at once,
when you've already got some of your own?"

A hopeful thought fluttered through Neva's head. Maybe there was a way to protect
Bud and Belle. She blurted, "Take them to
Violet's family." Surely Warren hadn't married another product of the orphanages,
someone all alone the way both he and
Neva had been before they found each
other.

Mr. Caudel shook his head. "Both of Mrs.
Shilling's brothers died of influenza when
they were still boys. All that's left of her
family is a widowed mother who's in poor

25

health. The woman isn't up to taking on three children either. She cried some, but she told the sheriff it was better if the children came to you."

Better for whom? Warren must have been wild with fever when he'd given instruction to bring those children to her.

Mr. Caudel leaned toward the trio of pale, sad faces. "Watch your toes now. I'm closing the hatch." The boy pulled his sisters close, and the little girls burrowed into their brother's coat front as Mr. Caudel fastened the gate. "I'll take them back to Beloit. The sheriff can arrange to send them on the train to an orphans' home."

Neva stared at the wood planks, seeing instead the hopeless expression on the boy's face. Her stomach spun, and she planted both palms against her apron, pressing hard.

Mr. Caudel picked up the lantern and offered her a sheepish half smile. "Don't feel bad about not being able to keep your nephew and nieces. 'Specially since it's pretty clear to me you never even met these kids before today. Besides that, you're hardly the only one making use of the state's homes for orphans. With so many people out of work, lots of folks are handing over their kids for someone else to clothe and feed. So don't you worry one bit, Mrs.

Gaines. Violet's mother will understand, and I'd wager even Warren and Violet wouldn't hold it against you."

Warren's voice echoed from the past. *"Don't take on so about not having more children, Neva. Even the doc says it's not your fault. I don't hold it against you."* But he must have. How else could she explain the presence of Charley, Cassie, and Adeline?

Mr. Caudel, the lantern swinging from his hand and making shadows dance, started for the front of the wagon.

"Mister?"

The quavering voice carrying over the edge of the wagon halted the man. He angled his head toward the bed. "Yeah, Charley? What'cha need?"

"Adeline needs the toilet."

Mr. Caudel, grimacing, looked at Neva. "Do you mind?"

Did he really think she would deny a small child the chance to relieve herself? "Of course not."

He glanced across the gray yard. "Where's the outhouse?"

Warren tore down the outhouse the day after their water closet was installed. "We have indoor plumbing. Bring her on inside." Then, without thinking, she added, "Why don't you all come in. It's past suppertime.

Have the children eaten?"

"No, but I can give them some of the jerked beef and saltines I packed for the ride over here."

Such an unpleasant offering for small children. If she was going to send them off to an orphanage, she could at least feed them a decent meal first. "Save your beef and crackers. Share our supper instead."

His thick, dark brows descended. "Are you sure? There's four of us, you know."

She forced her stiff lips into a smile. "That's fine. The food's not fancy — vegetable stew and biscuits — but there's plenty."

"Mister!"

The frantic cry seemed to prod Mr. Caudel into action. "Coming, Charley." He glanced at Neva while he unlatched the gate. "Thank you, Mrs. Gaines."

She wasn't Mrs. Gaines, but she nodded in reply and inched toward the back door. "Just bring them on up — staircase on the left at the end of the hall. You'll find the bathroom at the top of the stairs, then follow your nose to the dining room."

Jesse Caudel

At the base of the stairs, Jesse lifted Adeline and settled her on his hip. She was wiggling

28

like nobody's business, panic widening her blue eyes, and her short legs probably wouldn't get her up the stairs fast enough. He took two steps at a time and called over his shoulder to the other kids. "Come on now. Hurry."

Charley held Cassie's hand and the pair trailed Jesse up the narrow staircase. A peek inside the open doorway at the top of the stairs revealed a claw-foot tub, porcelain sink mounted on the wall, and a pull-chain toilet. He set Adeline on the floor. "Go on in."

But Adeline, still dancing in place, held her hand toward her brother. Charley ushered both little girls into the water closet. He closed the door in Jesse's face, which was fine. The less he had to do for the little orphans, the better.

Not that he disliked the Shilling kids. Over his hours with them they hadn't been an ounce of trouble. But he'd already paid his dues in caring for youngsters that weren't his own. No sense in getting too entangled with these three.

The toilet flushed three times — apparently Adeline wasn't the only one with a need — before the door opened and Charley guided the girls onto the landing. Jesse said automatically, "Did ya wash your hands?"

Without a word Charley aimed his sisters for the sink. He grabbed Adeline around the middle and lifted her so she could reach, and Cassie stood on tiptoe. When the girls finished, Charley made use of the soap and water, then dried his hands on his trouser legs instead of the towel hanging next to the sink. They stood in a little group and looked up at Jesse with questioning eyes.

A funny lump settled at the back of his throat. He cleared it with a rough *ahem*. "Well, c'mon then. Food's this way." The smell of biscuits and stew drew him easily. He guided the children through a nicely furnished parlor — there was even a harpsichord lurking in the corner — and into the dining room. The girl he'd seen in the window bustled around the table, setting out tin plates. The boy who'd gawked down at them slumped in one of the polished high-back chairs.

The girl sent a shy smile over all of them. "Momma and I will bring out the food in just a minute. Please sit down." She scurried through a doorway on the far wall, and her whisper carried from the room. "They're done in the water closet, Momma!"

Jesse looked at the boy. "Does it matter where we sit?"

He shrugged, his hazel eyes slits of distrust.

Mrs. Gaines bustled into the room with a covered china tureen in her hands. She flicked a mild scowl at the boy. "Gracious, Bud, where are your manners? Stand up and introduce yourself to our guests." She placed the tureen in the middle of the table and hurried back to the kitchen.

The youth rose slowly, as if his joints were rusty. With his mouth set in an unsmiling line, he extended his hand to Jesse. "Good evening, sir. I'm Bernard Shilling. Everyone calls me Bud."

Jesse experienced an inner jolt, but he hid it with a smile and gave the boy's hand a firm shake. "Nice to meet you, Bud. I'm Jesse Caudel."

"You one of the out-of-work folks passin' through on the way to a big city?"

The question could be considered insolent, but Jesse decided to answer anyway. But just a half answer. "Not exactly." Bud's forehead puckered. Jesse pretended not to notice and put his hand on Charley's narrow shoulder. "Bud, this is Charley, Cassie, and Adeline Sh—"

"And here are the biscuits!" Mrs. Gaines's shrill exclamation cut off the rest of Jesse's introduction. She settled an oval platter

31

towering with golden biscuits next to the tureen and gestured her daughter forward. "Belle, put that butter and jam on the table and then fetch the milk pitcher. I would imagine these children would like a glass of milk. Am I right?"

Her smile seemed overly bright, but the three little Shilling children nodded. "Good. Mr. Caudel, children, please sit down. As soon as Belle returns with the milk pitcher" — Belle entered on cue — "we'll ask the Lord's blessing and eat."

While Belle circled the table and poured milk into the waiting cups, Jesse helped the two little girls onto side-by-side chairs across from Bud. Charley eased into the chair next to the sullen youth. Belle slid in next to the little girls, and Mrs. Gaines took the chair at the foot of the table. That left two seats open — the one beside Charley and the one at the head of the table. But there was no plate at the head. Jesse moved past it and sat next to Charley.

Mrs. Gaines folded her hands, and all five children followed suit as if they'd done it dozens of times together before. She sent a tight smile to Jesse. "Mr. Caudel, are you a God-believing man?"

Those he worked with might give a different answer, but the Caudels had raised him to honor God, so he nodded.

"Would you mind asking the blessing?"

He hadn't prayed in a good long while and he was pretty sure he'd sound out of practice, but how could he say no without seeming like a clod? So he gripped his hands together and closed his eyes. "God, that is, dear heavenly Father, we thank Thee for this food and for the kind woman who fixed . . . um, prepared it. We ask You — Thee? — to bless it that it might nourish our bellies. Bodies! Amen." His breath whooshed out with the final word.

Mrs. Gaines echoed, "Amen."

If she found his bumbling prayer offensive, she kept it hidden. She rose and lifted the cover on the tureen, releasing a billow of steam and a mighty good scent. Jesse's stomach tightened in anticipation.

Mrs. Gaines ladled thick gravy swimming with chunky carrots, potatoes, peas, and tomatoes onto Belle's plate. "This simmered so long the broth nearly dwindled away, but that will make it easier to eat with a fork. Belle, pass the biscuits, then hand me the little girls' plates. Bud, get the butter and jam going around the table. Pass your plates, Mr. Caudel and Charley, and I'll dish you up."

Even the littlest girl waited until everyone

had a full plate before picking up her fork. The kids had been taught manners, that was for sure. They ate without saying a word, swiping their mouths with their napkins between bites, and sipped their milk instead of guzzling. Bud and Belle sent long looks across the table at each other and quick sidelong ones at their mother and the guests, but they didn't talk either.

Jesse ate in silence, too, partly because the stew tasted good and partly because a cloud of tension hovered over the table. If Mrs. Gaines quit poking at her food and said something, he'd answer, but he wouldn't start a conversation even though questions rolled in the back of his mind. How long had she been widowed? The four fine china plates stacked on a sideboard near the table gave him the impression she'd intended to serve supper to that number of people tonight. So who was the fourth if not her husband?

He surmised Bud and Belle were her children — their resemblance to her couldn't be denied, the same way Charley had Warren Shilling's straight dark hair and Adeline and Cassie were blond, blue-eyed miniatures of Violet — but then why had Bud introduced himself as Shilling instead of Gaines?

He stifled a snort. And why did he care? As soon as they were done eating, he'd get somebody to help him unload the furniture from the back of the wagon, put the kids on the feather mattress, and head to Beloit. Given the late hour, they'd probably sleep instead of cry, the way they did half the drive over here. He hadn't liked being so helpless against their sorrow.

He used a biscuit to mop up the remaining smear of gravy on his plate and then offered Mrs. Gaines a smile. "That was real good, ma'am — best stew I've had in ages."

She colored, dipping her head, but he wasn't sure if pleasure or embarrassment caused the reaction. "Thank you, Mr. Caudel. There's more if you'd like a second serving."

He did, but the three Shilling kids were done eating. They fidgeted in the chairs. He should get on the road. "I've had plenty, thank you."

Belle stood and reached for the tureen. "Want me to fix a plate for Poppa and then put out the share-kettle, Momma?"

The woman's face blazed pink. "Don't worry about fixing a plate. Just fill the kettle. Take the remaining biscuits, too. Unless . . ." She aimed a questioning look at Jesse. "Would you like to take some along to munch on while you travel?"

Curiosity writhed through him. If she was a widow, who'd Belle mean by "Poppa"? He started to ask, but a different question popped out instead. "What's a share-kettle?"

Belle smiled. "Momma always makes extra food for supper and then puts out a soup pot so the men who hop off the train have something to eat."

Jesse jerked his gaze from Belle to Mrs. Gaines. "You feed the hobos?"

His prayer hadn't offended her, but apparently his question did, because her lips pinched into a grimace. She said quietly, "Yes, Mr. Caudel, I do."

"Sometimes she even takes sandwiches down to the shantytown by the river and passes them out." Bud tapped a half biscuit against his plate, dotting the puddle of gravy with crumbs. "Our pop doesn't like her doing it. Says those men'll never learn to take care of themselves if she molly-coddles them. But she does it anyway. She's making herself an easy mark."

Belle glared at her brother. "Bud, for shame. The hobos carved a cat on the lean-to's wall. You know what that means. We ought to be proud we have such a kind mother."

"Bud, Belle . . ." The woman's voice held

36

a mild reprimand. The boy hunkered in his chair and Belle hung her head.

Mrs. Gaines slipped her arm around Belle's waist and faced Jesse. "Since I started putting out what Belle likes to call the 'share-kettle,' there have been fewer thefts from root cellars and fewer beggars knocking on back doors in our neighborhood. I see that as a positive change. Besides, as a Christian I believe it's my duty to assist the poor and downtrodden. My family has been abundantly blessed. It's only right we should share some of our bounty."

She spoke boldly, with assurance, but as soon as she finished her little speech, her face went white and she clutched the bodice of her dress with one trembling hand. If Jesse read her correctly, she was about to be sick. He jumped up, lifting Charley by the arm.

"You youngsters say 'thank you' for the supper."

In unison, Charley and Cassie mumbled, "Thank you." Adeline put her finger in her mouth and huddled against Charley's side.

Jesse prodded the children toward the parlor. "Ma'am, if you'd tell me where to unload the furniture and things from the wagon, we'll be out of your way in a short time."

Her hand lifted from her bodice and stretched toward him. "Mr. Caudel, wait."

CHAPTER 3

Neva

Neva glanced across the faces of Warren's children — all five of them — and then turned to the deputy. "Could we speak privately?"

He looked at the children, too, uncertainty playing on his square face.

"Belle and Bud can entertain Charley, Cassie, and Adeline for a few minutes." They should get acquainted. They were half siblings. Her chest constricted. "Come with me, please." She headed for the apartment door.

To her relief, he followed her. She led him down the stairs and into the hallway connecting the store to the backyard. Warren had installed incandescent sconces on the hallway walls two years ago. They rarely used them — once the store was closed for the evening, they spent their time in the apartment — but Neva was grateful for the lights this evening. She didn't want to visit with a stranger in the dark. She turned the key on one brass sconce and stood beneath its soft glow.

Mr. Caudel remained at the far edge of the circle of light. "Ma'am, not to be rude, but I don't have a lot of time to spare. I still need to unload that wagon, and then it's a forty-mile drive back to Beloit. Sooner I get going, sooner I can get those kids tucked into a warm bed somewhere." He frowned. "Sure hope the Shillings' neighbor is willing to put them up a few more nights till the sheriff finds an opening at —"

"Leave them here." Neva nearly blasted the words. His mouth agape, Mr. Caudel stared at her. She swallowed and said more calmly, "The children, I mean." Oh, how her chest ached, but she would do the right thing. "Warren wanted them to be with me. And I know why."

"You do?"

She nodded. "I grew up in an orphanage. A fine one with loving caretakers. I can't fault them for anything they did for us." Thanks to the Jonnsons, she'd been well fed, sheltered, educated, and taught to love the Lord. "But living in an orphans' asylum isn't the same as living with a family. Those children . . ." She swallowed the knot filling her throat. "They need a home."

His brows descended. "Folks without any kids of their own visit the orphanages, you know — pick out youngsters to take home and raise. Young as the Shilling kids are yet, it could happen for those three."

Yes, it could. She'd seen children from the Dunnigan Orphans' Asylum leave with new parents. But the Jonnsons had insisted on brothers and sisters remaining together. Not all orphanages followed the same policy. And given the country's challenges, fewer people were willing to assume responsibility for needy children. Hadn't the trains from New York that once flooded the plains with parentless children stopped running because people no longer freely opened their homes?

Neva shook her head. "It isn't likely, Mr. Caudel, and you know it. I can't in good conscience let them go to strangers."

He frowned. "But aren't you a stranger to those youngsters, too?"

"I am." She hung her head for a moment, gathering her thoughts. Then she faced him with her chin held high. "But I have a . . . connection . . . to them. More than a stranger off the streets would have. It won't be easy to raise five children by myself." *Dear Lord in heaven, what am I doing?* "But I've raised Bud and Belle mostly by myself.

41

And I have a business that will provide for the children's needs. They can stay."

Mr. Caudel sucked in a long breath, held it for several tense seconds, then let it ease out while he shook his head. He chuckled. "Mrs. Gaines, I don't know if I should admire you or question your sanity. But you taking those kids is what Warren Shilling wanted, and I suppose I shouldn't argue with the dead."

She formed a weak smile. "No, I suppose you shouldn't."

"Now, can I ask you something?"

His tone held an edge. She wanted to refuse, but her head bobbed in a jerky assent.

"You said you were a widow woman, but your kids both talk about their pa like he's still around."

Neva's frame went hot and then cold. "Yes. They . . ." She bit her lip, blinking rapidly against tears. "They don't know that their father isn't coming home. He's been away. On business." Everything she said was true, so why did she feel like the biggest fraud in the world? "I haven't found the time to tell them . . . yet."

Compassion warmed his expression. He edged toward her, lowering his voice to a raspy whisper. "You need to tell 'em as soon as possible. Something like that? They need to know."

She nodded, and one tear slid down her cheek. She swept it away with her fingertips. "I'll tell them tonight."

He straightened, turning businesslike again. "All right then. The Shilling kids'll stay with you. But what do I do with all that plunder in the back of the wagon? It needs to stay, too."

Since the merchant wagon would no longer fill the barn, the furniture could go there. Would the hobos who sometimes slept on the hay bother the fine items? Maybe even steal them? Not all of the unemployed men traveling through were honest. But she had no other choice. "Everything can go in the barn. I'll send Bud across the alley to ask for help from the Randall boys. They're young, but they're tall and strong for their ages. Between the four of you, you should have the wagon emptied in no time, and then you can be on your way."

Bud Shilling

Bud accepted the nickel from Mr. Caudel. "Thank you, sir."

The man nodded. He dropped silver coins into Leon's and Leroy's waiting hands.

Neither of the Randall boys said thanks — they just pocketed their nickels and trotted off toward home, socking each other on the arm. For once they weren't socking Bud. He appreciated that even more than the nickel.

Bud trailed Mr. Caudel to the wagon. The man climbed up on the seat, gripped the reins, and released the brake. Bud called, "Ain'tcha forgetting something?"

He glanced down. His hat brim sent shadows over his whole face, but Bud thought he frowned. "What's that?"

Bud huffed out a disbelieving laugh. "Those three little kids you came with." He'd never seen such peculiar kids. The whole time he and Belle were alone with them, they didn't say a word. Just huddled together like they thought a bogeyman was under the sofa.

The man on the wagon seat sent a glance at the kitchen window, then aimed his gaze forward. "Your ma will explain." He flicked the reins, making a clicking sound with his tongue, and the horses pulled the wagon out of the yard.

Bud scowled after the wagon for a moment, considering running after Mr. Caudel and demanding answers. But he'd worked up a sweat carting that furniture to the barn, and the cool air was making his moist skin pop out in goose flesh. He set his feet toward the store instead.

He entered the family apartment and bellowed, "Ma!"

Ma came tiptoeing up the hallway from the bedrooms. She pressed her finger to her lips and pulled her eyebrows down in disapproval. "Don't holler, Bud. You'll wake the children, and they need their rest."

"They're staying here?"

She nodded.

Bud stared at his mother. Her face was all pink but her lips were white. She looked plenty guilty. "Where'd you put 'em?" They only had three bedrooms — Ma and Pop's, Belle's, and his.

"Never mind that right now." She took hold of his elbow and tugged him toward the kitchen. "Come here. I need to talk to you and your sister."

Bud dropped into one of the chairs at the little worktable in the corner. He looped his arm over the chair's back and chewed the inside of his cheek. Ma guided Belle away from the sink to the table. And the dishes weren't even done yet. Ma was going to let talking come before cleaning? A funny feeling crept through his stomach.

As soon as Belle and Ma sat, he asked,

"What's the matter?"

Belle put her hands in her lap and fiddled with her apron. "Have we done something wrong?"

Ma put her hand over Belle's and smiled. A fake smile. "No, sweetheart. But I need you both to listen carefully. Will you do that?"

Belle nodded fast but Bud snorted. "Just hurry up and tell us."

"There's no easy way to say this, so . . ." Ma took a big breath. Tears made little pools in her eyes. "Children, your father isn't coming home."

Belle blinked. "You mean tonight?"

"I mean . . . not ever."

Belle jerked her hands out from under Ma's.

Bud unhooked his arm and stood up so fast the chair fell over. "That's not true." Pop was gone a lot, but he always came home.

Ma reached for both of them. Belle caught hold, but Bud folded his arms over his chest and glared at his mother. Tears fell from her eyes. From Belle's, too. Ma spoke soft and kind. "I'm sorry, but it is true. While your father was in Beloit, he ate some tainted meat. It made him very sick. The doctor couldn't save him."

Belle sagged against Ma and wailed. Bud wanted to wail along with her, but he had to be the man now. Hadn't Pop told him every time he left on his sales route, *"You're the man of the house while I'm gone, Bud. Take good care of your mother and sister."* He'd be the man of the house forever now. He sniffed hard.

Ma rubbed Belle's back. "They already buried him in Beloit, so we won't have a funeral."

Belle pulled loose for a minute. "Can we at least go visit his grave? Put flowers on it?"

That guilty look came over Ma's face again. "Maybe. Someday. But it's a long way to Beloit, and we have the store, so . . ."

Belle buried her face on Ma's shoulder.

Bud leaned on the table. His shaky legs didn't want to hold him up. "Did Mr. Caudel tell you about Pop?"

Ma nodded.

"And he brought those kids, too."

"Th-that's right."

"Why'd he bring 'em here?"

Ma pressed her cheek against Belle's head and closed her eyes.

He picked up the chair and sat. "Why, Ma? Why are they here?" He used his deep-est man-voice, and for once he didn't

47

squeak in the middle of his sentence. Ma looked at him. His throat went tight. He'd never seen such begging in her eyes.

She took hold of Belle's arms and set her aside. She used her handkerchief to dry Belle's face, and then she wiped her eyes. Bud wriggled with impatience. When he was about to yell the question again, she said, "They're here because your father wanted Charley, Cassie, and Adeline. He wanted them to be with us."

He pictured the boy and the two pigtailed girls in his mind — quiet and acting scared. More like little ghosts than flesh-and-bone kids. Why would Pop want them? Especially since he already had Bud and Belle. Pop always said Bud would take Ma's place in the business someday. He promised they'd change the Main Street Mercantile sign to "Shilling & Son" as soon as Bud was old enough. Never once had Pop said "Sons." Always "Son." Just Bud.

Belle sat with her head tipped to the side and her face scrunched up the way she did when she was thinking deep, but she didn't say anything.

Bud couldn't stay quiet, though. "How do you know Pop wanted those kids?"

Ma's lips quivered like she was trying not to cry. "Mr. Caudel said so."

"Maybe he lied. Pop never said anything about bringing home more kids."

Ma's cheeks went white. "Mr. Caudel didn't lie, Bud."

He clenched his fists. "How do you know?"

Belle glanced from Bud to Ma to Bud again. "Why would he fib to us, Bud?"

"I don't know." Bud thumped the table with his fist. Hard. It hurt, but he didn't care. "But it don't make sense to me, that's all. Why would Pop want another boy when he already has — had — ?" He bit down and held the other words inside.

Ma got up and moved between their chairs. She squatted down and put her arms around their shoulders. Belle leaned in. Bud wanted to lean in, too. The thought of Pop never coming home again made his chest ache something fierce. His nose burned, too, the way it did when Leon and Leroy picked on him at school. But he sat stiff and straight. Like a man.

"I know this isn't easy. It's all right to be sad and to cry." She looked right at Bud.

He gritted his teeth.

She went on in a sorrowful but steady voice. "We'll mourn and we'll miss y-your father." Her hand closed down tight. "But God will give us strength. We'll be all right."

Bud bolted to his feet. "I'm going to bed."

"Bud?"

He froze in place but didn't turn around.

"Go in quietly. Charley's already asleep in there."

Swinging his arms, Bud headed for the hallway. He'd scoop that kid up and carry him out to the sofa. He didn't have room in his bed — or his life — for some other "son."

CHAPTER 4

Beloit, Kansas

Jesse

By the time Jesse reached Beloit, the clock
on the courthouse tower showed two twenty
in the morning. Four more hours and he'd
report for work. Tiredness made his bones
ache. Or maybe being bounced all day on
the hard wagon seat was to blame for his
discomfort. Give him a saddle — or a cush-
iony Model T seat — instead. But all things
considered, he had it pretty good. Better
than that widowed shopkeeper in Buffalo
Creek who'd just taken on three extra
mouths to feed.

He drew the horses to a stop in the dirt
yard outside the livery stable. Streetlamps
gave him a good view of the looming stable,
but not even a flicker of light showed behind
any of the windows. Old man Campbell was
probably snoring in his bed. Jesse sighed.

Even though it would give him some extra minutes for sleep if someone else saw to the horses, he wouldn't bother the owner. He knew how to unhitch and stable a team.

He climbed down, trudged to the front of the wagon, and put his hands to work releasing the horses from their traces. He performed the task without conscious thought. Growing up on a farm in Nebraska taught him lots of things, most of which he'd hoped to never use again once he moved to the city. He led the horses to the wide door and unfastened the catch.

The stable's interior was dark as a tomb and just as quiet, but the scant light creeping through the glass panes from the street-lights helped him locate an empty stall. He sent both horses inside, then closed the stall door behind them. They nickered and he said, "Hush that. Go to sleep." He didn't stick around to see if they followed his directions.

Now on foot, he plodded stiffly along the quiet streets beneath the faint glow of street-lamps to Hersey Street and the courthouse. He'd bed down in one of the empty jail cells instead of going home. The courthouse was closer, and the jail cots weren't too uncomfortable. Not if a fellow was tired enough. And tonight, he was tired enough to sleep on a pile of rocks.

He used his key and entered through the back door of the stately stone building. The sheriff's office door stood ajar, and one of the night deputies, Denton Gentry, sat with his feet propped on the corner of the desk, hands linked on his belly and head drooping southwest. Jesse cleared his throat, and the man jerked — head up, arms outward, feet in the air, mouth so wide Jesse spotted the silver fillings in his back molars.

Jesse burst out laughing.

Gentry righted himself in the creaky wooden chair and scowled. "That ain't funny, Caudel. You shouldn't sneak up on a man that way."

He hadn't sneaked, and Gentry shouldn't have been sleeping. "Any empty cells available tonight?"

"Three o' the six. Peck hauled in some fellas for fistfighting at the train depot. We locked 'em up and they're sleepin' off their mad." Gentry glanced out the doorway. "You got a prisoner with you?"

"Nope. Gonna sleep here. Just got back from Buffalo Creek."

"Ah. That's right. You drew the short straw and had to deliver the Shilling orphans." The man worked his lips in and out, making his fuzzy mustache flare and flop like a butterfly stretching its wings. "Everything go all right?"

Jesse wouldn't have called the delivery all right. The evidence of Neva Gaines's distress had pestered him the whole drive back. "As well as it could go, considering. Had me a long day, that's for sure." He yawned, inching in the direction of the cellblock. "And I'm on foot patrol at six thirty, so . . ."

"Gonna follow a long day with a short night, huh?"

Jesse shrugged. Wouldn't be the first time he caught a short night's sleep, but being a deputy beat planting seeds and slopping hogs even if law keeping had its difficult moments. Like delivering those kids to Buffalo Creek.

Gentry waved at him. "Go. Catch some sleep." He snickered. "I just might do the same."

"Don't let Sheriff Abling catch you snoozing."

Jesse ignored the man's grunt and entered the first cell. Not even bothering to kick off his boots, he flopped across the cot and closed his eyes against the electric bulbs glaring from their twisted cords overhead. *Sleep, Caudel. Six o'clock'll be here before you know it.*

A steady *drip, drip* from a leaky faucet created an inharmonious lullaby. The mildewy scent clinging to the block walls mingled with the smell of dust and sweat on his clothes — a foul perfume. He'd slept in the cellblock dozens of times in his fifteen years of being a lawman and had always drifted right off despite the lumpy cot, intrusive sounds and smells, and always-glowing lights. But tonight, no matter how his tired body wished for rest, sleep evaded him.

Something didn't sit right about Shilling's sister. If her name was Gaines, why had her son introduced himself as Shilling? Why hadn't she told her son and daughter about their pa dying? She seemed like a caring mother, but a caring mother wouldn't hide something that important from her kids, would she?

When the cook hired by the city to feed the prisoners came in banging a wooden spoon against a pot at six that morning, Jesse was still awake with unanswered questions rolling in the back of his mind.

Buffalo Creek, Kansas

Arthur Randall
Thursday morning Arthur buttoned his brown tweed vest, adjusted his silk tie, and shrugged into his suit jacket. Ordinarily he

didn't wear a jacket on weekdays. A tie and vest were dapper enough for Buffalo Creek. But when a man went to make a business deal, he needed to look his best. That included a jacket. He stepped in front of the tall oval mirror on Mabel's dressing table and grimaced. He also needed neatly combed hair.

He left the dressing room and crossed the wide hall to the bathroom. His comb still waited on the edge of the sink, and he applied it to his thick, dark hair, smoothing the strands straight back from his forehead. Threads of silver had begun to make themselves known at his temples in the past year, but he didn't mind. He still looked years younger than his father had at the age of thirty-nine. By thirty-nine Pa was gray haired, stoop shouldered, and worn out. Another way Arthur was unlike Casper Randall.

As he applied the trimming scissors to his mustache, his older son's excited chatter from last night played through his mind. *"Should've seen it all, Dad. Bedsteads and bureaus, a carved rocking chair, even a fainting couch. All of it topnotch! You figure the Shillings are going into the furniture business? Won't do us much good to have competition right next-door."*

Pride puffed Arthur's chest. The boy had only just turned seventeen, but Leroy had made a keen observation — one his father wouldn't ignore. Right now Randall's Emporium was the only furniture provider in the entire Buffalo Creek township. That is, if one didn't count ordering from the Montgomery Ward or Sears and Roebuck catalogs. He snorted. As if a person could make a sound decision by looking at black-and-white drawings on a catalog page. Seating oneself, fingering the embellishments, lifting the table leaves and exploring the joints — that was the way to choose furniture. He wanted to hold the corner on furniture sales in Mitchell County.

He dropped the scissors in the little wooden box on the corner of the washstand, rubbed sandalwood-scented oil between his palms, then slicked his palms over his head until every strand of hair glistened. Then he returned to the dressing room and checked his reflection again. Ah, better. Hair lying in place, clean-shaven cheeks and neatly trimmed mustache, crisp white collar and perfectly centered mustard-colored tie. The suit was brand-new, so he didn't inspect it for sweat stains or loose threads. He gave a satisfied nod. Nobody would ever guess he'd grown up in a shack near the coal mines in

Pennsylvania.

He strode up the hallway, giving the boys' bedroom doors raps with his knuckles as he passed. "I'm heading across the alley to talk to the Shillings. Make sure you get your-selves to school on time."

From behind both doors, grunts sounded.

Arthur paused with his hand on the carved newel cap. "And, Leon, I better not hear about you putting a snake in the teacher's desk drawer again."

Muffled laughter carried from behind Leroy's solid raised-panel oak door.

Leon's door popped open and his son peered out. "Don't worry, you won't hear a thing about snakes. Too hard to find 'em now that winter's coming on." He shot his father an impish grin before ducking back into his room.

Arthur made his way to the kitchen by the enclosed back staircase. His housekeeper was already bustling around, preparing breakfast, and she pointed silently to the coffeepot, her way of letting him know the brew was ready. He gave a brusque shake of his head and strode through the screened porch to the back door. Frowning, he paused with his palm pressed to the freshly painted screen door frame.

Leon's teacher visited at least once a week

carrying stories of his boy's shenanigans. She'd pestered him the year she had Leroy, too. Sour-faced old maid. She didn't appreciate him saying the boys were merely high spirited. He didn't appreciate her telling him they were undisciplined. He and Miss Neff would never agree, just as he and the previous teacher hadn't agreed, and the one before that. He shook his head, emitting a little huff of annoyance. Buffalo Creek was a nice town. Why couldn't it attract teachers who had better things to do than complain about his boys? Maybe he'd run for the school board next term. Then he could fix things.

He gave the screen door a whack that sent it flying open and descended the three wooden steps in a trot. The door slapped into its casing behind him. He'd think about joining the school board later. For now, he had something else to fix.

He crossed the backyard, his polished shoes crushing leaves and picking up dust. The Kansas wind hadn't started blowing yet — too early — but the billowing clouds in the east promised another windy day. Maybe he wouldn't unfurl the canvas canopy. He liked the striped canvas. No other business on Buffalo Creek's Main Street had such an up-to-date sunshade. But he wouldn't risk having it ripped from its metal braces by the infernal wind.

He came alongside the Shillings' barn, and he couldn't resist stopping to peer through the dusty four-pane window. The choice proved dissatisfying. With the slanting sun bouncing off the windows, all he could see was his own reflection. He snorted and took off again, his arms swinging and his chin thrust forward in determination. He'd see that furniture. He'd buy that furniture and bring an end to Shilling's intention to start selling furniture.

Arthur reached the back stoop and thumped the door a half-dozen times with his fist. Moments later the patter of footsteps reached him, and then the curtain on the door's window was whisked aside. Mrs. Shilling herself peered out at him, her face reflecting surprise.

He pasted on his most charming smile — the one he used to coax customers into looking at a more expensive piece of furniture. He mouthed, *May I come in?*

A *click-squeak* indicated she'd turned the lock, and then the door opened. She stepped aside, inviting his entrance with the action. "Good morning, Mr. Randall. What can I do for you?"

By the look on her face, she wasn't thrilled

to receive company at seven thirty on a Thursday morning, but she was too polite to say so. Polite and comely. That Shilling was a lucky man. Arthur pushed aside his jacket flaps and tucked his thumbs into the pockets of his vest. "I'd like to speak to your mister. Could you send him down?"

The woman winced — a curious reaction. "He . . . isn't here."

Had he mixed up the dates? He sent his thoughts backward. Shilling's merchant wagon rolled out of town August thirty-first, so according to the schedule he'd kept for the past ten years, he should've rolled in yesterday. "Has he been delayed somehow?" Arthur frowned. The mercantile owner better not be bringing another load of furniture.

She turned her gaze away from him. "If you don't mind, I prefer not to talk about the reason for Warren's absence. It's . . . personal."

Arthur pinched his brows together. This situation was mighty suspicious. What were they plotting? He snapped, "Personal? Or is it business? I don't imagine you'd want to divulge any business-related secrets, would you?"

She sighed and faced him again. "Mr. Randall, I —"

"My boys tell me your barn is full of furniture. Quality furniture." He leaned in, narrowing his gaze. "And your husband isn't here even though he ought to be, seeing how it's a new month and that man keeps to his schedule the same way a rotary watch keeps time. So where is he, Mrs. Shilling?"

Something glinted in her hazel eyes. Anger? Frustration? Probably a little of both. But who inspired the emotions — him or her husband?

He repeated, "Where is he?"

The glint became a blaze. Her cheeks turned rosy, and she balled her slender hands into fists. "He's in a grave."

Arthur drew back so abruptly his back popped.

She nodded, her expression fierce. "That's right. He won't be coming home again."

She pointed at him, surprising him with her fervor. In the fifteen years he'd known her, he'd never seen her be anything but demure and kind. Even when he pestered her husband to sell out so he could expand his emporium — and he'd pestered Warren Shilling a lot — she never expressed a hint of indignation or impatience. But at that moment, sparks flew from her. Would she poke him in the chest with her finger? He took a shuffling step backward.

"So now you know the truth. But, Mr. Randall, I expect you to keep that information private until I've had the opportunity to speak to Reverend Savage." Her stiff frame wilted, and the spark in her eyes dimmed. Pleading replaced the ferocity of moments ago. "My children and I need a few days to accept Warren's death before the entire town hears about it. Will you allow us time to mourn privately?"

He'd lost Mabel more than six years ago, but he remembered his desire to hide from the world when he finally realized she was gone for good. Unexpectedly, sympathy twined through him. He offered a stiff nod.

A sad smile tipped up the corners of her lips. "Thank you." She gestured to the door. "And now, if you'll excuse me, I need to see to my children." She hurried off.

Arthur let himself out and crossed the yard slowly. So Shilling was dead. What a shock. How had he died? Maybe his wagon overturned. Or maybe someone robbed him. All kinds of shady characters roamed the roads these days, looking for ways to line their pockets. Any number of dangers could have befallen the man while he traveled.

Alongside the barn he halted in his tracks.

Giving his forehead a whack, he inwardly berated himself. He'd intended to ask to see the furniture, make an offer on it. But Mrs. Shilling's proclamation of her husband's demise distracted him.

He started to go knock on the door again, but the remembered image of her stricken face changed his mind. He might be calculating when it came to business dealings, but he wasn't hardhearted. A woman in the throes of mourning couldn't make prudent decisions. Besides, if he asked now, the town might accuse him of taking advantage. He couldn't tarnish his reputation as a fair businessman.

Arthur set his feet in motion, a plan forming in the back of his mind. He'd give Mrs. Shilling a few days of privacy, just as she'd requested. He'd be supportive and sympathetic. Then, when a decent amount of time had passed — a week, maybe two — he'd make on offer on the furniture and the store. A woman couldn't operate a business all on her own. She'd welcome his proposition, thank him for his generosity, and then step out of his way.

CHAPTER 5

Neva

Belle was filling the sink with hot water when Neva entered the kitchen. She glanced at the worktable where the children had been eating when a knock on the door interrupted their breakfast. Warren's three youngsters, attired in the nightshirts Neva had scrounged for them last night, were still in their seats where Neva had left them, but Bud's chair stood empty. She crossed to the sink. "Where's your brother?"

Belle made a face. "He went to his room." She held out a bowl. Hardened oatmeal formed a lumpy island in a sea of milk. "This is Bud's. He didn't eat. Not even a bite. Said he wasn't hungry. Said not to pack him a lunch either." Her forehead puckered. "I told him he's gotta eat or he'll get sick. He wouldn't listen."

Neva pulled in a slow breath, inwardly praying for wisdom. She'd sent up a dozen similar prayers during her sleepless night. She hoped God delivered the needed discernment soon.

She put her hand on Belle's shoulder and gave a gentle squeeze. "Your brother is mourning. When the sadness eases, his appetite will return."

"When'll the sadness ease, Momma?" Belle whispered the query, her voice raspy. Her gaze flicked toward the three quiet children at the table, then settled on Neva. Her eyes looked luminous, swimming with unshed tears. "Feels like I've got a boulder on my chest. Could hardly breathe last night. That's sadness, isn't it?"

Neva placed a kiss on her daughter's temple. "Yes, sweetheart, that's sadness. I feel it, too." Her chest held a pile of boulders — a mass of sorrow, regret, guilt, and anger. The sorrow might crumble easier than any of the other emotions. She spoke staunchly, as much to herself as Belle. "But God is faithful to comfort us in our time of need. Lean on Him, and He will sustain you."

"Yes, ma'am."

"Finish clearing the breakfast table, please. You and Bud can stay home from school today if you like." If they stayed home, the teacher wouldn't notice their melancholy bearings and ask questions

Neva wasn't ready to answer.

"Thank you, ma'am." Belle went on clearing the dishes, her motions slow, as if every cup and bowl were filled with concrete.

Neva turned her attention to the children at the table. Their bowls were empty. Sorrow didn't seem to be affecting their appetites. But maybe they were too young to fully comprehend their parents were never coming back. She forced a smile. "Did you get enough breakfast?"

Charley nodded, but neither Cassie nor Adeline responded.

Neva slipped into Bud's chair. Since Charley was oldest, she addressed her questions to him. "How old are you children?"

The boy gave his head a little jerk that sent his long bangs higher on his forehead — a tactic Bud often used when Neva let him go too long between haircuts. "I'm eight. Cassie's six and a half. Adeline just turned three."

The anger-boulder in Neva's chest grew heavier. So many years she'd been deceived by her husband. How could she have been such a fool? She pushed those thoughts aside. "So you must be in the third grade then, and Cassie is in the first?"

He nodded, his hair flopping over his eyes again.

Neva came close to pushing the heavy brown strands — as richly brown as Warren's — away from the child's face. She gripped her hands together. "Then you and Cassie will be in the same class at school. With Miss Franklin." Bud and Belle had loved Miss Franklin.

Charley peered at her through his thick fringe of bangs. "We goin' to school?"

Neva preferred not to send them. At least not yet. But she wasn't sure what to do with them all day either. She had a store to run. If Bud and Belle were home, they could mind the children while Neva saw to the customers' needs.

She shook her head. "Not today. Maybe . . . on Monday." She'd talk to the preacher Saturday evening, let him share the news of Warren's passing with the congregation Sunday morning. Then she and the children could start their new routine on Monday. Yes, that would be best.

"So we're stayin'?"

The question stated softly, almost emotionlessly, contrasted with the apprehension etched into the child's features. Neva's mother-heart stirred. "Yes, Charley. You're staying."

"You sure?"

She nodded.

" 'Cause that boy, Bud, said we was going to an orphans' home."

Neva shot a questioning look at Belle.

Her daughter's cheeks turned rosy. "Bud was just talking. Sort of . . . musing."

Neva closed her eyes for a moment. She'd speak with Bud, but first she needed to assure these children they'd found a home. Or had they? Yesterday evening she'd acted impulsively, driven by remembrances of her own orphaned state and lifelong desire to be part of a family. Now, in the light of day, after a night of tossing and turning, her fierce determination to honor Warren's dying request and care for his children seemed much less sensible.

She looked into Charley's brown eyes. Then at Cassie and little Adeline, who sat silent and wary. She received glimpses of herself in their uncertain little faces. She sighed. "You don't need to worry." She wouldn't take them to an orphanage. Never an orphanage.

For long seconds Charley stared at her as if trying to read her soul. Then he nodded — one quick, emphatic bob of his head. He rose. "May we get dressed now? My feet are cold."

"Yes. Go ahead. Your clothes are in Belle's room." Bud had set Charley's things outside his bedroom door last night, and Neva had been too weary to do battle.

The trio trudged off together, the girls holding Charley's hands and crowding so close they nearly stepped on his toes. But he didn't push them aside. Not the way Bud sometimes elbowed Belle to give him space. When they reached the doorway leading to the dining room, Charley stopped and peered over his shoulder at her. "Ma'am?"

Neva swallowed unexpected tears. Such a polite little boy. Warren and Violet had done well in raising him. "Yes, Charley?"

"The man who brought us here said we were going to Aunt Neva. Is that you?"

Neva nodded.

"Then we should call you that — Aunt Neva?"

She had no siblings and neither did Warren. She'd never hear any other child call her "Aunt Neva." The title was better than anything else. "That would be fine."

Charley aimed a solemn look at his sisters. "Hear that? She's Aunt Neva."

Cassie glanced at Neva, a bashful smile curving her lips. " 'Kay."

Charley tugged on Adeline's hand. "You understand, Adeline? You call her Aunt Neva."

Adeline spoke around the fingers in her

mouth. "Tant Neba."

Belle released a short, amused giggle.

Neva's lips twitched with the desire to smile, but she managed to squelch it. No sense in shaming the little girl. "Go on and get dressed now."

The children shuffled around the corner, and Neva turned to her daughter. "Since you're staying home today, you can finish the dishes later. Please fetch your brother. We need to have a talk."

Bud

"You better come. Momma's pretty mad."

Bud remained in his unmade bed, hands behind his head and elbows pointed at the ceiling. "Don't much feel like talking. You can tell Ma so for me."

Belle folded her arms over her skinny chest and scowled. No matter how hard she tried to be fierce, it never worked. She was too soft looking — wavy brown hair combed back and twisted into a long, thick braid, smooth cheeks, full rosy lips. The Randall boys said Belle was downright pretty, and even though he didn't like Leon and Leroy talking about his sister, Bud silently agreed. But right now she didn't look pretty to him. She looked as much a nuisance as those three little kids who'd shown up last night.

"Get outta here, Belle."

She pressed her lips together good and tight and glared at him.

He glared back.

She let out a huff, whirled around, and hurried off, calling, "Momma! He won't come out!"

Bud held his breath and counted off the seconds. One, two, three, four, five —

Ma stomped through the doorway with her hands on her hips. Ma was soft looking most times, too, but right then she looked almighty fierce. "Bernard Warren Shilling, if your father was here, you —"

Bud sat up so fast the bed springs twanged. "If Pop was here I'd ask him why he wanted those snot-nosed kids. But he's dead, so I can't ask, and nobody else can tell me, so I don't wanna talk about it."

Ma's mouth stayed open but no words came out. She didn't look fierce anymore. And while she was quiet, he might as well say everything on his mind.

"I don't want that kid sleeping in my room. I don't want him wearing my hand-me-downs like he did last night. I don't care if I've outgrown that nightshirt. It's mine, not his, and he had no right to it." He balled his hands into fists. His tense muscles made him quiver from head to toe, but his tongue worked just fine. "Pop said when he's not here I'm the man of the house, and that means I'm in charge. So I'm telling you to send that kid somewhere else. Send him to . . . to the Dunnigan Asylum. They'll take him just like they took you when you were a kid."

"I can't send him to Dunnigan."

Bud scrunched his eyes to slits. "Why not? Trains run every week. They go right through Brambleville." He'd been sassy a few times with Ma, especially in the last year, but he'd never been so outright disrespectful. Deep down, guilt nibbled at him. Especially when her chin wobbled like she was trying not to cry. He looked to the side so he didn't have to see if tears came into her eyes.

"Mr. Dunnigan died last year, Bud. The Jonnsons weren't able to buy the property, so it was sold. The orphanage is closed." Ma sounded sad.

Sad because of the way he was treating her? Because Mr. Dunnigan had died? Or because she regretted not being able to send Charley away? No matter, her reaction softened him a bit. He eyed her again. "There are other orphanages. You don't have to send him to Dunnigan." He sucked in a big breath that puffed out his chest.

"But he's got to go, Ma. He can't stay here."

She took two fast steps in his direction and caught him by the shoulders. He'd grown some in the past year. She hardly had to dip her head to look him in the eyes. "You listen to me, young man, and listen good. Charley, Cassie, and Adeline can stay here. They will stay here. The last thing your father said to anybody before he left this earth was for those children to come here to us. So we aren't going to send them away."

"You can keep the girls if you want to." They'd stay in Belle's room. What did he care about the girls?

Ma shook her head. "Think for a minute. How would you feel if someone came along and made you leave Belle?"

Some days he thought he wouldn't mind getting away from his sister, but be away from her forever? The reality of it didn't sit so well. He gritted his teeth until his jaw hurt.

Ma squeezed his shoulders. Not a "you better behave" squeeze like Pop used to give him, but a "please understand" squeeze. "Those children lost their folks."

He'd lost his father.

"They're with strangers, and they're scared and confused."

Fear rolled through Bud's chest. What would they do without Pop?

"Remember the Scripture from Matthew when Jesus was teaching? He said whatever we do to the least of these, we've done it to Him." Ma's hands held tight, almost desperately, as if she needed him to keep herself steady. "Think about that, Bud, when you're tempted to tell those children they aren't welcome here. Would you say such a thing to Jesus?"

The nibble of guilt became a gnaw. His stomach hurt and he felt trapped. He ducked away from his mother's grip and turned his back on her. "I don't feel so good."

"You're probably hungry. Come to the kitchen and eat something."

He shook his head. Food wouldn't help. Not at all.

Ma sighed. Her warm breath eased past his ear, reminding him of the hundreds of good-night kisses she'd aimed at his temple. He wished he could throw himself against her and cry like he'd done when he was little. The big old lump of hurt and mad and sad needed to come out.

The *pat-pat* of feet on hardwood told Bud that Ma was moving toward the door. "All right, suit yourself. I'll be going down to

75

the store soon, but you and Belle can stay home from school today."

He hadn't intended to go anyway.

"Crawl back under your covers and rest a bit. Then when you feel better . . ." Her voice changed from resigned to resolute. "Push your bed over against the wall and move your bureau next to the window."

Bud spun around and gawked at his mother.

"You'll need to make room for Charley in here."

CHAPTER 6

Beloit, Kansas

Jesse

Jesse poured his third cup of coffee for the morning and lifted the thick mug to his mouth. He swallowed and made a face.

Sheriff Abling looked up from the array of paperwork scattered across his desk and grinned. "What's the matter, Caudel? Find a bug in the brew?"

"Nope. It's just stout." Too stout. Gentry always put way too much ground beans in the pot. But Jesse took another long draw anyway. He needed something to keep him awake. While making the early rounds with the other day deputy, Rye Hamby, he'd yawned so big Hamby said he looked like a baby robin hoping for worms. When he was wide awake and alert, he didn't appreciate Hamby's penchant for joshing a fellow. He especially didn't appreciate it when he was half-asleep and sluggish. Hopefully the coffee would not only perk him up, but it'd restore his good nature, or he might give Hamby a less than good-natured jab in the ribs with his elbow.

"Well, slosh some water in it and then sit down for a minute. Need to talk to you about something."

Jesse disregarded the sheriff's suggestion about watering down the coffee — foul tasting it might be, but full strength was better for him today — and crossed to the wooden chair facing the desk. "Everything all right?"

"Oh, sure, sure. Just had a question or two about Buffalo Creek." The man leaned back and ran his hand over his coarse gray hair. The wiry strands popped right back up as soon as he released them. Jesse had always thought Abling's hair grew like prairie grass — toward the sun. Abling locked his hands behind his head and rocked gently. "What did you think of the community?"

Jesse scratched his cheek. "Kind of hard to say. I wasn't there hardly long enough to form much of an opinion."

Abling chuckled. "Oh, come on, Jesse."

Jesse? Abling always called his deputies by their last names. The casual use of his given name put him on alert.

"You've worked here . . . what? Six years now?"

"Six and a half."

"Yep. Six and a half years. And I've got pretty familiar with your abilities. Observation is one of them."

Jesse couldn't decide if he was more flattered or flustered by his boss's statement. He forced a short laugh. "Guess all those hours I spent walking behind a horse and plow helped with that. You either focused on the horse's hindquarters or busied your eyes elsewhere."

Abling laughed heartily. He smacked the desktop, sending a few papers sideways. "That's another thing I've always liked about you — you don't toot your own horn. In this line of work it's easy to get self-important. Some men think the badge gives them the right to be bossy or condescending. I've never witnessed that attitude in you."

How had Abling moved from asking about Buffalo Creek to describing Jesse's attributes? He set the now-cool mug of coffee aside. "Um . . . thank you."

The sheriff leaned forward. "So what did you observe about Buffalo Creek in your short time there?"

Jesse replayed images of the town in his

memory. "It's a middle-sized community — smaller than Beloit but bigger than Cawker City or Tipton. Seems like a well-cared-for town. Clean streets, uncluttered yards." The weeds were even trimmed in the alley he drove through. "Main Street has quite a few businesses. Mostly limestone, but a few are clapboard buildings with false fronts." Including the mercantile. He shrugged. "No boarded-up windows that I noticed. So I'd say from the looks of things, they're flourishing pretty well despite the hard times."

Abling nodded, his expression serious. "What about the residents?"

He recalled people lifting a hand in greeting as he drove up the street in search of Shilling's mercantile. "Townsfolk seemed friendly enough. Probably hardworking too, based on the appearance of the town in general." And if they were all as bighearted as Neva Gaines, it'd be a dandy community to call home. Jesse angled his head. "Why're you asking about Buffalo Creek?"

"Lemme be square with you, Jesse."

Jesse again. He fought the urge to squirm.

"You didn't draw the short straw the other night. I rigged it."

Jesse drew back and frowned. "Why would you do that?"

"Because I wanted you to see the town.

80

And I knew if I sent you, no matter the hour, you'd see it. Really see it."

The answer made no sense. "But why'd I need to see it?"

"Because they're looking for a sheriff, and I'd like to recommend you for the job."

Jesse stood. "Me?"

"Yep. You."

Jesse took a backward step. "What about Hamby? Or Frager? They've both been here longer than me. And they're older, too."

Abling rose and rounded the desk, talking as he came. "I know you're young yet, but I wasn't much older than you when I took over as sheriff here in Beloit. Hamby and Frager are good deputies, but they still rely too much on my feedback to make decisions."

He placed his hand on Jesse's shoulder. "I've watched you. You've got a knack for dealing with folks — calming them when they're rattled, sorting out the truth from a pack of lies, all without them even realizing you're doing it. You've got the abilities to lead. I think you'd make a fine sheriff. The question is, do you want the job?"

When he'd left his family's Nebraska farm, Jesse hadn't headed out with any greater ambition than to never stick a seed in the ground again. He pretty much stumbled into the position of deputy in Belleville, a town just over the Kansas border, and he thought it fine to have a job where he got to tell people what to do instead of being the one given orders. Over the years serving as a lawman in four different Kansas towns, he never once set his sights on sitting in the sheriff's chair. Not the way Hamby or Gentry seemed to do. But the thought of stepping into such an important position intrigued him. And scared him, too.

"You've got a little time to think about it. A week for sure, maybe two. The current sheriff over in Buffalo Creek — man name of Dodds Schlacter — is fixing to retire. By the end of October at the latest. He'd like somebody to step in a week or so ahead of him vacating the office to get comfortable with the town before he takes off his badge for good. Him and me have already talked, and he's given your name to the city council. They said if I approved you, that was good enough for them."

Abling could have gotten smug about his fine reputation in Mitchell County, but not an ounce of arrogance colored his tone. Jesse admired the man for his levelheadedness. If Jesse took on the position of sheriff in Buffalo Creek, he'd hope to be half as good at keeping order while keeping a humble spirit as Gene Abling.

The sheriff chuckled. "You're awful quiet. What're you thinking?"

Jesse decided to be honest. "I'm wondering if I'm ready for that kind of responsibility." Back on the farm, he'd carried responsibility — seeing to livestock, working the fields, watching over eight younger siblings. Ma and Pa had always trusted him. As a deputy, he'd had different kinds of responsibilities, and he couldn't recall one time his supervisor had chided him for shirking his duties. Most folks would say he was a capable man. But a sheriff? Could he really be a sheriff?

"Tell you what, how 'bout you drive over to Buffalo Creek and shadow Sheriff Schlacter for a day or two?" Abling's eyes twinkled. "Nothing like sitting in the saddle to give you a real feel for the ride."

Buffalo Creek, Kansas

Neva
Neva turned the cardboard sign hanging on the front door to Closed, then pulled the shade, sealing herself away from the street. She rested her forehead against the yellowed shade and released a long sigh. Had any day ever stretched as long as this one? Over the

years, she'd grown accustomed to seeing to the store by herself. But supervising five children between duties as well as carrying the heaviness of sorrow weighted her until she feared her frame would collapse.

What she wouldn't give to be able to take an hour-long soak in the claw-foot tub, up to her chin in Dreft bubbles, with *Anna Karenina* as her only companion. But those hours of leisure were gone now. Too many responsibilities awaited.

Forcing her leaden legs into motion, she headed for the staircase. Although she'd intended to wait until Saturday to share the news of Warren's passing with Reverend Savage, she needed her minister now. She climbed the stairs as slowly as a turtle climbing a mountain and scuffed into the apartment. Belle, along with Warren's three children, sat in a circle on the parlor rug playing pick-up sticks.

Neva touched Belle's hair, and her daughter looked upward. "Will you be all right for a little while longer? I need to run an errand."

Belle nodded. "Do you want me to put supper on the table?"

Beans and salt pork had been simmering on the stove since noon. It could stay there awhile yet, but the little ones would likely be hungry. "Yes, go ahead and eat. Fill a plate for me, and then put the leftovers in the icebox."

Belle's eyes widened. "Not out in the lean-to?"

Neva swallowed a knot of regret. With three extra mouths to feed, she wasn't sure she should continue to take care of hobos. "Not this time." She turned away from her daughter's puzzled face and glanced around the room. "Where is Bud?"

Belle grimaced. "In his room. He said he doesn't like to play pick-up sticks." Her tone turned knowing, and Neva understood the unspoken meaning. Bud had always enjoyed the game that required a steady hand and keen eye. He didn't like playing with Charley, Cassie, and Adeline.

Neva started to ask if Bud had brought in the children's clothing trunks from the barn, but she decided to ask Bud instead. When she peeked in his room, she discovered him curled in a ball, sound asleep. Despite her frustration with her son's surly behavior earlier that day, mother-love washed over her. He looked so young, so helpless, so innocent. She couldn't bear to disturb him. So she tenderly pulled the quilt over his sleeping form. As she turned to leave the room, she spotted the children's trunk shoved in the corner. The lid was up, and the contents were all askew as if someone had been riffling through it.

She cringed. If she didn't refold things now, she'd be forced to iron out the wrinkles later. She tiptoed to the trunk, knelt, and busily began straightening the little dresses, shirts, and trousers. Every item was store bought — not one flour sack, hand-stitched garment in the entire trunk. Apparently Warren had been as adamant with Violet about purchasing quality clothing for the children as he'd been with Neva.

"I don't want any child of mine to feel shamed by what they have to wear." Warren's voice rose up from the past and growled in her memory. *"I don't care what it costs. They'll be dressed in the best."*

She held up one tiny frock made of ivory lace with a satin underslip and trimmed with pink satin rosettes. Her heart panged. He'd certainly chosen the best for little Adeline. A prettier child's dress she'd never seen. Neva sighed and placed the folded dress in the trunk. As she pressed it gently on the stack, her knuckles bumped something sharp. Frowning, she pushed the clothing aside and encountered a scrolled gilt frame. Her hands began to tremble even before she gripped the frame's edge and lifted it out.

With the shade pulled on the window, only a minimal amount of light came through, but it was sufficient. She sat gazing down at a photograph of Warren and a lovely young woman. She whispered, "Violet." Her chest tightened until taking a breath was torture, but she couldn't tear her gaze away from the image. No wonder Warren had fancied her. With large eyes framed by thick lashes, delicate cheekbones, and a heart-shaped face, she could be a model for china dolls.

The photographer had colorized the portrait, giving Violet rosy cheeks and a touch of blue in her eyes. For a moment it seemed as though the woman were looking back at Neva, studying her, finding her lacking. She would not have this portrait in her house!

She pushed to her feet, pressing the offending image against her rib cage, and scurried to her bedroom. She started to toss the frame into the trash bin, but something brought her frantic movements to a halt. How many times had she longed for a photograph of the ones who'd given birth to her? To her knowledge, no images of her parents existed. Could she destroy this image, knowing it was the likeness of her children's father? And what of Charley, Cassie, and Adeline? Could she, in clear conscience, steal something so precious from them?

Neva lowered her head and closed her eyes, squeezing the frame so tightly the metal cut into her palms. No, she couldn't send it to the burn barrel. But neither could she leave it in the trunk where one of the children would find it, take it out, display it.

With jerky steps she moved to her closet, opened the door, and shoved the photograph clear to the back of the narrow shelf above the row of clothes hooks. Shadows hid it from view. No one else ever went into her closet. The photograph could stay concealed until the day Warren and Violet's children were grown. Until then, no one needed to know Warren had paired himself with such a lovely creature as the woman named Violet.

If she'd needed the support of her minister before, Neva needed it even more desperately now. She quickly donned a fresh dress — the nicest in her closet, admittedly trying to compete with the captured image of Violet — and covered her hair with a feathered felt cloche. Then she donned her best kidskin gloves and set off for the little parsonage tucked behind the clapboard chapel where she and her family worshiped each Sunday.

As she walked through the late-evening shadows, she practiced what she would say to Reverend Savage. No matter how she phrased it, the truth was ugly. Could she really divulge something so awful to a man of God? Halfway there, she almost turned around and went back home, but the deep need to purge herself sent her forward again. Besides, where else could she unload this burden? She'd never share her concerns with Warren again. Bud and Belle were still children. She couldn't rely on them for emotional support. Reverend Savage was a first-time preacher who'd stood in the pulpit not yet two full years, but he'd told his congregation they were always welcome to bring their concerns to him. She had to trust he had been sincere.

Neva knocked on the parsonage door, and moments later the minister's wife opened it. A wonderful aroma drifted to Neva's nose, and high-pitched chatter carried from around a corner. She'd interrupted their dinner. She drew back, chagrined by her thoughtlessness.

But Lois Savage offered a bright smile and ushered her over the threshold. "Please come in, Mrs. Shilling. What brings you out this evening?"

Neva wrung her hands together. "I . . . I'd hoped to speak to the reverend. But it can wait."

The younger woman tipped up her head and laughed, her chin-length blond hair swishing along her jaw. Her carefree action sent a shaft of pain through Neva's middle. Lois leaned close, her eyes sparkling conspiratorially. "To be honest, Ernie will welcome the chance to escape the table while the children are eating. They always seem to spill something on him."

The comment stirred memories of Bud's and Belle's toddler days. Neva's heart panged. "Well . . . if you're sure."

Lois touched Neva's elbow, the gesture like a sweet balm. "I'm sure. Wait right here." She hurried off on scuffed Mary Janes.

Only a few seconds later Reverend Savage bustled around the corner, wiping his mouth with a crumpled napkin. He tossed the napkin on a little table beside a wooden rocking chair and came straight at Neva, both hands extended. "Mrs. Shilling, Lois said you needed to talk to me."

Neva allowed him to cradle one of her hands between his warm palms. "Yes. If you have some time."

"Absolutely." He gently tugged her toward

the sofa stretching along the front windows. "Have a seat and —"

Neva jerked free of his grasp. "Not here."

His dark brows descended.

"I need to speak to you privately." She whisked a glance toward the doorway from which the sounds of children's voices and Lois Savage's soft reprimands continued to drift.

He gave a solemn nod. "All right then. We can go to my office."

They walked together to the church — he with a light step and Neva moving as though she trudged through a foot of sludge. He used a key to open the back door and gestured her inside. He led her up a short, dim hallway to a door on the left. He pushed the door inward and then reached past her to punch the button on the wall.

Light flooded the small space. A large wooden desk, its top nearly hidden by lined notepads and open books, filled the middle of the floor. He held his hand toward a pair of wooden chairs huddled in the corner. Neva gratefully sank into the closest chair's sturdy seat, and he took the opposite chair, his lips curving into a smile.

"Here now. Is this better?"

At least now no one would overhear her shameful confession. She nodded.

"Good. What's troubling you, Mrs. Shilling?"

His voice carried authority and kindness. Neva found her stiff muscles relaxing a bit. "I received some disturbing news yesterday. I hoped if I told you, you'd be willing to share the news with the congregation on Sunday."

Concern crept across his features. "Of course. What is it?"

"Warren is dead." She hadn't allowed the word *dead* to leave her lips when she talked to the children or to Mr. Randall. Stating the word so baldly stabbed like a poker through her middle. Unconsciously she released a little gasp of pain.

At once Reverend Savage reached for her hands. He held tight, his grip giving her strength.

"He died of botulism a week ago and they buried him in Beloit. A sheriff's official brought his belongings and also three small children. Warren —" Her tongue froze. Shame and anger and disgust crashed through her. She couldn't tell the minister her husband had fathered children with another wife. She stammered, "W-wanted to raise them." That was truth, wasn't it? She dropped her gaze to their joined hands rather than peering into the preacher's

92

sympathetic face.

His hands tightened on hers. "I'm so sorry for your loss, Mrs. Shilling. Of course I'll tell the congregation. Is there anything else I can do for you?"

Make it all be a dream. But not even a minister could work miracles. Neva, head low, shrugged.

"What about the store? Will you sell the mercantile?"

The question startled her into looking at him again. "Why would I sell it?"

Genuine confusion pinched his brow. "How will you operate it on your own?"

"I've operated it on my own half of each year since 1926." Even as she spoke, worrisome thoughts trailed through her mind. Warren had always paid their bills on his months in town and left envelopes of cash for her to distribute during his months away. She'd never ordered coal for the furnace or paid the electricity. He'd also brought supplies to restock the shelves on his return. He'd never told her where he ordered them, and she'd never felt the need to ask. Twice today she'd disappointed customers with her inability to fill their complete orders. All of the things Warren had done she'd now have to do on her own.

Tears filling her eyes, she wilted on the

chair. "The children and I need a means of income. Our home is above the store. I can't sell the mercantile."

"I admire your determination, but I confess I'm concerned for you." The sincere compassion glowing in his eyes brought a second rush of tears that rolled down her cheeks. He pulled a square cloth of white cotton from his trouser pocket and gave it to her.

While she mopped her face, he said, "Running a business is challenging under the best of circumstances. But without any help? During these days of economic trouble?" Although kindly uttered, the words fell like lashes. "Maybe selling the business right now wouldn't be wise considering how few people would have the funds to buy it. But are you sure you want to keep it open? Do you have family who might be able to take you in for a while until you can decide what's best for you and your children?"

Neva shook her head, misery twining through her chest. "I'm an orphan. My only family was Warren."

But she hadn't been his only family.

She shoved that thought aside and continued. "I must rely on myself. I have to keep things as stable as I can for Bud and Belle. They've already lost their father. I won't make them leave the only home they've ever known."

He nodded, his lips forming a soft line of understanding. "What of the other children you mentioned — the ones you said Warren wanted to raise?"

Her hands began to tremble. She'd told Bud the children would stay, but she hadn't yet considered how much more she would need to do in the mercantile. Taking on Warren's responsibilities in the store as well as seeing to the needs of three additional children was too much. No one would fault her for sending those children away. Especially not if the minister thought it wise.

She blurted out a question. "What should I do?"

CHAPTER 7

Bud

Bud curled his fingers over the battered hymnal tucked in the little slatted shelf on the back of the pew in front of him, eager to sing the closing hymn. Because then he could leave. The walls of the church had never seemed closer, tighter, than that morning. How could Ma and Belle sit there with their Bibles open in their laps, acting like everything was hunky-dory when the whole world was upside down? Pop was dead, three kids who'd somehow won his father's affection were smashed together in a row between him and Belle, and Ma had hardly slept or eaten since the sheriff's officer — who right now sat on the pew closest to the doors — showed up with that wagon full of furniture. He nearly snorted. If there was a God up in heaven, He must be as much a bully as Leroy and Leon Randall to let so many bad things happen at once.

"Before we close today, I have something of importance to share with you."

Bud released the hymnal and slunk low in the seat.

"One of our church families has experienced a tremendous tragedy. Mr. Warren Shilling, owner of the Main Street Mercantile, succumbed to illness in Beloit almost two weeks ago and was laid to rest in that town's cemetery."

Murmurs rippled across the room. People turned around to stare. Bud aimed his gaze at the hymnal and ordered himself not to cry.

"He leaves behind his widow, Mrs. Neva Shilling, his son, Bud, and daughter, Belle."

Bud already knew what the preacher would say — Ma had warned him and Belle before they took off for service that morning — but hearing it all said out loud still stung worse than being attacked by a hundred hornets. He folded his arms tight over his chest and held back the roar of fury that tried to escape his throat.

"Mrs. Shilling also told me her husband took on the care of three orphaned children — Charley, Cassie, and Adeline — who are currently staying with the Shillings here in Buffalo Creek."

More murmurs, some sounding confused

and some holding approval, rose from the people in the pews.

Bud flicked a glance at Charley and caught the boy scowling. If people weren't watching, he'd give the kid a good jab with his elbow. Charley had landed in high clover as far as Bud was concerned, being chosen by Pop and then taking over half of Bud's room. If anybody ought to be scowling, it should be Bud. He clamped his jaw hard and stared at the hymnal again. When would they sing the closing song? He wanted out of here.

"Mrs. Shilling and I are working on a memorial service for her husband. When the time and day is settled, we'll put an announcement in the Buffalo Creek *Examiner,* so please be watching." He paused, and Bud's fingers inched toward the hymnal. Preacher Savage sent a slow look across the congregation. "Before going home today, please take a moment to offer condolences to Mrs. Shilling and her children."

Bud's fingers curled into a fist. Nobody better talk to him! What would he say back?

"Also be in prayer on how to follow the biblical instruction to see to the needs of widows and orphans."

His stomach whirled. He didn't want to be an orphan.

"Let's ease our dear sister's burden with our loving support."

A knot of tangled agony and fury filled his throat. Nothing would ease the burden of not having a father anymore.

"Now please rise, take out your hymnals, and turn to page 119, 'What a Friend We Have in Jesus.'"

Finally! Bud held the hymnal open, but he didn't sing. He couldn't. Nothing would sneak past the lump in his throat. Charley didn't sing either, but Cassie and Adeline added their squeaky voices to the song, sometimes singing the wrong words and notes. The congregation sang all four verses, and Bud's desire to bolt grew stronger with every line. By the time they reached the closing words, he was ready to climb out of his skin.

He slapped the hymnal into its spot and pushed past the three little orphan kids. Ma reached for his arm, but he ducked away from her grasp and charged up the aisle, ignoring the sympathetic looks and extended hands of others in church.

He smacked the door open and plowed onto the porch, ramming directly into Mr. Jesse Caudel's backside. He grunted with the impact, bounced backward, and caught hold of the porch railing to hold himself upright.

The man turned and gave him a surprised look. "Bud . . ." He glanced at the door before looking at Bud again. "Why aren't you in there with your mother?"

"There's plenty of folks in there with her." He'd seen them all swarming toward their pew. "She don't need me."

"I think you're wrong about that, son."

Heat exploded through Bud's middle. He snarled, "I'm not your son." If the man snapped at him for being rude, he wouldn't apologize. Nobody should be calling him something only a father should say.

"You're right. I'll just call you Bud from now on. How's that?"

Too surprised to answer, Bud just stared at the deputy.

"Bud Shilling . . ." The man's tone turned to musing. "I'm tryin' to figure this all out. I thought your mother's name was Gaines. But in there the preacher called her Mrs. Shilling."

Bud curled his lips into a sneer the way he'd seen Leroy Randall do. "My ma was Gaines before she married my pop. Now she's Neva Shilling."

Mr. Caudel's eyes narrowed. Just a tiny bit. Almost so tiny Bud wasn't sure he really saw it. "So your pop was Warren Shilling."

Was. Bud broke out in a cold sweat. "I gotta go." He lunged forward.

Mr. Caudel's thick hand came down on his shoulder and held him in place. "I won't pretend to know what it's like to lose your pop."

He spoke soft. Gentle. But his hand was hard. Firm. Bud stood stone still beneath the weight of it.

"I'm guessing it's made you sad. And even angry. You probably think it wasn't fair."

Bud gritted his teeth. Fair? Not even close.

"I bet you're even tempted to wallow in unhappiness. Maybe try to make everybody else unhappy, too, hoping if they aren't happy, it'll somehow make you feel better." His fingers pinched tight, not painful but definitely attention grabbing. "But, Bud, that's wrong."

Bud aimed a slit-eyed scowl at the man, the face he'd been using to send Charley scuttling to his own half of the room every time he tried to talk to Bud.

Caudel didn't even wince. "You're hurting. That's all right. Losing your pop is reason to hurt. But it's not a reason to hurt others. Keep that in mind." He finally let go.

Bud leaped from the porch and ran for home like the Randall boys were on his tail.

Jesse

Jesse stepped to the edge of the porch and watched Bud hightail it up the street. Uncertainty pricked. Maybe he shouldn't have been so frank with the boy. He hardly knew him, after all. But if everything he suspected was true, Neva Gaines — he shook his head and corrected his thoughts — Neva Shilling would need all the support and kindness she could get. Bud's self-centered mourning would only add to his mother's pain. Regret for the way he'd treated his own ma soured his stomach. He'd hate to see Bud carry the same regret.

The church door opened, and Jesse moved to the side with his toe propped against the bottom corner of the door to hold it in place. Parishioners trailed past. Most turned a glance in his direction, and he nodded a hello to each, noting how many bobbed their heads or offered a curious smile in reply. The youngsters galloped out, some whooping to release their pent-up energy the way his younger sisters had when leaving church services, but every last one of the grownups from young to elderly was quiet. Subdued. Rightfully so, given the news they'd just heard about one of their own.

Something warm stirred through Jesse.

The townsfolk's lack of idle chatter, their sorrowful furrowing of brows and dabbing of eyes, endeared them to Jesse. They were a caring lot. It'd be a pleasure to serve such people. That sheriff job was becoming more comfortable by the minute.

The flow of people ended, and Jesse peeked inside. Mrs. Shilling was talking to the preacher and a young woman he surmised must be the preacher's wife from the way she held on to his elbow. Two little towheaded toddlers clung to the woman's skirts. Mrs. Shilling's daughter stood several feet away, surrounded by Warren and Violet's youngsters. He shouldn't stare. If they caught him, they'd think he was spying. But somehow he couldn't pull his gaze away. Something about the two separate circles of people bothered him.

He watched until the woman released the preacher's arm and enfolded Mrs. Shilling in a hug. He slipped halfway behind the door, angling his gaze away, while Mrs. Shilling and the cluster of children filed past. He sneaked a glance at their retreating backs and frowned.

Mrs. Shilling moved with her spine stiff and her face aimed straight ahead, her hand looped through Belle's elbow. Belle held the hand of the younger of Warren and Violet's

103

girls, and the other children trotted along behind.

He chewed the inside of his cheek, recalling how Belle had seen to the little ones through the church service, hushing them when they whispered and letting Adeline rest her head on her shoulder. He'd often looked at their row of heads — he couldn't seem to help himself — and not once had he caught Mrs. Shilling acknowledging the children's presence.

The warm feeling the townspeople inspired dissolved, and a lump of discomfort replaced it. She'd taken Charley, Cassie, and Adeline into her home, but it seemed she was holding them away from her heart. And he was pretty sure he knew why.

The thud of footsteps pulled Jesse from his musing. He stepped from behind the door and encountered the preacher on the other side of the threshold.

The man's face immediately lit with a smile. "Well, good morning! Or maybe I should say good afternoon." He chuckled. "I believe the noon hour has passed." He held out his hand. "I'm Ernest Savage, minister for the Buffalo Creek Chapel."

Jesse shook hands with him. The handshake was brief, firm, and told him a lot about the preacher's strength. "Good afternoon. I'm Jesse Caudel."

"I'm glad you stayed long enough for me to meet you, Mr. Caudel." The man spoke as energetically as he had from behind the pulpit, lending evidence of his genuineness. "My wife, Lois, already took our children home — as Lois would say, they'd worn out their 'sit' — or I'd introduce her." He pushed aside his suit coat and slipped his hands into his trouser pockets. "We don't get many visitors to Buffalo Creek. What brings you to town?"

Jesse had never established the habit of sharing his personal business with strangers, but he figured he could trust a preacher. "I guess you could say I'm nosing around, getting a feel for the community. I might be stepping into Sheriff Schlacter's shoes."

Preacher Savage blew out a soft whistle. "Big shoes to fill. Folks around here have a lot of respect for Dodds Schlacter." He looked Jesse up and down. "But I'm a pretty fair judge of character, and something tells me you'd do a fine job in his stead."

"I'd do my best. That's all I can promise."

A smile lit the preacher's eyes. "That's all any of us can promise, isn't it? Of course, believers also claim Philippians 4:13, 'I can do all things through Christ which strengtheneth me.' " He tipped his head, his gaze holding Jesse captive. "Are you a believer, Mr. Caudel?"

"Call me Jesse."

"You didn't answer my question."

Jesse grinned. The man was tenacious. "I suppose I didn't."

The preacher laughed. "All right then. I won't push. But I will invite you to have dinner with my family and me."

"Well, I —"

"If you're going to be our new sheriff, I'd like the chance to get acquainted."

Jesse considered the invitation. The man's face — still young, earnest, honest — held an expression of openness that was hard to resist. If Jesse intended to make Buffalo Creek his new home, being friendly with the town's clergy couldn't hurt. And this man ministered to Neva Shilling. He could shed light on the strange circumstance of her being called Mrs. Warren Shilling when the folks of Beloit recognized another woman in that position.

Jesse nodded. "Thank you. I think I'd enjoy taking a meal with your family."

CHAPTER 8

Jesse

Jesse dropped his napkin beside his plate, leaned back, and released a satisfied sigh. "Thank you, ma'am. That was a very good stew." Not as flavorful as the vegetables-only stew he'd eaten at Neva Shilling's table, but full of tender chunks of chicken and topped with moist dumplings. His stomach was achingly full.

"I appreciate your kind words, Mr. Caudel." Mrs. Savage's smile crinkled into a grimace. "And thank you for being understanding about the broth Jenny spilled on your trousers. We've yet to make it through a meal without a mishap, but usually the children spatter their father's clothes rather than a guest's. I'd be happy to launder them for you."

Growing up on a farm, Jesse had definitely had worse things spattered on his britches. He waved a hand in dismissal. "No worries, ma'am. They're still learning."

She shot a warm smile at him, then lifted the little girl from her highchair while the little boy climbed off his stool. With the girl wriggling in her arms, she addressed her son. "Come along now, Benji. It's time for your nap." Both children wailed as she ushered them out of the room. Somewhere up the hallway a door closed, muffling the protests.

Preacher Savage shook his head, an indulgent chuckle rumbling from his chest. "I'm afraid those two inherited my orneriness. My mother says I was a 'holy terror' when I was a boy and it's nothing short of a miracle that I became a 'holy sharer' as an adult."

Jesse laughed. During the hour-long meal, he'd grown fond of the young minister and his entire family. He couldn't recollect the last time he'd felt so at ease with folks he'd just met. "I imagine your mother's very proud of you, being a minister and all."

"No more than yours must be, having her son become a lawman."

Jesse's chest constricted, and he coughed out a short laugh. "To be completely honest with you, Preacher, my ma was plenty upset when I left farming. She and my pa both expected me to stay close and help work their land. Matter of fact, that's why they picked me from the group of orphans on the train. They had a whole herd of girls, but no boys. They took me home so they'd have a son big enough to help."

Everyone in Severlyn had known he was adopted, but he'd never told another soul about his humble beginning or how he'd become the Caudels' boy since he'd left the Nebraska farmstead. But it felt right — safe even — telling Preacher Savage. Jesse shrugged. "They're good people and I appreciate the upbringing they gave me, but I guess you could say farming just wasn't in my blood."

From behind the closed door up the hallway, Mrs. Savage began singing a lullaby. The melody was a homey sound, one that brought a feeling of peace to the room. Dinner was over and he ought to leave, but instead he settled himself more comfortably in his chair and toyed with his empty coffee mug. "What do your folks do for a living, Preacher?"

"Please call me Ernie. You aren't a member of my congregation. Yet." His dark eyes sparked with mischief. "And since I'm calling you Jesse, it only seems fitting."

"All right. Ernie." The name put images of the holy terror he must have been in Jesse's head, and a grin tugged at his mouth.

"So is preaching in your blood, or did you come by the job another way?"

Ernie crossed to the stove and poured himself another cup of coffee, talking as he went. "I come from a family of teachers. My mother taught in a little one-room schoolhouse before she married my father, my older sister teaches the youngest grades in Wakarusa, and my father is still teaching at a secondary school in Topeka." He slid back into his chair and cupped the mug with both hands. "I planned to be a teacher, too. Even got my certificate. But then a lightning bolt hit me and let me know I was on the wrong path."

Jesse gawked at the man. "A . . . a lightning bolt? You mean, a real lightning bolt?"

Ernie nodded. "It struck the ground about seven yards behind me. The current went in through my feet and out my hands. Singed some of my hair off, too, but luckily it grew back. Left scars on my hands and feet, though." He held out his hands. Pale pink splotches decorated the center of each palm. "The shock knocked me unconscious, and while I was out I had a dream. Or maybe a vision. I can't say for sure, but a Voice told me, 'Tell them how I saved you.' After I recovered, I enrolled in divinity school and trained to become a minister of the gospel."

He picked up his mug and took a slow sip. "Buffalo Creek Chapel is my first placement."

Open-mouthed, Jesse stared at the preacher for several seconds, gathering his senses. Then he shook his head. "I bet your congregation listens close when you tell that story."

Ernie chuckled. "I've never told them."

"But you said the voice told you to —"

" 'Tell them how I saved you.' That's right." His eyes glinting with fervency, Ernie rested his elbows on the table and leaned closer to Jesse. "And I do. I tell them how Jesus saved me from my sins. You see, Jesse, I survived that lightning bolt, but it weakened my heart. Doctors tell me it's likely my body will wear out early. But my soul will live forever with my Savior. That's the message I share, because that's the message that matters. And that's why I asked you if you're a believer. Lightning bolts or not, your body will wear out one day, too. Is your soul ready to meet your Maker?"

Jesse drew back. "Whoa there, Reverend, I'm not one of your parishioners. No need to preach at me."

In the space of a heartbeat, gentle warmth replaced the intense glimmer. "I'm sorry. I said I wouldn't push, didn't I?"

"Yep. You did." Jesse watched Ernie closely for signs of the preacher returning. Seeing none, he braved a comment. "You like being a minister."

"Very much. I suppose it's something like being an officer of the law. We both try to help people."

Jesse released a wry chuckle. "Of course, not all people appreciate the help."

Ernie raised one eyebrow and aimed a steady look at Jesse. "No, they don't."

Jesse hurried on. "You're awfully young yet. What — thirty? Thirty-one?"

He grinned. "Twenty-eight."

"Twenty-eight . . ." Seven years younger than Jesse. "You've got a wife, children, and an entire congregation depending on you. Seems like a pretty big responsibility."

"No more than an entire town depending on a sheriff."

"I suspect church members need different kinds of help from their minister than folks do from their sheriff." He'd help and move on to the next problem. A minister had to stick with the problems to the very end. "It must wear on you."

Ernie sipped his coffee, his brow scrunching. He set the cup aside. "Some days are more difficult than others — like today, telling everyone about Warren Shilling. It's hard to understand why he was taken so soon."

Jesse went immediately on alert. "He owned the mercantile here in town?"

"That's right. I'm sorry you never got the chance to meet him. He was a good man — an honest businessman, a leader in our community, and a pillar of the church."

The praise took Jesse by surprise. Ernie must have been unaware of Warren's other household. Given the ages of the children, it stood to reason Shilling had married Neva Gaines first. Which meant his marriage to Violet was a farce. If Ernie knew, he'd surely brand Warren Shilling a scoundrel rather than a saint. "Do I remember you saying he leaves a widow and two children?"

"Yes."

"But there were five children with Mrs. Shilling this morning."

"That's right. Warren spent every other month on the road, selling goods to people who lived far from town. In his travels, he apparently encountered children who needed a family and decided to take them in." A look of wonder bloomed on Ernie's face. "Can you imagine? These days people are struggling to get by, but he willingly assumed responsibility for those poor little waifs."

Jesse managed to squelch a snort.

"When he took ill, he made arrangements for them to come here to Buffalo Creek. So now they're with his wife." Ernie blew out a breath, shaking his head. "Such a shame that he passed away. Mrs. Shilling will certainly struggle without him, and Bud, Belle, and the three little ones have suffered a great loss."

An image of Mrs. Shilling walking ahead of Charley and Cassie, ignoring little Adeline, flashed in his mind. "Mrs. Shilling isn't going to raise those kids on her own, is she?"

Ernie turned aside. "Only Mrs. Shilling can answer that question. I'm praying for her to have discernment."

She'd need more than discernment if she decided to raise her husband's illegitimate offspring.

Mrs. Savage tiptoed into the kitchen and sank into her chair. She aimed a weary smile across the table at the two men. "They're sleeping. It only took five songs and three storybooks."

Ernie grinned. "A new record."

She sighed. "Indeed." Then she glanced at Jesse's cup and said brightly, "Would you like another cup of coffee before we bid you farewell, Mr. Caudel?"

Jesse swallowed a laugh. Such a subtle way

114

of asking him to go away. "No, thank you. I'm already sloshing." He rose and extended his hand to Ernie. "I've enjoyed visiting with you, Preacher, and with your lovely wife. Thank you for the kind invitation."

Mrs. Savage blushed a becoming pink. "You're welcome at our table any time, Mr. Caudel."

As long as he didn't overstay his welcome.

She began clearing the dishes, and Ernie escorted Jesse through the front room. At the door he gave Jesse's shoulder a solid smack. "If you decide to make Buffalo Creek your home, I hope you'll consider attending our chapel regularly. Man does not live by bread alone, but by the words of God."

Jesse grinned. Ernie had slipped into preacher talk again. "I'll consider it, but my duties might keep me otherwise occupied on Sunday mornings." In Beloit an officer was on duty every hour of the day, every day of the week. Jesse wasn't a stranger to working on Sundays.

"I'll have you know Sheriff Schlacter is a member of the Episcopal Church on the other side of town and he rarely misses a service." Ernie shrugged, smiling. "I think you'll discover pretty quickly Buffalo Creek is a quiet town peopled with folks who don't get into much mischief. Sundays are our day of rest, so they're especially quiet."

Whether he'd intended to hint he wanted to join the other community members in rest or not, Jesse decided to take the statement as his cue to leave. He grabbed the doorknob.

"And, Jesse?"

The preacher-tone entered Ernie's voice once more. Jesse sent a slow look in his direction.

"I'll pray for you to have discernment about becoming our new sheriff."

He didn't take much stock in praying. The prayers his parents sent up for abundant crop yields or for the next baby to be a son hadn't gone any farther than the ceiling to his way of thinking. But he'd been taught manners. "Thank you."

"I'll also pray for your soul. It needs a Savior."

He wouldn't tell this sincere young minister that he'd rather depend on himself. He said his good-byes and headed up the quiet street toward town and the sheriff's office. Sheriff Schlacter had given him a key so he could come and go as he pleased during his stay. The small jail in the back of the office served him well as a hotel room. Which was good since the hotel in town charged a dollar a night and he hadn't been given any kind of expense account.

A cool breeze brushed his face and teased his hair — a pleasant, almost-welcoming touch. His boot heels thudded on the raised walkway, creating a hollow sound that echoed against the storefronts and offered him some company. He let his gaze drift up and down both sides of the street, once again noting how neatly kept everything appeared. His first, brief impression of the town hadn't changed during his few days here. Would more time tarnish the image of peace and community pride? Somehow he hoped not. Seemed there ought to be places left in the world where a fellow could relax and trust the outside to truly reflect the inside.

He rounded the corner for the sheriff's small office. Outside the office on the boardwalk, a boy in blue dungarees and a brown corduroy jacket crouched on his haunches, shooting marbles in a chalk circle. Jesse took a wide step to avoid trampling him, and the boy looked up in surprise.

Jesse looked back with equal surprise. "Charley Shilling . . ." He balled his fists on his hips in mock exasperation. "What do you think you're doing out here by your-self?"

Charley straightened, still pinching a red-and-white aggie between his thumb and index finger. "Nothing much. Just staying out of the way."

Jesse didn't like the answer. He placed his hand on Charley's skinny shoulder. "Does your aunt Neva know you're out here?"

"Huh-uh."

"She'll worry if she looks for you and can't find you." He couldn't be certain he was right, but this boy needed some assurance. "I think you should head on back to the mercantile."

"I don't wanna." Charley stepped from beneath Jesse's hand and kicked a cloudy-blue marble into the street. He squinted over his shoulder at Jesse like he was taking aim. "Can I ask you something?"

"You've got a tongue. Go ahead and ask."

"Aunt Neva's not really my aunt, is she?"

How'd he managed to walk into this conversation? Weariness washed over him. Jesse sighed and plopped onto the bench in front of the sheriff's office. "What makes you ask that?"

Charley inched toward Jesse, his somber gaze on the marble, which he turned this way and that. "In church the preacher said

Aunt Neva was my daddy's wife. If she was my aunt, she'd be my daddy's sister."

So he'd reasoned out some of it. But Jesse hoped he hadn't figured out the whole thing. No eight-year-old boy should have to face such truths about his own father. He caught the hand playing with the marble and pulled it downward. Charley shifted his attention to Jesse. Jesse offered a nod. "You're right, Charley. But you know, there's no law that says the title 'aunt' can't be used for women other than your ma's or pa's sister. Sometimes it's used because it's more personal —"

Charley crinkled his face in confusion.

Jesse sought a word the boy would understand. "It's friendlier than saying 'Mrs. Shilling.' And it's more polite than calling an adult by her first name. Does that make sense?"

"I guess so."

"So it's okay for you to call her Aunt Neva."

Charley examined Jesse's face for several seconds. Then he ducked his head. "My daddy said for us to call her Aunt Neva?"

"Yep."

"And he wanted me and Cassie and Adeline to be with her?"

"That's what he told the doctor in Beloit,

and that's what the doctor told me."

Charley squirmed in place, his chin pressed to his left shoulder. "A boy's always supposed to do what his daddy says. But . . ."

Jesse caught Charley's chin and lifted his face. "What's the problem, Charley?"

"Bud's there, too, and he doesn't like me. He doesn't want me around. He told me to git. That's why I'm out here." Twin tears rolled over the boy's lashes and down his reddened cheeks. "I can't do what Daddy wanted and do what Bud wants. I don't know what to do."

Hadn't Bud listened to anything Jesse had told him earlier? That boy needed to grow up some. Jesse planted his hands on his knees and pushed himself upright. "Well, what you're gonna do right now is scoop up those marbles and put 'em in your pocket before someone steps on one and takes a tumble. Then I'll walk you back to the mercantile and have a talk with your aunt Neva — see if we can't find a way to set things right between you and Bud."

Charley chewed his lower lip. "You think you can do it?"

Jesse wouldn't be much of a sheriff if he couldn't settle a disagreement between two still-wet-behind-the-ears kids. But he wouldn't make a promise he couldn't keep. "Let's just get goin', huh?"

CHAPTER 9

Neva

Neva stared at the list of items written in her neat script. Such a long list. So many supplies needed. Why hadn't she noticed how empty the shelves were getting? She whispered to the quiet room, "Because I've never had to worry about it. Warren always arrived in time to fill them." A sob built in her throat. "Oh, Warren . . ."

The words on the page began to waver and dance. She propped her elbow on the counter and rested her forehead against the heel of her hand, her eyes closed.

"Will you sell the mercantile?"

Reverend Savage's question haunted her. She'd said no. She'd meant no. Even with her eyes closed, she knew exactly what she'd touch if she stretched out her hand in any direction. To the front, candy jars. Behind, medicinal cures. On the right canned goods and on the left bins of dried beans. She didn't even bother to test her memory so certain was she of what her fingers would find.

Eyes still closed, head low, she allowed her thoughts to transport her backward to the day she and Warren said their vows before the justice of the peace at the Belleville courthouse. That same day they'd ridden in a stagecoach to Buffalo Creek, and he carried her over the threshold of this very mercantile. She only eighteen, Warren a worldly twenty-two, they'd opened their business with the confidence and energy of youth. And they'd made it a success. This mercantile was more than a store. It was her home, her refuge, her security.

"Will you sell the mercantile?"

She jerked upright and shouted a reply at the half-filled shelves. "No!"

Someone tapped on the front door. A deep, masculine voice called, "Mrs. Shilling? Are you all right in there?"

Embarrassment flooded her. Who could be out on Sunday afternoon? Everyone treated the Lord's day as a day of rest in Buffalo Creek. She scurried across the floor, smoothing her hair as she went, and pulled up the shade. Mr. Jesse Caudel stood on the other side of the glass. She jolted in surprise. What was he doing back in town?

He jiggled the doorknob. "Open up, please."

She shook her head. "It's Sunday. I'm closed."

"I don't want to buy anything. I need to talk to you."

On his last visit he'd sent her down a pathway of confusion and anxiety. She couldn't take one more piece of bad news. "No."

His eyebrows formed a sharp V. He half turned and, to Neva's second shock, tugged Charley from behind him. Then he pointed to the doorknob again. This time Neva opened the door.

Mr. Caudel gave Charley a little push into the store and stepped in behind him. He kept his hand curled over the boy's shoulder. "I found Charley up the street a ways, playing marbles on the sidewalk. Since nobody else was out, I thought it would be better if he came on back."

Dried tears stained the boy's cheeks. He leaned against Mr. Caudel's hip, his head low, and peered at her sheepishly through his fringe of bangs. He had Warren's straight walnut husk–colored hair.

She jerked her attention to Mr. Caudel. "I didn't even know he was gone."

"I kind of figured."

The statement held no rancor, but defensiveness rose within Neva anyway. She folded her arms over her chest. "I've spent my afternoon doing inventory. I instructed the children to go to their rooms after lunch and entertain themselves quietly as is fitting on the Lord's day. I assumed they would all obey."

Charley hunched his shoulders. The collar of his jacket hid the bottom half of his face, but his velvety-brown eyes lined with thick black lashes continued to silently plead with her for . . . what?

She sighed. "Go upstairs, Charley, and stay there now."

Charley didn't move. Mr. Caudel gave his shoulder a nudge, and Charley bobbed his head. "Yes, ma'am." He trudged off.

Neva waited until his plodding footsteps on the stairs faded, and then she turned to Mr. Caudel. "Thank you for bringing him back. I'll make sure he doesn't wander off again." She opened the door for him.

He pushed the door closed. "I haven't talked to you yet."

She needed to finish taking stock of her merchandise, peruse the catalogs for the best prices on canned items and dress goods, and jot a few notes for the memorial service Reverend Savage insisted the community needed to say a proper good-bye to Warren. She pulled the door open and gestured to the sidewalk. "I don't have time to talk."

"Make time."

If only she could manufacture time. Then maybe she'd have a better chance of keeping the mercantile afloat. "Mr. Caudel, I —"

"Charley told me Bud told him to 'git.' That's why he was outside by himself."

Cool air, carrying a few crisp leaves and dust, whisked through the open door. She didn't have time to sweep again. Neva closed the door with a snap. "I'm sure Bud didn't intend for Charley to leave the mercantile. The boys share a room now, and Bud hasn't yet accepted the arrangement. He probably wanted Charley to stay on his own side of the room."

Mr. Caudel frowned. "So you think it's all right for Bud to order Charley about?"

Of course she didn't. She'd spoken with Bud multiple times in the few days they'd been together about the need to be kind to Charley and the little girls. But none of this was Jesse Caudel's business. "I can see to my children without your interference."

He had the audacity to chuckle. "I'm not so sure about that. Or I wouldn't have found Charley up the street by himself and you unaware that he was gone."

But Charley isn't my child. The words formed in her head and nearly spilled from her mouth, but guilt held them back. She should have known he'd left the mercantile. A good mother didn't let children wander off alone. A good wife didn't lose her husband to another woman. She winced against a stab of pain, her eyes slipping closed.

"About Charley . . ."

Neva looked at the man. Sunlight sneaked through a gap in the window shades and painted a ribbon of yellow along his side, emphasizing his tall, sturdy frame and drawing attention to the shadow of whiskers on his cheek. He seemed formidable, yet in his blue eyes she glimpsed a hint of tenderness. She focused on his eyes.

"He's trying to sort things out, but he's still a little confused."

His comment confused her. "Sorting out what?"

"Relationships." Mr. Caudel shifted slightly, removing himself from the sunbeam's path, and hooked his thumb in his trouser pocket. Even though he wore a plaid shirt in place of a deputy's uniform and no star shone on his chest, he looked every bit the lawman in his posture. "He asked me if you were really his aunt, but he'd already reasoned you couldn't be because the preacher called you his daddy's wife instead of his sister."

Neva broke out in goose flesh.

"I don't think he's grasped the whole truth of the situation, and honestly I hope he doesn't. Not until he's a good bit older."

"Wait." Neva's head spun. She lurched to the apple barrel and perched on its edge. "What do you mean by 'the whole truth of the situation'?"

He released a small huff of breath. "I stood by while a minister in Beloit spoke words over Warren and Violet Shilling's graves. I carted their youngsters to you at Warren's dying request. I know full well that your husband took up housekeeping with another woman. That's the whole truth, isn't it?"

She sent a frantic glance toward the staircase, then darted to the front window and peeked out. No one around to hear. Relief sagged her knees. She staggered back to the barrel and sank down. There was more — things Mr. Caudel couldn't know. She'd driven Warren to Violet. His desire for a big family couldn't be met any other way. The whole truth included her failure.

She sat in silence, deep remorse stealing her ability to speak.

Mr. Caudel stepped close. "Isn't it?" He spoke gently, the simple question falling like cottonwood seeds along the creek bank.

Neva's chin quivered. Her dry, aching throat resisted a reply, but somehow she croaked out, "He had children with another woman, yes." Then strength borne of desperation propelled her from the barrel. She gripped his forearms. "And you cannot tell anyone. I won't devastate Bud and Belle with their mother's betrayal."

He frowned. "Don't you mean their father's betrayal?"

Neva rushed on. "Warren's children are innocent of wrongdoing, but if people find out, they will suffer in his stead. The truth must stay buried with Warren, Mr. Caudel."

He slowly shook his head. "That's not the kind of thing that can be hidden. Those three kids upstairs are living evidence of what Warren did."

Why couldn't he understand? She pushed away from him and gripped her hands together in a prayerful position. "You're the only one who knows. Because you live in Beloit, you know. But no one in Buffalo Creek knows. No one in Buffalo Creek has to know. They'll only know what they're told, and —"

"So you're gonna lie to everybody?"

The question took the wind out of her. She slowly slid onto the apple barrel again. "No." She swallowed. "No, I won't lie. I just won't tell . . . the entire truth."

He raised his eyebrows and gazed at her with an expression of uncertainty. "Not so sure that isn't the same thing as lying."

She wasn't either. But what else could she do? She wasn't foolish enough to believe Warren's indiscretions would be overlooked. They would trickle onto her, onto Bud and Belle. Instead of condolences, she'd be offered condescension. She'd suffered it before — folks turning up their noses at the orphans living in the Brambleville asylum, expecting the worst because they didn't have parents. One woman had even pointed at them on a visit to town and spat, *The sins of the fathers will be visited upon the children to the third generation!*"

The Jonnsons had assured her and the others that the woman was wrong, but Neva still carried deep within her the hurt of that moment. She would never condemn her children to such treatment.

She pulled in a fortifying breath and straightened her spine. She met Jesse Caudel's gaze and spoke with a boldness she

130

didn't know she possessed. "My children will be protected, Mr. Caudel. No one in Buffalo Creek will ever be given reason to suspect Charley, Cassie, and Adeline are anything more than three orphans taken into Warren's care out of concern and compassion."

The man scrunched his lips to one side, his forehead puckering. "Well, now, I think somebody in town's gonna know."

She closed her eyes for a moment, gathering patience. "Yes, I'm aware that Charley will know. And Cassie and Adeline, although they're so young they may forget their other family completely in time. But as far as Charley is concerned, I —"

"I wasn't speaking of Charley, ma'am. I meant me."

She flipped her hand. "You're just passing through." A sudden worry descended. She rose. "You are just passing through, aren't you?"

A grin, somehow both sardonic and sympathetic, creased his face. "I'm not so sure about that, ma'am."

CHAPTER 10

Jesse

"I might be taking the position of sheriff here in Buffalo Creek." Jesse took no pleasure in the defeat that fell across Mrs. Shilling's features.

She lowered her head and covered her face with one slender, chapped hand. A soft moan escaped her lips.

Part of what she'd said — about her children suffering because of their father's behavior — cut him. He'd experienced some of that treatment himself, even in Severlyn, by a handful of folks. He didn't understand it, but an ugly stench followed anyone who didn't have two parents to call his own. Mrs. Shilling seemed most concerned about Bud and Belle, but Jesse's concern spilled over on Charley and the two little girls. All five of those kids could face some real scorn if the folks of Buffalo Creek discovered Warren Shilling's unfaithfulness.

He crossed to the window and peeked out the slit between the sash and the sturdy canvas pull shade. He glimpsed the same neat, well-kept storefronts he'd admired earlier. He'd felt at peace on the street, as if he walked in a place of serenity. Maybe, just maybe, this town would be the one spot where folks would understand, would accept and support instead of accuse and shun. But then again, the folks of this town were as human as the ones in any other city. Warren Shilling's deception might give them reason to drop their kindliness and take on disparagement instead.

Jesse glanced over his shoulder at Mrs. Shilling. Sagging forward, eyes closed, face buried in her hands, she looked as forlorn as Charley had. The sympathy he'd felt for the little boy surged up again and spilled over on the woman. He clopped across the floor and went down on one knee in front of her. "I won't tell."

Her head jerked up as fast as if someone had lit a firecracker under her. Her wide, gray-green eyes fixed on him, hope aglow in their pale irises. "Y-you won't?"

"Nope."

"Oh, Mr. Caudel, you —"

He raised one hand as if making a pledge. "Now, listen. As an officer of the law, I'm beholden to the truth of situations. So if someone straight-out asks me if those kids were spawned by Warren Shilling, I won't be able to say no."

Her face crumpled. Tears swam in her eyes.

He dropped his hand to his bent knee to keep it from cupping her flushed cheek in a gesture of comfort the way he had one of his forlorn little sisters. "But unless someone straight-out asks, I won't say a word about how they came to be here with you. Fair enough?"

She sniffed and flicked her fingertips beneath her eyes, clearing the tears. She nodded. Not with real confidence, but resignation. Still, it was agreement.

Jesse pushed upright. He plucked the lid from the jar of black licorice whips and helped himself to two strings. After digging a nickel from his pocket and sliding it onto the counter in payment, he moved toward the door, twirling the candy. "I'll go and leave you to your inventory now."

His gaze drifted across the shelves. Lots of empty spaces. Did she really make a living in this store? It was half the size of the one Shilling had owned in Beloit and didn't appear to have even a tenth of the goods.

He nipped off the end of one piece of

licorice and settled the spicy chunk of candy in his cheek. "Um . . . is this place gonna be able to support you and five youngsters?"

Her brow puckered briefly, and then understanding dawned on her face. "The shelves are so bare because I've done a good business this past month. They need re-stocking."

"So you've got an order coming then?" He couldn't be sure why he cared so much about her success, but he suspected it mostly had to do with Charley. The little fellow reminded him of himself at that age — a little lost and a lot uncertain. He wanted that boy well cared for. He needed to know Mrs. Shilling would do it.

She moved to the counter and fingered a sheet of paper. The bow formed from her apron strings hung crooked, the one imperfection in her otherwise crisp appearance. "Not . . . yet."

"Why not?" If she didn't have money to buy supplies, she had no business taking on the responsibility of three extra kids, and he'd tell her so.

With lightning speed she whirled around and aimed a glower in his direction. "Since you're privy to my other secrets, you might as well know this one, too. Warren always brought supplies." She lifted the paper and waved it. "I'm familiar with what belongs on these shelves. I know to a single ounce of salt exactly what I need. But where to get it and how to bring it here? Therein lies my quandary, Mr. Caudel."

Was that all? He swallowed the soggy lump of licorice. "You order from Kansas City and pick it up from the train station in Beloit." He took another bite and shrugged.

She stared at him as if he'd cursed. "It isn't that simple."

He waggled the licorice whips at her. "Seems pretty straightforward to me, ma'am."

Mrs. Shilling lifted her face toward the ceiling and heaved a mighty sigh. He'd seen his ma do the same thing when she was exasperated. But he couldn't think of one reason why the storekeeper would be exasperated with him. He'd told her what the Beloit businessmen did — what her former husband probably had done hundreds of times over the years — and it worked just fine.

"Mr. Caudel, to order supplies I have to know which businesses provide which goods. For me to pick them up from Beloit, I need a wagon and the time to make the trip there and back." She gestured broadly, her hands stirring the air. "Who will mind the store while I'm away? If I close, I lose customers. If I don't find a way to provide what people need, I lose customers. Are you beginning to see the larger problem here?"

It took every bit of control Jesse possessed not to laugh at her. The situation wasn't funny. Not even close to funny. But her stern expression and pose didn't fit with her neatly pressed yellow dress all decorated with cream lace at the scooped collar and cuffs or her wavy reddish-brown hair brushed back into a fat bun at the base of her skull. He jammed a four-inch-long piece of licorice into his mouth to stifle his chortle and nodded. "Yes, ma'am. I see."

"Good." Suddenly her frown faded into a pleading look that chased every bit of humor from Jesse's thoughts. "Mr. Caudel, when you brought the children here, you said Warren's store and stock had been sold to pay outstanding debts."

"That's right." Too bad, too. She could have used those goods to fill her shelves.

"How would I go about ascertaining that all of his debts are now covered?"

He paused midchew, thought for a moment, and then swallowed. "I suppose you could put a notice in local newspapers, asking creditors to speak up." He angled his head. "Have any debtors from around here approached you about taking care of unpaid bills?"

She shook her head. "No. But until you mentioned a sale to cover debts, I assumed Warren operated on a strictly cash basis with everyone. He always gave me envelopes with cash to pay for coal, electricity, and incidentals on the months he was on the ro—" Bold red splashed her cheeks. "I mean, when he was in Beloit with . . ."

Jesse nodded to spare her the pain of admitting what her husband had been doing. "Unusual for him to have cash at the ready, considering he was keeping two businesses afloat." His thoughtless remark planted seeds of fretfulness. He could tell by the way she bit down on her lip and turned sharply away.

He added quickly, "Of course, you said this place does well, and the mercantile in Beloit was always bustling. I'm sure he brought in a good amount of profit at both places — enough to pay his bills in Beloit and give you money for the bills here."

She peeked at him from the corner of her eye. "Do you think so?"

Jesse forced a light chuckle. "Well, now, unless he was robbing banks, it's the only logical explanation."

She straightened, smoothed one slim hand

over her hair, and gave a brusque nod. "Yes. Well. I'll visit Mr. Starkey at the telegraph office about posting notices, just in case."

"Actually, if there are any outstanding debts, unless your name is on the lien, too, you aren't responsible for his bills. So when you make that notice, be sure to include his, er, demise. That way you won't be contacted by unscrupulous folks trying to grab an easy dollar."

"All right. I will." Her shoulders rose and fell in a heavy sigh. "Now, I have work to do. I found a stack of catalogs from vendors under the counter, and I need to hunt for my best bargains. So . . ." She raised one eyebrow at him.

He battled a grin. He was destined to be shooed away by females that day. "Then I'll leave you to it."

"Thank you." She pattered to the opposite side of the counter and bent over, disappearing from view.

He called to the empty space where he'd seen her last. "Oh, by the way, there's a freighting company in Beloit — Sutherland Freighting. They send wagons all over Kansas. They could probably deliver your goods from the train station."

She popped up like a puppet on a stage. Her face was chalky except for two bright circles of rose in her cheeks. "I can't possibly use a Beloit company."

Ah. Because of Warren. Jesse blew out a breath, the scent of licorice filling his nose. That man was probably causing more problems from the grave than he had in life. He gentled his voice. "Well, ma'am, using a company right there in Beloit will be the least costly to you since it's the closest railroad town. I'm familiar with Brax Sutherland and his crew. They're trustworthy. They'll treat you fair."

She raised her chin slightly. "I cannot use a Beloit freighter."

Jesse shook his head. "All right, all right, do it your way. But, Mrs. Shilling?" He pointed at her again with the candy. "I think you're biting off more than you can chew, and your kids" — he wisely didn't mention Warren's three — "are gonna be the ones affected most. Maybe you need to really think through whether keeping this business and keeping Charley, Cassie, and Adeline is best for all of you."

Neva

Neva chose not to attend the Sunday evening service. Instead, she gathered the children in the parlor and read aloud from a Bible storybook they'd had on their well-filled bookshelf since Bud and Belle were no older than Adeline. The stories were really too simple for her twins at their age, but she hoped hearing some of the familiar tales would remind them of former happier days and let them drift off to sleep with good memories playing in their minds.

The children lined up on the sofa across from Neva's rocking chair — Bud slouching at one end, Charley sitting erect on the other, and Belle in the middle with a little girl tucked beneath each arm. Cassie and Adeline had taken to Belle like ducklings to a mother duck.

The sight of Belle so at ease with the little ones made Neva's heart ache and sing at the same time. Belle now had the little sisters she'd long prayed for, but knowing how they came to be was a wound that might fester forever in Neva's soul.

She read the story about Joseph and his jealous brothers. She chose it for the similarities between the story characters and the children in her parlor — both groups of siblings came from the same father but different mothers. Would Bud see a bit of himself in the brothers who callously tossed their younger brother into a pit and then sold him to passing slave traders? His repeated yawns and dramatic sighs said the story bored him rather than touched anything inside of him.

When she closed the book on the father's anguish at the loss of his favorite child, her stomach was rolling in anxiety. But she forced a smile as she rose from the chair and slid the book into its place on the shelf. "All right now, off to bed, all of you. School tomorrow."

Bud sat straight up, making the sofa springs whine in protest. "Are we all goin'?"

Neva pressed both palms to her middle in an attempt to calm her jumping stomach. "All but Adeline." What would she do with Adeline while the others attended school? Warren hadn't started traveling until Bud and Belle trooped off to the Buffalo Creek School, so she'd had help when they were small. Would the three-year-old behave all day in the store?

Bud stomped over to Neva. He folded his arms over his chest, his jaw set at a stubborn angle. "I think I oughta be done with school."

Neva recognized a storm brewing. She stepped past Bud and addressed the others. "You children get into your nightclothes and under the covers. Belle will tuck you in."

Belle, ever sweetly helpful, ushered Charley, Cassie, and Adeline up the hall.

Neva turned to Bud and gave him her firmest frown. "Exactly what do you mean you think you should be finished with school?"

"I'm fourteen." Bud's voice cracked in the middle of stating his age. His face flushed pink. "Same age Pop was when he quit school and started workin'."

Why had Warren told the children about his rowdy youth? He'd glamorized being on his own, grasping manhood well ahead of his time. How Warren loved to boast about successfully squirreling away enough money to purchase this building outright and open their business. She wished he'd talked more about the hard side of growing up too fast.

"Your father didn't have a choice. His parents died, and he was left on his own. But I'm here to take care of you, and I want you to get a full education. Maybe even attend college someday."

Bud rolled his eyes. "You can't do everything by yourself, Ma. If you wanna keep those kids Pop picked out, then you're gonna need help in the store." He squared his shoulders and jabbed his taut chest with his thumb. "So I'll quit school and become a storekeeper. Pop always said the business'd be mine and his someday anyway." The hard

143

edge of Bud's voice wavered, a touch of hurt creeping in. He swallowed. "Might as well claim my half now."

Neva wrapped her son in her embrace. His slim, lanky frame felt so different from the little-boy softness she remembered. Sharp shoulder blades rested beneath her palms, and his chin connected with her collarbone. It wouldn't be long before she'd look up to him. She sighed against his temple and pulled back, her lips quivering into a sad smile.

"Bud, I know you want to help, and I appreciate your offer. But you're still a boy."

He opened his mouth as if to protest.

She pressed one finger to her mouth to silence him, then went on softly. "Just as you and your father planned, this mercantile will be yours someday." She'd hold on to it for him somehow. "After you've finished school. After you've grown into manhood. Your father would not approve of you giving up your education to work."

"Pop did just fine as a businessman even without schooling!"

He'd done better than either she or the children had even realized — running two businesses and supporting two families at the same time. How had he managed it when so many other businesses were failing? She wished he'd shared his secrets for success with her. She could use the knowledge. But he'd held many secrets from her.

She pushed down the rising tide of bitterness and prayed for Bud's cooperation. "Yes, he did, but he told me many times he wished he'd had the chance to finish his education because he would have been better prepared to open his own business. Education was important to him, Bud, and it's important to me, too. It should be important to you."

He aimed his rebellious glare to the side and growled out, "I don't wanna go. Not with those kids."

"Neither Charley nor Cassie will be anywhere near your classroom. You probably won't even see them all day." She caught hold of his arm and gave it a little shake. "But you will walk them to and from school, and you will be kind to Charley when you're in your bedroom together. Your father wanted those children. This is their home now."

Bud yanked loose and stomped up the hallway. The slam of his door echoed through the entire building.

"Maybe you need to really think through whether keeping this business and keeping

Charley, Cassie, and Adeline is best for all of you."

Mr. Caudel's parting statement exploded through Neva's mind. Bud resented the children's presence so much. Should she consider taking them to an orphan's home? She raised her gaze to the papered ceiling, envisioning God in His heaven looking down. "Where's the discernment for which Reverend Savage promised to ask? Why are You withholding it from me?"

CHAPTER 11

Arthur

Leon and Leroy slapped their forks onto the table, bounded out of their chairs, and reached for the schoolbooks stacked precariously on the edge of the dry sink.

Arthur released a stern, "Ahem!"

Both boys halted in their tracks and turned toward the housekeeper. "Thank you for breakfast, ma'am," they chorused in a flat recital.

Mrs. Lafferty, unsmiling and always weary looking no matter the hour of the day, gave a nod of acknowledgment and then returned to swishing a damp cloth over the linoleum countertops.

"Bye, Dad." Leon offered the farewell. Leroy slammed out the door, and Leon darted after him, hollering, "Hey! Wait up!"

Arthur sat holding his cup of coffee beneath his chin and staring at the back door. Pencil marks climbed one side of the jamb, indicating the boys' heights at each birthday through Leroy's eleventh and Leon's ninth year. The marks looked ridiculously low considering how tall both boys had gotten in the years since their mother died. In his mind's eye Arthur could still see them as scrawny boys, rising on tiptoes so the marks would be higher than reality. He remembered Mabel's soft laugh and chiding voice. *"Here now, that's cheating. You'll be taller next year. Wait and see."*

The leftover smells of bacon, eggs, and biscuits — Mabel's standard weekday breakfast — hung heavy in the room. The sound of a woman's leather-soled slippers scuffing on the polished floor, her starched apron whisking with her movements, joined with the aroma and carried Arthur backward in time. He jerked his face in the direction of the approaching woman, expecting to see Mabel coming to collect the dirty dishes.

The sight of Mrs. Lafferty's wrinkled face, her lips set tight in an unsmiling line, sent the fanciful imaginings for cover. What was he thinking? Mabel had never been one to hold her tongue. She was always talking, laughing, scolding, sometimes even nagging, depending on her mood. But silent? He snorted. No one would ever mistake the taciturn housekeeper for his vibrant Mabel.

148

He set the half-empty coffee cup aside and rose, then stepped out of the way of Mrs. Lafferty's reaching hands. She wasn't a talker — he didn't think she'd said more than a dozen words in all the years she'd worked for him — but she was efficient. His house never sported a speck of dust, hot and tasty meals were always on the table, and he and his boys walked out the door wearing clean, pressed clothes every day. He had no complaints.

Except for occasional loneliness. Two rambunctious boys and an efficient housekeeper could never take Mabel's place.

He removed his jacket from a peg beside the door. "I'm off to the emporium." He spoke out of habit, not expecting a reply, but somebody needed to disturb the unearthly quiet. "I'll be here at eleven thirty for lunch." Of course he would be. He never deviated from his routine.

Mrs. Lafferty lifted the stack of dishes and turned toward the sink without a pause.

Arthur sighed. He shrugged into the jacket, plopped his hat on his head, and aimed himself for the back door. His gaze connected with the faded pencil marks. Mabel's cheerful voice chirped through his memory again. *"You'll be taller next year. Wait and see."* Sadness threatened. She hadn't gotten to see. And Arthur hadn't recorded it.

He gave himself an inward push. Why was he standing here lost in the past? He had a business to run — a business to build so his boys would have something to carry into the next generation. His old man certainly hadn't left him anything of worth. Just a trunk of coal dust–smudged clothes, a tattered Bible, and an outstanding balance at the company store.

With his jaw set in a determined jut, homburg placed at a jaunty angle on his head, and shoes as shiny as a new penny, he set out the door for work.

Instead of crossing through the alley, as was his usual custom, he rounded the house and stepped onto the sidewalk. No sense in getting his shoes all dusty after Mrs. Lafferty had done such a fine job making them look like new. He inhaled the morning air, letting its cool crispness chase away the melancholy reflections that had taken hold of him after breakfast.

Two boys swinging tin lunch pails, their shoelaces flapping, dashed past him, and he started to holler at them to watch where they were going, but a movement ahead stole his attention.

Mrs. Shilling's son burst past the overgrown lilac bushes at the corner, looked both ways, then darted across the street. Seconds later the boy's sister emerged from behind the cluster of bushes. Two younger children — a boy and a girl, both strangers to Arthur — accompanied her. Belle Shilling reached for the younger ones' hands. The little girl took hold, but the boy backed away and shook his head. Belle leaned down a bit, seeming to reason with the boy, but he linked his hands behind him, out of reach.

Arthur stifled a chuckle. The boy possessed a stubborn streak. Or maybe an independent one. Either way, it tickled him to watch the brief battle of wills. The school bell rang, and Belle put her hand on the boy's back to propel him forward. The three hurried off together. Arthur watched them until they went inside the brick schoolhouse.

With the sidewalk clear, Arthur proceeded to the corner. Why hadn't he heard about a new family moving to Buffalo Creek? The town had experienced a substantial population growth in the midtwenties when Fowler Marbleworks expanded their operation, but these days newcomers were rare. He'd need to seek the new folks out, let them know whatever they needed to set up housekeeping from the newest appliances to the most up-to-date parlor sets and everything in between, he had it.

Even though the boy and girl with Belle Shilling were much younger than his boys, Leon or Leroy would probably carry home information about them. His sons were aware of everything that went on school. They'd mentioned the Shilling twins had skipped some days of school and pondered if they were ill. Arthur knew the reason for Bud and Belle's absence, but he'd kept quiet, as Mrs. Shilling had requested. He could talk now, though, since their time of private mourning was over. It must be if she was sending the twins to school again.

That meant he'd be free to visit her, make his offer for the mercantile. Excitement stirred within him. His pa had been satisfied to live in a tiny shack, wear coal dust under his fingernails, never have two dimes to rub together. But Arthur had aspirations to be as rich as the town banker. Even richer. He knew how to do it, too, but he needed more space. He needed the Shilling mercantile — it was the most logical choice for expanding his emporium. He couldn't very well build on the south or west sides. He'd spill over into the street. The north side offered only four extra feet, much less than what he needed. But the mercantile adjoined his emporium on the east, and on its other side was an empty half lot also owned by the Shillings. All the space Arthur could possibly want stretched in that direction.

He unlocked the back door and, leaving the electric lights off, crossed through the shadows to his small office in the back corner of the store. He flicked on the lamp in his office, shrugged out of his jacket, and slid into his tall banker-style desk chair. As he did every morning before putting out the Open for Business sign, he checked his books to be certain his balances were still in the black. As always, they were.

Oh, his profits had declined since that horrendous Wall Street crash. But he'd been sensible enough to hoard his money in a safe in the cellar instead of trusting the banks, so he'd come out better than some. He still had his emporium. Eventually the economy would improve. Of course it would. In the meantime, he'd be content with the black numbers in his ledgers. Only the most astute businessmen kept a positive balance these days.

With a sigh he leaned back in the chair and rested his head on the high carved backrest. The regulator clock on the wall showed five minutes until opening time.

Mrs. Shilling opened the mercantile at nine o'clock, a half hour after he invited customers to visit. If things were quiet this morning — both in his store and in hers — he'd take a little break shortly after nine and plant a few hints about his willingness to take that cumbersome responsibility off her hands.

Neva

"Adeline, I know you're sad, but you really must stop crying." Neva lifted Adeline onto the edge of the counter and wiped the child's eyes and nose with a soft handkerchief — the third one of the morning. The child had started crying when Belle left for school an hour ago. First pitiful hiccupping whimpers, then body-shuddering sobs, and finally shrill, angry wails. "You'll make yourself sick if you don't quit, and you don't want to get sick, do you?"

"W-w-want B-B-Belle!" Fresh tears spilled down the little girl's reddened cheeks.

Neva dabbed the moisture away and battled breaking down in tears herself. She understood Adeline's angst, and sympathy for the little girl pinched her, but at the same time she wanted to lock Adeline in one of the upstairs rooms and let her cry it out on her own. Neva's ears were ringing.

Or maybe the front bell was ringing. A shadowy form filled the doorway behind the pulled screen. A customer wanted in.

Neva set Adeline on the floor and said sharply, "Stay right there," then hurried to the door and unlocked it. "I'm so sorry for the delay in opening this morning. I —" Her apology melted when she recognized the visitor. Arthur Randall never patronized her store. He made use of the larger grocery store on the other side of town — puzzling, given her close location to his house. He must have been bothered by Adeline's tantrum. Surely half the town had heard her screeching.

The man stepped past Neva and stopped, his frown landing on Adeline, who continued sobbing around her fingers. He pointed. "What is this?"

Neva hurried across the floor and lifted the child into her arms. Adeline fought against her, and she set her on the counter again. "I think it's fairly obvious that 'this' is an unhappy child."

He drew back. "Why, Mrs. Shilling, you snapped at me."

Yes, she had. Something she'd never done to a neighbor or a customer before. The morning had been harder on her than she'd realized. She closed her eyes for a moment and prayed for strength. "I apologize. It's been a rather . . . harrowing start to the day."

A grin of amusement grew on his lips. "Yes. I've heard."

"I'm sorry if her crying bothered you."

He tucked his thumbs into the little pockets on his striped vest. Arthur Randall dressed as impeccably as Warren always had. With his thumbs caught that way and his feet planted wide — a confident stance showcasing masculinity — he could have been Warren. His presence made her heart pine for her husband despite the hurt he'd caused her.

She turned her back on him and smoothed Adeline's tear-damp hair from her face. She'd apologized for disturbing the businessman. Would he now go away?

Boot heels thumped on the floor, but to her dismay he approached her rather than exiting. He leaned against the counter and bobbed his head at the toddler. "I suppose I should have said, 'Who is this?' I haven't seen this child before. Or the ones your daughter escorted to school this morning. Is there a new family in town?"

"Not exactly." She continued fussing with the little girl's fluffy blond pigtails, careful not to look Arthur in the face. The whole town would ask questions soon. She might as well practice giving answers. "Warren wanted the children. He arranged for them to come to me before he died."

Her conscience panged, which was silly, because every word was truth. She straightened Adeline's pinafore and quoted, " 'The LORD gave, and the LORD hath taken away . . .' " She couldn't add, *"Blessed be the name of the LORD."* That would be pure sacrilege.

His eyebrows rose the same way Reverend Savage's had. The way Jesse Caudel's had. The way she expected the entire population of Buffalo Creek would look at her when the news that she'd taken in three orphans spread. How many times would she have to see the evidence of shock before the reaction stopped irritating her?

She balled her hand on her hip. "Mr. Randall, do you need something?"

"As a matter of fact, yes, I do." He glanced around the store, an unreadable expression on his mustached face. "I'd like to take a gander at the furniture my boys tell me is stored in your barn. The pieces could be a nice addition to the stock in my emporium. That is, unless you intend to put them up for sale in your mercantile." A soft, amused *humph* left his lips. "You seem to have made room for larger items by clearing your shelves."

Heat filled Neva's face. She had her list ready, and she would visit the telegrapher's office and send orders to companies in Kansas City today. Once she figured out how to get the goods from the train station in Beloit to Buffalo Creek, her shelves would be full again. She didn't need Arthur Randall making sport of her. "I don't intend to sell furniture in the mercantile, but neither do I intend to part with the items."

At least, not yet, even though she had no use for another parlor set, dining room table and chairs, or anything else besides the children's beds and bureaus, which were already in the apartment.

"You have some sort of special attachment to them, do you?"

"None whatsoever." In all truth, just looking at the fine cherry and maple pieces made Neva's heart ache. Apparently Warren had spoiled Violet as much as he'd spoiled her. Yet she couldn't bear to let them go. She wouldn't pretend to make sense of her feelings. And she wouldn't attempt to explain them to Mr. Randall either.

He gazed at her silently for several seconds, not smiling but not frowning. Finally he angled his head and squinted at her. "Well, then, if you aren't willing to sell the furniture, would you sell the mercantile?"

Hot anger flooded Neva's frame. The frustration of dealing with Adeline's lengthy tantrum, the uncertainty of the future, her tiredness from lying awake worrying instead of sleeping all rolled into a cannon ball that she needed to release. She took aim at the smug target standing before her and fired.

"How dare you ask such a thing? Didn't my husband tell you again and again this store is not for sale? The answer still applies, Mr. Randall. Warren might be gone, but I am here, and I will never — I repeat, never — part with my livelihood and my home."

He gawked at her, eyes wide in surprise.

Aiming an imperious finger toward the door, she barked, "Now take your pocketful of money where it might be appreciated and kindly do not darken my door again unless you are here to place an order." She scooped Adeline from the counter and darted around the corner, willing the irritating man to find his way out without her assistance.

CHAPTER 12

Bud

Bud took his time walking home. Only three blocks from the school to the mercantile. If he ran he could make it in two minutes. Most times he ran, eager to get home and put on his starched cobbler apron and give Ma — or Pop on the months he was home — a hand in the store. Bud had always loved the mercantile. Especially the way it smelled, like apples and leather and spice. The same way Pop always smelled.

But everything had changed. Pop would never be home again. They'd never get to put "Shilling & Son" on the sign. If Pop had lived, would he have put "Sons" up there since Charley was here now?

Bud kicked a rock and sent it skittering up the street. Even though it wasn't nice, and even though he figured God would punish him for the thought, he wished he could kick Pop instead. How could he just up and die on them?

All day long, that's all he'd heard. *"I'm so sorry for your loss, Belle and Bud."* Miss Neff said it first, as soon as he and Belle settled in their desks. Then at recess and lunch, kids came up and said the same thing. Lots of the girls cried while they said it, and the boys looked down or off to the side and mumbled, embarrassed about being mushy. Even Leon Randall, who'd never said a kind word to Bud as far back as he could remember, had socked him on the arm and told him he was sorry to hear about his pop. Bud had come mighty close to socking Leon back — picking a fight so he'd have some way of getting rid of all the mad feelings floating around inside of him.

"Hey, Bud." One of his pals, Martin Buckwelder, tromped up beside Bud and nudged him on the shoulder. "Sure am sorry to hear about —"

Bud stopped in his tracks and glowered at Martin. "Yeah, yeah, I know." Why couldn't they all understand he didn't want to think about Pop being dead? Every time somebody said "I'm sorry," Bud's chest got tighter and tighter until it hurt to breathe. He wished people would just leave him alone.

Martin scratched his head, making his red

hair stand up. "You don't gotta get sore. I was just trying to be nice. The way Miss Neff said we should."

"When'd she say that?"

"When you and Belle were downstairs gettin' those two new kids enrolled in school."

Bud scowled and started walking again, dragging his heels so dirt sifted up and dusted the hem of his dungarees. "Well, you don't have to." No amount of nice would bring Pop back. It wouldn't send Charley away. "I don't even wanna think about it."

Martin jammed his hands into the pockets of his overalls. Martin always wore overalls, two sizes too big — hand-me-downs from older brothers. Most kids wore hand-me-downs or homemade clothes these days, but Pop always brought Bud and Belle store-bought clothes from one of the bigger cities. He must have done some shopping for Charley and the little girls before he died, because their trunk was full of new clothes. Bud's stomach writhed.

Martin sighed. "Guess I can't blame you. I don't get along all that great with my pa. He's always after me about one thing or another. But if something happened to him, I'd sure miss him."

Bud gritted his teeth.

" 'Course, you oughta be used to not having your pa around since he was gone so much. You might not even notice much that he —"

Bud broke into a run.

"Bud! Hey, Bud!"

Bud kept running until he reached the mercantile. He slammed through the front door, startling his mother and two ladies from church, who jolted and gaped at him the way Belle stared at spiders.

"Hello, Son." Ma could've scolded him for scaring everybody. But she held out her hand and beckoned Bud to come close. "Mrs. Hood and Mrs. Austin brought us some casseroles. Would you carry them up to the kitchen for me?"

"Yes, ma'am."

"And then come right back down. I need you to mind the store while I run an errand."

"Yes, ma'am." Bud lifted the tin containers and headed for the stairs.

Behind him one of the women said, "I'm sure your Bud and Belle will be a great comfort to you. What a blessing that they're nearly grown."

"My goodness, yes," the second woman said. "Why, if you'd become a widow when your children were small, you'd surely suffer much more than you are now."

Bud didn't see much comfort in their words. He hurried up the steps and into the apartment. Belle was on the sofa with Adeline in her lap, and Charley and Cassie had their schoolwork spread all over the floor. Bud stepped around their papers and entered the kitchen. But there wasn't any place to set the casseroles. Filled plates, pans, and baskets covered the table, the counters, and even the top of the Frigidaire.

He stomped back into the parlor, still holding the pans. "What's all that stuff in the kitchen?"

Belle gave him a wide-eyed look of amazement. "Food. Momma said people have been bringing things all day long. Isn't it wonderful?"

Why did people bring food when somebody died? He hadn't felt much like eating since he got the news of Pop's passing. Bud would rather just have Pop. "What am I supposed to do with these?" He held out the pans.

She shrugged. "Leave them on the dining room table, I suppose. Momma said she'd put everything away after supper."

Bud couldn't imagine where. He plopped the pans on the table and headed back downstairs. Mrs. Hood and Mrs. Austin had gone, and now Martin's mother was with Ma. But it didn't look like Mrs. Buckwelder had brought food. Just as well. They had enough upstairs to feed half the town. She was doing a lot of talking, though.

"I vow and declare, Neva, I can't imagine what Warren was thinking to take in extra children the way he did — and not even a word of warning to you ahead of time! Granted, the Good Book proclaims that children are an inheritance of the Lord, and of course my husband and I have our nine, but they came to us through, er, the usual means. Now you're expected to take care of some . . . some foundlings without the help of a husband? I wouldn't do it. No, indeed, I would not do it."

From the look on Ma's face, she wished Mrs. Buckwelder would've brought food instead of an opinion. Bud marched over. "Weren't you needin' to run that errand now, Ma?"

She turned a grateful smile on Bud. "Yes. Will you please excuse me, Naomi? I have to get to the telegrapher's office before it closes."

"Oh, sure, sure." Mrs. Buckwelder waved her hands at Ma. "Go right on, Neva. Bud here can see to my needs. Or . . . maybe he can." She scrunched her face the same way

Miss Neff did when the kids were acting up in class. "You seem to be short on stock."

"And that's why I'm going to the telegrapher — to place orders." Ma moved toward the door, removing her apron as she went. "I shouldn't be long, Bud." She hurried out the door.

Bud slipped his cobbler apron over his head, then donned his favorite hat — the one that smelled like Pop's hair tonic. "What did you need, ma'am? We're all out of sugar, but we've still got a good amount of flour and cornmeal." Martin brought corn muffins in his lunch tin every day. He said their family ate them for every meal. Bud moved to the shelf where a short stack of cornmeal bags waited.

"I do need cornmeal. A ten-pound bag should do."

Bud carried it over and laid it on the counter. "What else?"

"Well, now, let me think." Mrs. Buckwelder pushed her fuzzy red bangs from her forehead.

Bud waited, tapping his fingertips on the counter. Martin's ma always looked a little frazzled. Maybe having so many kids meant she didn't have time to comb her hair or iron her dresses. Maybe Ma would start looking frazzled now that she had five kids to see to instead of just two. The thought didn't sit so well.

He stopped tapping. "Mrs. Buckwelder, can I ask you a question?"

"You certainly may."

"You told my ma you wouldn't take care of kids that weren't your own. Why is that?"

She puckered her face. "Oh, now, I didn't intend for you to hear our conversation. But since you ask . . ." She leaned close. Close enough Bud could count the freckles on her round face. "Your own children come to you as infants. You raise them the way you want them to behave. You teach them and you protect them from, well, unsavory influences so you can be sure they behave the way the Good Book advises."

Apparently she didn't know that Martin sometimes smoked hand-rolled cigarettes behind the outhouse at school.

"But when you take in someone else's children, you have no idea what habits they might bring with them, what kind of teaching they've received. I wouldn't risk it. Not if I already had impressionable children in my house, like your mother has with you and your dear sister, Belle."

"So you think Pop was wrong to want those kids?" Bud held his breath while he waited for her to answer.

"I think your father, because he was a bighearted man, meant well. But I don't see how your poor mother will handle the added responsibility." She straightened her spine and lifted her chin. "And that's all I'm going to say about it."

Jesse

Jesse paid the telegrapher, then watched the man tap out the message he'd penned to the Beloit courthouse. He hoped Sheriff Abling would accept a telegraph as an official notice of resignation. He'd never been good at putting words on paper. Write a full letter? He nearly shuddered. Just coming up with the sentence needed to let his former boss know he'd decided to take the position of sheriff in Buffalo Creek had taxed him. But now it was on its way.

"All done, Mr. Caudel." The telegrapher, a slender man with a missing front tooth, turned from the machine and offered Jesse a wide smile. "Or should I say Sheriff Caudel?"

"I'm not sheriff until Dodds Schlacter vacates his office."

"Way I heard him tell it, he's ready at any minute. Now that you're here, he'll likely be out by sundown."

Jesse laughed. No doubt Schlacter would clear out fast. The office was already almost empty, with a pair of fishing poles leaning in the corner as a silent proclamation of what the man really wanted to do with his time. But it would take longer than sundown for Jesse to gather his belongings, load them in the back of his trusty '22 Oldsmobile flatbed, and transport them to Buffalo Creek.

He already had a place to put his few furnishings. Schlacter assured him he could take over the little shotgun-styled house behind the sheriff's office and make it his home. It'd been sitting empty ever since the sheriff and his wife bought a house outside of town where he could practice his shooting without fear of wounding a Buffalo Creek resident. He'd also invited Jesse to come out and shoot with him whenever he took a mind to. Jesse intended to take the man up on it. A sheriff should always be ready to aim straight and true.

The telegrapher stuck out his ink-stained hand. "Welcome to Buffalo Creek, Sheriff."

Jesse returned the handshake, then pulled in a deep breath and let it ease out. His first big breath as Sheriff Caudel. It felt good. He bid the man good-bye, slipped his Stetson in place, and stepped onto the sidewalk right in the path of Neva Shilling. "Excuse me, ma'am."

"Excuse me," she returned, her voice pleasant even though her face was set in a mask of worry. She reached for the latch on the screened door.

Jesse caught it first and held it open for her. She smiled a brief thanks and hurried in. Jesse let the door slap closed, but instead of leaving he loitered on the sidewalk. Using the tip of his pocketknife, he cleaned the bits of grime from beneath his fingernails and listened in.

"Mr. Starkey, I'm sorry to arrive so near your closing time, but I couldn't leave the mercantile until the children were home from school."

"Why, that's no problem, Mrs. Shilling. And let me tell you now that you're here, I was sure sorry to learn about Warren's passing. He was a good man, and I considered him a friend."

Jesse shook his head. That Shilling was one smooth character, winning the affections of two women and two entire communities. He'd not had any direct dealings with Shilling, but after he'd passed on, not a soul in Beloit said an unkind word about him. Now it was the same here in Buffalo Creek. It was enough to make a man wonder if he could ever really know a person, deep down.

"Thank you." Mrs. Shilling's voice wavered just a bit, and Jesse envisioned her holding tight to the awful truth while probably wishing she could degrade her dead husband at the top of her lungs. "I have three lengthy telegrams to send to companies in Kansas City, and then a short one I wish to send to every newspaper in Mitchell County."

Jesse paced, listening to the off-beat clicks of the telegraph. His nails were clean, and the clicks were still going. He pocketed his knife and moved to the edge of the sidewalk, pretending to take stock of the town, still waiting.

"There now, Mrs. Shilling, they've all been sent. When I get the receipt notices you requested from the vendors, I'll have my boy take them straight over to the mercantile."

Jesse eased closer to the door to catch Mrs. Shilling's response. "I appreciate that. Thank you."

"No problem at all. I'm glad to help. And if there's anything else I can do for you — anything at all — you just ask, all right?"

"Actually, Mr. Starkey, I do have need for someone to retrieve the stock I ordered

171

from the railroad station in Beloit and bring it to Buffalo Creek. We had a wagon, as you know, but according to the sheriff's official who brought word of Warren's death, the wagon was sold to cover a debt. Do you know someone nearby who owns a large wagon or farm truck who might be willing to drive to Beloit once a month for my shipments?"

"Right offhand, I can't think of anyone, but I tell you what . . ."

Feet pounded on the floorboards. Jesse couldn't resist peeking through the screen and spotted Starkey coming out from behind his counter. The wiry man caught Mrs. Shilling by the elbow and guided her to a large wooden board on the post office side of the building.

"You write out a little notice of what you need, and I'll pin it right up here. Everybody in Buffalo Creek drops by at least once a week to retrieve their mail. If there's someone in town who'd take on a job like that, you'll find out soon enough."

"Thank you, Mr. Starkey. I'll bring in a notice tomorrow."

Jesse leaped back when she headed for the door. The moment she stepped onto the sidewalk, he called her name.

She jolted and turned a wide-eyed look

on him. "You're still here?"

"Yes, ma'am, and I confess I eaves-dropped."

Her brows descended into a V.

"Listening in to find out if you'd decided to contact an orphans' home somewhere."

Now her lips pressed into a firm line.

" 'Cause if you were, I was going to volunteer to deliver the children." He shrugged. "It'd be better if somebody they already knew did the deed, don't you think?"

Her expression softened a bit. "I appreciate your concern for Charley and the girls, but as I've already told you, I'm keeping them with me. So you don't need to worry." She turned to leave.

He reached out and brushed her elbow with his fingertips. "Wait."

Very slowly she faced him again. The brim of her little hat cast a crooked shadow across her forehead, but the late-afternoon sun fully lit her hazel eyes, bringing out flecks of gold and green. "What is it?"

If he was going to be sheriff of Buffalo Creek, he'd need to meet the needs of the people, whatever those needs might be. Even transporting goods. "Well, Mrs. Shilling, I think I have a solution to your problem." He tipped his head to the side and grinned. "Would ya trust the new sheriff of Buffalo Creek to pick up your stock from Beloit?"

CHAPTER 13

Arthur

Arthur pushed the succulent pieces of pot roast around on his plate. Although the aroma tantalized him, he couldn't bring himself to take a bite. Not with the huge lump of fury filling the back of his throat. Who would have suspected sweet-natured Neva Shilling to become so surly and disagreeable? To point her finger at the door and demand he leave? To make him feel small and insignificant and even miserly?

He'd always known Shilling was stubborn. The man held to that mercantile the way a drowning man clung to a flotation device. But he'd expected Mrs. Shilling to be reasonable. Every time he recalled the way she'd sent him scuttling out the door like a dog with its tail tucked between its legs, his humiliation and aggravation grew.

"Maybe I asked too soon." He didn't realize he'd spoken aloud until both of the boys stopped eating and stared at him.

"What was that, Dad?" Leroy stabbed a chunk of roasted potato and jammed it in his mouth.

"Nothing." Arthur lifted his glass and took a long draw of the buttermilk. The liquid did nothing to cool the frustration stirring within him. He needed to think about something else. He drew on his standard weekday query. "How was school today?"

"Kinda sad, really." Leon put down his fork for a moment. "Miss Neff told us Bud and Belle's father died. Did you know that, Dad?"

"Yes. Yes, I did." He chopped a small bit of meat free of the thick slice, pierced it with his fork, then used it to draw curlicues in his gravy. "Very sad."

"It's kinda strange, don't you think, that they buried him in Beloit? I mean, our ma died in Beloit at the hospital, but we still buried her right here in Buffalo Creek." Leon took a bite of the roast and then spoke around the lump. "Why do you think they did that?"

"Maybe he died of something catching." Leroy used his fork as a pointer and jabbed it in his brother's direction. "Remember that drifter who came through last year — the one they found laid out cold under the water tower? As soon as the doc said he'd passed of diphtheria, the town councilmen buried him real quick instead of trying to send him back to his own town. They didn't want to risk spreading the sickness."

Leon turned to Arthur. "Did Mr. Shilling die of diphtheria?"

Arthur finally put the bite in his mouth. The meat was cold, the gravy starting to congeal. He made himself chew and swallow before answering. "What did Miss Neff tell you?"

"Only that he died. And then some kids who go to the same church as Bud and Belle said their preacher said he was buried in Beloit. But they're gonna have a service here later this week." Leon shrugged. "Don't know how you can have a service without a grave or a body to put in it. Will you go to the service, Dad?"

After the way he'd been treated earlier by the man's widow, Arthur didn't have much desire to attend a service honoring Shilling. But as a neighboring businessman, his presence would be expected. He nodded.

Leroy's face lit. "Think they'll close down school for the day? If they do, Leon and I could go trap some gophers. Bounty's up to thirty cents a pelt."

Arthur scowled at his son. "If they close

down school for the service, you'll go to the service."

"Aw, Dad . . ."

"And something else, Leroy." Arthur thumped his fist on the table, making the boys' milk cups bounce. "Leave gopher hunting to the youngsters who have need of the bounty money. You and Leon receive an allowance."

Defiance flickered across Leroy's face, but he pursed his lips and stayed quiet. Wise boy.

Leon gazed at Arthur in genuine confusion. "There's enough gophers for all the boys in town to catch a sack full every day and twice on Sunday. Why shouldn't Leon and me get in on it — earn a little extra spending money?"

Arthur turned his glare on the younger boy. "I'll tell you why. It's embarrassing when the two of you go traipsing into the sheriff's office with a sack full of little corpses. Poor folks take advantage of the vermin bounties." He'd trapped his share of coyotes for the pelts. The smell of the dead animals — the stench of poverty — lingered in his memory. He examined his palms, assuring himself no speck of coal dust appeared in the creases. He jammed his clean hands in the air. "We aren't poor folks."

The boy scrunched his lips into a scowl. "Jeepers, Dad."

"And no more of that slang language either." Arthur rose and flung his napkin onto his plate. "Speaking slang only makes a man sound ignorant. If you can't think of more appropriate words to express yourself, then open the dictionary and study." He strode from the dining room.

Leon's whisper followed him. "What's bugging him, Leroy?"

"Dunno. Better stay out of his way tonight."

"Don't worry. I will!"

Stifling a growl, Arthur entered the kitchen. Mrs. Lafferty looked up from the work counter, where she was kneading a mound of dough. Her expressionless face gave no indication that she'd overheard their conversation. But that didn't mean anything. He'd never met anyone as poker-faced and tongue-tied as this woman. He swallowed a snort. Mrs. Shilling could take a few lessons from Mrs. Lafferty.

"I'm going up to my study. I don't intend to come back down until breakfast tomorrow. Please lock the back door behind you when you leave." He waited for her nod of acknowledgment and then he pounded up the back staircase.

He kicked off his shoes and slid his feet into the leather slippers waiting just inside the door of the room originally intended to serve as a maid's quarters. The smooth soles whispered against the uncovered floorboards as he moved to the overstuffed chair lurking in one corner. A small table with a lamp stood beside the chair, and after plopping onto the soft cushion, Arthur clicked the scrolled brass lamp key to On. Yellow light flooded the space. Not that there was much to see.

A 1918 calendar — a Randall's Emporium calendar given to guests at his grand opening — hung from a tack, the only embellishment in the entire room. Mabel had never entered this room, claiming it cold and depressing. And that was part of the reason Arthur liked it. It was his space. His alone space.

He picked up the newspaper resting on the edge of the table right where Mrs. Lafferty had been instructed to leave it. He read every article from page 1 to page 4, scowling at some, shaking his head at others. At least with summer behind them, reporters had stopped writing about the drought. Such a weary topic. And what could anyone do about it? Nothing. Man had no control over whether it rained or not. A waste of newsprint, to Arthur's way of thinking.

The only article he read with real interest concerned the upcoming presidential election. His lips tugged upward into a grin. Wouldn't it be something if their very own Governor Landon landed in the White House? Of course, the odds were against it, knowing how the farmers in the Midwest supported Roosevelt. But Arthur enjoyed a few minutes of considering the celebration if good ol' Alf Landon actually won.

Arthur reached the last page and located his emporium advertisement. Sliding his finger along the print, he ascertained that all words were spelled correctly. The special of the week — PAY CASH! PAY HALF! — stood out in bold block print, just as he'd requested, with *On specially selected items* in small print underneath. No one had come in today with the ad in hand, ready to deal, but since most people read the paper in the evening rather than the morning, he expected to see more activity tomorrow. And if he didn't, he wouldn't use that ploy to entice customers again. There were many other ways of bringing people into his emporium.

Lowering the paper to his lap, he aimed his gaze at the yellowing calendar. Sometimes it was hard to believe he'd owned the emporium for eighteen years. Other times it seemed as though it should be longer. He chuckled, recalling how un-emporium-like the store had been when he and Mabel opened the doors for the first time. But he'd been wise enough to buy a building four times the size needed for his humble stock, purchased with the settlement money paid to every family member who lost a loved one in the mine collapse. He and Mabel had planned to grow the business every year, and they'd done it. Yes sir, they surely had. And now an important celebration awaited in the not-too-distant future.

January 1, 1938, would mark the twenty-year anniversary of the store's opening.

They hadn't celebrated the ten-year anniversary. Mabel fell ill for the first time just before Christmas in '27, and it hadn't seemed right to celebrate. Especially considering how involved she'd always been in the store. She loved teasing him by saying, *"You're a driven man, Arthur Randall, and it's me who steers you."*

He always blustered at her, but underneath he knew it was true. Her suggestions for organizing the show floor into room blocks, letting the customers envision how the pieces could be arranged in their own homes, gave the emporium an edge over the warehouse-type display he'd planned. Granted, he couldn't fit nearly as many pieces into the store her way, but it hadn't mattered. The store had flourished, partly due to the appealing arrangements and partly because of the vivacious hostess who greeted customers at the door and made them feel at home.

Oh, how he missed his wife . . .

He closed his eyes and sighed, willing the remembrances to flee his mind so he could concentrate on the future. Mabel was gone, but Leroy and Leon were with him. By the twentieth anniversary, he wanted the emporium expansion complete. He wanted to change the name from Randall's Emporium to Randall & Sons Emporium. His boys wouldn't need to leave their home town to carve a good life, the way Arthur had. They'd have their good life right here in Buffalo Creek. But he didn't have a lot of time left.

Leroy would graduate next May and Leon three years after him. Why, in five or ten years he could have a couple of daughters-in-law and even a grandchild. Wouldn't that be something? He stroked his mustache with one finger, smiling, imagining. He hoped the first grandbaby was a girl. He wouldn't mind having a little girl toddling after him, calling him Grandpap. But for the store to support all of them, he needed that expansion.

Smacking the newspaper onto the table, he bolted out of the chair and paced the small room. Wide-planked boards absorbed the fall of his feet, and he kept his head low to prevent clunking his forehead on the sloped ceiling. Back and forth he plodded, thoughts railing. His pride still stung from Mrs. Shilling's adverse reaction to his more-than-fair bid. Much to his perplexity, money obviously didn't entice her. Maybe he should bluntly and forcefully spell out all the difficulties of running a business single-handedly. No, given the backbone she'd exhibited today, she wouldn't respond well to strong-arm tactics either. So what should he do?

He came to an abrupt stop. Releasing a sharp huff of laughter, he shook his head. He'd been a widower for so long he'd completely forgotten what moved women. Females were emotional beings, susceptible to emotional manipulation. How had he coaxed Mabel out of a sour or melancholy mood? Not by scolding or threatening or even handing her a handful of cash. She responded to tenderness — whispered compliments, kind gestures, unexpected favors. She became putty in his hands when he nursed her feminine spirit. If it worked with Mabel, didn't it then stand to reason it would be effective with Neva Shilling as well?

He opened the little drawer on the table and withdrew a pad of paper and pencil. He slipped back into the chair, braced the pad on his knee, and wrote in bold letters across the top: *Ways to Woo the Widow.* He chuckled. If Mrs. Lafferty saw the heading, she would assume he was interested in matrimony. And so what? She wouldn't tell anyone, so his secret was safe.

He knew what he wanted, and he would get it in time for the emporium's twenty-year anniversary.

Neva

Neva found a place on the cellar shelves for every item friends and church members delivered during the day. At first she'd been uncertain about accepting the casseroles and hams and home-canned goods. So many people were struggling these days — should she take food meant for their families? But Lois Savage advised her to view the offerings in a different way.

"Please don't say no," the younger woman had said, holding out a quart jar of apple-sauce and a basket of home-baked bread. *"You'll rob me of the opportunity to bless you."*

When put into that perspective, Neva's guilt vanished and only appreciation remained.

Now, holding aloft the lantern, she scanned the variety of items and battled tears. Thanks to the town's generosity, she and the children needn't worry about meals for at least two weeks — a true blessing. Much more so than the offer from Mr. Randall to take the mercantile off her hands. What had he been thinking? Hadn't Warren told him no more than a dozen times in the past fifteen years? Now, more than ever, she needed the mercantile to provide for Bud and Belle.

She chewed her lower lip for a moment, regret striking. She'd blatantly used Mr. Randall as a mark for her frustration. Discourtesy didn't rest well on her conscience. Her dear foster mother, Christina Jonnson, had encouraged the children at the asylum to treat others the way they wanted to be treated. Neva wouldn't have wanted to be on the receiving end of such a tart diatribe as the one she delivered to Mr. Randall. But at the same time she was proud of herself for responding so staunchly. Maybe Arthur Randall would understand the mercantile was not up for sale. Not at any price.

She aimed the lantern's glow for the dirt stairs and climbed upward. Moonlight bathed the yard, providing enough light that she felt safe extinguishing the lamp. She turned the knob, shrinking the wick.

"Ma'am?"

The voice startled her so badly she nearly dropped the flickering lamp. She whirled around and held the tin lamp like a shield in front of her. Two shabbily dressed men with whiskered faces and uncombed hair stood a few feet away. The taller of the pair bobbed his head toward the cellar opening.

"Herb and me saw you putting food down there. A whole heap of food."

Neva nodded slowly. "That's right." The padlock for the doors waited in the grass near her foot, but they could easily overtake her before she managed to secure it. Her heart began to pound. "It's food for my youngsters. Bud and Belle, Ch-Charley, Cassie, and little Adeline. They're all upstairs" — she risked a glance toward the kitchen window, a square of yellow against the gray siding of the mercantile — "preparing for bed."

The man named Herb licked his lips. "Bet they're going to bed with full bellies, aren't they?"

"Y-yes." All but Bud, who still picked at his food rather than eating.

"Now, take Ansel and me." Herb inched toward her, wringing his dirty hands against his tattered jacket front. "We haven't had a decent meal in close to a week. Word up the line, though, is fellows can get a meal at the Main Street Mercantile in Buffalo Creek. Word is the lady owner is kind and giving." He took another step closer. A foul stench came with him. He apparently hadn't bathed in weeks. "Is all that a lie?"

Nausea rolled through her brought on by fear and the unpleasant essence clinging to the hobo. She hugged the now-dead lamp, inwardly praying for guidance on how to best handle the situation. She wouldn't wish hunger on anyone, but neither did she want them ransacking the cellar and carting off the things meant for her family.

"It's not a lie." She spoke slowly, amazed at how calm she sounded despite the fierce thud of her pulse. "You see that lean-to on the barn? That's where I put the soup kettle."

Both men craned their necks in the direction of the lean-to.

"Go look. There's a little woodstove out there. I use it to keep the kettle warm." *Go. Just go.* If they went to the barn, she should have enough time to lock the cellar and get inside.

"I'll go see." Ansel ambled off, leaving Herb standing guard. Moments later he hollered, "There's no kettle out here — just a cold stove!" He trotted to his buddy's side.

Neva inwardly groaned. Now what would she do? *Lord, protect me, please.*

No sooner had the prayer left her heart than another male voice, this one authoritative, intruded. "Just what exactly are you gentlemen doing in Mrs. Shilling's yard at this hour?"

Neva released a startled gasp. Her rescuer was Arthur Randall?

CHAPTER 14

Arthur

Arthur crossed the uneven ground to Mrs. Shilling's side. She gaped at him as if she were seeing a ghost. He swallowed a chortle and aimed a stern frown at the two hobos. "I asked you a question. What are you doing here?"

The ragtag fellows shifted in place, their shamefaced expressions pointed at the ground.

"They were looking for food," Mrs. Shilling answered.

Arthur folded his arms over his chest. "Just as I expected." He angled his body to shield her from the other men. "Listen up, both of you. Mrs. Shilling isn't running a bread line. She's a widow lady with children to feed. Before you hop on the next passing train, you carve an *X* over that drawing of the cat on the barn's lean-to. Then you spread the word that no one's to bother this lady again."

"No!" Mrs. Shilling removed a match from her apron pocket and lit the wick on her lamp. She held the lamp aloft and turned an insistent look on Arthur. "Don't be hasty. They didn't harm me. They're just hungry." She grimaced as she faced the men. "I realize the stove's cold this evening and there's no kettle out. The last few days have been busy. And taxing. I haven't had time to set out the share-kettle. But if you'll wait just a minute, I'll . . ."

She scurried down the cellar stairs, leaving Arthur to keep watch over the two bums. They watched, too, their furtive gazes flicking from him to the cellar opening. After only a few minutes, she emerged with the lamp in one hand and the other clutching the corners of her apron skirt together. The skirt hung like a pouch. She handed Arthur the lamp and then crossed quickly to the men.

"Here." She transferred a loaf of bread, some cheese, and a few apples to the men's dirty hands. "I know it's not the same as a hot meal, but I hope it will fill your stomachs so you can sleep without hunger pangs tonight."

Watching her treat those grubby bums with kindness, Arthur experienced a swell of admiration. She'd been clearly afraid of these two when he'd come across the alley, but compassion had conquered the fear. In those moments she reminded him of Mabel, and the remembrance was sweet. But somebody had to be stern. She'd apparently worn out her starch on him that morning, so he'd take the harsh role this time.

"Now that you've got what you came for, you scoot on out of here." Arthur took two steps toward the men, and they moved backward the same distance, cradling the food against their midsections. "And don't you tell any more of your ilk what Mrs. Shilling has in her cellar. Don't repay her benevolence by setting her up to be robbed."

"No, sir." The taller man shook his head hard. "We wouldn't do anything like that."

"We'll tell everybody to look out for the nice lady at the Main Street Mercantile, mister," the second one said. "You can count on it."

"All right then. Now go on."

The pair shot smiles of thanks to Mrs. Shilling and trotted up the alley. Shadows swallowed them within seconds.

Arthur crossed to the woman, discarding his stern countenance as he went, and offered her the lamp. "Are you all right? You looked pretty scared when I first got here."

She cradled the lamp against her apron bib and released a long, uneven breath. "They said they'd seen me fill the cellar with food, and I was afraid they might clean it out. They seemed so desperate." She tilted her head, her forehead crinkling. "How did you know they were out here?"

He pointed across the alley to his house, to the two square windows beneath the eaves. "I was working in my study. I happened to notice your lamp go out, and then there were three shadows in the yard." How fortuitous for him to have gazed out the window at that exact moment. Fate must intend for the mercantile to be his. "I decided it would be much less than neighborly not to come see if you were faring well."

She shook her head, still gaping at him. "Thank you. I find your concern . . ."

He offered a smug grin. "Touching?"

"Um, no."

His grin faded.

She laughed softly. "Confusing." She gently swung the lantern, making shadows dance. "I chased you out of the mercantile this morning. I was rude."

"Yes, you were." Arthur heaved a sigh and hung his head. "But I was pushy."

"Yes, you were."

He lifted his chin and gawked at her. To his surprise an ornery gleam lit her hazel eyes. He choked out a short laugh. "Mrs. Shilling, I believe you're taunting me."

The impishness instantly disappeared. "And I shouldn't be. I should thank you. I don't know what might have transpired had you not come over when you did. Thank you, Mr. Randall."

He bobbed his head in a chivalrous manner. "You're welcome."

"And . . ." She took a tiny step forward, bringing the toes of his slippers into the half circle of light cast by the glowing lamp. "Allow me to apologize for my less-than-charitable behavior this morning. I don't want to sell the mercantile. It's my means of supporting my family. But I should have refused your offer more graciously. For that, I am sorry."

How quickly one act of gallantry had softened her. He chuckled deep in his throat. "Oh, now, you'd had a harrowing morning with the little one so upset. I tell you what, I won't hold a grudge for your reaction if you won't hold a grudge about me asking to purchase the property."

She held out her hand. "Agreed."

He took it. Although her hand was small and delicate, her grip possessed strength.

He found himself reluctant to release her cool, slender fingers. How long had it been since he'd held a woman's hand? "Mrs. Shilling?"

"Yes?"

"How did things go today, keeping the little girl in the mercantile with you?"

She didn't need to answer. Her expression spoke volumes.

He chuckled again and gave her hand a little squeeze. "I believe I might have a solution to that problem."

Hope ignited in her face. "What?"

"Oh, not yet. I need to confirm it first." Arthur eased his hand from hers and took a slow backward step. "But if my idea works out, you'll be the first to know." He touched his forehead in a pretend tip of the hat. "Watch for me tomorrow morning, Mrs. Shilling. I'll pay you a visit, and this time you won't want to chase me from your mercantile."

Neva

By the end of the first full week in October, Neva and the children had established a routine that, if not cheerfully followed, was at least agreeable. Each morning by eight thirty, all five children trooped out the door,

195

and Belle delivered Adeline to the Randalls' housekeeper on the way to school. After school Belle retrieved Adeline and minded the younger children in the apartment or the backyard while Bud helped Neva in the mercantile. Poor Belle often played peacemaker because Bud continued to openly chafe at Charley, Cassie, and Adeline's presence. Since the youngsters weren't going anywhere, Neva did her best to keep them separate as much as possible and prayed for her son to accept their intrusion into his home.

For reasons Neva couldn't fathom, Mr. Randall began the habit of stopping by each day. In the midmorning "just to say hello," sometimes shortly after lunch with pastries baked by Mrs. Lafferty, and once in the evening armed with rope and a sanded board, which he used to fashion a swing in the old apple tree beside the barn. Given the unseasonably warm, dry weather, the children enjoyed it for hours after school.

She puzzled over her neighbor's odd behavior. In all the years she and the Randalls had lived with an alley between them, he'd never made any attempts to establish a friendship. Deep down, suspicion niggled. But she was letting Warren's choices color her feelings toward Mr. Randall. Just because Warren had proven untrustworthy didn't mean she should distrust everyone else she encountered. She and Mr. Randall had shaken hands and agreed not to hold grudges. Most likely he was only trying to prove he held no hard feelings about her unwillingness to part with the mercantile.

At odd moments guilt swooped in and attacked her. By holding on to the business, Neva forced Belle into bearing the weight of responsibility for the younger children. But not once did the girl complain, so Neva tried to ignore the unwelcome emotion and focus her attention on pleasing her customers. Fortunately, the townsfolk exhibited patience with her sparse shelves. She had more than a dozen lists of orders to fill as soon as her stock arrived. According to the telegrams sent by the Kansas City distributors, her goods would arrive in Beloit on the Friday morning train. She could only hope Mr. Caudel would deliver them to her that same day so she could distribute the orders on Saturday morning.

Friday at breakfast Neva set aside her coffee and addressed the twins. "Remember to come home at noon break, and no dallying. We'll only have a short amount of time for you to change into your Sunday clothes and get to the chapel for your father's memorial service."

Belle propped her chin in her hand. "I wish we had Poppa's wagon and horse. Sandy was such a nice old horse, and she could take us to church so much faster than we can walk."

Since the wagon came and went with Warren, Neva hadn't given it or the sorrel horse much thought. Warren was gone, so the wagon was gone. But Belle's comment raised a worry in the back of her mind. Apparently Warren had taken out loans to cover his expenses in Beloit, yet he'd paid cash outright for everything at the Buffalo Creek mercantile. Or she presumed he had. She didn't know what she would do if an official came to her door and held her accountable for bills in Warren's name.

"Why can't we just stay home this morning?" Bud's scornful question chased away Neva's inner reflections. "Seems silly to go for only half a day."

Belle tsk-tsked. "You know our grade has an arithmetic examination this morning. If we miss it, we have to make it up during noon recess on Monday."

Before Bud could voice an argument, Neva put her hand on his arm. "You're going to school this morning, and that's that. Just make sure you hurry back at noon. We don't want to be late to the service Reverend Savage has prepared."

Charley dropped his half-eaten biscuit on his plate. "Should I come back, too, Aunt Neva?"

Bud huffed. "Why?"

Charley frowned. "To go to the service."

"Why would you want to?"

Bud's derisive tone made Neva cringe. Charley seemed to shrink, too. She spoke kindly. "I think it best you stay at school, Charley. You and Cassie both."

"But —"

"You already attended a service with the people who live in Beloit, didn't you?" Neva felt Bud's narrowed gaze boring into her, but she kept her face aimed at Charley. At the boy's nod, she added, "Well, this service is for folks who live in Buffalo Creek."

Charley sucked in his lips and furrowed his brow. "Don't we live in Buffalo Creek now?"

"Well, yes, you do, but —"

"Then we should go, too." Charley stood, as if trying to make himself bigger. "He's our daddy, and —"

Bud rose, fists clenched, face reflecting fury. "Listen here, you little pipsqueak, don't you ever call my pop your daddy, you hear me? He had me a whole lot longer than he had you, and he was mine!"

Charley shrank back and Cassie began to cry. Apparently frightened by her siblings' reactions, Adeline joined her sister in wailing.

Belle slipped her arms around the little girls and glared at Bud. "Now see what you've done. You made everybody all upset." She turned a pleading face on Neva. "Momma, maybe we should all go. Maybe it would" — she glanced at Bud and Charley before pinning Neva with the same hopeful expression — "bind us together."

It pained her to deny her daughter's heartfelt request, but Neva could not sit in the service and maintain her composure with her husband's illegitimate offspring beside her.

Bud snorted. "You're such a Pollyanna, Belle. Nothing's ever gonna bind us together, so why don't you just shut up?"

"Bernard Warren Shilling!" Neva jolted to her feet. "Being upset is one thing, but speaking hatefully to your sister is another. Neither your father nor I have ever allowed such vulgar talk. Apologize."

He glared at her with his lip curled.

She smacked the table, making everyone except Bud jump. "Apologize!"

Seconds ticked by. Tense seconds, with

Cassie's and Adeline's muffled sobs the only intrusion in the otherwise deathly silence.

Finally Bud pulled in a breath that expanded his chest. He held it for a few more seconds and then eased the air out between his clenched teeth. Not until his shoulders had completely deflated did he speak. "I apologize." His flat, emotionless tone held little sincerity, but something akin to remorse flickered in his hazel eyes.

A sad smile quavered on Belle's full lips. "It's okay, Bud. This day's gonna be hard on all of us. I don't want to say good-bye to Poppa either."

Neva sagged back into her chair, her rubbery legs unwilling to hold her up any longer. Of course Bud's outburst came from his reluctance to truly believe his father was gone forever. She stared, amazed, at her daughter. Optimistic and also wise. Belle was growing into a mature young woman right in front of her eyes. And Warren would never see it.

Tears clouded her vision. Neva blinked twice to clear the moisture and then fixed Bud with a steady look. "Off to school now. You can eat a sandwich here with me before we go to the service." She turned to Charley. "I want you to stay at school all day. Belle will come get you when classes let out."

Both boys nodded, apparently too emotionally spent to argue.

Relieved at their acquiescence, Neva shifted her attention to Belle. A swell of tenderness nearly toppled her from her chair. She reached up and tucked a stray strand of red-brown hair behind her daughter's ear. "Can you wash the girls' faces and help them into fresh dresses?" Tears stained their round cheeks and the bodices of their frocks.

"Of course. Do you want my help with the breakfast dishes?"

"No. You'll be late for school. Just go on now. I'll see you at lunchtime."

Belle, still holding Adeline, leaned down and delivered a kiss on Neva's cheek. She whispered, "We'll be okay, Momma." She hurried out of the room with Cassie trotting on her heels. Bud and Charley, Charley well behind Bud, scuffed around the corner, and Neva was alone.

She rested her forehead in her hand. Bud's angry statement, *"Nothing's ever gonna bind us together,"* competed with Belle's sweet words of parting, *"We'll be okay, Momma."* As much as Neva wanted to emulate her daughter's confidence, she feared this time Bud was right.

CHAPTER 15

Jesse

Friday morning after his last breakfast at Garrett's Boardinghouse, Jesse cleared out the room he'd called home for the past half-dozen years. Funny how it didn't even pain him to do it. He'd thought himself happy in Beloit, and he expected to experience at least a twinge of remorse at pulling up stakes and moving on, but only a sense of excitement filled him.

When he finished loading everything on the truck, he paused for a moment and frowned at the small amount of items. Being a bachelor, always living in one room of a boardinghouse or a cramped furnished apartment, he never had need for much clutter. Still, it panged him a little to realize just how few things he had to call his own. Shouldn't a man have a little more to show for himself by the time he was thirty-five years old?

Slapping his hat back onto his head, he climbed behind the wheel of his truck and aimed it for the train station. The morning sun bounced off the hood of the truck and made him squint. Depending on how long it took him to load the goods he promised to transport for Mrs. Shilling, he'd be in Buffalo Creek by noon or a little after, which would leave him plenty of time to situate his belongings in the little house behind the sheriff's office.

As he rolled slowly toward the station's loading dock, he examined a sizable pile of crates, sacks, and barrels stacked at one end of the long, planked deck. His eyes widened. Was all that hers? He squinted and made out the word *Shilling* stamped on a couple of the biggest crates. He whistled through his teeth. She'd placed a large order all right. Maybe it was good his things hadn't taken up much space on the flatbed. He'd need all the room he could get for the mercantile's supplies.

He pulled his truck as close to the dock as possible. If he ended up transferring those crates and barrels by himself, it would be easier to slide them from the dock right onto the bed of his truck. He turned off the ignition and hopped out, and at once a man in dusty pants, scuffed boots, and blue shirt straining at its buttons emerged from the little shack next to the dock.

"Howdy. You the one pickin' up the Shilling order?"

Jesse held up his hands in surrender, grinning. "That's me."

"I had my boys put it all together here for you. Not an easy task. These things were tucked into three different freight cars." The man shook his head, blowing out a breath. "First time ever we got involved in a shipment for the Shilling mercantile, an' it happens after Shilling is dead. Kind of a strange state of affairs, wouldn't ya say?"

Jesse tossed a sack of flour over his shoulder and stepped to the front of the bed. "If Shilling didn't use the railroad, how'd he get his goods?"

The fellow grabbed one of the barrels and heaved it onto the flatbed. "Guess he bought 'em outright an' carried them on that wagon he always drove. Asked him one time how come he didn't let the rails carry his goods, an' he laughed. Said he could get a better price goin' face to face with dealers." He shrugged and reached for another barrel. "Guess he finally changed his mind about orderin' by telegram and lettin' the trains do the totin'. Too bad he ain't even here to see how easy it is."

Jesse could have explained where the goods were going and who'd actually ordered them, but he decided the railroad worker didn't need the information. He found it puzzling, however. The wagon Sheriff Abling auctioned off hadn't seemed large enough to accommodate the size of orders Warren Shilling would have needed to fill the shelves at two businesses. Something didn't make sense. He'd need to think on the situation some more.

When they finished transferring everything to his flatbed, Jesse offered the helpful fellow a fifty-cent piece as a thank-you, but the man backed up, shaking his head.

"I get paid well enough for my job, mister. Give that to whoever helps you at the other end." He chuckled. "Your job's only half done, you know."

Jesse gripped his back and feigned a groan. "I know, I know." With the man's laughter following him, he slid behind the wheel and cranked the engine to life. He held the truck at twenty-five miles an hour the entire distance from Beloit to Buffalo Creek, swerving to avoid potholes so he wouldn't bounce anything from the bed. Just shy of one thirty, considerably later than he'd expected, Jesse rolled onto his new town's Main Street.

He downshifted and slowed his truck to a crawl. Ahead, automobiles of every kind and at least two dozen wagons with horses or mules napping within the traces crowded the street. He eased the vehicle forward, fighting the clutch — his old truck did better at full throttle than moving at a snail's pace. Several wagons were parked clear up in the yard of the little chapel where Reverend Savage served. Jesse marveled at the sight. Half the town must be gathered there. Nuptials, burial, or revival?

The chapel's windows were all raised, and the door stood wide, braced open with a brick. He killed his engine right in the middle of Main Street lest its rumble disturb the ceremony taking place in the small sanctuary. Sticking his head out the window, he strained to hear the minister's voice. He caught two words — Warren Shilling.

He smacked the cracked steering wheel. Of course, the memorial service. Which meant Shilling's widow would be there. Which meant the mercantile was closed. Which meant he couldn't unload the crates until she returned. Which meant his belongings, which he'd put at the front of the flatbed rather than the rear, would have to stay put awhile longer. So much for getting his lodgings organized this afternoon.

But postponing his unpacking was small potatoes compared to what Mrs. Shilling and her children were doing. It wouldn't be easy, laying Warren Shilling to rest with no body and no peace. Because how could she have peace, knowing what her husband had done?

Parking in the middle of the street wasn't exactly legal, but he decided folks would understand, given the circumstances. So he hopped out of the cab and crossed the dead grass. He sat on the lowest porch riser and listened in. The same way they'd done at Shilling's graveside in Beloit, people paid their respects by sharing their thoughts about the deceased man.

"He was a straight shooter in his business dealings. You always knew you could trust Warren Shilling."

"What a gentleman he was, always in a suit and tie, always ready with a 'yes, sir,' or a 'no, ma'am.' We could do with more men like him."

"Last spring, even though we were behind on paying our account, Mr. Shilling let me take home vegetable seeds for our garden and even slipped a packet of marigold seeds in at no charge. He said folks needed a little beauty to feed the soul. What a kindhearted man . . ."

"If you needed a hand — digging a cess-pool, changing a tire, patching a porch roof — he'd take off his jacket, roll up his sleeves, and dive right in. He was never one to worry about getting his hands dirty."

Just like in Beloit, everybody said good things. Jesse could have countered every last one of the statements, but would it help? Probably not. And it would surely hurt Mrs. Shilling and her children. But keeping quiet wouldn't be easy. Not if people sang those praises to him. He'd never been able to hide his feelings. Whatever he thought showed on his face. His ma always said that was a good thing. A person shouldn't find it easy to deceive others, because it only led to heartache. Mrs. Shilling must be experiencing that truth right about now.

The accolades seemed to roll forever. Jesse's rear end was going numb by the time Reverend Savage's distinctive booming voice brought an end to the service with a prayer. Even though Jesse was outside, away from the others, he stood, bowed his head, and closed his eyes out of respect for the reverend and for the God to whom the minister spoke. Even for Mrs. Shilling, who'd been deceived. But not out of any respect for the deceiver. Shilling had given up any right to respect a long time ago.

A resounding "amen" completed the prayer. Jesse turned, expecting to see a flow of people exit the chapel, but the minister spoke again. "The ladies of our congregation prepared a fellowship luncheon that will now be served in the basement. Everyone is welcome to partake."

Apparently everyone chose to partake, because nobody came out. And who could blame them? Lots of folks scrambled to eat three meals a day. A free meal would be a big draw. But Jesse really wanted to get Mrs. Shilling's goods off the back of his truck. He scratched his chin. Should he interrupt the luncheon to ask for a key?

He didn't doubt she'd trust him to let himself in and out of the mercantile. He wasn't exactly a stranger to her. Or maybe . . . A fuzzy image took shape in the back of his mind. Before he barged in on the church ladies' luncheon, he'd find out whether his memory served him correctly.

He climbed back into the cab and coaxed the engine into turning over. Then he chugged the few blocks to the mercantile. As he had when he'd delivered the children, he drove through the alley to her back door. He glanced out the window as he rolled to a stop, and he couldn't hold back a grin. Sure enough, there it was, the way he'd remembered.

A clay flowerpot — the only flowerpot in the whole backyard — sat on one corner of the stoop. A clump of something long dead straggled over the pot's rim, but finger smudges on one edge of the pot let Jesse know someone had recently handled it.

He crossed the yard and tipped the pot. As he'd expected, a skeleton key lay on the gray concrete. He brushed it against his trouser leg to remove dust and then tested it on the back door. Moments later he used the pot to hold the door open, and he dragged in every crate, box, sack, and paper-wrapped bolt of cloth that had arrived at the train depot for Mrs. Shilling that morning.

He thumped the last crate to the floor and then paused, looking at the crowded area. Sympathy pricked him. She'd have quite a chore emptying all those crates. And to face the task after attending a service for her dead, philandering husband made it even worse. She'd be exhausted. Emotionally if not physically. But maybe he could help.

After two hours of frenzied activity, he was good and sweaty, so he borrowed the tin cup hanging on a bent piece of wire from the pump handle and cooled his throat with a drink and then his face with a splash. The water spattered his shirt front, too, but he didn't mind. It would dry. And it felt good despite the breeze blowing from the east.

He locked the door and returned the key to its spot, careful to place the pot exactly the way he'd found it. The next time he saw Mrs. Shilling, though, he'd advise her to hide the key somewhere else. If he'd discovered the key, someone else could, too. And someone else might not be entering the mercantile for honorable reasons.

With the delivery complete and the mercantile secure, he could go to his new home and get settled. Come Monday he'd step into the position of sheriff. Eagerness propelled him across the yard. Whistling, he slipped in behind the wheel and bounced his way out of the alley.

Neva

"Belle, shake a leg." Neva flicked her fingers at her daughter as if shooing flies. The luncheon and then responding to everyone's condolences had eaten up the entire afternoon. The school buzzer had rung nearly half an hour ago. Charley and Cassie would fear they'd been forgotten if someone didn't come soon.

"I'll hurry, Momma." Belle broke into a run.

Neva considered calling her back. The ribbon bow holding her hair in a fluffy ponytail had come undone at some point during the afternoon, and it flowed out behind her like the tail of a kite. Every Sunday Belle wore the inch-wide, cream-colored satin ribbon Warren had purchased during one of his away times. He'd bragged it cost him a full fifty cents. To replace it would cost dear. As she watched, the ribbon slipped from Belle's hair and fluttered to the ground. Neva pulled in a breath, swallowed, and turned to Bud.

"Let's go home, Son." The two of them fell into step together. Usually Bud dashed ahead or lagged behind. She couldn't remember the last time they'd walked side by side. To her surprise his stride matched hers, bringing a mixture of pain and pride. He was growing up so fast. She slipped her hand around his arm.

He shot her a startled look, but he didn't pull away. They walked in silence for a few moments. Then he said quietly, "Ma?"

"Yes, Son?"

"Isn't Charley big enough to walk back from school on his own? Belle and I made it just fine when we were eight."

For once no rancor colored his tone. Perhaps the service had mellowed him. It had achieved the opposite effect within her. She offered a sad smile. "Charley's different than you and Belle. He didn't grow up here in Buffalo Creek. Everything is still new to him."

Bud turned his gaze ahead and walked with firm, rhythmic steps. They'd traveled the distance of a block before he spoke again. "He's a real pest, you know."

Scolding words formed on Neva's tongue, but she held them back. She didn't want another argument.

"He follows me around at school during lunchtime. But he never says anything. It's like having a half-sized shadow." Bud crinkled his face as if he'd tasted something rancid. "Then at home, in my room, he sits on his bed and stares at me. Always quiet. Martin Buckwelder calls him a moron."

"Martin Buckwelder should have better manners." Neva frowned. "I hope you defend Charley when Martin is rude."

"Oh, Ma . . ." Bud made another face. "Martin's my friend. I don't want to make him sore."

"Well, Charley is your —" She stopped herself from saying "brother." She floundered for an appropriate replacement.

"Responsibility. He's part of our family now. Would you tell Martin not to call Belle a moron?"

"Sure I would."

"Well, then?"

Bud sighed. "Belle doesn't act like a moron. She doesn't deserve to be called one." He peered at her out of the corner of his eye. "Sometimes Charley does."

Neva stopped. Bud took another step, and she lost her light grip on his elbow. He angled a look at her over his shoulder. His hair had grown, and his bangs caught on his thick eyelashes. Instead of defiance, she read uncertainty in his gaze, and she couldn't bring herself to berate him for the unkind statement.

She stretched out her hand, and he held out his elbow. She caught hold and they started off again. Quiet. With matching strides. The mercantile waited on the next block. When they reached it, they'd get to work and the opportunity for conversation would slip away. Even if it meant another argument, she needed to instruct him, once again, to be kind to Charley. She opened her mouth to speak.

"Ma, can I ask you something?"

She pushed her comment aside. "Of course."

This time Bud stopped, drawing Neva to a halt beside him. He gazed at her with his eyes narrowed, as if it hurt to keep them open. "Did Pop adopt Charley and the girls?"

At least she could answer truthfully. "No, Bud, he didn't adopt them."

"Then why'd you tell us to have Miss Franklin record their names in the school records as Charley and Cassie Shilling? Don't they have some other name?"

How could Warren have done this to her, putting her in the awful position of lying to their children? If he were there at that moment, she would rail at him the way she'd never railed at anyone ever before.

Her hand trembling, she cupped Bud's smooth cheek. "They are Shilling, Bud, because your father wanted them to be Shilling. That will have to be explanation enough."

He stared at her for several seconds, unblinking, eyes still squinted.

Farther up the block, tires squealed, a car horn honked, and someone hollered, "Moron! Learn how to drive!"

Bud's lips twitched into a grin. "Want me to go tell him he's rude?"

Neva laughed. She couldn't help it. And it felt wonderful to release the burst of amusement. A tidal wave of love washed over her, and without thinking she grabbed Bud in a hug right there on Main Street.

He wriggled loose, then glanced right and left with his face glowing red. "Ma!" But his grin didn't fade.

She laughed again. "I'm sorry. Was that rude?"

This time he laughed with her. They covered the final few feet to the mercantile's front door with light steps. She unlocked the door and they stepped into the store, still chortling. But their laughter died in the same instant. Cold chills broke out from her scalp to her feet.

Empty crates were stacked beside the counter, their contents already on the shelves. The bean bins were full, the cracker barrel full, the sugar and flour barrels full. Canned peaches formed a pyramid on one end of the counter, and on the other end the glass candy jars each contained a fresh assortment. Although the gumdrop jar didn't seem to be filled to the top.

Neva stood as if rooted in place, hugging herself, and stared disbelievingly, while Bud moved slowly through the store, his mouth hanging open. Bud finished his circle and stopped beside the row of candy jars. He gaped at Neva. "Who did all this?"

She shook her head, shedding the ridiculous thought that struck the moment she entered the mercantile, and made herself think rationally. Given his previous solicitous acts during the week, she would suspect Arthur Randall if he hadn't been at Warren's service.

"And look at this." Bud picked up two dimes and held them out to Neva. "Whoever did all the work even left some money behind."

A smile tugged at Neva's lips. The missing gumdrops and the payment gave him away. "It must have been Mr. Caudel."

"You think so?"

She knew so. Neva nodded.

"How'd he get in here?"

"I don't know."

Bud whistled softly. "He sure saved us a lot of time."

Hours and hours of time. "He certainly did."

Bud lifted the lid on the closest candy jar and fished out a few jellybeans. "Want me to start on some of those orders folks left with you? We can use these crates and get them all organized for pickup tomorrow."

Neva gathered her senses. She hurried across the floor and took the candy jar lid from Bud. She clanked it into place, then turned him by his shoulders toward the staircase. "We'll get started on those orders after we've changed out of our good clothes and had a bite of supper." They could enjoy a leisurely supper, thanks to Mr. Caudel's thoughtfulness.

Bud trotted off.

Neva started to follow, but then she stopped and sent one more slow look at the mercantile shelves. Although shoved in haphazardly rather than in soldier-like columns, he'd chosen the correct locations for everything. So much he'd accomplished. He couldn't know unloading the goods onto the shelves was a task Warren insisted belonged to him.

In her mind's eye she could see Warren with his sleeves rolled above his elbows, a hank of thick dark-brown hair falling across his forehead, emptying crates with movements as efficient as any machine. She heard his chuckle and then his voice.

"You've got lots of inner strength, Neva, but you need to leave the heavy work to me. That's what husbands are for."

She covered her warm cheeks with her hands, both flattered and flustered. What had compelled Jesse Caudel to put away her stock? And why was Mr. Randall being so attentive and helpful? What did they want from her in return?

Neva closed her eyes and moaned. "Why did such a cynical thought even occur to me?" Would Warren's duplicity make her question every other man's intentions?

CHAPTER 16

Jesse

After unloading his belongings and organizing them in his new home, Jesse decided to treat himself to supper at Betsy Ann's Café, a diner tucked between the hardware store and the sheriff's office. How convenient to have an eating place so close to him. The house had a small Windsor stove with four burners and an oven the size of a breadbox — just about right for a bachelor. But if he was lucky, he'd never have to use it.

He entered the diner, removing his hat as he stepped over the threshold. The place was quiet, every stool along the counter and every booth empty. But that wasn't too surprising. Most families didn't have money to squander at cafés these days. Being alone, he probably ought to take one of those round stools, but instead he chose a booth in front of the window where he could watch the street.

A skinny woman with straggly dark hair streaked with gray scuffed out of the kitchen. She carried a coffeepot and a thick ceramic mug. Without asking she served him coffee, and then she announced in a flat voice, "The Friday special is Aunt Sue's famous chicken an' dumplings. Thirty-five cents a bowl. Coffee's on the house."

Jesse thought about asking to see a menu — if he was going to be eating here regular, he'd like to know what his choices were. But her unsmiling countenance didn't encourage conversation. He smiled. "Sounds fine."

Less than three minutes later she plopped a chipped bowl in front of him. No enticing aroma rose from it, but he thanked her anyway.

"You're welcome, mister." She worried her stained apron in her hands and stared at him through watery eyes. "You the new sheriff?"

"That's right. Name's Jesse Caudel."

"Betsy Ann Mullin. I own this place." No pride colored her tone or expression. Betsy Ann Mullin looked and acted as bland as the bowl of chicken and dumplings smelled. "You married?"

"No, ma'am."

"Me neither."

How did a fellow respond to a statement like that? He hoped she wasn't hinting.

She sighed. "Seems a shame. You look young enough to still catch a wife. If you get a hankering to marry up, let me know. I got two cousins of marriageable age."

He swallowed a snort of laughter. "Um . . . thank you, but being a lawman keeps me too busy to properly court a woman." And marriage meant all kinds of responsibilities he'd rather avoid. Much easier to keep the law than take care of a family.

She gave him one more long, searching look, then scuffed out of the dining room.

Grateful to have escaped a proposal, he picked up his spoon and took a hearty bite. And almost spat it out. No wonder the booths were empty. Betsy Ann was a mighty poor cook. If Aunt Sue's recipe was famous, it was likely for giving folks indigestion.

Even so, he ate every bite of the stringy chicken and rubbery dumplings and lifted the bowl to drink the thin, flavorless broth. Never let it be said Jesse Caudel wasted food. But he'd give learning to use that stove in his house some serious consideration. Or maybe he'd just visit the Shilling share-kettle.

He slid a quarter and a dime next to the bowl to pay for his meal, then added three pennies for a tip. He hollered a thank-you to the kitchen doorway, but Betsy Ann didn't answer, so he slipped his hat over his hair and vacated the café.

The sidewalks were almost as empty as Betsy Ann's booths. Friday nights in Beloit were active, with folks spending their dimes at the picture show or gathering in the park for free-will concerts or just window-shopping. But up the street in Buffalo Creek, the lights around the Bijou Theater's poster for *Red River Valley* were off. Gas lamps lit the grassy park and its weathered pavilion, but the area was quiet. Would Saturday night be more lively? In a way, he hoped not — less activity meant less mischief. But on the other hand, a fellow could get bored mighty fast with all this peace and hush.

He scanned the east half of the business district. Two teenage boys loitered beneath the streetlamp outside the drugstore, and farther up the street a trio of elderly men sat chatting on the bench in front of the bank building. The teens seemed no rowdier than the old duffers, so Jesse turned his attention to the west side of town.

Streetlamps dotted the sidewalks, but the businesses were dark. Except for one. Slivers of light escaped from around the lowered shades at the Main Street Mercantile. Apparently Mrs. Shilling was working. He hoped she wouldn't mind an interruption, because he needed to tell her to move that key.

He set out with wide strides, enjoying the thud of his boots against the sidewalk. He breathed in the musky air, cool with the arrival of evening but dry. With practice borne from years of keeping watch over a passel of younger sisters and then a town full of folks, he scanned the area, ears alert, muscles tense and poised for whatever action might be needed. But he reached the mercantile without a single reason to pause. Yes, sir, this was a peaceful town.

He tapped on the door, and within moments the corner of the shade lifted. Bud peeked out. The shade dropped, a lock clicked, and the door popped open. Bud didn't smile, but he did hold out his hand in an invitation to enter, so Jesse did.

"Good evening. Sorry to intrude. I can see you're working." Working they were — the whole lot of Shillings from the proprietress all the way down to Adeline, who held a feather duster and marched around waving it as enthusiastically as a band leader waved a baton.

Mrs. Shilling stepped from behind a crate,

wiping her forehead with the back of her wrist. "Mr. Caudel, I'm glad you stopped in. Thank you for not only delivering my stock but putting most of it away." She seemed extra animated compared to the café owner.

He grinned. "How'd you know it was me?"

She pointed at the gumdrop jar.

He squelched a chuckle and shrugged. "Ah. Well . . ."

She gave her hands a quick swipe with her apron and then extended them to him.

He took hold of her smooth, dry hands and gave them a quick squeeze before slipping his hands into his pockets. He scanned the shelves. She'd already removed a few things. "I hope I didn't mix up your system. I figured it would be easier for you to dive right back into shopkeeping if you didn't have to worry about unpacking."

A glimmer of uncertainty flashed in her eyes, but then she graced him with another smile. "It was a great help, Mr. Caudel. Thank you. But" — a trickle of self-conscious laughter spilled out — "how were able to do it? When I left for the service, I locked all the doors."

Jesse explained his means of accessing the building. "It'd be a good idea, ma'am, to move the key. That little pot sitting there all alone, serving no other purpose, is a red flag to a lot of people, some of an unsavory character. If you'd like, I'll help you find a safer hiding spot for your spare key."

"I appreciate your help. Especially considering . . ." She glanced at the children. With the exception of Adeline, who now whacked a row of cans with such gusto feathers flew from the duster, all had paused in their tasks and appeared to listen.

Her voice unnaturally cheerful, Mrs. Shilling continued, "There are so many strangers passing through these days. One must be safe rather than sorry, yes?"

He sensed she'd intended to say something else, but he wouldn't prod her into sharing. Not with their audience. "It's always best to err on the side of caution. That's my motto."

Belle stepped away from the crate she'd been filling and approached Jesse, a shy smile on her face. "Mr. Caudel, have you moved to Buffalo Creek for good?"

Jesse nodded. "As of today I sure have. I set myself up in that little house behind the sheriff's office, and I'm calling it home." He shrugged, aiming a sheepish grin at the girl's mother. "Such as it can be with mostly empty rooms. This is the first time I've ever had a whole house to myself, so I've never had need for many personal effects. I plan on stopping by Randall's Emporium tomorrow and see if he'll make a good deal on some used furniture."

Belle's forehead crinkled. "Mr. Randall only sells new furniture. My poppa only bought a few things from the emporium, because he said all of them cost a pretty penny. Maybe you should shop in a bigger city somewhere, the way Poppa did, to save your money."

The girl looked so worried for him Jesse couldn't help but try to put her at ease. "Well then, I just might talk your momma into letting me have a few of these leftover crates. They'd make fine chairs and tables in a pinch, don't you think?"

Belle's expression remained uncertain. Neva slipped her arm around the girl's shoulders and fixed Jesse with a pensive look. "I haven't paid you for delivering my goods."

He held up his hands. "I offered, remember? And I was coming from Beloit anyway so it didn't cost me anything extra to bring those things."

"I know, but I'd still like to repay you. You did me a great favor, retrieving the orders from the railroad and even putting the stock on the shelves." She bit the corner of her lip, flicking a frown toward the children. When she faced him again, she spoke in a near whisper. "The furniture you brought along with the children is still in my barn. Would you consider accepting a few pieces as payment?"

Jesse drew back. The furniture in the barn was nicer than anything his folks had owned. Nicer than anything he'd ever expected to own. "That's kind of you, ma'am, but —"

"If you'd like, you can consider them a loan."

"A loan, you say?"

She nodded, her eyes beseeching him. "That's right. They'll only go to ruin in the barn with its drafty walls and leaky roof. They'd fare much better in a house, so if you took them, you'd really be doing me a favor."

She was doing him the favor, and they both knew it. The stubborn side of him wanted to resist, but deep down he knew she was right — that fine furniture would go to rot if left in a cold, wet barn over the winter. But he couldn't take it unless she'd let him balance the give-and-receive scales.

"Mrs. Shilling, I'd be pleased to store your furniture in my house. I'll take good care of it while it's there. And as 'rent payment,' so to speak, you can consider me your personal drayman." If every Friday was as quiet as this one, taking one day a month to drive to the Beloit train station and back shouldn't be a problem.

A weak smile toyed at the corners of her mouth. "A drayman generally refers to a man driving a horse-pulled dray, not an Oldsmobile truck."

He chuckled. "All right, then. Your personal, er, truckman. How's that?" To his delight she laughed. It pleased him to coax laughter out of her, especially on this day, when she'd bid an official farewell to her dead husband.

"Actually I prefer the title drayman. It sounds more dapper. But either way I appreciate your service, and I would like to confirm our arrangement." She held out her hand.

For the second time that evening, Jesse curled his fingers around hers. They shook hands, with him mimicking her mock-serious frown, and then at the same time they smiled.

Across the room Bud cleared his throat.

She yanked her hand free and gave Belle a little push toward the crates. "Finish packing that order now. We want all the orders ready to go out the door when we open for business in the morning."

230

"Yes, Momma." Belle scurried back to the crate and lifted a sheet of paper.

Jesse needed to let them all return to work. He eased toward the door. "I'll fetch my truck and pull it around to the barn. Get started moving some of that furniture to my place."

"And then would you help me find a better place for the key? As you said, its current location is too conspicuous." An odd half-sad, half-hopeful smile climbed her pale cheek. "I suppose I can trust a sheriff to keep secret a suitable hiding spot."

After what her husband had put her through, the fact that she could trust anyone — even a man sporting a sheriff's badge — was nothing short of a miracle. He wove his way between the crates, heading for the back door. "Let's go do that right now, ma'am." He'd find a safe spot for that key. Nobody would bring harm to this family again. Not while he was on duty.

Bud

Bud slid open the barn door while Mr. Caudel pulled his flatbed truck up close. Pop had never put electricity in the barn even though he often talked about it. They'd never have electricity out here now. Ma

231

wouldn't think of it on her own, and he wouldn't mention it, because it meant talking about Pop.

Mr. Caudel peered into the barn, squinting. "Dark in there. Do you still have the lantern we used last time?"

Bud nodded. He felt his way to Pop's workbench along the west wall and located the lantern and a tin of matches. He tucked one match in the corner of his mouth the way Pop did, then used another one to light the lantern. He stretched up on tiptoes and caught the tin lantern on a hook in one of the ceiling beams. Not as good as electric lights, but at least they could see the furniture now.

Mr. Caudel sauntered in and moved from piece to piece, as if taking stock. "Awfully nice of your mother to let me use these things. I already thanked her, but I'd be beholden if you'd tell her again."

Bud shrugged. "All right." He leaned against the work counter, folded his arms over his chest, and watched the new sheriff. He was some taller than Pop and a little wider across the shoulders, but in some ways he acted like Pop — like he was comfortable all the time. How must it feel to just be comfortable?

He pushed off from the bench. "I need to

hurry up so I can finish helping Ma. Which things do you want? She said you were welcome to all of it."

The man chuckled. "I won't have room for all of it. It's a pretty small house. But to keep it from going to rot and ruin out here, we'll pack as much in as we can. The rest? Maybe your mother can cover them with canvas. Protect 'em at least a little bit."

How come this new sheriff cared so much about the contents of their barn? The old sheriff hadn't cared what was in a place unless something turned up missing.

Mr. Caudel paused beside the velvet settee and ran his hand across the wooden back. "This is heavy furniture. Would you like to get your friends to help again?"

"You mean Leon and Leroy?"

"That's right."

Bud snorted. "They're not my friends."

"No?"

"No." And Mr. Randall wasn't Ma's friend either, even though he tried to act like it. Bud didn't trust the father any more than he trusted the sons. "We don't need them anyway. I helped Ma carry the bedsteads and bureaus upstairs."

The man's eyebrows shot up. "You and your ma — all by yourselves — carried those walnut beds upstairs?"

If Bud wasn't mistaken, Mr. Caudel looked impressed. Unexpectedly, pride swelled. He fingered the sulfur end of the matchstick caught in his lips and rocked on his heels the way a detective did in a movie he'd watched over at the Bijou. The movie hero had seemed plenty tough. Bud wanted to look tough, too. "Yes, sir, we did. So I figure I can help you load these things on your flatbed without any other help."

The new sheriff grinned. "All right then. Let's get to it."

Bud would never tell how hard it had been to get the heavy furniture up the staircase in the mercantile. And he'd never tell how much it strained him to heft these pieces onto Mr. Caudel's flatbed. He hoped he and the sheriff had taken long enough in the barn that Ma and the kids got all the order boxes filled, because he didn't want to lift as much as a can of peas by the time he and Mr. Caudel shoved the last dining room chair onto the wooden platform. But even more than his muscles ached, satisfaction filled him. He'd done it.

Mr. Caudel wrapped twine around it all, gave a few items a tug, then nodded. "That oughta hold things. Especially since I'm only going a few blocks." He grinned and gave Bud a light whack on the shoulder.

"Good work there. You're as strong as any man twice your age, I'd wager."

The praise reminded him of something Pop would've said, and it raised a good feeling in the center of his chest. Bud toyed with the chewed-up matchstick to hide his smile. He inched sideways toward the barn. "Gonna blow out that lantern now, then head in and see how Ma's doing with those orders."

"Huh-uh. Hold up there."

Bud stopped, confused.

"You think I'm gonna let you get out of carrying these things into my house?" Mr. Caudel chuckled again. He waved one hand toward the barn door. "Go ahead and extinguish the lantern, lock this thing up, and then climb in my truck. I still need your help."

This time Bud didn't pinch back his smile. He just let it grow.

"If Betsy Ann's is still open by the time we're done, I'll take you in there and buy you a soda as a thank-you."

Bud grimaced. "Soda's about the only thing a person feels safe ordering in Betsy Ann's. She's a terrible cook. Folks around town say that's probably why she never married. Her husband would've ended up starving to death."

Mr. Caudel laughed. "Thanks for telling me. But you're an hour or two late." He clutched his stomach and made a terrible face. "I had supper there."

"The Friday special?"

"Uh-huh."

"Ma keeps sodium bicarbonate behind the counter. While I lock up, you might go get some from her."

He laughed again. Harder this time.

Bud grinned. He generally didn't like grownups laughing at him, but for some reason it didn't bother him so much tonight. Working out here with Mr. Caudel had almost been like working with Pop. He just might get to like this new sheriff after all.

Jesse

The clock on the wall showed twenty past eleven by the time Jesse finished arranging the furniture in the house. He would have been done earlier had he not taken Bud Shilling to the café for a bottle of Royal Crown Cola, but he didn't begrudge treating the boy. No one could say Bud wasn't a hard worker. His mother — and his father, if half of what Bud said about the man was true — had taught him the value of hard work. It'd been hard work for Jesse to keep a smile on his face while the boy bragged

236

about his "pop." His heart ached now, thinking how crushed Bud would be when he learned the truth. But he wouldn't hear it from Jesse. That was Mrs. Shilling's responsibility.

The little shotgun-style house had only three rooms — a front room, a bedroom, and a kitchen with a bare corner for a table and chairs. Someone, probably Dodds Schlacter, had tacked on a bathroom so small Jesse could sit on the toilet, soak his feet in the tub, and hang his face over the sink to brush his teeth all at the same time. But indoor plumbing was a luxury no matter how cramped the space.

He took advantage of the plumbing and then headed to his bedroom and shimmied down to his long johns. There'd been a good-sized feather mattress in the barn but no bedframe, so he'd spread the mattress on the floor. He flopped across it and released a sigh. Tomorrow he'd go to Randall's Emporium and buy the least expensive bedframe in the store. For now, though, sleep beckoned.

An electric lamp sat on one of the dining room chairs, which he'd had to bring into the bedroom because the kitchen was too small for all six chairs around the table, and the front room was too cluttered with other pieces of furniture. Jesse, yawning, rolled to his side and stretched his hand toward the lamp's key. A small gold plate attached to the underside of the chair came into his view, and he paused midreach and read the name of the chair's manufacturer: Rich & Baker.

He frowned. Where had he heard that name before? He forced his tired brain to think, think. He shook his head, aggravated with himself. The name was familiar, but he couldn't place why. He yawned again. Why worry about it tonight? He'd think about it tomorrow when he was well rested. He snapped off the lamp, sagged onto the mattress, and closed his eyes.

Behind his closed lids, the Rich & Baker plate glowed as bright as the Bijou's marquee. There was something important hiding in the recesses of his mind. But what?

CHAPTER 17

Arthur

Just as he did for every newcomer to town, Arthur sat at his desk and penned a note of welcome to the new sheriff. He slipped one of the flyers he'd commissioned from the newspaper office into the envelope with the note and carried it out to the floor where the boys were hanging the newest shipment of original oil paintings from street artists in New Orleans. No other furniture store in Kansas carried original oils from out-of-state artists. Maybe he should have included that on his flyer.

"Here, Leon. Take this over to the sheriff's office and give him our shtick."

Leon made a face. "Aw, Dad, do I hafta? It's embarrassing."

"Embarrassing to drum up business?"

Leon sighed. "Why can't Leroy do it?"

"Because I asked you." Arthur gave his son a little nudge on the shoulder. "Now

239

go. And smile when you deliver it."

Leon waved the envelope over his shoulder in farewell as he scuffed out the door.

Arthur hoped the boy wouldn't act like a hoodlum in front of the sheriff. Sometimes it seemed Leon was losing common sense instead of gaining it. He grabbed the feather duster from its hook and began the morning dusting routine. A mindless task, one that allowed time for thinking.

Having the boys offer new residents a welcome to town had been Mabel's idea. *"Folks might shoo away a salesman on their doorstep, but who can resist a charming young boy?"* She was right. Every note brought new business into the emporium. Sometimes only a lamp or décor item, other times an entire room of furniture, but always something. But when she'd come up with the idea, Leroy and Leon were only four and seven years old — little, cute with their missing front teeth, and eager to please.

Ten years later no one could call them "little." Tall, husky, pimple-faced, they'd long outgrown their cuteness. And their eagerness. Arthur scowled. Maybe he shouldn't have sent Leon after all.

The door burst open and Leon trotted across the floor. His face glistened with perspiration. He must have run both ways. "I saw him, Dad, and gave him the welcome. He said thanks, and he'll be in soon to look at our beds."

"You mean a bedroom suite?"

Leon shook his head. "Nope. Just a bed. He's got everything else he needs. That place is packed full." He grabbed the last painting from the crate, unwrapped it, and handed it to Leroy. "I'm pretty sure it's the same furniture we helped him put in the Shillings' barn."

Arthur dropped the feather duster and pounded over to the boys. "What?"

Leon jammed both palms in the air. "Don't get sore at me. I only did what you told me to. Not my fault he'd already got furniture at the mercantile."

Arthur balled his hands into fists. Neva Shilling claimed she didn't intend to sell that furniture, then she'd gone and done it anyway. This was how she repaid him for his kindness? He started for the door.

"Where you goin'?" Leroy hollered after him.

Arthur came to a stop. Indeed, where was he going? To berate the woman? To accuse her of stealing sales from him? Did he really want to sabotage his own plan to woo her out of her mercantile?

He changed course and snatched up the feather duster. "You've finished there. Start rearranging the window display now." Rotating stock — another of Mabel's ideas — made people think he'd gotten something new.

The boys exchanged glances, but they went to work without complaint. Frowning, Arthur stood and watched them for a few minutes. They moved the furniture with care, just the way he'd taught them, but they were such big, bumbling bruisers. It was time to discard Mabel's welcome plan. He scrunched his eyes closed, stifling a groan. The idea stung — as if he were discarding the woman herself.

"Hey you, get out of here."

Leon's sharp voice pulled Arthur from his ruminating. He opened his eyes and spotted Leon waving both hands at someone outside the window. Arthur strode over. "What are you doing?"

Leon turned his frown on Arthur. "Trying to make him leave. He'll scare off business."

Arthur looked out the window. The little boy he'd seen walking to school with Belle Shilling stood at the edge of the sidewalk, staring in at them. "He doesn't look so scary to me."

"He's weird, Dad." Leroy joined them.

"I've never seen a more peculiar kid. He follows Bud Shilling around with this look on his face that reminds me of a dog waiting for someone to throw him a bone. He gives me the creeps."

Arthur examined the boy. Small yet sturdy, with straight dark hair, big brown eyes, and round cheeks. He seemed more cherub than child. Especially when compared to the two overgrown whelps beside him. Arthur snorted. "There's nothing creepy about that boy. You two are the peculiar ones. Get back to work and leave him be."

With muttered grumbles, his sons obeyed.

Arthur opened the door and stepped outside. Next door, customers scurried into the mercantile with empty hands and staggered out carrying crates. Arthur's chest went tight. So much business . . . It'd be a lot harder to convince Mrs. Shilling to let the property go if she was making a good profit. He remained in the shade cast by the striped awning and watched the activity for several seconds. A movement in the corner of his eye pulled his attention away from the mercantile. The little boy held the lamppost with one hand and slowly circled it, his head low.

Arthur cleared his throat. The child stopped and lifted his face. Arthur smiled.

"Good morning. Nice day, isn't it?" Mid-October, and as warm and dry as early September had been.

The boy stared at him but didn't answer.

"You live next door at the mercantile, am I right?"

The boy licked his lips, his gaze flicking toward the mercantile and then returning to Arthur. He nodded.

Arthur, keeping a smile fixed on his face, gave the boy a thorough examination. Not one patch on his britches, shoes nearly scuff-free. He could use a haircut, but otherwise he seemed better cared for than many these days. "What's your name, son?"

"Charley. Charley Shilling."

So he'd already taken the Shilling name. "Welcome to Buffalo Creek, Charley."

Charley lifted his shoulders slightly, bringing the collar of his corduroy jacket up to his ears. "Thank you."

"I'm Arthur Randall. I own this furniture emporium. When you looked through the window, did you see anything you liked?"

The boy ducked his head. "I dunno."

Arthur was beginning to agree with Leon and Leroy about this child's strangeness. He took two ambling steps in Charley's direction. "So tell me, Charley, do you have big plans for the day?"

"I was gonna help people carry their groceries. But everybody's said the boxes are too big for me." He mumbled the words toward the ground.

Arthur cupped Charley's chin and lifted his face. The boy squinted against the sun. For one brief second, something in his appearance seemed vaguely familiar, but the remembrance scooted away too fast for Arthur to catch it. "Don't worry. You'll be big enough to help your ma by and by."

"My aunt."

Arthur frowned, uncertain he'd heard correctly. "What was that?"

"My aunt. She's Aunt Neva. She's not my ma. My momma's dead."

True sympathy eased through Arthur. "I'm sorry to hear that, son."

"My daddy's dead, too."

Arthur put his hand on Charley's shoulder. "Then I guess it's a good thing you've got your aunt Neva."

Charley sucked on his lower lip and didn't answer.

He stood gazing down at the child. Oddly quiet for a boy, but appealing with those big eyes. Young enough to stir feelings of protectiveness. No one with half a heart would send him scooting if he turned up on a doorstep.

Arthur gave a jolt. He glanced through his emporium's window. Leon and Leroy lounged on one of the sofas. He stifled a grunt. He'd deal with them later. Right now, he had something more important to do.

Curling his hand lightly around the back of Charley's head, he aimed the boy for the mercantile. "Come along with me, young man. I want to visit with your aunt. I think I have a job that's just the right size for a boy like you."

Neva

Neva glanced up from figuring Mrs. Wooster's lengthy order and stifled a groan. Here he came again . . . That man was making a regular nuisance of himself. But how could she send him away when he tried so hard to be considerate?

"Mrs. Shilling, good morning."

Apparently he didn't notice the customers in the store. She'd have to make him notice. "Good morning, Mr. Randall. Please give me a minute to finish with Mrs. Wooster, and then I'll be right with you."

His amiable smile remained intact. "Of course." He tipped his head at Mrs. Wooster. "Please take your time."

Neva found it difficult to punch the correct amounts into the cash register keys with

Mr. Randall leaning negligently against her counter, whistling softly. But she finished, wrote the total on a slip of paper, and showed it to her customer. "There you are, Maggie. Will that be cash or charge today?"

"Charge today, but Milton will be in at the end of the month to settle up with you."

"All right." Neva preferred cash, but she wouldn't chase off a steady customer. She recorded the purchase in the book, then slapped it closed. "Have a good day, Maggie. Bud, please help Mrs. Wooster carry her packages to her car."

With Mrs. Wooster on her way, Neva needed to see to Mrs. Roof, but she decided to take care of her neighbor first. Mrs. Roof wasn't the pushy sort, and Neva preferred to rid the mercantile of her large distraction.

She slid the charge book under the counter and aimed what she hoped was a convincing smile at her neighbor. "All right, Mr. Randall, what can I do for you?"

"Actually, I need something from Charley."

"Charley?" She finally noticed the boy standing near Mr. Randall, his big brown eyes reflecting as much confusion as she felt.

"I'd like to hire him." Mr. Randall propped his wide hand on Charley's shoulder and beamed at Neva. "I need a messenger — someone to deliver ads to the fine folks of Buffalo Creek. The job pays fifty cents a week. That's a good salary for a youngster."

Neva frowned. Arthur Randall threw his money around like a lasso. "Can't your boys do the deliveries?"

The man chuckled, shaking his head. "My boys are too busy working in the emporium to take the time for delivering ads. Now, take Charley here . . ." He gazed down at the boy with such fondness Neva experienced a stab of guilt she didn't understand. "He said he isn't big enough to carry grocery bags. But he's just the right size to carry a satchel of advertisements, don't you agree?"

If she said yes to Mr. Randall's request, she'd have one more reason to owe the man. The scale was getting far too unbalanced. "I don't know . . ."

He shot her a sharp look. "Are you using him here in the mercantile?"

Mostly she'd just asked him to stay out from people's feet since he didn't want to be upstairs with Belle and his sisters. "Well, no, but —"

"Then let me put him to work." He planted his elbow on the counter and leaned in. "You know what they say — idle hands are the devil's workshop. You wouldn't want him getting himself into trouble, would you?"

Heat seared Neva's face. Warren's hands were always busy, and he'd still managed to create more trouble than she ever would have imagined. "I —"

Mr. Randall straightened and placed his hand on Charley's head, tipping the boy's face upward. "Look at him, Mrs. Shilling. Can't you see how much he wants this job?"

Neva couldn't deny the hope shining in Charley's eyes. And if she let him go, she'd be free of the reminder of her husband's deviltry for a few hours. She sighed. "Charley isn't familiar with Buffalo Creek. He could get lost wandering around by himself."

"Hmm . . ." The man used his fingers to scrape his mustache down. "Learning the route would familiarize him with his new town. He'd get to know everybody. In no time he'd feel right at home. Wouldn't that be good for him?"

If she didn't give a direct yes or no soon, the persistent man would use up her entire morning. She came out from behind the counter and bent down to address Charley. "Do you want to deliver advertisements for

Mr. Randall?"

Charley nodded.

"Well, you can't do it by yourself." She didn't intend to speak so sharply, but her tone held a bite anyway. "If Belle is willing to go with you — and that means Cassie and Adeline have to go, too — then you can take the job."

"Splendid!" Mr. Randall rubbed his palms together. "Run up and fetch the girls, Charley, then come on over to the emporium. I'll have the satchel ready for you."

Charley darted off, wearing the biggest smile Neva had seen since Mr. Caudel brought him to her a week and a half ago. The boy's delight should please her. But it didn't.

CHAPTER 18

Jesse

He wouldn't officially wear the sheriff's badge until Monday, but Jesse decided to spend the weekend pretending it was already pinned to his chest. Might as well become familiar with the town and let the town become familiar with him. He might take a chance on the Saturday special at Betsy Ann's while he was out. His attempt at pancakes hadn't gone so well that morning, and he was hungry enough even to eat more of Aunt Sue's famous chicken and dumplings.

Buffalo Creek acted a lot more like Beloit on Saturday. Cars and wagons crowded the street. Businesses had their doors propped open with bricks. Every place he passed, with the exception of Betsy Ann's Café, seemed a beehive of busyness. He stepped through every door, doffed his hat to the ladies and shook the men's hands, meandered a bit to see what was available, and then set out again.

He didn't bother entering Main Street Mercantile, though. His glance through the open windows showed Bud and Mrs. Shilling buzzing around, both looking frazzled. They didn't need one more person underfoot when the little store was already so crowded. But he'd go by again later, buy a few groceries to fill the shelf in his kitchen. He might also ask Mrs. Shilling for a few simple recipes. Including one for pancakes.

His stomach growled, and he winced. There was one other place besides Betsy Ann's for a fellow to grab a bite to eat — the Oakes Hotel out on the edge of town. According to Dodds Schlacter, the dining room served up a good meal three times a day, but it was pricey. Twice as much as Betsy Ann charged, and a full mile's walk from the sheriff's office.

He stood on the sidewalk, thinking about the money remaining in his pocket. He'd start drawing his salary on Monday, but he'd only draw a half wage for his first month. As sheriff of Buffalo Creek, he'd earn forty dollars more a month than he had as a deputy in Beloit, but he shouldn't get too free with his spending. He'd never rented a whole house, paid for utilities, or supplied himself with groceries for an entire month. He could very well use up that extra money real quick. Especially if he spent seventy cents for every meal.

Jesse sighed. Lousy cooking or not, it made more sense to eat at Betsy Ann's Café. He set his feet in motion in the direction of the diner. Halfway there he caught sight of a small entourage coming up the sidewalk. Charley, with a leather pouch hanging over his shoulder, led the group. Belle came next, pulling a wooden wagon. Adeline rode in the wagon, and Cassie lagged at the rear.

Charley's gaze met Jesse's, and his face lit. He broke into a trot. "Hi, Mr. Caudel!"

Jesse smiled at the boy's flushed face and sweaty hair. "Hi to you." He flicked the strap on the pouch. "What'cha got there?"

"I got a job." Charley dug in the pouch and withdrew a sheet of paper. He shoved it at Jesse. "Here you go, compullments of Randall's Emporium."

Belle eased up alongside Charley, the wagon wheels rattling. "Compli-ments. Re-member?"

Charley offered an embarrassed grin. "Anyway, it's for you from Mr. Randall."

Jesse took the smudged paper. "I thank you, Charley, but I already have one of these. Mr. Randall's son Leon dropped one by this morning with a note welcoming me to town." He hadn't made it by the emporium yet, but he would before closing time. He needed to get that mattress up off the floor before critters took a notion to chew on it, and he hoped Arthur Randall might be able to help him understand why the manufacturer Rich & Baker continued to niggle in the back of his mind.

"Oh." For a moment Charley's face fell. Then he shrugged and took the page back. "I'll save it for someone else then." He puffed up. "I'm taking them to every house in town."

Jesse released a low whistle. "That's a pretty big job for a little —"

Charley scowled.

Jesse amended, "— man."

"I can do it." He shifted the bag to his other shoulder. "As soon as I learn all the streets, Aunt Neva says Belle won't have to come with me. I'll be able to go by myself."

Belle appeared as frazzled as her mother and brother had. Jesse pointed to the wagon. "Have you pulled that thing around all morning?"

She sighed. "Yes, sir. Momma said I couldn't leave the girls behind. She had to work and couldn't watch them. But it's too far for Adeline and Cassie to walk, so Mr.

Randall loaned us the wagon. Adeline really likes riding in it." She glanced at the little girl, then whispered, "She's heavier than she looks."

Cassie scampered up next to Belle. "Belle won't let me ride with Adeline. She says I make the wagon too hard to pull."

Jesse crouched down to Cassie's level. "Why don't you try taking turns with Adeline?"

Cassie crossed her arms over her chest and poked out her lower lip. "Adeline doesn't take turns."

Jesse ruffled the little girl's soft hair, then straightened and addressed Belle. "Since it's lunchtime, you kids should run on home and eat something with Bud and your ma. Start out again after your arms have had a chance to recover."

"Momma never takes a Saturday lunch break. The mercantile is too busy."

Worry nibbled at Jesse. "But you all will eat something, won't you?" Growing children needed to eat.

"We've got some leftover pork and beans in the refrigerator. I'll heat them for us."

Charley made a face. "Beans make my insides rumble."

Jesse couldn't stop a laugh from blasting. The boy's expression . . . "Beans have that effect on me, too, Charley." He scratched his chin. Belle looked worn out, but the kids had to eat. "I'm heading over to the café for a sandwich and a bottle of pop. You kids wanna come with me?"

Belle said, "We don't have any money."

Charley perked up. "I do! Mr. Randall gave me fifty cents to deliver his advertisements."

Jesse shook his head. "You keep your money, Charley. The sign at the café says today's special is a bologna or cheese sandwich." And only ten cents. He grinned at Charley. "Does bologna make your stomach rumble?"

"I don't know. I've never had bologna."

Jesse turned a dumbfounded look on the boy. "You've never had bologna?"

"Me neither." Belle cringed. "One of the church ladies brought over a ring of bologna, but Momma put it out for the hobos. Poppa always said bologna was 'poor man's fare.' He wouldn't let us eat it."

Charley stared at Belle in amazement. "My daddy said that, too."

"No bologna then." Jesse took the wagon handle from Belle and turned the group toward Betsy Ann's Café. "We'll have cheese sandwiches with our soda pop. Let's go."

Neva

Neva turned the sign to Closed a half hour early and pulled the shade. A yawn stretched her mouth, and she sagged against the doorframe as the breath heaved from her lungs. She couldn't recall the last time she'd been so tired. What a good day. What a good, good day. Her money box contained enough to pay the invoices on her most recent deliveries and then some. The charge book showed several sizable purchases, which meant the promise of more money coming in. And, best of all, she was so tired she should be able to sleep instead of lying awake worrying.

Bud took the broom from the corner. "Sure hope Belle has supper ready. I'm half-starved."

Neva gave a jolt. Had the children come back for lunch? Belle wouldn't have bothered to come into the mercantile, as busy as things had been, but Neva should have heard them trooping up and down the stairs. Even little Adeline's light steps sounded like an elephant tromping on the old, creaky stairs.

Neva looked at the tin ceiling, listening. Complete silence overhead. She frowned at Bud. "Was your sister here at lunchtime?"

He shoved the broom's bristles across the

floor. "I don't know. I was too busy to notice."

Neva whisked her apron over her head and moved for the staircase. As she rounded the corner, the back door burst open, and Belle, followed by the three younger children, clattered in.

Belle sent her mother an apologetic look. "Is it five o'clock already, Momma? Charley wanted to get as many papers delivered as we could, and then we took the wagon back to Mr. Randall's. He wanted to know where all we'd been. I didn't realize it was so late."

"You're not late. I closed early."

Belle blew out a little breath, smiling. "Oh, good. I'll get supper started right away then. Is it all right if I heat the ham-and-potato casserole Mrs. Wooster brought over? It'll go good with the leftover peas in the Frigidaire."

"Whatever can be heated quickly is fine. The children must be famished." Neva put her hands on her hips. "Why didn't you bring them back for lunch?"

Belle herded the children toward the stairs. "Mr. Caudel took us to the café for a sandwich."

"And pop!" Cassie added. Apparently they'd had strawberry pop, because she and Adeline wore pink mustaches.

"Hold still for a minute!"

The entire cluster of children froze. Neva waved her hands at the younger ones. "Go wash up. Charley, help your sisters." She waited until the trio departed. Then she aimed a frown at her daughter. "You let Mr. Caudel buy your lunch?"

Belle's cheeks turned pink. "I tried to talk him out of it, Momma, but the children were hungry, and the mercantile was so busy. So I —"

Someone banged on the front door.

Neva sighed. Maybe she wouldn't close early. "Go get supper started. We'll discuss this later."

Belle scurried off, and Neva returned to the door. Jesse Caudel stood outside, frowning at his timepiece.

She opened the door, and he jerked to face her, surprise registering on his face.

"I thought you stayed open until five on Saturdays."

She stepped back, gesturing for him to come in. She snapped the door closed behind him, though, and turned the lock. "I am usually open until five, but the traffic had slowed so much after an especially hectic morning and early afternoon, I decided to lock up early."

"Oh." He took a step backward. "If you're

too tired to do business, I can come back on Monday."

Why did he always have to be so accommodating? She wanted to be mad at him. "That's fine. I have enough energy to put together one more order."

He grinned and pushed his hat to the back of his head the way Bud wore Warren's old hat. The rakish angle made him seem far too young to assume responsibility for maintaining law in an entire town.

She turned and headed for the remaining few empty crates. "What do you need?"

The clop of his feet followed her. "To be honest, ma'am, I'm not real sure. I've never had my own kitchen. The boardinghouse owner didn't allow cooking in our rooms, so this is my first time to fend for myself."

Neva picked up a crate and faced him. "So you have no idea what grocery items you want?"

He shrugged, the gesture boyish. "No, ma'am. But I trust you to put together something that will meet my needs for some simple meals."

Neva stared at him for several seconds, unwilling to believe he had no idea what to buy. "You bought lunch for my children today."

A slow grin grew on his cheek. "Yes, but

260

no need to thank me. I enjoyed their company."

She frowned. She hadn't intended to thank him. "It was kind of you, I'm sure, but we had food here. They didn't need to eat somewhere else."

The grin faded fast. "I didn't feed them bologna."

Now she drew back in surprise. "Who said anything about bologna?"

Jesse glanced at Bud, who had finished sweeping and began straightening cans on the closest display shelf. "Belle. And Charley. Apparently neither of them had ever tasted it before. So I got them cheese sandwiches instead. I . . . I hope cheese was all right."

Obviously there was more to the story than what he was telling. But tiredness stole her desire to understand. She plopped the crate onto the counter. "If you want ease in preparation, I suggest a variety of canned goods — meat, vegetables, and fruit. Do you have an oven?"

He nodded.

"Then I'll give you some potatoes. Baked potatoes are easy and they go with anything. You can even dice a leftover baked potato and fry it for your breakfast. As for breakfast, oatmeal is a simple choice. Or boxed

261

cereal. We carry Post Toasties and Rice Krispies — both are popular with my customers." She began gathering the items and laying them out on the counter for him to choose. "You can either arrange delivery of milk from the dairy, or I can add a few cans to your order. Whichever you prefer."

"What about pancakes?"

She paused with her hands around two cans of condensed milk. "Pancakes?"

He nodded. "I tried to make some this morning with water and a little flour I found in a tin in one of the cupboards, but they burned. I like to never scraped it all out of the pan."

She could well imagine. She returned to the counter and plunked the cans next to the crate. "Mr. Caudel, you need more than flour and water to make pancakes. You use flour, oil, an egg, milk, or water. And then you put oil in the pan to keep the batter from sticking."

He cringed. "I sure messed that up."

She ducked her head so he wouldn't see her smile. "There is a simpler solution."

"What's that?"

She crossed to a shelf and pulled down a box of Bisquick. "I don't generally stock this because it's considered a luxury item around here, but it's perfect for you. This is premixed for biscuits or pancakes. All you add is water or milk. See here?" She pointed to the back of the box and the easy-to-follow directions. "Just do what this says, and you should have pancakes you'll be able to eat." She put the box in his crate. "Would you like syrup or jam to put on your pancakes?"

"Both."

She laughed softly. "You and your sweet tooth."

He grimaced, his cheeks blotching with pink. "Yeah, pretty bad, isn't it? I can't ever remember getting store-bought candy when I was a kid, but my ma made taffy every year at Christmas. Never could get enough of it to suit me."

For reasons she didn't understand, his admission created an uncomfortable ache in the center of her chest. She turned to the row of jam jars. "Strawberry, peach, or marmalade?"

"Anything but marmalade."

He made marmalade sound like a dirty word. Neva almost laughed. "Strawberry then. It's the sweetest." She punched each item into the cash register, each click and clang intrusive in the now-quiet store, and he put everything in the crate. She placed two loaves of bread on top without asking if he wanted them, but he didn't take them out. She wrote the total on a slip of paper, then subtracted sixty cents and handed him the paper.

He frowned at it. "What's this?"

"Your bill."

"No. I mean what's this amount you took off? Some sort of discount?"

"That is what you paid for the children's lunch."

He shook his head.

She raised one eyebrow. "Mr. Caudel, do not lie to me. I've lived in Buffalo Creek for a number of years, and I'm familiar with Betsy Ann's specials. She charges ten cents for a sandwich and five cents for a bottle of pop. Four children means four sandwiches and four pops. Sixty cents."

He shook his head again. "Cassie and Adeline shared a sandwich and a bottle of strawberry pop. Belle and Charley each had a sandwich, but they shared a Royal Crown Cola. So your figure is off." He plucked the pencil from her hand and scratched through the sixty cents. "Three sandwiches and two bottles of pop comes to forty cents." He wrote the number down, then added it back into her total. "And it was my treat. So you aren't taking it off my bill."

She raised her chin and squared her

shoulders. With her uncombed hair strag-
gling along her cheek and her dress wrinkled, she might not look like a formidable
opponent, but she could be as stubborn as
a mule when provoked. "Mr. Caudel, I —"

"You're a proud woman. I understand
that." He spoke so kindly her shoulders
began to wilt. "But I wanted to treat the
kids. It was my idea. You don't owe me
anything." He dug in his pocket and withdrew several bills and coins. He laid the payment on the counter and reached for his
crate.

"Just a minute."

He froze in place.

She snapped a small brown bag open and
then popped the lid on the gumdrop jar.
She scooped three handfuls of the sugar-
coated drops into the bag, rolled the top,
and placed it in the crate. He aimed a
questioning look at her.

"My treat." She swished her palms together. "Turnabout is fair play."

A grin broke across his face. "Thank you,
Mrs. Shilling." He inched toward the door.
"And now I've kept you long enough. Go
on up and have your supper. Enjoy your day
of rest tomorrow. Bye, Bud."

"Bye, Mr. Caudel." Bud held the door
open for the man and then closed it behind

265

him. He sent a smirk to Neva. "He ramrod-ded you just like Pop always did."

Neva sniffed. "I'm going up to help Belle with supper. Finish cleaning and then turn out the lights." She hurried off before her son witnessed her succumbing to tears.

Jesse

Jesse balanced the crate of groceries on one hip and opened the front door to Randall's Emporium with the other. Arthur Randall himself bustled over before the bell swing-ing above the door stopped clanging, a genial smile on his face.

"Leon said you'd be coming in, but I'd just about given up on you, Sheriff." The man chuckled. "You made it in the nick of time. I'll be locking up in another five min-utes."

Jesse grimaced. "Sorry. Time got away from me today."

"No worries." Mr. Randall slipped his thumbs into the little pockets of his vest. "Leon says you need a bedframe, correct?"

"Yes, I do." He set the box on the floor by the door. "Nothing fancy, though. The bedroom at my place is too small for any-thing more than a simple frame."

"Well, follow me, and I'll show you what I

266

have in stock."

Jesse glanced at the various furniture arrangements as he trailed behind the man. He couldn't resist releasing a low *whew.* "You've got some nice things in here."

Randall flashed a grin over his shoulder. "I try to provide my customers with some of the finer things in life. Even though most folks in the Buffalo Creek township are farmers or quarry workers, they still deserve a bit of luxury, don't you think?"

"I suppose. I don't need anything too luxurious, though."

"I've got simple things, too, Sheriff." Randall stopped next to a stained pine bed and rested his hand on the headboard. "Like this one."

"How much?"

"Eleven dollars and fifty cents. Now that doesn't include a mattress, but I will throw in the matching bedside cabinet." Randall leaned in, his mustache twitching. "If you don't have indoor plumbing, you can tuck a chamber pot out of sight behind that cabinet door."

Jesse laughed. "I have indoor plumbing, but I reckon I could tuck my gun or maybe a snack in the cabinet." His bag of gumdrops would fit behind the square raised-panel door nicely. He pulled his money purse from his pocket, counted out the amount, and handed it over. "There you go."

"Thank you, Sheriff." The man rolled the bills around the coins and held the wad in his fist. "Shall I have my boys bring the pieces over to your place? No extra charge."

"Sounds good."

"Fine, fine." Randall clapped Jesse on the shoulder. "I'm glad we found something that suits. Is there anything else I can do for you? Maybe a painting for the wall or an entry table?"

He had no need for decorative items. Jesse shook his head. "No, thanks." He ambled toward the front door.

Randall moved alongside him. "Well, if you ever find yourself in need of other furniture, please trust Randall's Emporium to meet your needs."

Jesse came to a stop and faced the store owner. "Say, have you heard of Rich & Baker furniture?"

Randall's eyebrows shot high. "Rich & Baker? That's high-dollar furniture."

He should have surmised that by the quality of the pieces jammed into his house. "Do you sell their things?"

The man pursed his lips. "Their things are a little too, er, high class for most folks around here. But if you're interested, I could look into —"

Jesse held up his hand. "Don't bother. I just wondered if you knew about them."

"I'm sure every furniture salesman in the US knows about Rich & Baker. Or at the very least knows about the theft from their warehouse."

Jesse's scalp began to prickle. "Theft?"

"Yes, sir. Five, maybe six years ago some officials came here to search my store." Randall made a face. "They said they were searching every furniture dealer in the state, but it didn't make me feel any less violated. As if I would sell stolen goods!" He shook his head. "They didn't find anything here to match the description of the stolen pieces, but I wasn't surprised. I only buy from reputable dealers, never out of the back of a wagon."

The back of a wagon . . . Jesse forced a smile. "Glad to know there are honest businessmen left." He stuck out his hand and Randall took it. "Thanks for staying open for me. I'll be at the house whenever your boys are ready to deliver the furniture."

He grabbed up his crate and headed out onto the sidewalk. Across the street the telegraph office lights were still on. Jesse broke into a trot. He'd bother one more

Buffalo Creek business owner before returning to his house.

CHAPTER 19

Bud

Bud moved up the hallway on bare feet toward the kitchen, drawn by the smell of bacon and eggs — Pop's favorite breakfast, and his, too. Ma was at the stove, already dressed in her Sunday clothes. Except she didn't have her hat on yet. And she wore a bibbed apron. She must've gotten up really early.

He moved directly to the stove and stuck his nose close, drawing in a deep breath. "Mmm. Smells good."

Ma lifted a piece of meat from the sizzling pan with a fork and laid it on the plate already heaped with at least a dozen slices of crisp-looking bacon. Little grease bubbles bounced and popped on the wavy strip. She winked at him before pushing more shriveling lengths of bacon around in the pan. "I thought we deserved something special for breakfast after all the work we did yesterday."

Bud grinned. He liked it when Ma talked to him the way she would a grownup. "So all this is just for us? The others get gruel?" He waggled his eyebrows at her the way he'd seen Pop do.

A grin curved Ma's lips, but her eyes didn't light the way they used to when Pop took to teasing her. "I think we'll need to share. They worked, too. Just not in the mercantile."

Bud could have argued that walking around town shoving papers at people wasn't the same as carrying full crates and cleaning. And Charley got a whole fifty cents for the job. Ma only gave him and Belle a quarter a week for their allowance, and they worked a heap sight harder than Charley had. The words rolled on his tongue, eager to escape, but he swallowed them. Ma looked tired even after a full night's sleep, and she was fixing him a special breakfast. He'd repay her by not fussing. The decision gave him a good feeling inside.

"Would you run down to the cellar and get me some apples? A half dozen of the firmest ones, please."

"What'cha gonna do with those?"

This time when Ma smiled, it looked more real. "Fry them in butter with some brown sugar."

Saliva pooled under Bud's tongue. He licked his lips. "This is gonna be the best breakfast ever!"

Ma laughed. Propelled by her happiness, Bud darted to his room for his slippers and robe, then charged down the stairs. He reached for the back door lock, but a draft flowing up the hallway that led to the store stopped him short. He angled a frown toward the dark mercantile. Had he left the overhead fan on last night? He replayed his final actions in the store and recalled giving a little hop to catch the pull chain. He'd turned it off.

He moved to the bottom riser and started to call for Ma, but then he clamped his mouth closed. Ma was busy. And wasn't he the man of the house? He'd explore things by himself. Slowly, his heart thudding like a bass drum, he pushed the button for the hallway sconces. The sudden light made him wince, and he squinted as he moved in the direction of the shadowy mercantile.

Clear at the front of the store, a strange pale glow formed a narrow path on the gray floor. Bud squinted harder, trying to make sense of it. And then understanding fell like

273

the ceiling on his head. He stopped so quick his soles slid on the floor. He tried to yell for Ma, but his throat was too dry.

"The sheriff . . ." He gasped the words. "We need the sheriff." Without another thought Bud raced out the open front door and up the street.

Neva

How long did it take to fetch a half-dozen apples from the cellar? Neva glanced over her shoulder, frowning. She needed to core and slice the apples before she could fry them, and she wanted to get them in a pan before she woke Belle and the children.

Using her apron as a heat shield, she transferred the platter of bacon and the bowl of scrambled eggs to the warming oven. She poured the bacon grease into a can and then used a rag to wipe the pan clean. For a moment she stood motionless with one ear turned toward the doorway, listening for Bud's feet on the stairs. Nothing.

She sighed and crossed to the Frigidaire for the butter. She spooned a blob into the pan but didn't set it on a burner. No sense in scorching the butter. She returned the butter bowl to the refrigerator and then listened again for Bud. Still nothing.

She shook her head, impatience teasing her. Where was that boy? Had he gone back to bed? She started for the hallway to peek in his room, but muffled noises from the lower level captured her attention. She changed course and moved to the stairway instead. As she descended, the whisper of voices — one excited, one low pitched and calm — crept around the corner. Her confusion mounting with every downward step, she sped her progress and broke into a clumsy trot when she reached the bottom of the stairs.

The voices became more clear and recognizable as she moved up the hallway in a brisk stride. Apparently Bud had been distracted by an unexpected visitor. She burst into the room, located her son and their guest behind the counter, and then huffed out a little breath. "Mr. Caudel, what are you doing here this morning?"

He and Bud wore matching expressions of dismay and remorse. Mr. Caudel started to speak, but Bud rushed at her and began blabbering. "Ma, I fetched the sheriff. Somebody broke into the mercantile last night. They took the money box."

Nausea attacked. Neva clapped her hand over her mouth and reached out for her son. He gripped her hand and held tight.

Mr. Caudel approached and touched Bud's shoulder. "Go up and pour your mother a cup of coffee, Bud. Add a splash of medicinal whiskey if you've got it."

"Pop kept a bottle behind a box of rags in the barn."

Warren? Whiskey? Would the surprises never cease? She shook her head. "No. No spirits."

Mr. Caudel gently shifted Bud toward the hallway. "It'll help calm your nerves."

"No!"

He grimaced. "Bud, get that coffee, huh?"

Bud darted off.

Mr. Caudel took hold of her elbow and guided her to the counter. "Catch hold there, ma'am, until you get your bearings. This isn't the best way to start a day, is it?"

His soothing demeanor did her more good than an entire bottle of whiskey could. She drew in several slow breaths and brought her racing pulse under control. She finally found the ability to answer his question. "No. No, it surely isn't."

Only last night she'd fallen asleep thanking God for bringing so many customers to the mercantile, secure in the knowledge she would be able to care for her children as well as Warren had. Now her security had crumbled, and betrayal swept over her with as much force as a stout Kansas wind.

Bud shuffled into the mercantile, cradling a cup between his palms. He held it out to Neva. "Here you go, Ma. No whiskey — just black coffee."

Neva would pour out that whiskey as soon as she had the strength to cross the yard. She took the cup and sipped the liquid. It didn't help, but she offered Bud a wobbly smile anyway. "Thank you, Son. Now go get dressed. And wake the others, too."

He stood gazing at her with his brow furrowed, clearly unwilling to leave her.

She forced a smile. "I'll be all right. Go on, now. We don't want to be late for church."

"We're going?"

"You're going?"

Bud and Mr. Caudel spoke at the same time, their voices expressing matching incredulity.

Neva set the cup on the counter and bounced a firm look over both of them. "Of course we're going." She needed prayer and a reminder of God's presence.

Bud shrugged, but he headed around the corner. His feet thudded on the stairs, and soon the patter of footsteps overhead assured her all the children were awake and readying themselves for the day.

Mr. Caudel wandered over to the door. He seemed to examine it closely. Neva remained next to the sturdy counter, uncertain her shaky legs would support her if she tried to walk. She wished she had a stool to sit on, but Warren had never wanted any chairs in the mercantile, claiming a place to relax would encourage sloth.

She shoved aside memories of Warren and focused on the new sheriff. "Did they break the lock?" Would the town locksmith be willing to replace it for her on a Sunday? If he did, he'd probably charge extra. Would she be able to afford it?

"The lock's not broken, ma'am." Mr. Caudel crouched and peered one eyed at the locking mechanism. "It wasn't jimmied either." He rose and aimed a puzzled look at her. "No broken windows. The back door was still locked up. Since this door was standing wide open, I have to assume it's how he came in and went out. And far as I can tell, that's exactly what he did. He just . . . came in."

Neva frowned. "You mean the door wasn't locked?"

"That's how it appears."

"That can't be."

He clopped toward her, his boot heels as loud as her thundering pulse. "I'm sorry,

278

ma'am, but I'm afraid it is. Otherwise there'd be signs of breaking in. There aren't any."

She desperately needed a chair. She worked her way to the opposite side of the counter and sank down on the edge of the slanting bean bins. Burying her face in her hands, she battled tears. How could she have been so careless?

His scuffing footsteps approached, and then a hand touched her wrist. She opened her eyes to find him on one knee before her, an apology etched into his features.

"It was my fault. I came in after you locked up. If it hadn't been for me coming in after you'd closed, that door would've been secure."

"No, no." She raised a hand in dismissal. "I know to check the locks before turning in. I was just so tired . . ." She was tired now, too. Tired of unpleasant surprises.

"Do you have any idea how much was in the money box?"

She swallowed a knot of anguish. "I'll have to review my receipts from yesterday, but I know it was more than thirty dollars." Thank goodness not everyone had paid cash. She could count on the charge customers bringing in money later in the month. But what would she do for now?

She had bills to pay, and she needed money to place next month's orders. The weight of responsibility bowed her forward.

"Ma?"

Bud's voice jarred Neva into raising her head and pasting on a smile. "Yes, Son?"

He held out his hands, showing her his clothing. "We're all dressed. And the kids are hungry. Should Belle and me go ahead and feed them?"

Belle and me. Never had Bud offered to help put a meal on the table. Nor had he offered to do anything kind for the younger children. Perhaps this robbery had one good result.

Mr. Caudel stood and pulled Neva to her feet. "Lock this door behind me, then go up and feed your family. I'll come back this afternoon, and we'll write up an official report. Maybe we'll get lucky and somebody will have seen something — strangers loitering on Main Street or . . . something."

Neva's pulse gave a leap. "I wonder . . ."

Bud crowded close. "What, Ma?"

She put her arm around her son's shoulders and addressed Mr. Caudel. "Earlier this week two men — hobos who'd jumped off the train — came to the backyard looking for food. They said they'd been watching me." Recalling the statement, she involuntarily shuddered. "I gave them some bread, apples, and cheese, and Mr. Randall ordered them to catch the next passing train. Do you think they might have stuck around, hoping for something more?"

"Randall . . . Arthur Randall from the emporium?"

"That's right."

"He saw them, too?"

Warmth flooded her cheeks the way it had when her neighbor came charging over to rescue her. "Yes."

Mr. Caudel gave a decisive nod. "I'll get a report from him, then, too. I can't guarantee you'll see that money again, Mrs. Shilling, but I'll do my best to find whoever took it and recover as much as possible." He headed for the door in his typical wide stride. "Lock this now. We don't need to invite a second intruder."

Neva scurried after him and closed the door firmly. Then she turned the lock, checked the door to be certain it held, and finally turned around.

Bud stared at the door. Horror widened his eyes. "Ma . . . I did it. I let them in, didn't I?"

CHAPTER 20

Jesse

Jesse, with Dodds Schlacter's help, spent much of Monday and Tuesday talking with folks who lived near Main Street and searching for clues that might lead him to the mercantile's thief. But even with their efforts combined, they discovered nothing helpful. By Wednesday Jesse had to conclude the money was gone, carried away in the pockets of the drifter who'd pilfered it. He stopped by the mercantile late that afternoon to give Mrs. Shilling the bad news.

The mercantile was quiet except for the squeaky overhead fan turning a lazy circle and the soft *thump-thump* of cans being settled on a shelf somewhere out of sight — probably Bud doing some restocking. Although Mrs. Shilling would probably prefer a crowd of customers buying her wares, Jesse was grateful for the chance to talk to her privately.

He crossed to the counter, where she was filling brown paper sacks with flour and weighing them. She paused in the task and watched his approach. No glimmer of hope showed in her hazel eyes. At least it seemed she wasn't expecting good news. He grimaced. Did that make his visit better or worse?

Leaning on the edge of the counter, he looked straight into Mrs. Shilling's stalwart face. "I wish I had something better to tell you, ma'am, but Sheriff Schlacter and I agree that whoever stole the money is long gone, and he was wily enough not to leave a trail. We're giving up trying to find him."

She bowed her head and nodded. "I understand."

Bud came flying from behind the tall shelves, his cheeks and neck mottled with red. "Whaddaya mean you're giving up? Sheriffs don't give up. I read about them all the time in the dime novels. Every lawman always says, 'I will find that man.' What kind of a sheriff are you?"

Mrs. Shilling reached for him. "Bud . . ."

He ducked away, his eyes still blazing. "You can't quit. We need that money. How're we supposed to keep this place going without it? You gotta keep trying, Mr. Caudel. You gotta."

283

The boy's voice cracked, and Jesse thought his heart cracked at the hurt and betrayal creeping through Bud's angry explosion. "I'm not giving up completely. I'll keep listening for clues that will help me figure out who stole your ma's money. But I've worn out my available resources. So I have to let it go for now."

Bud rammed his fingers through his hair, disheveling the wavy locks. "If they'd busted that door down instead of just walking through it, we'd have heard. We could've come downstairs and caught 'em in the act. We'd still have our money." The boy's chin wobbled, and he blinked hard and fast.

"Whoa there, Bud." Jesse clamped his hands on the boy's shoulders and held tight even though he squirmed. "I'm grateful you and your ma didn't come down here that night. A man desperate enough to march into someone's place of business and steal is desperate enough to try to cover his deeds. You could've been hurt. Or even killed."

Bud stopped wriggling. His eyes widened. "Killed?"

"It's happened before." Only yesterday Sheriff Abling had called in response to Jesse's telegram and told him that a night watchman for Rich & Baker warehouse had been shot during the break-in almost six years ago when several pieces of furniture, including a dining room set identical to the one in his house right now, were taken. The thief had never been found, the furniture never recovered.

Bud stared at Jesse with his mouth slightly agape for several seconds. Then he broke free of Jesse's hold and scooted a few feet away. "Betcha I know who did it. Betcha it was Leon and Leroy. They were next door all day Saturday, so they knew how many people came in here to buy stuff. They'd know we had a box full of money. And they'd know Ma never takes the money box to the bank until Monday."

Mrs. Shilling took one step toward Bud. "Son, you can't accuse our neighbors."

Bud snorted. "Some neighbors."

The boy's derision raised the fine hairs on the back of Jesse's neck.

The boy folded his arms tight. "They've never been nice to us the whole time we've lived here. Until Pop up and died. Then old man Randall comes over here, acting all chummy, and —"

Mrs. Shilling caught Bud's elbow and gave it a little shake. "Speak politely, young man."

Bud curled his lip into a belligerent smirk. "Don't you remember what Pop always said about the Randalls? They're moneygrub-bers. They don't care about anything except getting more and more greenbacks." He turned to Jesse. "Bet you didn't ask Mr. Randall about his boys, did ya? Bet you didn't ask them to empty their pockets." He narrowed his gaze. "And bet you won't, 'cause nobody ever wants to get on their bad side. So they just do whatever they want to." He whirled and ran from the store.

Jesse blew out a breath. He angled a glance at the boy's mother. "If you need to go after him, I'll mind the store for you."

She shook her head. "If it was Belle, I'd go. With her, talking helps. But with Bud . . ." Deep regret pursed her face. "Before the theft he and I had turned a corner in our relationship. He was taking on more responsibility here, being more respectful and cooperative. At least with me. But now we're back to the way we were, with him angry and resentful. I think it's because he feels he's to blame for leaving the door unlocked. I've told him again and again I'm the owner, so I should have checked it, but . . ." She held out her hands in futility.

Jesse chewed the inside of his lip for a moment, gathering his thoughts. "You think there's any truth to what he said about the

286

Randall boys? Do you think they might have been the ones to take the money?"

She laughed softly. "They already have more money than nearly anyone else in town. Why would they need to steal more?"

Jesse shrugged. "Because that's what moneygrubbers do?"

"Warren was friendly to their faces, but he often spoke ill of the Randalls behind their backs. 'Moneygrubbers' was one of the mildest titles he gave them. I never thought it was very nice, and his attitude prevented me from becoming friends with Mabel Randall." A sad smile graced her face. "I think sometimes he was jealous of their success. In many ways Warren was a moneygrubber, too." Her cheeks bloomed pink. She ducked her head. "And I've said too much."

Jesse forced a chuckle to cover the troublesome ideas taking shape in his mind. "No worries, ma'am. Law enforcement officers are trained to keep secrets. I won't repeat what you said."

She offered a weak smile. An explosion of angry voices burst over their heads. She looked at the ceiling. "Uh-oh." She inched toward the hallway, her beseeching gaze pinned on him. "Does your offer to watch the store for a few minutes still stand?"

He nodded. "Go ahead. Take the time you need. I'll stay right here until you get back."

She darted off.

Jesse waited nearly a half hour before Mrs. Shilling and Bud returned. The woman wore a look of determination, and the boy seemed both surly and defeated. Jesse didn't ask questions, but as he left, he made a decision. He couldn't do anything about the missing money, but maybe he could help restore peace between the mother and her son. After all, he'd contributed to the conflict by interrupting their lockup routine. The least he could do was try to repair the damage.

The next day Jesse began a routine of greeting the students as they arrived at school. Then he came back in the afternoon to supervise their leave-taking. At first he did it just so he could single Bud out for a quick chat or friendly smack on the shoulder. But the more he thought about it, the more sense it made to get friendly with all the youngsters in Buffalo Creek.

Kids who knew him and liked him would be less prone to cause trouble in town, so he worked to build camaraderie with all of them, from the little ones on up. As the days progressed, he learned their names, and they began running up to greet him instead of waving at him from afar. No matter how many children commanded his attention, Jesse always reserved an extra dose for Bud. Even when the boy acted standoffish.

Jesse witnessed a lot. As Bud had hinted, the Randall boys ruled the playground without a word of rebellion from the other students. But Bud shouldn't complain about the Randall boys, because he gave Charley the same lordly treatment, refusing to let the younger boy join the Kick the Can or marble games. He did enlist Charley when they played blindman's bluff, making him the blind man and being especially rough in taunting him.

At times Jesse battled the temptation to grab Bud by the collar of his jacket and shake him until his teeth rattled. But he wasn't the boy's father. He couldn't take on a punitive role without sacrificing the opportunity to build a friendship with the boy. So he encouraged Charley to talk to Aunt Neva about Bud's behavior and secured promises from the sad-faced boy that he would try.

When he engaged Bud in conversation, Jesse shared tidbits of his childhood, being overrun with pesky little sisters and the regret he carried for the times he wasn't as kind as he should have been. Yet Bud continued to use Charley as a target for his resentment and frustration.

As Halloween approached — Jesse's first holiday in Buffalo Creek — he became especially diligent in making his presence known at the school. In Beloit, hoodlums had sometimes broken shop windows and the globes on streetlamps, spread trash in people's yard, and otherwise vandalized the community. Having spent time shooting marbles and playing catch and riding on the merry-go-round with them, he hoped the young people in his new town would decide to forgo mischief that night. And if they didn't, he would have to show them a different side of being sheriff and let them suffer the consequences of their actions.

Friday morning, the thirtieth of October, Jesse drove to the filling station and pumped twelve gallons of gas into his truck's tank. The station's owner, Rob Geary, ambled out and watched Jesse work.

"Getting yourself a full tank?" The man raised his eyebrows and shifted his stained Western-style hat on his head. "Big spender, you are. Most folks just put in enough to get by."

"Driving to Beloit today. I wouldn't want to run out."

"Reckon not. What's in Beloit?"

He intended to spend some time with Sheriff Abling, picking the older man's brain regarding the suspicions he harbored about Warren Shilling, but nobody needed to know that just yet. Maybe never.

He grinned. "Picking up a few things for Mrs. Shilling's mercantile." Her order was a lot smaller this time than last, thanks to her shortage of cash. He hoped she'd have enough goods to carry her a full month. Jesse removed the nozzle and handed it to Rob.

The man held the nozzle the way a bride held a bouquet of flowers. "So she's planning to keep that place going?"

Jesse twisted the gas cap into place. "As far as I know."

"Well, I'll be . . ."

Jesse flicked a glance at the man. "There some reason she shouldn't?"

"She's a woman."

Rob's statement made Jesse laugh. "Well, that's true enough, but there's no law, is there, that a woman can't run a business?"

"S'pose there isn't, or Betsy Ann Mullin would've been in jail a long time ago." Rob draped the nozzle over the hook and leaped back when it dripped on his shoe. He folded his arms over his chest and frowned. "But seems to me women are made more for matrimony than owning businesses. Now Betsy Ann, being over forty and kind of homely and set in her ways, the likelihood of her getting hitched is slim to none. But that Mrs. Shilling — Why, she's a fine figure of a woman, still young. And she's got youngsters to raise. I can't believe she doesn't want to sell that place and look for a new husband." The man's expression turned wily. "You thinking about taking on a wife who's got a herd of kids ready to call somebody Daddy?"

Jesse grimaced. "Now don't start matchmaking, huh? I'm not in the market for a wife."

Rob held his hands wide, smirking. "Me? Matchmaking? Huh-uh. I'll leave that to my missus." He lost the teasing look. "Gotta tell you though, Sheriff. Folks around town been talking about how good you are with youngsters, meeting up with 'em on the playground and making friends. More'n one of the ladies has mentioned how you an' the Widow Shilling would make a good pair."

Jesse swallowed a sharp retort. All small towns had one thing in common — people loved to gossip. Mostly because there wasn't much else to do. "That poor woman's only been widowed a few weeks. I figure she needs some time to recover."

What woman would want to marry a lawman, knowing he could be called to duty any time of the day or night? If he did marry, he wouldn't choose a widow with children. He'd paid his debt helping to raise somebody else's kids.

He clapped Rob on the shoulder. "Besides, I'm happy being on my own, and you can share that at the barber shop the next time you go in for a shave."

Rob barked out a laugh. "All right then, Sheriff. Enjoy your drive to Beloit. Hope that widow woman appreciates all you do for her."

Jesse climbed behind the wheel, offered a wave, then pulled out of the station. He parked in front of the mercantile and left the engine idling while he jogged across the sidewalk and entered the store. A few customers browsed the shelves, but Mrs. Shilling separated herself and met him near the threshold.

"I'm heading out now." He patted his pocket, where he'd tucked her list of orders. "I'll get the boxes from the depot. Is there anything else you need while I'm there?"

"Not a thing. But are you sure you should leave now?" Worry lines formed a V between her fine eyebrows. "The schoolchildren have grown accustomed to you being on the playground as they arrive."

Jesse grinned. "They'll survive one day of me not being there. Besides, by leaving early I'll be back by lunchtime. Then I can go over to the school and hand out those licorice whips I had you order as my Halloween treat to the youngsters." He hoped there'd be enough in the jar for him to enjoy some of the whips, too. "But that means I need to get going."

She shook her head, backing up. "All right, all right, I'll quit pestering you. Drive carefully, and thank you again for being my drayman."

Jesse lifted a hand in farewell and returned to his truck. The entire automobile quivered, as if eager to get on the road. He hoisted himself into the cab, pressed the clutch, and put the truck in gear. It groaned forward, and he rumbled out of town.

The drive on Highway 14 didn't offer much in the way of views, but Jesse didn't mind. It was peaceful out here, farmland stretching in all directions. Nothing was growing now with fall in full swing, and nothing was green, because the rains had avoided the area for far too long. But he still liked looking across the rolling prairie and watching hawks trace circles against the clear blue sky.

He reached Beloit and followed Court Street until it turned north and became River Street. When he rattled across the train tracks, he thought he heard someone grunt. He stopped on the far side of the tracks, listening, but the wind blowing through a tiny crack in the window combined with the noise of the trains' stacks sending up steam covered anything else. He shook his head. He hadn't grunted and he was alone, so his mind must be playing tricks on him. He put the truck in gear and pulled up in front of the brick depot.

Mrs. Shilling's crates were stacked on one corner of the porch. Jesse hopped out and left his door wide open. He waved one of the workers over. "Hey there! Can you help me load these onto my truck?"

"Sure thing, mister." The man moved past the truck, sticking out his hand to give the door a push. Then he sidestepped around the door, holding up his palms. "Whoops! Sorry there. Didn't mean to close you up inside." He ambled toward Jesse.

Jesse sent him a puzzled look. "Who're you talking to?"

He poked his thumb over his shoulder. "Your kids. Reckon they'd rather not be shut up in there while you're —"

"My what?" The startled exclamation left his mouth at the same time Charley Shilling leaped from the truck cab. While Jesse gawked in amazement, Cassie slid out behind him. Charley grabbed her hand, and the two of them took off running as if the devil himself were on their tails.

CHAPTER 21

Jesse

"Charley! Cassie! You get back here!"

They kept running, heading straight for the middle of town.

Stifling a growl, Jesse took off after them. If Charley'd been alone, Jesse wouldn't have had a chance, but Cassie slowed him down. Jesse pounded up to them and scooped Cassie into his arms. The little girl shrieked.

Charley whirled around. A look of fury pinched his face, and he charged at Jesse. Charley pounded on Jesse's ribs with his fists while Cassie bucked worse than a bronco, still screeching like a banshee.

Jesse tossed the little girl over one shoulder and grabbed Charley by his jacket collar. "Here now, that's enough. Behave yourselves."

The fight left the boy as quickly as it had risen. He aimed his pleading face upward. "Let us go, Mr. Caudel, please? Can't you let us go?"

With her brother calm, Cassie must have figured it was time to stop fighting, because she went limp. Jesse set her on the ground next to Charley, then crouched in front of the red-faced pair. He held their wrists, though, just in case they took a mind to tear off again. His boots weren't made for running over the rough ground. The soles of his feet throbbed.

He gave their skinny wrists a yank. "What in blue blazes do you two think you're doing, stowing away in my truck and then running off like that? You oughta be ashamed of yourselves."

Cassie leaned toward Charley and rested her cheek against his shoulder. His lower lip trembling, Charley glared at Jesse. "There wasn't any other way for us to get to Beloit. Except to hop a train like the hobos. And Cassie's too little for that. So we had to get in your truck."

Jesse couldn't imagine scrunching into the small slice of space behind his seat and staying quiet for the entire drive. Charley must have been mighty desperate to plan such a stunt. "But why?"

Charley jerked his face away from Jesse and pressed his chin on the top of Cassie's head. Jesse waited, but the boy didn't answer.

Jesse released Cassie and tugged Charley several feet away. Cassie made as if to follow, but he pointed at her. "Stay put." Blue eyes wide, she froze in place. Jesse planted his palms on his knees and looked eye to eye at Charley. "You'd best start talking, boy, because I'm running out of patience, and when my patience taps out, I just might turn you over my knee." An idle threat — Jesse would never raise his hand to this miserable child — but he hoped the risk might motivate Charley to talk.

The boy took several shuddering breaths as if gathering courage. He blurted, "I was going back to my old house. I was going to run Daddy's store. I know Daddy said I'm supposed to stay with Aunt Neva, but I don't want to. She doesn't like me."

There were lots of things Jesse could say. The house and store belonged to someone else now. Charley was far too young to run a business. But he focused on the boy's last statement. "Charley, she likes you. Doesn't she take care of you?" Always clean, well-fed, neatly dressed, Charley was walking proof of Neva Shilling's meticulous care.

"She doesn't like me." He folded his arms and stuck out his chin in a defiant stance.

If Charley had claimed Bud didn't like him, Jesse would understand. Bud wore his dislike for Charley as openly as Jesse wore his badge. He straightened and plunked his balled fists on his hips. "You aren't making an ounce of sense, Charley. How can you say Aunt Neva doesn't like you?"

Charley imitated Jesse's pose, glaring up while Jesse glared down. "She never looks at me when she talks to me. And when I try to talk to her like you told me to — you know, about how Bud is mean at school — she says, 'All right, Charley. I'll take care of it.' But she never does. I know she never does, because it never changes." The boy's tough demeanor began to melt. "And it never will. Bud doesn't want me there, and Aunt Neva doesn't want me either. So I'm gonna stay here in Beloit, where my friends are."

Jesse glanced at Cassie, who hunkered on her haunches building a little hill out of rocks. "What about Adeline?"

Charley cringed. "She would've cried if I made her leave Belle. I'm gonna wait for a while, let her grow a little bigger, then I'll go back and get her."

Jesse hated to topple the boy's plans, but somebody had to. And he was the only one there. He sighed and laid his hand on

300

Charley's shoulder. "Listen, Charley, I'm sorry you aren't happy with Aunt Neva. But you can't stay in Beloit."

"Why not?" He sounded more inquisitive than insolent.

"Because you don't have a house here anymore. Or a store. Those things were sold after your daddy and momma died."

"Why?"

How did one explain debt to an eight-year-old? Jesse scratched his cheek. "Well, because those things didn't really belong to your daddy. They belonged to the banker."

Charley screwed up his face in confusion.

"Your daddy took out loans from the bank to buy the house and the store. He hadn't paid back the loans yet, so when he died, the banker had to sell the buildings to get his money back."

"So somebody else is living in our house?"

Jesse nodded.

Charley stared at Jesse for several seconds, unblinking. He shrugged. "Well, then, I'll go to the banker and ask for money to buy a new house for Cassie and Adeline and me."

Jesse's patience wore out. He gripped Charley's jacket and turned him toward the truck. "A banker won't lend a boy your age enough money to buy a house. You'll have to wait until you're grown up, out of school, and have a good-paying job. Until then, you're going back to Buffalo Creek and your aunt Neva. Cassie, let's go."

The little girl abandoned her rock pile and trotted over. Jesse caught her hand, and he marched the kids to his truck. The bed was already loaded, and the worker was nowhere in sight, so Jesse lifted the kids into the cab and climbed in behind them.

All the way back Charley sat so stiff and quiet, Jesse wondered if he even breathed. Cassie wriggled some but she didn't talk either. That suited Jesse fine. Dealing with the pair of stowaways stole his chance to talk to Sheriff Abling. Now he'd have to make an expensive telephone call to get his former boss's advice. He gripped the steering wheel and counted the miles until he could leave the runaways in their classroom.

He pulled up to the school. Kids swarmed the playgrounds. "Looks like we got here in time for noon recess." Neither Charley nor Cassie had eaten lunch, but Jesse decided that wasn't a cruel consequence for their morning's misbehavior. "Hop out, and go tell your teacher you're back. I'll let your aunt Neva know you're both safe and at school. She oughta be happy to hear it."

Charley reached past Cassie for the door

handle. He muttered, "She won't care."

Jesse grabbed Charley's sleeve. "Are you sure about that?" The boy turned a look of such misery on Jesse, his heart rolled over in his chest. True or not, Charley believed Neva Shilling didn't want him around. He held tight to Charley's sleeve, thinking. "Are you sure you don't want to stay with her?"

The boy nodded so fast his hair bounced.

"Well, there is one other place I could take you."

"Where?"

Was he doing the right thing? Either he'd set Charley up for another disappointment — because Mrs. Shilling had made it clear she wouldn't let the children go to an orphanage — or he'd convince Charley he was better off staying in Buffalo Creek. He drawled in a near whisper, "An orphans' asylum."

Both children gazed up at him with wide eyes.

"It's not what your daddy wanted. And you wouldn't all be together the way you are at the mercantile. Charley, you'd have to stay with the boys, and Cassie and Adeline would stay with the girls. But you wouldn't be here anymore. Is that what you want?"

Charley gnawed his lower lip. "I . . .

dunno."

At least he hadn't jumped at the chance. Jesse patted his arm. "Tell you what. You've only been here a month. That's not much time to settle into a new place. Let's give it . . . three months altogether. Until Christmas. You promise not to run off again, and I promise I'll take you to an orphanage after Christmas if you still aren't happy here." He stuck out his hand. "Deal?"

Charley sucked in a big breath, staring at Jesse's hand. Then his breath whooshed out, and he grabbed hold with a strength greater than Jesse would have expected from such a young boy. "Deal."

Relief nearly collapsed Jesse. "Good." The bell rang, beckoning the school kids to return to their classrooms. "Pop that door open and get going. Behave yourselves." He watched the pair run toward the schoolhouse, hand in hand. When the door closed behind them, he put his truck in gear and pulled away. He'd unload these goods for Mrs. Shilling, and then the two of them would have a serious chat.

Neva

The rumble of a truck's engine alerted Neva to Mr. Caudel's return. She darted to the front door and propped it open with a painted brick, then stepped onto the sidewalk. Over the morning the temperature had cooled, and she crisscrossed her arms to block the breeze.

The truck rattled into silence, and Mr. Caudel slid out of the cab. He rounded the bed and reached for the closest crate. "Run next door and see if Randall will lend a hand."

An odd greeting, different from his customary genial smile. But perhaps he'd encountered some difficulty on the road that had resulted in a sour mood. If he was anything like Warren, it would wear off in time.

She scurried up the sidewalk toward the emporium. Although she preferred not to ask favors of Mr. Randall, his nearness made him a likely choice. And he'd be willing. He'd been more than ingratiating over the past month, despite her attempts to keep him at a distance.

The man's face lit brighter than a full moon on a black night when she stepped through the emporium doors. He came at her, hands extended. "Mrs. Shilling! How good to see you. What can I do for you today?"

She slipped her hands into her apron

pockets. "Would you assist Mr. Caudel in carrying my orders into the mercantile?"

His smile didn't dim. "Well, of course I will. Of course." He gripped her elbow and guided her out the door and along the sidewalk. "I'm more than pleased to assist you." He stepped to the end of the bed, rolled up his sleeves, and snatched up a large crate.

Neva stood out of the way and watched the men cart everything into the store. Such an incongruous combination they were — Mr. Randall in his crisp white shirt, wool trousers, and matching vest, and Mr. Caudel in tan dungarees and his customary chambray shirt with a tin star pinned over his left breast pocket. But they coordinated their movements as well as if they'd worked together a dozen times before, never blocking the other's passage. Within fifteen minutes the bed was empty, and a stack of crates and boxes climbed one side of the back hallway.

When they finished, Mr. Randall pushed his sleeves into place and aimed a cheerful smile in her direction. "There you are, Mrs. Shilling. Another month's goods ready to disperse to eager customers. If you need anything else, remember I am ever at your disposal." He strode out the door.

Neva turned to Mr. Caudel, who remained next to the stack of boxes, fanning himself with his hat. He seemed even more stern when juxtaposed against Mr. Randall's zealous jollity. She stayed beside the counter and offered him a smile she hoped might take the edge off his bad humor. "Thank you for bringing my orders from the train station. Did you already retrieve your jar of licorice whips? If not, I'll begin opening crates and find it for you."

He assumed a negligent pose — elbow on a crate, leg bent, and toe planted on the floor, hat held against his thigh. "Don't worry about the licorice just yet. Let me tell you what I retrieved for you."

She didn't care for the bite in his tone. "What's that?"

"Charley and Cassie."

She pursed her lips. "That's old news."

"Not as old as you think." He stepped away from the crates and moved to the end of the counter. He plopped his hat on top of the cast-iron cash register and stacked his arms on the counter's edge. "I retrieved them this morning. From the train yard in Beloit."

"What?" Neva shook her head. "That's ridiculous. I sent them out the back door with Bud, Belle, and Adeline at eight o'clock

307

just as I always do. How could they be in Beloit?"

"They sneaked into my truck and rode there with me."

If it wasn't for his serious expression, she'd think he was playing a prank in honor of Halloween. "You mean they —"

"Yep. Hid behind my seat. Then when I stopped, they got out and hightailed it for town." He tipped his head at a cocky angle, peering at her through narrowed eyes. "You know why?"

"N-no."

"They wanted to go back to their old house. Because Charley says you don't like him."

"Nonsense." She tried to blast the word, but it came out on a quavering note instead.

"Is it?" He eased closer, his squint-eyed gaze holding her captive. "I've watched Bud torment that boy on the playground, and I've told Charley to tell you how he's being treated. He said he's told you, and you promise to take care of it, but it never changes. That little boy is as unhappy as any kid I've ever seen. The only time he smiles is when he's delivering fliers for Mr. Randall. Probably because he's away from the mercantile and Bud."

Defensiveness rose from Neva's chest and

spilled out her mouth. "Bud has reason to resent Charley. He doesn't understand why his father needed another boy. Now, with his father gone, he feels accountable for taking care of his sister and me. He sees Charley, Cassie, and Adeline as unnecessary intrusions."

"Is that how you see them?"

"No!" Her voice was so shrill it pierced her ears. She winced.

"Are you sure?"

No, she wasn't sure. But she wouldn't confess it to Jesse Caudel. She sighed. "I'll have another talk with Bud about the way he treats Charley."

"And you'll talk to Charley? You'll tell him you don't want him to leave?"

She focused on a bag of rice sitting off-kilter on the shelf. "Yes."

"Mrs. Shilling?"

She glanced at him.

His lips formed a grim line, and a warning glimmered in his eyes. "When you talk to him, look him in the face so he'll believe you. Because I made a deal with the boy. If he's still this unhappy at Christmastime, I promised to take him and his sisters to an orphanage. If you're serious about keeping them, you need to make some changes. Because I'll keep my promise. I guess we could say you're pretty much on borrowed time with those kids."

She clamped her mouth tight and held back the protest rising in her throat.

"And something else . . ."

She whirled to face him and snapped, "What?"

His forehead pinched into a sharp V. "You have some really nice furniture in your apartment. Is any of it made by Rich & Baker?"

Chapter 22

Neva

When the children returned from school, Neva quickly put a handwritten sign, Be Back Soon, in the window and sent the three youngest ones upstairs for a snack. Then she took Bud and Belle into the storage area under the stairs, where they would have privacy. With Mr. Caudel's warning about taking Charley and the girls to an orphanage still ringing in her ears, she went directly to the point.

"Bud, you're to start treating Charley with kindness and respect. No more tormenting him at school or in your room when the two of you are alone."

Bud jerked a scowl at Belle. "Tattletale."

Belle's eyes flew wide. "I'm not a tattletale."

Neva grabbed Bud's arm. "Your sister hasn't said a word. I hear the things you say to him when you think I'm not listening.

311

And Sheriff Caudel told me he's seen you mistreating Charley on the playground."

Bud gawked at her. "Sheriff Caudel tattled on me?"

"That's right. He also told me Charley and Cassie hid away in his truck, intending to sneak out when he reached Beloit so they wouldn't have to live with us anymore."

"Oh, Momma . . ." Belle covered her mouth with her hand. Tears pooled in her eyes. "Charley told me he wanted to walk Cassie to school by himself to prove he could do it. I didn't know they were gonna run off."

"It isn't your fault, Belle. You've been nothing but kind to all three children." Neva turned her stern frown on her son. "But if Bud doesn't change his ways, Sheriff Caudel intends to take Charley, Cassie, and Adeline to an orphans' home."

"So let him take them. We can't afford to keep them here." Bud yanked free and waved his arm toward the closed door behind him. "I saw the crates in the hallway. There's not enough to last a whole month. And you know November's a busier month because of Thanksgiving. We need more stock, not less."

Neva stood speechless. Bud had paid more attention to storekeeping than she'd realized.

Her son shoved Warren's hat brim upward and glared at her as he continued, his voice changing from harsh to pleading. "Folks are gonna start going across town to the big grocer instead of coming to us if we don't keep our shelves stocked. We can't keep our shelves stocked unless we have money to buy goods. And the more children you have to feed and clothe, the less money you'll have." He swallowed, his Adam's apple bobbing in his lanky neck. "Let 'em go, Ma."

"I can't."

"Why not?"

"B-because they —" A hand seemed to close around Neva's throat, stealing her ability to breathe. If she told the twins the truth about the children, would Bud finally come to accept their presence? "Because they're your . . . your brother and sisters."

Both Bud and Belle stared at Neva in confusion. Belle asked, "How can that be?"

Neva's dry throat resisted speech, but she forced the words out. "They were born to your father and a woman named Violet. When your father left in his wagon, he wasn't selling goods to people in the county. He was driving to Beloit to spend a month with his other family. Charley, Cassie, and Adeline are your half brother and sisters."

Belle stared in mute horror, her face white.

Bold red crept from Bud's neck and filled his cheeks. "That's not true. Pop didn't — He wouldn't —" He gritted his teeth and growled.

Would Neva's heart survive witnessing her children's distress? She wished she could have one hour with Warren to tell him how much harm he had brought to her. Her thoughts carried her backward in time. Every night of his months in Buffalo Creek as they slipped into bed, he'd kissed her and whispered how much he loved her. How could he have deceived her so callously? Warren's idea of loving was certainly different than hers.

She reached for the twins, but both shied away. She blinked back tears. "I know it hurts to hear such a thing about your father. But please know it had nothing to do with the two of you. He loved you. He was proud of you. He just wanted . . . more." More than she could give.

Her chest ached with a ferocity that defied description. She stretched out her arms, and this time they allowed her to cup their cheeks with her trembling hands. "We both wanted more children. I couldn't give them to him, but Violet could. And did. In giving your father children, she gave you a brother and two sisters. She gave you a . . . a gift. Don't you see?"

Bud slapped Neva's hand away. "This is all a dirty lie. You're the one who wanted more kids, not Pop. You're making this up so you can keep those blasted kids. Well, fine." He threw the hat onto the floor, then wrenched the door open and stumbled out of the storeroom, yanking the cobbler apron over his head as he went. "You want them? Keep them. But I'm not sticking around and listening to you tell lies about my father." He wheeled around the counter and stumbled for the door.

"Bud!"

Belle's frantic cry shattered Neva's heart. She pulled her daughter into her arms and rocked her as she sobbed. "Shh, darlin'. Hush now. Remember what you told me the day of your father's memorial?" She kissed Belle's moist temple once and then again. "You said we'd be all right."

Belle's slender frame shuddered within Neva's embrace. She rasped, "Pray, Momma. Please, pray."

Neva automatically closed her eyes. "Dear Lord . . ." But no other words came. She didn't know what to pray. She clutched Belle close and hoped God would understand the wordless groaning of her heart.

She was empty.

Arthur

Arthur, throw rug in hand, opened the door and stepped onto the sidewalk. He raised the rug to give it a good shake, and Bud Shilling careened directly into the rectangle of woven wool. The rug flew one way, and Bud bounced the opposite direction, his arms flailing.

"Here now." Arthur grabbed Bud's elbow and helped him catch his balance. When the boy stood on two feet without wobbling, Arthur chuckled. "What's your hurry? Is the mercantile on fire?" He started to retrieve the rug, but something in the boy's face made him pause mid-motion. "What's wrong?"

Bud's chin quivered. Tears winked in his eyes. His entire body trembled.

Arthur took hold of Bud's arm again and, leaving the rug on the sidewalk, pulled the boy into the emporium. He guided him between displays of furniture, well away from the big plate-glass windows. Then he removed his handkerchief from his breast pocket and pushed it into Bud's hand. "Blow."

Bud stood there letting the white square

of cloth dangle like a surrender flag.

Arthur nudged his hand, urging it upward. "Go ahead. Blow."

Bud blew, then swiped his eyes. He wadded the handkerchief in his fist and stared outward, his mouth set in a scowling line.

"Feel better now?" Arthur already knew the answer — despondency was written all over the boy's face — but he had to say something. They couldn't stand there like a pair of statues.

Bud shook his head.

Arthur smoothed his mustache, examining Bud's stiff posture. "If blowing your nose doesn't help, maybe blowing your top will."

Bud shot a startled look at Arthur.

He feigned surprise. "What's the matter? Hasn't anyone ever told you to go ahead and lose your temper?"

"No, sir. Ma's always telling me not to lose it. Pop said the same thing." Bud hung his head. His fingers convulsed on the rumpled handkerchief.

"Telling youngsters not to lose their tempers is something parents like to do. I tell my boys to keep a grip on their tempers, too. But can I be perfectly honest with you?" Arthur took hold of Bud's shoulders and eased him onto the foam cushion of the floral Duncan Phyfe sofa. He hitched his pant legs, settled himself on the matching chair, so he was close but not too close, and went on as if Bud had answered in the affirmative. "I've discovered holding all that anger inside isn't always the best idea. Gives me terrible indigestion. So sometimes I have to let it out. Especially when it's been bubbling for a while."

Something was bubbling in this boy. He kept a tight enough grip on the handkerchief to pop its seams. His jaw muscles bulged as if he were biting down on a strip of boot leather, and his cheeks were mottled with red. When he blew, it wouldn't be pretty. Arthur would keep him here until he'd let it out so Mrs. Shilling wouldn't have to witness it. Women never handled men's outbursts very well.

Arthur bumped Bud's knee with his fist. "Blow."

Bud angled his head and peered at Arthur through his heavy bangs. "If I do, you gonna do like the sheriff and go snitch to my ma?"

"Nope." Arthur held up his palm. "Scout's honor."

"You were a scout?"

He laughed. "No. I'm afraid I was already close to your age now when the Boy Scouts got started back in 1910. I thought it was

318

for little kids." And there were uniforms and dues, things that cost money his family didn't have.

"You're pretty old, then."

Arthur swallowed a chortle. "I suppose so. But old or not, I've always admired the organization. Admired their oath, too, especially the part about helping other people. That's why I started this business — to help people make their homes inviting, comfortable places to live."

Bud squinted slightly. "I thought it was because you could make lots of money."

The boy was certainly candid. Arthur smiled. "That's a happy result, too."

"My pop said you were after our mercantile because you're a moneygrubber."

Maybe too candid. Arthur's smile faltered. "Is there something wrong with wanting to make a decent living?"

The flame of fury that had started to flicker during their conversation flared again. "No. A man takes care of his own — that's what Pop always said. But try telling that to my ma. She won't listen to me. She's gonna keep those kids even if it means we all end up in shantytown. And I don't believe that they're my brother and sisters. Pop wouldn't —" He jerked to his feet and shoved the handkerchief at Arthur. "Here. I gotta go." He started for the door.

Arthur followed. "Bud, I meant it when I said I admire the Boy Scout oath about helping people. If you ever need anything, you can —"

Bud stopped but he didn't turn around. "Mr. Randall, just remember you said you wouldn't snitch to my ma. Pretend like I was never here." He whacked the door open and stormed out.

Arthur moved to the window. Bud paused at the edge of the sidewalk long enough to glance left and right and then took off across the street at a dead run. He kept going until Arthur lost sight of him. But Arthur remained there, staring blindly after the boy, with the sentence Bud hadn't finished, *"Pop wouldn't —,"* playing through his memory. Pop wouldn't . . . what?

He finger combed his mustache, trying to make sense of the boy's prattle. Just prior to the comment, he'd said his mother called the three children living at the mercantile his brother and sisters. Awareness descended. Surely Warren Shilling hadn't —

His knees gave way, and Arthur dropped into the closest chair. Of course! That explained why he'd thought young Charley looked vaguely familiar. The boy had Warren's hair, eyes, and solid build. Over the years he'd heard tell of men, mostly railroad men, who had families all up and down the line. But he never would have suspected it of his very own neighbor. Poor Mrs. Shilling. How could she even hold up her head, knowing her husband was a philanderer?

An unexpected coil of protectiveness wound itself through him. Over the past weeks even though she resisted his gestures of friendship, he'd begun to admire her. He didn't understand why she held with such tenacity to that mercantile, but he respected her for working so hard. She'd even won his regard by giving food to those two ragtag men the sheriff feared might have come back and stolen her money.

Even if she'd known they would rob her blind, he suspected she still would have handed the food over. That's the kind of woman she was — kind and giving and unselfish. Kind enough even to open her home to her husband's children by another woman. Why, Mrs. Shilling was exactly the kind of woman he would seek if —

Arthur stood so abruptly his back popped. What was he doing now, mooning over her? He straightened his tie beneath his chin, smoothed down his vest, and cleared his throat. He'd set out to win the mercantile from her, not be won by her. He needed to reevaluate his motives and his method.

The clock mounted on the bank tower across the street showed two minutes until five. Close enough to lock up for the evening. He pulled the shades, locked the door, and turned out the lights. Instead of going home, he entered his little office and opened his books for an end-of-the-month evaluation.

October sales had been slow, but by unloading a few of his older pieces to a warehouse in Topeka, he'd still squeaked out a profit. He stared at the number, dollar signs flashing in the back of his brain. Once again Bud Shilling's voice swooped in — *"you're a moneygrubber."*

Arthur smacked the book closed and announced to the empty room, "Better a moneygrubber than a philandering scoundrel." But somehow the statement didn't make him feel better. A philanderer was motivated by lust. And a moneygrubber was, too.

CHAPTER 23

Neva

Bud's empty chair taunted Neva during supper. Where was he? The entire month of October had been mild, but over the day an increasingly colder and stronger wind had stirred, promising a chilly night. He had run out the door with his jacket but no hat, no gloves, no scarf. She fully expected him to skulk through the door when the supper hour arrived, but they'd been at the table for thirty minutes already, and still no Bud.

Dear Lord, don't let him have hopped a train . . .

The prayer formed in her head without conscious thought, and she released a gasp as it took shape. Surely Bud wouldn't —

"Momma, what's wrong?" Worry pinching her brow, Belle gazed at Neva.

Charley and Cassie paused in pushing their stewed tomatoes around on their plates and sent furtive glances from Belle to Neva.

Only Adeline continued happily eating. Or, rather, smashing her tomatoes into a lumpy paste with the back of her fork.

Neva had never allowed her children to play with food, but she didn't scold the child. Belle's question still hung in the room, unanswered, and Neva decided to give an honest response in the hope it might communicate the seriousness of running away to Charley. "I'm very worried about your brother. I don't know where he is, and I don't know if he's coming back."

Belle reached out and covered Neva's wrist with her warm fingers. "Of course he'll come back. He's just" — she flicked a look across the table at Charley and Cassie — "upset. When he calms down, he'll come home."

"Wh-why's he upset?"

Neva couldn't bring herself to answer Charley's question. She rose. "It looks as though everyone is finished eating. I'll clear the table. Belle, would you help the children prepare for bed?"

Charley's lower lip poked out, but he slid out of his chair and headed for the hallway without a word of argument. Belle lifted Adeline from her chair, and Cassie followed Belle from the dining room, leaving Neva alone. She gathered the dishes, battling the desire to cry loud and long until every bit of suppressed emotion found release.

She hadn't allowed herself to cry when she received the news of Warren's death. Nor had she cried at his memorial service. She wanted to be strong for her children. But now Bud was missing. Mr. Caudel had threatened her, then asked questions about her belongings that left her confused and concerned. Her strength was waning, and if she knew no one would overhear, she would wail at the top of her lungs.

She slapped the plates onto the washstand and pounded to the head of the bedroom hallway. "Belle?"

Her daughter poked her head from the girls' room.

"Leave the dishes. I'll wash them when I return."

"Where are you going?"

"Out." She turned and headed for the staircase. Belle would assume her mother was hunting for Bud, and for the moment Neva would allow the misconception. She would explode if she didn't give vent to the storm raging within her.

She snatched her shawl from a hook near the back door and stepped into the yard. The wind tugged at the woven fabric, nearly ripping it from her hands, but she held tight and managed to unlock the cellar door with one hand. Opening it proved tricky given the strength of the cold breeze pushing against it, and she grunted with exertion. She created an opening large enough to step through and hurried down the steps, allowing the heavy door to slam into the frame above her.

Immediately she was plunged into darkness, but she didn't care. She felt her way along the cool dirt wall past the storage shelves to the small table and bench tucked in the far corner. By the time she sank onto the bench, her eyes had adjusted enough to make out murky shadows. She set her gaze on the sturdy overhead beams keeping the earth from collapsing into the cellar and pulled in a shuddering breath. As her air released, a racking sob came with it. Then another, and another, her body jerking with each mighty heave.

She wailed, and she socked the air with her fists, and she screeched out her hurt and fears and frustrations to the sturdy walls, which swallowed the sounds and kept them secret. She cried until her voice was hoarse and her chest ached, and then she sagged over her lap and buried her face in her apron skirt.

The wind's whistle crept through the

cracks around the cellar door, but otherwise the space was silent. Almost ethereal in its quiet. For a moment Neva considered staying down here all night, away from the mercantile and its responsibilities, away from her children, who depended on her, away from Warren's children, who were not a gift no matter what she'd tried to tell Bud and Belle, away from the uneasy feelings the sheriff's questions had raised. But, in time, reality descended. She couldn't stay hidden away. Her business and the children needed her.

She sat upright, wiped her face clean with the apron, and forced her weak legs to straighten. She inched her way to the stairs, praying as she went that she'd find Bud in the house, dipping into the pork roast and potatoes. After securing the cellar door with its padlock, Neva hurried into the house and up the stairs. Approaching footfalls from the upstairs hall gave her heart a hopeful lift. She burst around the corner, her son's name hovering on her lips.

Belle met her instead. "You're back. Did you find Bud?"

The hope departed in a swoosh that left Neva's heart bruised. "No. He hasn't returned?"

Belle shook her head. "But the children

are in bed. Charley's reading one of Bud's dime novels — he said he wasn't sleepy. But Cassie and Adeline are already asleep. I read them a story and sang a song. Then I gave them each a good-night kiss, and they drifted right off."

Neva pulled Belle into her embrace. "You're going to make a wonderful mother someday, sweetheart. Thank you for taking such good care of the little girls."

Belle rested her head on Neva's shoulder. "It's not so hard." She pulled loose and smiled sweetly at Neva. "Somehow your good-night kiss at the end of the day always made it easy for me to drift off to sleep. So I just do for them what you used to do for me."

Neva gave a start. Belle's innocent comment — "used to do" — stabbed like a knife. She knew exactly when she'd given up the practice of entering the children's room at bedtime and giving them a kiss, praying with them, and whispering wishes for pleasant dreams. The same day Jesse Caudel delivered Charley, Cassie, and Adeline to her back doorstep. She'd gone an entire month without kissing her children good night so she wouldn't feel obligated to bestow the same treatment on Warren's offspring. But she'd stolen something precious from Bud and Belle.

A second bout of tears threatened.

"Momma, I know you're worried about Bud." Belle slipped her arms around Neva's waist and hugged her tight. "Why don't you ask Sheriff Caudel to look for him? He has a truck, so he can cover more area than you could walking."

It would be humiliating to confess that another child had run away from her today, but Belle's idea was sound. She needed help, and the sheriff was the most sensible choice.

"I'll do the dishes for you, and while I wash, I'll pray for Bud to come home."

Neva kissed Belle's temple, pressing her lips to her daughter's sweet-smelling hair for several seconds before letting go. "Thank you. I'll lock the door behind me." She pointed at Belle, frowning. "You stay inside until I return."

"Of course, Momma." Belle hurried around the corner.

Neva stood in the empty hallway, staring at the doorway where Belle had disappeared. She should apologize. She'd spoken more harshly than she intended. Did she really expect Belle to behave with such disregard for her feelings? Certainly not. She shouldn't allow her frustration with Bud to trickle over on Belle.

Nor should she allow her frustration with Warren to trickle over on Charley.

The realization hit like a bucket of ice water dumped over her head. Chills traveled from her scalp down her body to the backs of her calves, and then she went warm all over, awareness bringing a rush of shame. Mr. Caudel's demand that she look at the boy when she talked to him swept through her mind, and she bowed her head. She never looked Charley full in the face. Because every time she did, she saw Warren. Gazing at Charley made her relive her husband's betrayal. Charley wasn't responsible for his father's choices, yet she'd used the little boy as a target for her anger.

Oh, she hadn't been cruel to him. Not like Bud. But she'd talked around him and over him. She'd pretended he wasn't there so she could pretend Warren hadn't lain with another woman. She'd been wrong. Hurtful. Insensitive. She owed Belle an apology, but she also owed one to Charley. And she'd give it to him, just as soon as she found Bud. Her son needed to witness his mother humbling herself to his half brother. Bud needed to see how to release a grudge.

She clattered down the stairs for the second time that evening. But when she

330

stepped out the back door, she didn't aim her steps for the sheriff's office.

Arthur

Arthur and his sons spent the blustery evening in the parlor, reading. The boys sprawled on their bellies on the carpet, Leon absorbed in an article in *Practical Mechanics* about building a battery and Leroy scowling his way through Tolstoy's *War and Peace,* his latest assignment from Mr. Pearson.

Arthur sat in front of the fireplace in his favorite chair with his ankle propped on his knee, the most recent copy of *Fortune* open across his thigh. The cover feature about photography hadn't captured his attention, but he carefully studied every word of the article about economic royalism.

Times had changed since Hoover's campaign theme of a chicken in every pot and a car in every garage. Nowadays folks were lucky to have a pot, let alone a chicken to put in it. And cars? He snorted. Around Buffalo Creek there were more cars sitting idle in fields with empty gas tanks than being driven up and down Main Street. Whoever won the '36 election would have his hands full putting the nation back on its

331

financial footing.

The knock on the front door brought all three of their heads up. Arthur glanced at the grandfather clock standing sentry in the corner and frowned. Who would call at this hour?

Leroy bounced up. "I'll get it, Dad."

Arthur set the magazine aside and waylaid his son. "Finish your chapter. I'll see who's at the door." He was glad he'd chosen to go himself when he found Neva Shilling on his doorstep. "Mrs. Shilling, come in."

Cold wind propelled her over the threshold, and she shivered as he closed the door behind her. "I'm sorry to bother you."

Arthur touched her back with his fingers, urging her into the parlor where the fireplace warmed the room. "Mrs. Shilling, as I've tried to tell you, you are never a bother." He scowled at his sons. "Boys, get off the floor so we have room to walk in here. Take your books to your rooms and —"

"No, please stay." Mrs. Shilling held out one hand in a silent entreaty to Leon and Leroy. "You might be able to help."

The boys plopped onto the sofa, and Arthur guided Mrs. Shilling to the chair Mabel had claimed as hers. No one ever sat in it, but it seemed to fit Mrs. Shilling nicely. Arthur returned to his chair and gave his neighbor his full attention. It wasn't difficult. Even with wind-tossed hair, red-rimmed eyes, and worry lines furrowing her brow, she was a fine-looking woman.

"With what do you need help, Mrs. Shilling? Some furniture moved or some crates unloaded?"

She clutched her shawl closed over her bodice with shaking hands. "Bud left several hours ago and hasn't returned. I'm at a loss as to where to search. I thought since Leon is in Bud's class, he might have some suggestions."

Arthur stood. "Leon, Leroy, put on your coats and take the flashlights from the closet. Go to the sheriff's place first, tell him Bud is missing, and ask for his help."

The boys scrambled for the hall tree.

"And, boys?"

They paused but quivered like a pair of eager puppies.

"Take my firing pistol with you. Make sure it's got a blank in it. When you find Bud, point it in the air and shoot it off." He turned a warm look on the woman seated in Mabel's chair. "The sound will bring comfort to his mother."

"Sure, Dad." Leroy grabbed Leon's arm and pulled him out of the room.

Arthur crossed to Mrs. Shilling and

perched on the corner of the coffee table. Her worried frown and the tears brightening her eyes stirred him to compassion. "Mrs. Shilling, try not to fret. I'm sure my boys will know where to search. They'll find him."

"I appreciate you sending them out. It should be my responsibility, but —"

He tsk-tsked, shaking his head. "I take responsibility, too. Bud and I had a little chat earlier today. Afterward I watched him run up the street. Maybe if I'd gone to get you right then, you could have caught him and brought him home instead of suffering this worry."

"Bud . . . came to you . . . to talk?"

In less serious circumstances he would laugh at her genuine befuddlement. But she needed his assurance, not his amusement. He briefly explained Bud's run-in with the rug, which was probably in Nebraska by now, thanks to the wind. "He seemed to need a friend, someone to simply listen." He shrugged. "I tried to meet the need."

She gazed at him with her mouth slightly open, her eyes wide. He couldn't decide if appreciation or mere shock motivated the reaction. He decided to respond as if she was appreciative.

"I was happy to give him a place to release

some pressure, so to speak. Sometimes a boy just needs to talk to a man. Bud is welcome to come to me anytime." A surprising warmth filled him as he spoke. He truly meant what he said.

Her mouth closed, but her eyes stayed fixed on him. The log in the fireplace rolled, sending up a shower of sparks and releasing a snap. The coziness of the room, their close proximity, her hazel eyes gazing intently into his face wove a web of intimacy around Arthur unlike anything he'd experienced since Mabel's death.

He braced his palms on his knees and leaned forward slightly, watching her for signs of withdrawal. She blinked, but she didn't shrink away. A slow smile pulled on his mouth. "Mrs. Shilling?"

"Yes?" Her simple reply wheezed out, as if she'd just finished running a footrace.

His smile tugged a little higher. "Would it be all right if I called you Neva?"

CHAPTER 24

Bud

Bud huddled under the big oak tree south of town with his arms folded across his middle, his teeth chattering so hard his jaw hurt. He was cold. And hungry. And tired. And even a little scared. But he wouldn't go home.

Why'd it have to go and get so cold so fast? Stupid wind, pushing at him.

Stupid kids, pushing into his life.

Stupid Ma, calling those kids his brother and sisters.

Stupid Pop, spawning those kids and then up and dying on them.

Bud pulled up his knees and pressed his back more firmly against the tree. The bark bit through his jacket, and a lumpy root poked him hard on his rump. He hadn't chosen the best spot to spend the night, but the full moon had ducked behind a cloud of dust about an hour ago. Now he couldn't see well enough to continue on safely. The old tree, with a trunk so big he and Belle couldn't reach around it and hold hands, would have to do.

While the tree limbs clacked together and the wind howled, Bud closed his eyes and tried to sleep. Somewhere nearby a night bird began to call. Its repetitive song became words in Bud's mind. Two words, over and over. *Stupid Pop. Stupid Pop.* His nose started burning, a sure sign he was going to cry. He sniffed hard, rubbed his nose with his fist, and then put his hands over his ears to block the bird's cry.

Bud didn't want to think of his pop as stupid. He loved Pop. The days Pop drove away were awful and the days he came back like a birthday, Christmas, and a trip to the circus all at once. He loved watching Pop with customers in the store — always smiling, joshing with the men and making the women blush with his compliments. He loved following Pop around in the barn, loved how Pop would say, *"Come here, buddy o' mine. Let me show you how to grease wheels so they don't squeak when you roll up the road."* He loved how Pop would show him and then let him try for himself. He loved hearing Pop say, *"Good job!"* with a booming, proud voice.

Had Pop done those same things with customers at the Beloit store? Had he called Charley "buddy o' mine" and taught him how to do things, too? Had he told Charley, "Good job!" with the same pride as he showed for Bud?

Bud's nose started burning again. He loved Pop, and he hated him. Hated him even more than he hated being picked on by Leon or Leroy, more than he hated lima beans, more than he hated Charley. How could he love Pop and hate him so much at the same time? It didn't make sense.

Stupid feelings . . .

His backside started to throb where the root dug in. He lay on his side and curled up like a roly-poly bug. Tucking his hands into his armpits, he willed sleep to take him someplace far, far away.

Neva

Sleep was impossible. Neva alternately paced the floor of the mercantile, prayed, and emptied crates to keep herself occupied. With each pass near the windows, she paused to peer up the street, hoping to see one of the Randall boys guiding Bud home with a flashlight or Sheriff Caudel's pickup with Bud riding in the cab.

At midnight Arthur — not Mr. Randall, because in a moment of weakness she'd agreed they should call each other Arthur and Neva — came by to tell her he was making his boys turn in. He'd promised to keep driving the streets in his Packard, however, and for the first time since he started his daily visits and kind deeds, she gave him a truly heartfelt thank-you.

By the time the bank clock rang out with two resounding bongs, she'd emptied every crate, her shelves were stocked, and exhaustion sagged her spine and her spirits. She dragged the cracker barrel close to the window and sat, then rested her forehead against the cool glass. Her eyes burned, and she rubbed them every few minutes, but she refused to close them. She might miss seeing either the sheriff or Arthur return with Bud.

When the clock bonged four in the morning, Neva forced her stiff body from the barrel and limped to the storage space under the stairs where she'd hung her wool coat, the one Warren had given her two Christmases ago, with the real fox fur collar. She gritted her teeth as she slipped her arms into the sleeves, recalling how she'd squealed with delight upon opening the box and discovering the lovely coat. Wearing it now nauseated her, but it would keep her warm even against the most vicious wind.

She fastened the carved ivory buttons all the way to her throat, pulled up the collar, and marched to the front door. As her fingers curled around the handle, her good sense returned. She couldn't leave. Not with Belle and the children asleep upstairs. Belle was capable of watching the others, but sometime during the past hours Neva had vowed to stop leaving the care of Charley, Cassie, and Adeline to Belle. The added responsibility wasn't fair to the girl, and Neva had to make amends. She'd do so by assuming the role of caregiver. Not aunt or mother but caregiver. It was the best she could do, but she intended to pray for God to open her heart to more. She could only trust He would do so in time.

Leaving her coat on, she returned to the cracker barrel, sat on its edge, and sighed. Her breath steamed the glass. She swiped it clean with her coat sleeve and then gazed out at the quiet scene. The street seemed so forlorn with its dim lamps forming fuzzy circles of light like dandelion puffs. The gusting wind turned dust into writhing snakes that slithered along the bricked street. The old building popped and moaned against the wind's force.

Neva shivered. She hugged herself, gently rocking on the barrel. Such a storm. And somewhere out there, all alone, Bud was in the midst of it.

Bud

The ground beneath him vibrated. Drowsy, Bud grimaced and burrowed his face into his elbow. A horn honked, and someone — Mr. Randall? — hollered his name. Bud scrambled to his feet and plastered himself against the tree. His heart pounding, he blinked against the night and watched from the corner of his eye as the Randalls' Packard slowly rumbled near, the headlights skimming the dry grass along the road.

"Bud? Bud? You out there, Bud?"

Light crept up on Bud's right, and he held his breath until it transferred to the other side of the tree and appeared to float away. Mr. Randall kept calling, but his voice got fainter and fainter until it faded clear away.

With a sigh Bud slid down the trunk and sat for a moment, letting his galloping pulse return to normal. The wind was still blowing, but while he slept, the moon had sneaked above the dust. He could make out his surroundings well enough to walk without smacking into a tree or a building. If

Mr. Randall was driving up and down the roads, chances were Ma had sent others out, too. He needed to get away from the places cars could go.

He gripped the tree and leaned out on one side and then the other, looking, listening. No headlights, no car engines. It was safe to move on. But to where? If he remembered right, the road ran north and south. He didn't want to follow the road, so he needed to go either east or west. He scanned the two possibilities.

To the east was cleared farmland. Easy for walking even in the dark, but there was nothing to shield him from the moonlight, nothing to duck behind if a car happened along. To the west was a windbreak of trees. It'd be rougher traveling. Scrub bushes and low-hanging branches would probably try to catch him. But if he stayed in the windbreak, he'd just look like one more shadow to anyone who drove by.

The decision made, he took off at a lope for the thick, scraggly growth. He was right about the trees and such grabbing at him. Branches scratched his face and snagged his jacket. A branch like a skeleton's finger reached down and caught his hair, and it took him a good three minutes to work himself loose. Maybe he should've asked

Ma for a haircut before he set out.

Once free of the pesky branch, he slipped his jacket over his head the way a war chief huddled in a blanket. His hair didn't get hooked again, but his sheepskin collar did. He was probably leaving little tufts of wool behind, like Hansel and Gretel's breadcrumbs from the story Ma had read him and Belle when he was little. A grin of fond remembrance pulled at his cheek.

His steps slowed to a stop. He let his jacket slide back onto his shoulders. The wind tore at his hair and bounced little branches against him, but he stood there and let the leafless branches smack him. What was he doing taking off like this? Where did he think he'd go? Sure, he sometimes talked big about striking out, finding a job, carving a future the way Pop had when he was only fourteen. But deep down he didn't want to be alone. And Ma would be half-sick from worry by now.

He gritted his teeth and forced a growl. Let her worry. She shouldn't have taken in those kids. She shouldn't have let Pop go off every other month. She . . . She . . . He hung his head. The anger wouldn't rise. In its place was a heaviness he couldn't toss aside. He was lonely out here. He wanted his mother.

Off to the right in the distance, a flickering light caught Bud's attention. He squinted at it, his tired brain struggling to identify its source. Headlights? No. Then there'd be two lights. And this one wasn't the right shape, more square than round. Ah, a window — or a lamp behind a window. Which meant there was a farmhouse, and somebody was awake.

His heart gave a hopeful stutter. Maybe the farmer would have a telephone he could use to call the sheriff's office and ask Sheriff Caudel to come get him. Or maybe the farmer would be willing to take him into town. Most of the farmers had shopped at the mercantile a time or two, and he didn't know of anybody who didn't like Ma and Pop. Surely the farmer would do him a favor if he said he was Warren and Neva Shilling's son.

Bud worked his way out of the windbreak and broke into a trot over the uneven ground, moving directly toward the square of light. When he'd gone half the distance between the trees and the farmhouse, a bobbing circle of light emerged from the house's tall shadow and began floating toward the lurking gray shape Bud surmised was the barn. Apparently the farmer, with a lantern in hand, was heading out to do early chores

— probably to milk. Hunger pinched Bud's belly. Maybe he'd even get a little something to fill his stomach.

Bud forced his tired legs into a dead run and waved both hands over his head. "Hey! Hey, mister!"

The bobbing circle stopped. A harsh voice broke through the murky predawn. "Who's out there?"

Without slowing his pace, Bud choked out his name. "B-Bud — Bud Sh—"

"Whoever you are, you're trespassin'! This is private-owned land, and you got no right to be on it!"

Bud stumbled to a halt. His lungs were heaving so hard he couldn't catch his breath. He braced his hands on his knees and tried again to speak. "Mister, I'm —"

"You're a dirty trespasser, that's what you are!" The lantern's glow began bouncing toward the house, twice as fast as it'd gone before. "I'm fetchin' my shotgun. If you're still out here by the time I get it in hand, you can figure on receiving a backside full of buckshot!"

Bud gave up trying to explain himself. Fear sent him running again, away from the farm, back toward the windbreak, where he could hide among the brambles. He tripped and fell flat. Stiff blades of dried grass speared his palms. He hissed in pain and rolled to his side, cradling his stinging hands against his chest.

Kaboom!

The blast of a shotgun launched him to his feet, and he took off again, panting in fear, his palms burning like someone had lit a match to them. His feet pounded against the ground in rhythm with his thudding pulse. Another explosion shattered the night, its echo filling Bud's ears, and he screeched. He risked a glance over his shoulder, certain he'd see the farmer right on his tail, but there was no one behind him. And suddenly there was nothing under his feet.

Bud's arms flew over his head as he rapidly descended into blackness. He scrambled for a handhold but came away with nothing more than clumps of dirt and broken fingernails. For a fleeting moment he wondered if he'd found the Alice in Wonderland hole. He hadn't liked the book all that much when Miss Franklin read it to the class, and now that it had become his reality, he liked it even less. But instead of falling free into another world, his feet met a solid surface. The impact jarred him all the way up his spine, and pain exploded through his hips.

For several seconds he just stood, or lay — he couldn't be sure since his body was wedged so tightly and the fall had muddled his brain — with his arms above his head and tried to calm his ragged breathing. Dirt filtered into his nose, making him cough. His eyes burned. He wanted to rub them, but when he tried to bring his arms down, his elbows caught. The close walls around him prevented movement.

He blinked a dozen times to clear them of dirt. It helped some. He leaned his aching head back as far as he could and squinted. Mostly all he saw was black. But far above him, a dim circle of pinkish gray gave him a tiny glimpse of the morning sky coming awake. He hoped some of the light would find its way down to him and give him an idea of how to get out of . . . Out of what? Where was he anyway?

Through rapid blinks he examined his surroundings. Not much to it — just a circular space, narrow, with crumbling dirt walls. An old well, maybe? If so, lucky for him they'd been suffering a drought. It was dry as unbuttered toast down here. At least he didn't have to be afraid of drowning. Even so, he didn't want to stay.

He tried grabbing the walls and pulling himself up, but his fingers were bleeding. It hurt too much to dig them into the hard walls. So he tried pushing with his legs. Pain stabbed through his hips and lower spine. He sucked in a sharp breath and went limp. The shooting pain changed to a dull throb. Bearable. Maybe he should just stay put until night fell again. Give his legs a chance to recover.

That farmer would likely be watching all day, and he'd shoot as soon as he saw Bud's head pop up from the ground. Besides, he was tired. A good rest would give him the strength he'd need to pull himself out of here.

Yes, it was a good plan. He'd just rest up and wait until the dark came back. Bud tipped his head against his upraised arm, using it as a pillow, and closed his eyes.

CHAPTER 25

Jesse

Jesse thought he'd felt bad when he couldn't find the thief who took off with Mrs. Shilling's money, but it couldn't compare to the way he felt telling her he hadn't been able to find her son. Arthur Randall kept a grip on her elbow, which Jesse surmised was the only thing keeping her upright. Her red eyes and haggard face told him she hadn't slept a wink all night.

She gazed at him in complete helplessness, her hazel eyes swimming with tears. "Do you think he . . . he might have hitched a ride on one of the passing trains?"

Back home when his little sisters wailed over some calamity, he imitated them and called them crybabies. But he had no desire to treat Mrs. Shilling with such unkindness. She'd already been through enough. Funny how he could easily stir up sympathy for a woman he'd only known one month and had never manufactured it for the little girls who called him brother.

He grimaced. "I suppose anything's possible. There were at least two trains through town last night." One tear rolled down her cheek. Jesse, stung by the sad sight, hurried on. "But it'd be dangerous to try to hop one of those locomotives, and Bud's not a foolhardy boy. I think it's more likely he spent the night in a farmer's barn somewhere. He's probably tuckered out and sleeping in a pile of hay. When he wakes up and wants breakfast, he'll make his way home."

"Why, sure." Randall added his booming opinion. "That would explain why he didn't answer when we called his name — he was sound asleep. We'll watch for him this morning. And if he isn't here by noon, the sheriff and I will go out again, won't we, Sheriff?"

Jesse had used an entire tank of gas last night, but he'd spend another two if he had to. What kind of sheriff couldn't track down a fourteen-year-old runaway boy? "Absolutely. Now, ma'am, it's time to open your doors to business, so I —"

"I'm not opening today!"

Jesse started to tell her losing business wouldn't help her any, but Randall cut him off.

"Now, let's think this through, Neva."

Jesse jolted. Neva? Since when had the furniture seller and the mercantile owner become so familiar?

"Saturday is your busiest day. If you don't open your doors, customers will go to the big grocer instead. What would Bud tell you to do?"

Mrs. Shilling rubbed her lips together, blinking fast. The moisture in her eyes disappeared. She sighed. "Bud has learned the mercantile business well. He'd say let the customers come in."

"Then that's what we'll do." The man beamed at Mrs. Shilling.

She shook her head. "You have your own business to operate today. Saturdays are busy for you, too."

"Well, let's compromise, hmm? I'll have Leon help me, and I'll send Leroy over here to help you." Randall shook his finger at the woman, as playful as Jesse had ever seen him. "But only until Bud shows up. Then that boy needs to do his duty to make up for the worry he put you through."

A slight blush colored her cheeks. Jesse sent a puzzled glance across the two of them. A night of no sleep sure affected people in peculiar ways. He cleared his throat. "As I started to say, I'll get out of your way. Hold on to hope, Mrs. Shilling."

Her weak smile thanked him, and he strode onto the sidewalk. Last night's wind had finally died down, but the cold temperature it blew in remained. He pulled his twill jacket closed and buttoned it all the way up, then tugged his hat more firmly onto his head. The Stetson was getting a bit battered from everyday use, but he liked it and didn't want a sudden gust to steal it from him. He aimed himself for the little house where Pastor Savage lived. He needed help, and he suspected the young preacher would offer it.

The minister's wife answered his knock. Her face reflected surprise, but then she smiled and invited him in. "I'll fetch Ernie for you." Mrs. Savage headed for the doorway leading to the kitchen.

Jesse removed his hat and waited. The heat rising from the steam radiators felt good, and the smell of coffee warmed him even without taking a sip. The little house defined the word *home* and left Jesse feeling a bit melancholy. But it was probably only tiredness stirring the strange emotion.

The young minister rounded the corner from the kitchen, his hand extended and a big smile on his face. "Jesse! Or should I call you Sheriff Caudel? I hope you've come to talk to me about church membership." The man's eyes twinkled.

Jesse hated to put a damper on the preacher's good humor, but he didn't have time for idle chitchat. "No, I'm here about one of your members — Mrs. Shilling." He shared about Bud's disappearance, the long night of fruitless searching, and Mrs. Shilling now greeting customers without enjoying a bit of rest. "She's pretty worn out and I am, too. I'd like to try to grab a little sleep, so I wondered if some of your church members might lend a hand. Maybe the men could go out looking for the boy, and maybe a woman or two could offer to keep the mercantile open today so Mrs. Shilling can take a break, spend time with the other kids."

"I'll make some calls. I'm sure people will help." Ernie angled his gaze over his shoulder and called, "Lois? Would you come here, please?"

Lois hurried into the room, her face pursed with concern. "What's wrong?"

"We need to pray. Let's form a circle." He caught his wife's hand, then stretched the other one toward Jesse.

Without thinking, Jesse took hold, and Mrs. Savage moved close to grab his other hand. The reverend and his wife bowed their heads, and Jesse automatically followed suit.

"Our dear heavenly Father and eternal God." Ernie spoke in a strong, confident voice that raised a strange wave of longing in Jesse's chest. "I praise You for being all-knowing and all-caring. I praise You because right at this very moment You hold young Bud Shilling in Your sight. You are there with Bud, keeping him safe, and You are with Bud's mother, easing her worry and instilling a sense of calm. Your Spirit is here with us as well, almighty God."

Jesse drew in a slow breath, and a sweet essence filled his nostrils. Somehow he knew in the center of his soul the minister's words were true. God's Spirit was here, right in their midst. His stiff shoulders relaxed, and a flood of peace flowed through him as Ernie continued.

"I ask You to endow Jesse with strength and wisdom as he seeks this missing boy. Guide him, Father, in this search and in every other aspect of his life. To You will be all praise and glory when Bud is found and returned to his mother's arms. Amen."

Mrs. Savage echoed, "Amen," and Jesse repeated the closing, his voice breaking slightly with the utterance.

Ernie released Jesse's hand and turned to his wife. "Lois, get out the church directory and start making calls. We need to get as many men as possible combing the area in and around Buffalo Creek." She bustled off, and Ernie aimed his serious gaze at Jesse. "While I was praying, I received an image of a dark place, a place that left me feeling hemmed in. I don't know what it means, whether it pertains to you or to Bud. I intend to spend more time in prayer seeking clarification. But I felt led to share it with you."

Jesse took a hesitant step backward. "Visions only happened in Bible times." But being in a dark place, hemmed in, closely described the way he felt whenever he allowed his thoughts to drift to his childhood and youth.

Ernie chuckled softly. "I'm glad you're familiar enough with the Bible to know what is meant by a vision. I can't honestly say that's what I received, but I can tell you that when these images come to me in prayer, they hold meaning." He put his hand on Jesse's shoulder. "It isn't meant to frighten you — God seeks to save and uplift, not destroy and discourage. So don't go away filled with worry. Take heart. God is trying to speak to you, Jesse."

Jesse moved away from the minister's gentle touch, which seemed to hem him in

355

as effectively as any dark place he could imagine. "Since you're getting a search team organized, I'm going to lie down for an hour or two. Then I'll set out in my truck again." His throat tightened, and he spoke more to himself than the young preacher. "We've got to bring that boy home."

Arthur

The black-and-orange sign Arthur had placed in his store window two days ago to draw people in on Halloween day — "Spooktacular Savings on Halloween!" — was, from all accounts, successful. Not once during the entire morning was the floor empty of shoppers, and sometimes more than one family was browsing at the same time. The best Saturday all month.

Leon grinned as widely as a carved jack-o'-lantern as he helped carry out a slightly damaged arts-and-crafts dining set to the new owner's waiting wagon. Between trips he whispered excitedly, "Paddin' your pockets good today, huh, Dad?" Even marked at half price, the set would bring a five-dollar profit. Previously Arthur would have beamed in reply and mentally counted the coins, but somehow the thrill eluded him. He couldn't tear his mind away from

Neva, from Bud, from the desire to protect them both.

Not that he thought Neva was a hothouse flower in need of cosseting. Perhaps the many months of caring for her family and the mercantile without a husband's presence had built a strength in her that left her capable of functioning on her own. Arthur didn't wish weakness upon her, yet he wanted her to need someone.

He wanted her to need him, because in the past weeks he had discovered within himself a deep need for a wife. But not just any wife.

A young couple with a crying baby entered the store. He doubted they'd stay long. He gave Leon a little push toward the couple. "See what they need. I'm going to the outhouse."

He slipped out the back door and moved to the outhouse, but instead of going inside he leaned against its weathered gray siding and let the cool air flow over him. He whispered, "I want Neva. Not for her property. For her companionship."

With a sigh he aimed his gaze at his emporium. The biggest business on the street, not counting the Oakes Hotel at the far end of Main Street. Such pride he'd always taken in keeping the lap siding painted bright white, his windows sparkling, his sidewalk swept, and the tile foyer with tiny blue squares spelling "FURNITURE" gleaming against a white background. Making the emporium the most successful business in Mitchell County was his biggest dream. And suddenly, inexplicably — even disappointingly — it all seemed so unimportant.

Arthur pushed off from the outhouse wall and returned to the store.

The couple with the baby were gone. Leon bounded over, his lips twisted into a disgusted scowl. "I showed them six lamps for less'n three dollars apiece, and they didn't buy any of them. Said they were gonna get one from the Sears and Roebuck catalog."

Arthur shrugged. "They'll probably end up paying more than three dollars with the shipping costs, but it's their choice. We can't make people buy."

Leon's mouth dropped open.

Arthur ignored his son's stunned response and crossed to the front door, bouncing his fist on the backs of sofas and chairs as he went. "I'll be back in a few minutes. I'm going to check on Leroy, make sure he's following Mrs. Shilling's instructions."

Chapter 26

Neva

By the end of the day, Neva was glad she had opened the store. The flow of customers kept her mind too busy to wallow in worry. Some visitors to the mercantile didn't come to make purchases, but she appreciated their presence anyway.

Reverend Savage came in and prayed with her and Belle. Shortly after the preacher left, Mrs. Lafferty arrived and offered to take Charley, Cassie, and Adeline for the day. Charley refused to go, insisting he wanted to help in the mercantile since Bud wasn't there, and Neva found the courage to meet his gaze when granting her permission.

Mrs. Hood and Mrs. Austin, whose husbands went out in search of Bud, brought in a basket of sandwiches and fruit at lunchtime and then minded the store so she, Belle, Charley, and Leroy could take a break and eat in peace. Even Arthur stopped in to make sure she was holding up. After spending the whole night hunting Bud without success, he had every reason to be grumpy, but his pleasant bearing and kind words warmed her.

Neva learned the true meaning of community on that Halloween Saturday in 1936, a day when her heart ached even more fiercely than it had the first raw days after Warren's death. People could have been judgmental, could have questioned her parenting or criticized Bud. Instead they showered her with sympathetic understanding. Never would she forget the compassion of her friends and neighbors, and when Bud returned, she would sit down with him and pen notes of thanks to every person who had offered an act of kindness that day.

At six o'clock she locked the door and turned the sign to Closed, but she left the window shades up and the electric lights on. If Bud traipsed into town, he would find a warm glow welcoming him home. She, Belle, and Charley walked together to the Randalls' house to retrieve Cassie and Adeline from the housekeeper's care.

Leon answered their knock and led them to the dining room. To Neva's shock, Arthur and the little girls sat together at the dining room table, drawing with Crayola crayons on large sheets of brown wrapping paper.

Arthur glanced up, and a smile broke over his face. "Well, hello. Is it quitting time?" He pulled his timepiece from the little pocket on his vest, checked its face, then nodded. "Sure enough. After six already." He slid the gold disc back into his pocket and rose. "I hope you don't mind. I sent Mrs. Lafferty home when I returned from work. She usually only stays until noon on Saturdays, so I hated to keep her much longer."

He gestured to the paper and crayons. "Belle, Charley, come over here and help Cassie and Adeline finish their flower garden. Cassie tells me Charley is very good at drawing frogs, which every garden needs to keep the pests away. I'm sure Belle can add some beautiful roses or maybe some butterflies."

The pair looked at her for permission.

Neva nodded. "Go ahead." The two slipped into chairs and picked up crayons.

Arthur rounded the table and cupped Neva's elbow. "Let's go to the parlor. You can tell me the latest developments on the search for Bud."

"There's not much to tell, I'm afraid." The

worry she'd held at bay during her busy day tiptoed in and formed a knot in her throat. "One of the men said he found what appeared to be tufts of wool on some low-hanging branches at a windbreak northeast of town. I'd like to think they came from Bud's jacket — it has a sheepskin collar and lining. But I'm afraid to get my hopes too high."

He offered her the same chair she'd sat in yesterday evening, and then he seated himself on the sofa. Elbows on his knees, he fixed a serious look on her. "Would you like me to drive out and search more fervently?"

She smiled despite her deep heartache. Why had she allowed Warren's opinion of their neighbor to form her judgment? Arthur Randall was a very caring man. "That isn't necessary. Sheriff Caudel said he would drive out, snoop around, talk to farmers living near the windbreak. If Bud is somewhere in the area, I have to trust the sheriff will find him."

Arthur gave the back of her hand one quick, impersonal pat and then sat up. "I'm sure you're right." He yawned behind his hand. "Oh, please forgive me, Neva. The lack of sleep is catching up with me." He chuckled. "Leon and Leroy have already gone to their rooms. I won't have to worry about them going out and performing Halloween pranks this year."

She'd give anything to be worrying about Bud sneaking out to soap windows or turn trash bins on their sides. She rose. "I should go. The children haven't had their supper yet, and —"

He stood quickly. "I fed the little girls."

Embarrassment smote Neva. "Did they beg for food?"

"They didn't have a chance. Mrs. Lafferty told me to give a portion of the brisket and steamed cabbage to them." He shook his head, wonder lighting his eyes. "Mrs. Lafferty has worked as my housekeeper since the week after Mabel died — over six years now. And she's spoken more in the past two weeks than in all those six years combined. Do you know why?"

Confused, Neva held out her hands in silent query.

"Because of Adeline. She adores the little girl." He frowned, his expression pensive. "She never took to Leroy or Leon. Even when they were younger. Maybe they were too rambunctious for her. Or maybe it was my fault. I certainly never encouraged them to develop any kind of relationship with her." He seemed to drift somewhere inside himself for a few seconds. Then he gave a little jerk and a smile brightened his countenance. "So thank you for letting Adeline spend the school hours with Mrs. Lafferty. It helps you, of course, but I think her presence has been a gift to the lonely older woman."

A gift . . . She'd told Bud and Belle the younger children were a gift. Now Arthur said the same thing. Something in Neva's chest pinched and held. Was it time for her to begin seeing them as her gift, too? "I really should take the children home. Belle and Charley need their supper, and I want to be there if Bud comes back."

"*When* Bud comes back," he corrected, his voice gentle yet firm. "What did Sheriff Caudel tell you? Keep your hope alive, Neva."

She smiled. "I will. Thank you."

He glanced out the front window. "Dusk has fallen. Let me get a flashlight and I'll walk you all across the alley. It is Halloween, and I wouldn't want any ghosts or goblins to carry you away."

Now she laughed. Amazing she could find something amusing enough to warrant laughter, but somehow he'd coaxed it from her. Something flickered in his eyes — something she couldn't define, but it chased any thought of laughing far away. She hurried to the dining room, calling for the children. They all needed to go home.

Jesse

Jesse knocked on the farmhouse door and waited. Between his fingers he held one of the bits of fluff Tim Austin had found caught in some brambles just west of the farm. For Mrs. Shilling's sake, he hoped the farmer saw a boy wearing a jacket with a fuzzy sheepskin collar.

No one answered, so he knocked again, harder this time, and finally a voice hollered from inside. "All right, all right, don't break the door down. I'm coming." It swung open, and a grouchy-looking man wearing trousers and suspenders over grimy long johns glared at Jesse. "Who're you?"

Jesse tapped his badge with one finger. "Sheriff Caudel from Buffalo Creek. Are you Silas Deering?"

"That's me. Am I in some kinda trouble?"

"Can I come in?"

The man poked a button next to the doorjamb, and a bulb sputtered to life above their heads. He joined Jesse on the porch. "You out patrolling, looking for Halloween pranksters? They don't usually come all the way out here. Enough places in town to keep them busy."

"Actually, I'm looking for a runaway boy." Jesse held out the puff of creamy wool. "One of the men from town found this in the windbreak at the edge of your property. We think it came from the boy's jacket. Have you seen him?"

"A boy? Wearing a woolly jacket?" Deering scratched his cheek. His fingernails rasped on his thick whiskers. "Can't say that I have."

"Do you mind if I look around a little bit?"

Deering grabbed the rusty handle on the screen door and squeaked it open. "Meander all you want to. Just don't wake my chickens." He let the door slam shut and then the light went out.

Jesse released a short huff of laughter. There sure were some interesting characters in the world. He eased off the porch and, beneath the light of a round, bright moon, started around the corner of the house.

An automobile — the banker's Bentley if Jesse's tired eyes were seeing things correctly — bounced along the road, stirring dust in its wake. The driver hit the horn repeatedly. Jesse changed direction and trotted to the road. The vehicle pulled to a stop next to Jesse.

Samuel Griggs cranked down his window

and reached out for Jesse's sleeve. "Sheriff, we need you in town. Some blasted kids started a fire in a barrel behind the hotel. Matt Oakes caught them and has them corralled in the hotel's washroom. He's threatening to put their clothes through his wringer washer. With the kids still in them."

Jesse considered telling Griggs to let the hotel owner do whatever he wanted to the mischief makers, but if the banker drove all the way out here to fetch him, he should probably go. He back-pedaled toward his truck. "Go back to town, Samuel, and see if you can convince Matt to wait until I get there."

"I will. You better hurry. When Matt gets upset about something, he's worse than a raging bull." The Bentley's tires screeched in protest with the banker's three-point turn, and then the car chugged toward town.

Jesse sent one look across the Deerings' property, torn between rescuing Matt — or, more accurately, the kids from Matt's wrath — and looking for Bud. But as sheriff he owed more than one resident his attention. The search for Bud would have to wait.

Bud

A car horn's nasally *meep! meep!* pulled Bud to wakefulness. He opened his eyes, cringing against the gritty feeling when his eyelids scraped over his eyeballs. Way above him velvety black and three wavering dots — stars — filled the little circle where, between long snatches of restless sleep, he'd watched the sky change color. It was night again. He could sneak out.

He stiffened his back muscles and tried to dig his fingers into the dirt walls. His hands didn't respond. Confused, he tried again. Nothing happened. He couldn't feel his hands. Or his arms. Not at all. Panic rolled through him. Had his arms fallen off while he slept?

He squinted through the darkness and made out the shape of his deathly white fingers draping above his head. Relieved, he let his head sag back and he closed his eyes. He still had arms. And hands. But for some reason they were useless.

Bud popped his eyes open and gritted his teeth. So he'd have to push himself out with his feet. When he was little, Ma teasingly said he was half monkey because he could walk his way up the wall all the way to the ceiling by bracing his feet on opposite sides of the narrow bedroom hallway. He hadn't done his wall climbing for a long time, but he remembered how to do it. He would monkey-climb out of this hole.

When he'd landed, his legs had ended up one on top of the other, with his right foot flat and his left toe pointing down. He'd wriggled enough earlier in the day to get his feet side by side, which relieved the deep pressure in his hips. He twisted again, hissing against the pain that shot across his lower back, working to plant his feet on the sides of the wall.

He struggled, squirming, grunting, willing his soles to catch hold. His body shifted, but instead of working his way up, he slid several inches down. He froze, his heart hammering against his ribs. How deep was this hole? Could he fall all the way to the center of the earth, where the teacher said a ball of red-hot lava always boiled?

A sob broke from his chest. He'd gotten stuck in things before. Under his bed, up in a tree, even on the roof of the barn one time. And every time Pop had rescued him. Bud choked out, "Pop . . . I need you, Pop. I need you."

But Pop was dead. He couldn't rescue Bud this time. He'd die down in this hole.

Even though the racking sobs hurt his back something fierce, Bud surrendered to the need to cry. Between bouts of helpless crying, he whispered Pop's name, begging Pop to come, to pull him out, to help him.

He wanted his pop so bad. And in the middle of his crying, he remembered what Ma had told him and Belle. *"We'll miss y-your father. But God will give us strength."*

Pop was dead and gone. He couldn't help Bud anymore. But Reverend Savage and Bud's Sunday school teacher and Ma said God was always there.

"God, help me. Oh, please, God, help me." His weak cries gained strength, and even though speaking was like dragging nails across his dry throat, he called out at the top of his voice, "Help me! Help me!"

Eyes open and gaze fixed on the tiny patch of star-studded heavens, Bud petitioned the Father with his whole heart and the entire strength of his lungs. "Help! Help me! Help!"

CHAPTER 27

Jesse

Thank goodness Halloween came only once a year. It took nearly thirty minutes of cajoling before Matt Oakes calmed down enough to let Jesse take the fire-starting teens out of the hotel's laundry. After giving the boys a stern lecture about the hazards of playing with matches, he delivered them into their parents' hands. Then he aimed his truck for the farm where the wool tufts had been found.

On his way out of town, he encountered two kids, one of whom carried a dead raccoon by its tail. His badge compelled him to stop and ask what they intended to do with the stiff creature. After several minutes of hemming and hawing, they reluctantly confessed they were going to put it on Miss Neff's front porch. Jesse didn't figure the spinster teacher would appreciate finding a raccoon — dead or alive — on her porch, so he told the kids to toss it in the back of his truck and go home. The raccoon landed with a dull thud, and the boys trotted off in the opposite direction. Jesse could only hope they were going home.

As he put his truck in gear, he shook his head. Kids . . . Why did they find such pleasure in stirring up havoc? The boys Matt Oakes collared could have burned down the whole hotel with their stunt. These two with their raccoon could have given poor Miss Neff apoplexy. And Bud's shenanigans would give his mother gray hair. The same way Jesse's thoughtless behavior had been responsible for more than half the gray hairs on Norma Caudel's head.

His truck rolled over a rut in the road, bouncing him in the cab. He appreciated the jolt, because it sent his thoughts of Ma and the farm in Nebraska from his mind. Turning his focus to the area illuminated by his headlights, he pushed on the gas, eager to reach the Deering place and snoop around.

An old rattletrap of a pickup lurched into Jesse's path and stalled. Jesse let out a yelp of surprise, swerved, and slammed on his brakes. His engine died, but to his relief he'd missed the pickup. Fury quickly replaced the relief. Probably more kids out stirring up trouble.

He leaped out of his cab and stormed to the driver's side. "What are you doing driving around in the dark with your headlights off? Up to no good, huh?"

Instead of a sheepish teenager, farmer Deering sat behind the wheel. The man glared at Jesse. "My headlights ain't worked in more than a year. As for somebody being up to no good, that's true enough, but it isn't me. I was coming to get you."

Jesse blew out a breath. Would this night never end?

"Somebody's out at my place hollering like a peacock and keeping me and my missus from resting."

"Hollering like a peacock?"

The farmer grunted. "Yes. You know how a peacock yells. Heeelp! Heeelp!" His eyebrows formed a V. "Whoever it is won't shut up, an' he's hidin' so good I can't find him. You'd better come put a stop to it."

Awareness struck as hard as a fist in his gut. Jesse curled his hands over Deering's windowsill. "Mr. Deering, I'll go to your place, but I need a favor from you."

The V got even tighter. "What's that?"

"Drive on to town. Go to Reverend Savage's place. He lives in the little clapboard house behind the chapel at —"

"Third and Main. I know, I know."

"That's right. I need you to —"

"Me and the missus sit in on the preacher's sermons at least once a month."

Jesse resisted clamping his hand over the man's mouth to keep him quiet. "Would you tell Reverend Savage to round up as many men with flashlights as he can? Tell him to get everybody out to your place."

The farmer's eyebrows shot upward. "You putting together a posse to catch some ornery youngster playing a Halloween prank? You take your job mighty serious, don't you?"

A grin threatened, but Jesse managed to squelch it. "Yes, sir, I do. Now hurry. We don't want to lose track of your prankster."

"You got it, Sheriff. I'll send 'em. You can bet I will."

Neva

While Belle and Charley ate leftover sandwiches from the lunch basket, Neva supervised Cassie and Adeline's bath. When they were clean and dry and smelled sweetly of lavender from the soap, she helped them dress in flannel nightgowns and combed their silky hair into pin curls. Although outwardly she smiled, inwardly she battled tears the entire time. Taking care of the little girls brought back precious memories of Belle's toddler-hood. When the doctor removed Neva's womb from her body, she'd mourned the lost opportunity for more little ones to raise. Why had she held herself aloof from these two for so long?

Adeline stood trustingly between Neva's knees, and Cassie sat on the edge of the bed, watching Neva form the little swirls of hair and pin them in place. Cassie didn't say a word, but her big blue eyes held myriad questions.

Neva paused now and then to offer the six-year-old an assuring smile, hoping the child would understand what Neva's actions intended to say — she would take care of them. She would love them.

As she finished Adeline's last curl, someone pounded on the mercantile door. Neva set Adeline aside and hurried up the hallway. She met Belle, who came from the kitchen.

"Do you think it's Bud come back?" Belle sounded breathless.

Neva paused long enough to touch Belle's cheek. "I don't know. Pray, Daughter."

Charley trotted up to Belle, and the two of them followed Neva down the stairs and through the lit mercantile. Hope multiplied with every patter of Neva's soles against the floor. But Reverend Savage stood outside. She swallowed her disappointment and opened the door.

The minister remained on the sidewalk. He shot an uncertain glance across Belle and Charley. "Mrs. Shilling, could I speak to you privately?"

Horrible thoughts filled Neva's mind. If he'd brought bad news, Belle and Charley shouldn't hear it. She shooed the children toward the stairs, then gestured for Reverend Savage to step inside. She hugged herself, silently praying for strength. "What is it?"

"It might be nothing, but . . ." The man gripped her upper arm, his warm hand offering the strength she'd requested. "Sheriff Caudel asked for help out at the Deering farm — the closest farm to the windbreak where Mr. Hood found those little bits of wool. Deering said he and his wife heard somebody hollering for help, and Jesse — that is, Sheriff Caudel — told Deering to round up a 'posse.' I'm pretty sure the sheriff thinks it's Bud calling for help."

Neva gasped.

He gave her arm a gentle squeeze. "Maybe I shouldn't have said anything until we knew for sure, but you asked me to keep you apprised of any new information."

"I'll get my coat."

"Now, Mrs. Shilling, there's no sense in you going out in the cold. It could just be someone playing a prank. It is Halloween, after all."

She couldn't stay in the apartment if her son was in the cold dark calling for help. "It will only take me a minute. Will you drive me out?"

An understanding smile creased the man's face. "Of course I will. Why don't you gather up blankets, a jug of water, maybe a sandwich or two. While you do that, I'll make sure my flashlight is in working order. We'll probably need it."

"I'll be ready when you return."

The minister left, and Neva hurried for the staircase. She rounded the corner and found Belle on the first riser, Charley a few steps higher. She frowned at the pair. "You listened in?"

Belle nodded. She clasped her hands together beneath her chin in a prayerful pose. "Momma, do you really think it might be Bud calling for help?"

Reverend Savage's warning spilled from Neva's mouth. "It could be someone playing a Halloween trick. But just in case, I'm going out."

"I want to go, too."

"No, honey. It's too cold. Besides, some-one has to stay here with the younger ones."

Belle hung her head. "Yes, Momma."

Charley thumped down the stairs to Neva's side. "I wanna go with you."

Neva shook her head. "It's too late for you to be out."

"I don't care. I gotta go. I made Bud run away."

"You didn't make Bud run away. It was his choice to go."

Charley poked out his lower lip. "He was trying to get away from me."

Neva couldn't argue. She'd be sharing falsehoods. She sought a way to reassure the child.

"Let me go with you, Aunt Neva. I wanna help find him." All obstinacy faded, and such yearning filled the boy's face Neva couldn't turn away. He whispered, "Please?"

Neva touched Charley's shoulder. "All right. Put on your heaviest coat and your hat and gloves. Get Bud's hat and gloves from your closet, too, and bring them along. He'll likely need them when we find him."

"Yes, ma'am!" He raced up the stairs.

Belle tipped her head. Both curiosity and approval shimmered in her eyes. "Why'd you say yes to him, Momma?"

Neva gathered her thoughts. "I suppose

I'm finally seeing Charley as a real little boy with real feelings and wants and needs. I can't — I won't — ignore him anymore." She looped arms with Belle and started up the stairs. "Now help me put together a pack of things Bud might need when we find him, hmm? Then pray Charley and I get to bring your brother home."

Jesse

Reverend Savage sent a dozen men to the Deering farm, and Jesse didn't end up needing any of them. At least, not to find the mysterious caller.

The instant he leaped from his truck cab, he heard the sound Deering had claimed sounded like a peacock. Even though the full moon smiled down in silent amusement, even though it was Halloween and he'd already dealt with tricksters, even though the voice calling for help was weak and wavering and ghostly, Jesse knew — *he knew* — this was no prank. The caller might not be Bud Shilling, but whoever it was needed rescuing.

He cupped his hands beside his mouth and bellowed across the landscape. "Keep calling! I hear you!" Within seconds the call came again, and Jesse gave a whoop. "That's right! Holler! Holler!" He snapped on his flashlight and trekked across the ground in the direction from which the sound seemed to come.

Sweeping the light from side to side, he searched for anything out of the ordinary. Every few steps he encouraged the stricken person to keep yelling, and the voice rewarded him with a stream of "help, help, help, help."

Jesse paused, trying to make sense of what he heard. The continuing cries were raspy, even weak, but they seemed to be getting louder. That should mean he was getting closer. But no matter where he turned his flashlight's beam, all he saw was uneven ground studded with dried stalks of what might have been corn, some wild grasses, and a lot of shriveled weeds. No sign of a person.

He stayed rooted in place and hollered, "Who are you?"

"Bud. Bud Shilling."

Jesse's heart launched into his throat. It didn't sound like Bud — more like an old man who'd smoked cigars his whole life. But he decided to believe him anyway. He waved the flashlight beam around in frantic jerks. "Bud, it's me — Jesse Caudel. Tell me where you are."

"I'm here. I'm here!"

Jesse frowned. Why did the boy's voice seem to carry from a distance? He lifted the flashlight, sending the beam farther out. But Bud didn't appear in its path. "Where, Bud? Walk toward my flashlight."

"I — I can't. I'm stuck in a hole."

A hole . . . Underground? Jesse jammed the light directly in front of his feet. "Call out, Bud! Don't stop!"

"Help me! Help!"

Jesse inched forward, holding the flashlight the way a water witcher held a divining rod. He'd traveled fewer than a dozen steps when the light skimmed a circular opening perhaps eighteen inches across. He knelt beside it and aimed the flashlight into the cavity. The beam fell on a boy's dirty, pale face.

Eyes closed, hands curled above his head, Bud continued to grate through chapped, bleeding lips, "Help. Help. Help."

"I see you, Bud!"

Bud released a long, shuddering sigh. Then he fell silent with his mouth still drooping open.

"Bud?"

No movement. Not even a flicker of an eyelid. Worry slammed through Jesse's chest. Had he arrived too late?

Headlights pierced the darkness — townsmen arriving. He propped his flashlight next to the hole, then leaped up. "Bud, help's coming. Hold on. We're gonna get you out of there. Just hold on, Bud, all right?"

The boy didn't answer.

Jesse turned his face to the sky. "If You're up there, heed Bud's words. Help him, God." He swallowed. "Help me help him."

CHAPTER 28

Neva

Reverend Savage's car lagged at the end of the procession of vehicles. Neva bit her fingernails to the quick, willing him to hurry, hurry. It seemed an eternity passed before he pulled his car up at the edge of the road. Even before the engine rattled into silence, she grabbed the door handle and leaped out.

A group of men, flashlights in hand, gathered around the sheriff's pickup. Jesse Caudel's voice rose from the center of the group. "Do any of you have shovels with you?"

"I do, Sheriff!"

"Me, too."

"Get 'em. I've got rope and —"

The two men darted off, and Neva pushed her way through the throng. She grabbed Mr. Caudel's arm. "You found him?"

He didn't look happy to see her. "I did."

His gaze lifted, seeming to search the faces of the men. He waved Reverend Savage forward. "Ernie, stay here with Mrs. Shilling."

"Take me to him!" Neva yanked the sheriff's arm. "Take me to him now!"

He took hold of her shoulders. "Mrs. Shilling, where he is . . ." His face was white, his eyes blazing in the harsh light from the dozen flashlights aimed toward them. "You don't want to see him that way."

Reverend Savage, holding Charley by the hand, leaned close and lowered his voice to a deep rumble. "Jesse, I don't want to tell you your job, but it seems to me Bud needs to see his ma as much as she needs to see him. Let's all go."

Mr. Caudel blew out a breath and stepped away from Neva. "Fine. We're wasting time here." He turned to the men and raised his hand. "Come on — out there where I left my flashlight. He's in the bottom of a narrow shaft. I think it's an old well."

They all swarmed toward the dim beam of light pointing at the sky.

Stiff grasses snagged Neva's stockings, and the cold breeze made her ears ache, but she moved as quickly as she could at the head of the group, taking two steps for every one of Mr. Caudel's. Reverend Savage held to her elbow, helping her navigate the rough terrain. She kept her gaze pinned to the flashlight's beam, her heart pounding out prayers of both praise and petition.

When they reached Mr. Caudel's flashlight, she broke free of the reverend's grasp, dropped to her knees, and planted her hands on either side of the hole. "Bud?" The dirt beneath her knees broke loose and bounced into the opening.

Mr. Caudel grabbed her and pulled her away. "Be careful! We don't want to bury him alive."

Neva gasped and covered her mouth with her hands, her imagination conjuring horrendous pictures.

When he spoke again, he gentled his tone. "It's a very narrow shaft, Mrs. Shilling. We don't want it to close. Please stay back." He entrusted her to Reverend Savage and then returned to the dark opening.

Mr. Hood and Mr. Geary stooped over on opposite sides of the hole, each holding flashlights and peering downward. Hood asked, "How're we gonna do this, Sheriff?"

"I'll drop a rope to the boy, tell him to hold on. We'll pull him out."

Geary shook his head. "He looks awfully weak. Maybe one of us should go down with the rope — bring him out."

Hood gawked at the gas station owner. "What're you thinking, Geary? That hole's not big enough for any of us. We'd end up stuck on top of him, and then two people would need rescuing."

Geary balled one hand into a fist. "Then what do you suggest?"

"Digging a second hole and tunneling across. It's gonna take space to carry that boy up and out."

If Reverend Savage wasn't in her way, she'd snatch up the rope or a shovel and rescue Bud herself. When would they stop talking and start doing?

Hood scanned the circle of men. "Where's Deering?"

Geary snorted. "He went to his house, said he was going to bed."

"We might want to get him out here. He'll know if this is a dried-up water well or a shaft for an oil derrick. I can't remember if he's one of the fellows who bought into that rumor of an oil boom out here in the twenties."

Geary spun on the man. "What difference does it make?"

Hood shrugged. "If that's a shaft for a derrick, and if they found petroleum down there, it could still be leaking gas. We'd need to get that boy out fast. Even with several of us digging, it'll take the rest of the night to dig down far enough to get below him and then make a tunnel to connect the two holes. If there's gas down there, then —"

"It's a dried-up well," Geary said with a sneer, "not an oil-derrick shaft. Deering probably pulled the pump when the water source went dry."

Neva couldn't stay silent. She bounded forward and took Mr. Caudel by the arm. "Enough talk! Get my son out of that hole!"

A moan carried from the bottom of the well.

Every man yanked his gaze toward the opening.

Neva's pulse scampered into double beats. She gripped Mr. Caudel's arm with every ounce of strength she possessed. "Please. You've got to hurry."

The sheriff grabbed the coil of rope he'd pulled from the back of his truck and marched to the hole. As he tied the rope into a loop, he called, "Bud? Bud, can you hear me?"

Another moan rose. Neva pressed her fingers to her mouth, blinking back tears. He sounded so weak, so ill. She closed her eyes and prayed as Mr. Caudel called directions to Bud.

"All right, listen to me."

Hear me, God. Save my son.

"I'm gonna drop this rope down. I need you to slip it over your head and under your arms."

Hold him, dear Father, in Your loving arms, and bring him to safety.

"Do you understand, Bud?"

Give him strength, God.

"I . . . I understand. But I can't do it. My arms . . . my hands . . . I can't feel 'em. It's like they're not even there."

Bud's raspy confession weakened Neva's knees. She stumbled forward, impatience writhing through her. "I'll go after him. Send me down."

Mr. Caudel shook his head. "You're not a large woman, but that hole isn't big enough even for you. None of us here are small enough to fit. Bud'll have to grab hold, or we'll have to dig that second hole."

The men with shovels moved forward in readiness, their gazes aimed at the sheriff.

"I'd fit."

Every gaze shifted to Charley, who stepped forward with his big brown eyes flitting from one face to another. He stopped next to Neva and Mr. Caudel and held out his hands. "I'm little enough to fit in the hole, aren't I?"

Neva's heart rolled over in her chest. She

touched the boy's hair. "Charley, you're too little. You aren't strong enough to pull Bud out."

His chin quavered. "But I wouldn't have to pull him out. I'd just put the rope on him. Then Mr. Caudel and the others could pull him out."

Mr. Caudel went down on one knee in front of Charley. "You're a very brave boy for offering, but —"

Reverend Savage moved behind Charley and put his hands on the boy's shoulders. He looked fervently into Mr. Caudel's face. "Jesse, Bud is in a dark place. He's hemmed in, and he needs rescuing. In front of you is a willing rescuer. Use him."

The two men stared at each other, both as still as statues. The breeze lifted the collars on their coats, and from the windbreak a turtledove cooed and its mate answered, but neither seemed aware of their surroundings. The others remained silent, too, and Neva almost held her breath, sensing the unspoken communication that sizzled between the preacher and the sheriff.

Mr. Caudel bowed his head briefly, heaved a tremendous sigh, and then looked again at Reverend Savage. "All right." He rose and caught Charley by the arm. "Come with me, son. We'll rig you up and send you after Bud."

Bud

Something landed on Bud's head and rolled down his cheek. Another something, bigger than the first, hit his shoulder, and then a small shower sprinkled his face. He wanted to bat away whatever it was, but his hand refused to move, and he grunted in aggravation.

Opening his eyes, he gingerly shifted his face toward the opening, where only a little while ago flashlight beams had blinded him. There was still light, but a big blob of something blocked most of it. Thin fingers of light that shifted from one edge of the hole to the other sneaked past the black blob.

More bits pelted him, and a large chunk — earth, Bud now realized — clunked him on the chest. Panic rolled through him. Was the wall caving in? He opened his mouth to yell, but only a grating whisper emerged. "Don't bury me. Please don't bury me."

"It's okay, Bud. I'm not gonna bury you. Gonna getcha out."

Bud blinked and squinted at the shape bobbing above him. Slowly his brain registered what his eyes were seeing. Not a blob, but a person. A person coming facedown, arms stretching toward Bud, and bringing bits and pieces of the dirt walls with him.

Sheriff Caudel's voice boomed from above. "Bud, keep your eyes closed so you don't get dirt in them. Charley will let you know when he reaches you."

Charley? Grit rained down and Bud grimaced, closing his eyes and pressing his face against something soft — his own upraised arm. Why couldn't his arm feel his face? He tried again to close his fingers, to move his hands, but nothing happened. Would the doctor have to cut his arms off because they were dead? Even though Bud was fourteen years old, practically a man, he started to cry.

"Don't cry, Bud. You'll be all right. Don't worry."

Charley . . . comforting him. Bud had never been so humiliated and so humbled at the same time. The feelings made him cry even harder, which turned out to be a good thing, because the tears washed the dirt bits out of his eyes.

"Okay, Bud, I got you."

He did? Bud forced his eyes open. Charley dangled right above him and held on to his hands. And Bud couldn't feel a thing.

"Gonna put this rope over you. Hold still."

Caught like a cork in a bottle, Bud didn't have any choice about holding still. The rope slid down Bud's arms, but it didn't even tickle. It scratched the back of his neck, though, when Charley looped it behind his head. Charley made little grunting noises as he worked the rope to Bud's armpits and then tugged it until it bit into Bud's flesh. Bud winced.

The little boy cringed. "Sorry if that hurts you, but it's gotta be tight. Mr. Caudel said so. We don't want it fallin' off when you're halfway out of the hole."

Bud didn't want that either. "I'm all right."

"I know." A slight grin lifted one corner of Charley's mouth. Pop used to grin crooked that way when he was tired or worried about something or even teasing. Charley grabbed Bud's hands again.

Bud wished he could feel it. He needed to feel it. The deadness scared him and made him sad all at once.

"We're ready!" Charley's shrill cry echoed against the close walls and made Bud's ears ring. "Close your eyes, Bud. We're going up."

And then the rope went tight. Bud couldn't feel Charley's hands on him, but he felt that rope. Even through his jacket, it bit into his underarms and beneath his shoulder blades. He gritted his teeth and held back a moan. Eyes closed to block the clumps of dirt that peppered his face, he didn't know he'd been pulled free until arms wrapped around his torso and lowered him flat on his back.

He opened his eyes to a circle of men holding flashlights and Ma leaning over him, tears streaming down her face. She stroked his hair and his face while she cried and murmured his name. He tried to talk but no sound came out. His throat had worn out just like his arms. So he worked his lips, shaping the word *Ma* again and again while her warm tears dribbled onto his cheeks.

Then another face leaned in — Charley, all puckered up with worry. Dirt smudged his forehead and cheeks. Dirt clumps matted his hair. His chin was scraped and bleeding. Bud turned away from Charley's face, and his gaze landed on Charley's ankles. His trousers had ridden up and his socks sagged down. In between, a raw, ragged line showed where the rope used to pull the two of them out of the hole had burned into his skin.

He'd never been nice to Charley, but the boy had come down after him. Those well walls might have fallen in. On both of them. Charley had risked his life to come after Bud. Now he sat there bruised and bleeding, but instead of feeling sorry for himself, he looked at Bud with concern.

Bud turned his head and met Charley's worried gaze. He formed a different word. *Why?*

Charley gave him Pop's tired grin and lifted one shoulder in a lopsided shrug. " 'Cause you're my brother."

A sob left Ma's throat, a sound as raw as the wounds on Charley's legs. She grabbed hold of Charley and held him. Rocked him. Pressed a kiss on his temple. Charley burrowed into Ma's embrace and wrapped his arms around her neck as tight as that rope must've held Bud. Both of them cried. Neither of them were looking at him anymore, but Bud mouthed it anyway.

Thank you, little brother.

CHAPTER 29

Jesse

Something inside Jesse seemed to break loose. He knew he needed to put Bud in one of the vehicles and get him to the doctor. But he couldn't tear his eyes away from the scene at the center of the wavering beams of light.

The way Mrs. Shilling held Charley — snug to her breast, lips pressed to his temple — carried him back to Severlyn, Nebraska, and the woman he'd called Ma but had never really accepted as a mother in his heart. She'd tried to hold him close like Mrs. Shilling now held Charley, but he'd pushed her away. If not physically, then emotionally. Resentful because —

His thoughts jammed. Why had he been resentful? The Caudels had given him their name, had sheltered and fed and nurtured him with the same attention they gave their birth children. But somehow he'd built up walls around himself.

Standing there in the moonlight, witnessing Mrs. Shilling openly embrace her husband's illegitimate son, he battled a desire to swing his arms outward, knock down his walls, remove himself from the hemmed-in place he'd created, and be as free as Bud must feel right now with the wind on his face.

Jesse lurched forward and slipped his arms under Bud's shoulders and knees. He rose with his burden and barked out orders as he strode toward Ernie's vehicle. "Somebody find some scrap lumber in Deering's shed or barn and get that hole covered so no one else tumbles into it. Preacher, get Mrs. Shilling and Charley and let's get Bud to the doctor."

The doc should check Charley's legs, too — Jesse hadn't done a good job of protecting the boy's skin from the rope's bite. His open wounds were an invitation for infection. "Come on, everybody, move!"

Urgency — to see to the boys' needs but also to find his way out of his dark places — chased Jesse across the field and rolled in his chest all the way to town. He reached the doctor's house first, and he banged on the door until the doctor groggily answered. The man came to full wakefulness when

Jesse told him who was coming to see him and why. Within a few minutes he'd dressed and readied his examination room.

Ernie pulled up with Mrs. Shilling and the boys. Jesse trotted to the car, amazed his legs still worked, given the little sleep he'd enjoyed over the past two days and the tension of the evening. Maybe God had answered when he asked for help. The thought brought an element of peace Jesse found both welcome and confusing.

He carried Bud into the house, and Mrs. Shilling followed with her arm around Charley's shoulders. Jesse placed Bud on the examination table and turned to leave, but Mrs. Shilling reached for him.

"Mr. Caudel, I know you have other duties, but could you go to the mercantile and let Belle know we've found Bud? She'll be awake, waiting for me to come home."

"Reverend Savage and I will go together." It would give him some time to talk to the preacher without anyone overhearing. He closed the door behind him and approached Ernie, who leaned wearily against the foyer's paneled wall. "You all right?"

"I'm fine." The preacher grinned. "Tuckered, but more grateful than anything. Our prayers have been answered. The lost is found."

"And he was in a dark place, hemmed in, just like you said." Jesse eased toward the door. "I told Mrs. Shilling I'd let Belle know where her ma and brothers are. Would you . . . come, too?"

Something glimmered briefly in Ernie's eyes. He clapped his hand on Jesse's shoulder. "Your automobile or mine?"

Jesse got the odd feeling the young preacher already knew about the restlessness niggling in Jesse's heart and had advice to offer. And Jesse was ready to listen. "Do you mind driving?" The way he quivered from head to toe, he'd likely run them onto the sidewalk.

"Not at all." The two ambled across the doctor's yard to Ernie's waiting car. They slid in, Ernie cranked the engine to life, and he pulled onto the street. He sent a lingering look left and right, then flashed a grin at Jesse. "Awfully quiet. Looks like Halloween's over."

"Good." Jesse wasn't up to handling even one more conflict tonight. If Buffalo Creek proved as active every night as this one had been, he'd petition the town's council to hire a deputy. Or two. He sagged against the seat. "Sure am glad Bud's safe. Hope that boy stays close to home from now on for his ma's sake."

He cringed as the words left his mouth. Mrs. Shilling's stricken face as she'd begged him to find her son had closely mirrored his mother's face the day he'd set out from the farm. He'd never gone back. Did his ma lie awake at night, worrying and praying over him?

Jesse jerked upright. "Ernie, I . . . I did a terrible thing."

Ernie had turned into the alley behind the mercantile. He pulled up beside the Shillings' barn, turned off the engine, and angled his face to Jesse. "I'm not a priest, Jesse. You don't need to confess to me. You can talk to God Himself."

"I know." Frustration smote him. He popped the car door open. "I better go tell Belle about Bud." Light shone behind the kitchen window. As Mrs. Shilling had said, Belle was awake. "Then you'd better go back to Doc Zielke's place. Mrs. Shilling and the boys will need a ride home."

Ernie caught Jesse's sleeve. "Come to service tomorrow morning, then have dinner with Lois and me. I can see you need to talk, but it's late. You also need rest. Let's plan on visiting tomorrow, all right?"

Although Jesse's tormented thoughts needed release, he recognized the sensibility of Ernie's suggestion. A night's rest would do him good, and the preacher needed his sleep, too, or he might yawn in the pulpit. "All right."

He hurried across the lawn to the mercantile's back door, a flicker of hope following him. Maybe, just maybe, tomorrow he'd find a way out of his dark, hemmed-in place.

Had Ernie prepared this sermon in advance, or had last night's events prompted it? Either way, Jesse listened in rapt attention to Jesus's parable of the prodigal son. He'd heard the story before. His entire childhood and youth, his adoptive parents carted him off to church every Sunday. But this morning the story took on a deeper meaning.

Holding his Bible open in one palm and lifting his other to the congregation, Ernie paced on the raised dais. "Can you picture it? Consider the father at the window, watching with expectation, never once losing hope that he would see his son appear on the horizon. Look at his face creased with longing. Can you hear his heart beating in anticipation? Can you feel his yearning?"

Jesse's pulse beat a thrum in his ears. His chest grew tight.

"And then one day — oh, joyous day! — the father's diligence was rewarded. His son! His son!" His eyes alight, Ernie pointed to the back of the sanctuary. "Look!"

Every person seated in the pews gave a little jolt. Several turned their heads in the direction Ernie pointed, and Jesse couldn't keep from looking, too, fully expecting to see a bedraggled young man with sunken cheeks and a defeated spirit standing in the aisle.

"Here he came . . ."

Jesse turned forward again, his gaze pinned on the minister's shining face.

"And when the father saw him, what did he do? He ran." Tears pooled in the minister's eyes. His clutched the Bible to his chest, an expression of wonder blooming on his face. "He ran to his son, and he swept him into his arms. Oh, how foul that boy must have smelled after wallowing in a pigpen. The filth clinging to his clothes must have transferred to the father's fine robes. But did the father shy away?"

Jesse, almost without conscious thought, shook his head.

"No. No, he didn't. He kissed his son, and he placed his own robe over the boy's shoulders, and he called for a celebration because the lost had come home!" Ernie pulled in a breath and let it go with a satisfied *ahhhh,* the way a man did when he'd just finished a good meal. Then he moved to the pulpit with slow, measured steps, his head low. He laid the Bible on the wooden stand, placed his hand over it, and lifted his gaze to the congregation again.

"This story is a parable meant to illustrate a biblical truth. The truth is this. The father in the story is our Father God. The son is any person who has strayed away. The welcome the son received? The embrace, the kiss, the robe, the ring, the fatted calf?" A smile grew on the minister's face. "That's what waits for anyone who turns his feet toward the Father."

Ernie tapped the Bible, nodding as if agreeing with some private thought. "The father ran to greet his son upon his return. Right now God stands with open arms, watching, waiting, ready to run and meet you on your return trek. Are you ready, dear brothers and sisters? Are you ready to run to the arms of the Father?"

He yanked up the hymnal lying on the edge of the podium. "Rise. Let's sing together, 'Turn Your Eyes upon Jesus.' As we sing, as the Spirit leads, you come. Come to His arms."

The organist played the opening bars, and the congregation began to sing. " 'O soul, are you weary and troubled? No light in the darkness you see . . .' "

The words wrapped around Jesse, stirring to life a longing unlike anything he'd experienced before. He wanted to go. He wanted to return to the Father, but there was something else he had to do first.

Jesse snatched his hat from the seat, settled it on his head, and hurried out the doors with the words " 'And the things of earth will grow strangely dim, in the light of His glory and grace' " ringing in his ears.

Arthur

From his spot at the end of the very last pew, Arthur watched the sheriff scurry from the church building. He considered going after the man and asking if there was an emergency. Just to assure himself nothing more had befallen Neva Shilling. He'd come to church this morning in the hopes of seeing Neva. Perhaps sitting with her. But she wasn't here.

Back when Mabel was alive and the boys were young, he'd attended church regularly. Then Mabel passed away, and it had proven too challenging to keep the boys quiet without his wife's help. Within a short period of time, churchgoing lost its appeal. Lazing at home — rising late, puttering around in his bathrobe and slippers, doing nothing he didn't want to do for a solid day — on his only day away from the store replaced the habit.

But as he listened to the worshipers singing in harmony, he realized he'd been missing something by staying away from service. The message had spoken to him. The words of the song now reminded him of the faith Mabel held dear. The faith he'd once viewed as important. Just like the son in the parable, Arthur had strayed. Oh, he hadn't wallowed in a pigpen or otherwise wasted his life. But he hadn't honored God. He'd only honored himself.

Moneygrubber. The word Bud Shilling used to describe him returned and flayed him with its selfish meaning.

" 'Turn your eyes upon Jesus . . .' "

Arthur shifted his gaze to the cross hanging on the wall behind the pulpit. A lump filled his throat. He wanted more than a successful store. He wanted more than a bank account as big as the local banker's. He even wanted more than a new wife. Arthur wanted a new life.

The song ended, and Reverend Savage held up his hands as if under arrest. "Before our closing prayer, I have an important announcement. Please, everyone, have a seat."

Arthur sank back onto the hard pew, as

did everyone else.

"Some of you already know this news because you were involved in last night's activities."

A few heads bobbed, apparently the ones referenced by the preacher.

"Last night — or I could say early this morning —"

A few chuckles rumbled.

"Neva Shilling's boy, Bud, who had been missing since Friday afternoon, was found trapped in an abandoned well at the Deering farm."

Concerned mutters rolled through the room, and Arthur caught the back of the pew in front of him, ready to launch himself out of his seat.

"Bud spent the night with Dr. Zielke, and I stopped by there this morning for a report to share with you. The doctor said the boy popped his hip out of its socket when he fell, so he'll be moving slowly for a while. He has several scrapes and bruises and was mildly dehydrated. According to the doc, his worst pain came from his arms and hands. The well was a mighty small space, and since he couldn't move much, the circulation got cut off from his limbs. As he's regained feeling, Bud has been pretty uncomfortable. But the doc assured me he's going to be just fine, and I ask each of you to send up a prayer of thanks that one of our very own members had the chance to welcome home a lost son."

Applause broke out across the congregation, and Arthur couldn't resist joining in. Warmth rolled through him, a feeling of togetherness with these people.

Reverend Savage beamed a smile and waved his hands again, bringing the celebration to a close. "Please go by the mercantile during the week and share Mrs. Shilling's joy. For now, let's close in prayer."

At the minister's "amen," Arthur headed for the door, determined to be the first to share in Mrs. Shilling's celebration. Two women moved into his path, and he stifled a growl. He trailed them closely, anticipating his chance to step past them, and although he didn't intend to eavesdrop, their voices filtered to his ears anyway.

"After they got Bud out of the well, Matthew said the littlest boy called Bud Shilling his brother. At first he didn't think much of it — they all live together, you know. But . . ."

"But what, Marta?"

"Matthew said he took a good look at that little boy, and I think he's right."

"Right about what?" Eagerness sharpened

the second woman's tone.

They'd reached the bottom of the porch steps. Arthur could move around them now. But his legs refused to carry him forward. He held his breath, waiting for the answer with as much impatience as the woman.

"Matthew said that youngster is the image of Warren Shilling himself. Now Matthew wonders if it's a bald lie that Mr. Shilling took those children in. Matthew thinks Mr. Shilling is their father."

The second woman gasped, her eyes wide. "Oh, Marta!"

Arthur had heard enough. He shot across the churchyard in the direction of the mercantile. He'd check on Neva, ask after Bud, offer his congratulations the way the minister had encouraged, but then he'd let her know what he'd overheard. If one person was talking, it wouldn't be long before the whole town was abuzz. And he wouldn't let the gossip blindside her if he could help it.

CHAPTER 30

Neva

Neva couldn't recall the last time she'd slept until midmorning. Having arisen too late to ready herself or the children for church, she chose to take a leisurely bath and then read a Bible story to Belle and the children in lieu of attending service. She missed worshiping with fellow believers, and she fully intended to be in church next week, but after their stress-filled weekend, the quiet, unrushed time at home was a balm to her spirit.

They ate lunch early since they'd slept through the breakfast hour, and while Neva washed dishes, Belle got out the puzzle cubes from the bookshelf. The children scattered them across the parlor floor. Neva listened to them chatter and giggle, and she found herself smiling, enjoying the sounds of their happiness. Such a blessing to be completely at peace with their presence.

When someone knocked at the back door shortly after noon, Neva hurried downstairs, expecting to find Dr. Zielke bringing Bud home. Instead Arthur waited on the little stoop. The moment she opened the door, he stepped across the threshold and took hold of her hands.

"Neva, I heard the good news about Bud."

Startled yet touched by his affectionate gesture, she released her mixed emotions in a girlish giggle. "Yes, Sheriff Caudel found him last night in an abandoned well."

"How frightening for him."

She gently pulled back on her hands, but he didn't let go. Another nervous giggle escaped her throat. "It was, but the doctor says he will be fine. I'm so relieved."

"As am I."

The sincerity in his expression warmed her. She stopped trying to remove her hands from his grasp. "I'm surprised word reached you already. Even for Buffalo Creek, it seems the news traveled fast."

"Reverend Savage informed the congregation at the close of this morning's service."

Had she heard correctly? Arthur Randall had gone to church?

"He wanted us to celebrate Bud's safe return with you." His forehead briefly pinched, and he released one of her hands

409

to comb his fingers through his thick mustache. "I heard that good news, and then I heard something else. I thought you should be aware of the speculations made by at least one of the men who helped rescue Bud from the well."

Still silently rejoicing in her neighbor's choice to attend worship service, Neva only half listened.

"Apparently one of the men recognized the similarity in appearance between Charley and Warren. As we were leaving church, I overheard his wife tell another woman they're beginning to wonder if Charley is Warren's son rather than a foundling."

"Mm-hmm."

Arthur frowned and gave Neva's hand a little tug. "Neva, listen to me."

She set aside her inward reflections and gave him her full attention.

"I'm afraid, given the speed with which news travels in our small town, it won't be long before everyone will be looking at Charley and wondering the same thing."

She frowned. "Wondering what?"

Arthur shook his head, a bemused grin making him appear boyish. "I didn't think you were listening." The teasing look disappeared and worry replaced it. "People are talking about Charley." He paused. "And

Warren." Another lengthier pause. "And their true relationship."

She gazed at him blankly for a moment. Then she gave a start. "You mean they wonder if Charley is Warren's son?"

His breath whooshed out. "Exactly."

A month ago she would have dissolved into anguish at the thought of people discovering the secret. But the past days had changed her. Charley, Cassie, and Adeline weren't flesh of her flesh, but they were related by blood to Belle and Bud. That made them family. She no longer cared who knew. She shrugged. "Let them wonder."

Arthur's jaw dropped. He lost his grip on her hand and took a step backward, connecting with the edge of the open door. He pushed the door closed and then aimed an astonished look at her. "You don't mind if they . . . if people . . ."

She raised her chin. "I'm done being dishonest with myself and with my children. Charley, Cassie, and Adeline are Bud and Belle's half siblings. Their father was in the wrong, but the children are not to blame." Awareness bloomed in the center of her heart, and she finished with boldness. "And neither am I. Warren's choices were his and his alone."

Arthur shook his head. "I'm not sure

411

everyone will see it that way."

Neva nodded. "Some will look askance, finding fault." She'd done it herself. "But I can't control other people's actions. If they choose to be petty or meanspirited, then they'll have to account for their own consciences. But if I choose truthfulness, my conscience will be clear. That's what matters to me."

For several silent seconds he gazed at her with his lips pursed tight and his forehead furrowed. Then he released a little huff of breath. "I think you're making a big mistake. In a town the size of Buffalo Creek? With the majority of its population closely tied to church? It's been a good long while since I sat in on sermons, but I remember some rip-roaring ones on the Ten Commandments. Preachers especially like pounding the Bible about adultery and the harm it brings. It's one thing to keep the children. It's another to let people know from where they came."

He took her hands again and squeezed. Urgently. Beseechingly. "Please consider what you're doing. The very supposition of illegitimacy can bring out ugliness in folks. If they know for sure the children were born out of wedlock, they won't hold back on their judgment. Not on them. Or on you."

■ ■ ■ ■

Jesse

Not until Jesse picked up the telephone receiver on the corner of his desk in the sheriff's office did he realize the foolishness of his action. He'd gotten spoiled to the convenience of the invention that allowed people to talk from miles apart. But he couldn't reach his folks that way. In all likelihood they didn't have a telephone in their farmhouse. Pa Caudel had barely made enough to buy seasoned wood for the woodstove that heated their drafty old house. A telephone was an extravagance beyond reach. Calling them wouldn't work. He'd have to contact them some other way.

His stomach growled, and he smacked his forehead. He was supposed to have dinner with Ernie and Mrs. Savage, and he'd taken off instead. His friend — he'd come to view the minister as a friend — would be worried if he didn't show.

Jesse locked the office and, leaving his pickup with its nearly empty gas tank at the curb, headed up the sidewalk in wide strides. Even if he arrived late, they'd let him sit at the table with them. The young couple was as good hearted as his parents were, warm and welcoming to everyone.

Jesse's heart lurched. Could the parable Ernie shared that morning be true even today? He'd been away for a long time. Lots longer than the son in the Bible. How long would a father wait before he gave up?

Anxiousness to settle things within his spirit sped his steps, and he reached the preacher's house winded, his lungs burning from breathing the cold air. His tap on the door brought an immediate response, and Ernie ushered him in.

"There you are! We held dinner for you. Lois insisted."

Jesse cringed. "I hope Benji and Jenny aren't getting too restless."

Ernie laughed as he led Jesse to the small dining area next to the kitchen. "Oh, those two didn't wait. Lois fed them as soon as we got home. They're already down for their afternoon naps." A stream of jabber carried from behind a closed door at the end of the hall, and a second little voice answered. Ernie grinned. "Well, they're down. The napping part will come later. But you won't have to worry about Jenny spilling gravy on your trousers today."

Jesse sat in the chair Ernie indicated, and Mrs. Savage bustled from the kitchen with a roasting pan. She placed the pan on the table and lifted the lid, releasing a wonderful aroma. "Venison stew. Nice and hot still. Let me get the biscuits and we'll eat." She hurried out again.

Jesse leaned toward Ernie. "I'm sorry I made you wait. I —"

"Here we are." Mrs. Savage came in with a plate of nicely browned biscuits and a bowl of creamy butter. She put the items next to the pan, slid into her chair, and turned an expectant look on Ernie.

He cleared his throat and folded his hands. His wife bowed her head, and Jesse tamped down the words that had formed on his tongue so he wouldn't trample Ernie's prayer.

They ate quickly, focusing on the food rather than conversation. That suited Jesse. The sooner they got their bellies filled, the sooner he could empty his mind of the troubling thoughts. He didn't even mind when Mrs. Savage sheepishly admitted Benji had knocked the pie she had prepared off the counter so she'd thrown it away. She offered a bowl of canned peaches as a dessert, but he declined, stating honestly that he was adequately filled.

"Thank you for the good dinner, and my

apologies again for being such a tardy guest."

Mrs. Savage offered a warm smile and began clearing the table.

Ernie wiped his mouth and dropped his napkin on the plate. "And now I'd like to know what sent you scurrying out of church this morning."

So he'd seen Jesse's hasty departure. He squirmed.

"Did a mouse run up your pant leg?"

Despite the heaviness of his heart, he laughed. Ernest Savage had a way of putting a person at ease. "No, no mouse in my pant leg. But something . . ." He searched for a way to describe the feelings that had attacked him at the well's site and then crept over him during the sermon. "Something's eating at me. I need . . . help."

Ernie rose, all teasing wiped from his expression. "Let's go over to the church. It'll be quiet there."

They settled in the pew closest to the dais. If Jesse turned his head even a smidgen to the left, the wooden cross on the wall filled his vision. Ma Caudel always said the cross was a reminder of God's great love for mankind. The symbol offered him a breath of comfort.

"All right. Tell me what's bothering you."

Even though he'd spent much of the night wrestling with his thoughts, he still found it hard to put them into words. He hoped Ernie was good at deciphering. "The story — the parable — you told this morning. I think I'm like the son."

"How so?"

Jesse examined the minister's face for signs of condemnation. Seeing none, he continued. "I didn't ask for an inheritance." He snorted softly. "There wouldn't have been one to give anyway. The only thing my folks had an abundance of was youngsters." Images of the girls who trailed him, imitated him, irritated him, and called him brother flashed in his mind's eye. "Since I was the oldest, I was kind of the leader. They were always around me, always pulling at me, always needing me for . . . something."

"And that made you feel hemmed in?"

Jesse angled his head and stared at the cross. "Yeah. I hadn't really thought of it that way, but yeah. Since I came into the family half-grown, with four daughters already there, I never had the chance to just be. And every year and a half or so, another daughter came along until there were eight of them. Every time my ma's belly started to swell, I'd pray for a boy. Just one boy so I wouldn't have to be the only one, and every time a girl came along, I got more and more" — the emotion he'd identified the night before spilled out — "resentful."

He jerked his gaze to Ernie, and truths he'd never allowed himself to examine, let alone speak, poured from him. "Before the Caudels took me from the train, the woman who'd traveled with us orphans prayed with us — prayed for the people who would become our parents. She told us God would take us to the best families for us, and I believed it.

"But then, when I got to the farm and saw all those little girls, I figured the Caudels didn't want another child as much as they wanted a farmhand. I felt like God hadn't listened to the lady's prayers. But my folks were praying people. They took me to church, told me God loved me, told me I could talk to Him and that He wanted to hear from me. So I tried praying." For a brother instead of another sister, for a better crop so they'd have money in the bank to carry them through the winter, for a new pair of shoes when his old ones wore clear out. Countless prayers gone unanswered.

The lump of resentment in Jesse's chest swelled until it pained him to breathe. "God didn't listen to me any more than He had to the lady on the train. No more than He listened to my folks when they prayed. I stayed with Pa and Ma for ten years. And then I'd had enough of the hard life. I left."

Ernie's eyebrows came together in a sad line. "Did you ever go back?"

Jesse sagged forward, rested his elbows on his knees, and lowered his head. "No. Not even once. Been away now more years than I was with them. I don't even know if they're still alive." His last words emerged on a strangled note, the lump in his throat so big it nearly cut off his ability to speak.

Silence fell. The solid building blocked any sound from outside. Not even a whisper of wind intruded. During those quiet moments Jesse sat still, stiff, staring at the plank of pine between his boots and waiting for Ernie to rebuke him for his thoughtlessness. He readied defensive replies even though he knew he wouldn't say them out loud. Not to Ernie.

"Well, Jesse, I'm no expert, but it seems to me you're carrying around a heavy load of guilt."

Jesse nodded. He shouldn't have left Pa Caudel short handed. The older man needed him.

"But that's to be expected when we run away from God."

Jesse sat up. "I ran away from the farm. I

419

didn't run away from God."

Ernie smiled. "Really?"

Jesse thought for a moment. Had he left because the work was too hard or the sisters too many or because God hadn't responded the way he wanted Him to? He chewed his lip for a moment. "Well . . ."

Ernie clamped his hand on Jesse's shoulder. "One of the hardest parts of faith, to my way of thinking, is accepting that God knows what He's doing. We ask for things, we want our way, and when God does something else, we start thinking He doesn't care. But that's not the truth. He does care, Jesse. When He says no, He's being the parent who does what's best for the child."

Jesse raised one eyebrow.

He chuckled. "Do you think I give in to every whim Benji and Jenny set their minds to? Absolutely not. Does that mean I don't love them?" He squeezed Jesse's shoulder. Hard. "Absolutely not. And it's the same way with God. Only bigger, because He's so much wiser than I could ever be."

They sat in silence again, Ernie keeping a grip on Jesse's shoulder and Jesse staring across the room, his thoughts churning.

Ernie's hand dropped away. "Why'd you take off from church this morning?"

An embarrassed grin pulled on Jesse's

cheek. "I went to my office. Picked up the telephone. Was gonna call my folks. Tell them I'm sorry for leaving and not coming back." He snorted. "Pretty foolish. If they even have a phone, I don't know the number."

Ernie nodded, his gaze locked on Jesse's face. "You'll probably rest better when you've contacted them and made your apology, like the boy in the parable. In the meantime there's Someone else you need to talk to. No telephone required." He stood, the pew popping as his weight left it. "Talk to your Father, Jesse. 'But seek ye first the kingdom of God, and his righteousness; and all these things shall be added unto you.' Square things with Him. I think you'll be surprised what a difference it makes."

The minister strode up the aisle and out of the building.

Jesse sat for a moment with his elbows on his knees, his hands locked together, his head low. Then slowly, as if a gentle hand cupped his chin and lifted his face, he raised his gaze to the cross. A lump of longing tried to choke his airway. He groaned out, "God?"

CHAPTER 31

Neva

Neva kept both Bud and Charley home from school the week after Bud's rescue. Bud needed to rest his hip, which the doctor had popped back into place, and she feared Charley would break open his wounds. So she settled the boys in the parlor with books, puzzles, games, and the schoolwork Belle carried home each afternoon. She promised to check on them between customers, but she didn't check on them as often as she'd intended the first few days.

On Monday a steady stream of church folk, including the wife of each of the men who played a role in bringing Bud out of the well, came in with hugs and words of congratulations. Neva returned their hugs and tearfully thanked them for their prayers. With each visit she celebrated Bud's home-coming anew. She found such delight in the opportunity to praise God again and again for keeping her son safe.

Word of the rescue spread, and on Tuesday and Wednesday dozens of townspeople stopped by to tell Neva how glad they were about Bud's safe return. Most quizzed her for details about how Bud was saved, and Neva unrestrainedly shared how Charley volunteered to go after his brother. Her use of the word *brother* seemed to startle some, confuse others, and in several cases resulted in outright withdrawal. But Neva chose not to let the negative responses bother her.

Arthur stopped by at closing time Wednesday to see how the boys were healing. After spending a few minutes chatting with them, he took Neva aside and cautioned her about being too open. "Some folks aren't taking well to the truth, Neva."

"I appreciate your concern." His friendship and support meant more to her than she dared to admit. "But why should the children be forced to hide because of a shame that isn't theirs to bear?"

He argued with her — kindly but firmly — and she responded with equal firmness. Now that she'd chosen truth, no one would persuade her to turn back. Not even Arthur.

Thursday and Friday were slower, the tide

of congratulations finally ebbing and the flow of customers a mere trickle. Neva didn't mind. Less traffic meant more time to peek in on the boys. Each time she entered the apartment and found the pair with their heads close together, laughing over something silly in a book or puzzling over a school assignment, her heart swelled. Bud's resistance to Charley had melted away. Charley blossomed beneath Bud's attention. They were growing into a family in its sweetest sense, and she'd never been happier.

Saturday morning Bud begged to help in the mercantile. Recognizing his restlessness, Neva agreed. But he spent most of the morning perched on the apple barrel, watching passersby on the sidewalk while Neva dusted, reorganized the canned goods, and refilled the bean bins.

At noon Neva put out the lunch-break sign and instructed Bud to stay put. "I don't want you overdoing it on the stairs. I'll bring a sandwich down for you. Would you also like a piece of pumpkin bread? We still have half the loaf Belle baked yesterday."

"I'm not really hungry." Bud pushed off the barrel and limped to the counter. "Where are the customers?"

Neva smoothed his hair into place. She'd

given both boys haircuts earlier in the week. Bud looked so handsome. "Probably patronizing other merchants this morning. We aren't the only store in town, you know."

"Yes, but Saturdays are always busy. Except for today." Bud sent a scowling look toward the window. "How can we keep the place going if nobody comes in?"

"Oh, Bud." Neva laughed and gave him a quick hug. "It's just one quiet morning. Wait for the afternoon. I'm sure things will pick up."

But only two people entered the store the entire afternoon, and each purchased only a few items. When Neva totaled the sales for the week, she was startled to realize how little the mercantile had brought in. She'd mistakenly counted the flood of visitors earlier in the week as customers. How could she not have noticed the cash register went largely unused? But she carefully hid her concerns from Bud.

Sunday morning she took a loaf of bread from the mercantile shelves to make bread pudding for breakfast. The children considered it a treat. Only she knew it was a way to use up bread before it grew too stale to sell. After putting a pot of beans with a ham bone in the oven to slow cook, she and the children set out for church. They walked slowly. Neva didn't want to put too much pressure on Bud's hip.

Cars and wagons passed by on the streets, heading to places of worship. Neva smiled and waved at the drivers. Only one lifted a hand in reply. The others glanced in her direction, then looked ahead as if they hadn't seen her. Puzzled and a little hurt by what felt like deliberate snubs, Neva caught Adeline and Cassie by the hands and kept her gaze pinned on the church steeple.

They entered the chapel as the congregation was rising to sing the opening hymn. Neva ushered the children to their usual pew, where Mr. and Mrs. Buckwelder and their three youngest children spread out from the middle to the end opposite the middle aisle.

"Excuse me," Neva whispered as she eased into the pew.

Naomi Buckwelder glanced over, her mouth pursed so tightly it took on the appearance of a prune. She nudged her husband with her elbow. He fumbled the hymnal and frowned at his wife. Then his gaze bounced past her to Neva. A scowl knit his brow. He grabbed Martin by the arm and gave the boy a shove that forced him to collide with his brother and sister. Holly and Jim complained loudly enough to be heard over "Shall We Gather at the River?"

A few people cranked their heads around to gawk. The singing faltered.

With his face glowing nearly purple, Mr. Buckwelder crowded his family together at the other end of the pew, leaving nearly two-thirds open for Neva and the children. More than enough space. But Neva no longer wanted to sit there.

The singers began belting out the final verse. When the hymn ended, the minister would have the congregation sit. She didn't want to be standing in the aisle when everyone else was seated. The back pews were generally unoccupied, purposely left available for guests. With hand gestures and frowns, she turned the children toward the rear of the church.

Neither of the back pews was empty. On the right Jesse Caudel stood just inside the aisle. On the left Arthur and his sons stood toward the center of the pew. Without a moment's hesitation she urged the children in next to the Randalls.

The final line from the refrain rang out. " 'Gather with the saints at the river that flows by the throne of God.' " Hymnals clunked into trays on the backs of pews, and pews creaked as people settled in.

Neva lifted Adeline next to her as she

seated herself. Then she glanced across the row of heads — two blond, two russet, and one walnut-husk brown — at Arthur, who glanced back. He didn't smile as she'd expected him to. He looked worried. His expression chilled her, and she zipped her gaze forward.

Reverend Savage smiled at the congregation. "Wonderful singing this morning. And won't that be a glorious day when we, with all the saints who've gone before, gather beside the throne of God and worship Him throughout eternity?"

A few mutters rose in response, but no one offered a hearty *amen.*

The young minister's smile lost a bit of its shine, but he continued in a booming voice. "In less than three weeks, we will celebrate the Thanksgiving holiday with our families and friends. But why wait for a specific date on the calendar to express our thankfulness? Who would like to stand and share a reason for gratitude this morning?"

As quickly as a jack-in-the-box springing its trap, Belle stood.

Reverend Savage acknowledged her with a nod.

She licked her lips and sent a nervous glance across the gathered worshipers. "I'm grateful my brother is here in church with me today."

Someone a few pews ahead muttered, "Which brother? I hear she's got more than one." Someone else shushed the mutterer.

Belle laced her fingers together and hunched her shoulders. "Um, I was scared when Bud was gone. I was afraid he'd never come back, like Poppa. But Momma told me to pray, and I did, and he's here now. So I'm grateful." She sat.

Neva couldn't reach her with four children between them, but to her relief Arthur reached past Leon to give Belle's shoulder a little pat. She smiled shyly in reply.

"Thank you, Belle. I, too, am very grateful your brother is home." Reverend Savage held out his hands in invitation, scanning the room. "I'm sure Belle isn't the only one with a thankful heart today. Who else would like to share?"

A man near the front stood.

"Yes, Mr. Muck, for what are you thankful?"

"Actually, Preacher, I had a question. For Mrs. Shilling." Alfred Muck turned sideways. His narrowed gaze settled on Neva. "Back a month ago the preacher here told us your husband had died and he'd taken on carin' for three youngsters."

Reverend Savage stepped off the dais.

"Mr. Muck, I don't think —"

"But just last Tuesday" — Mr. Muck raised his voice — "when my missus went to the mercantile, the way Preacher Savage said we should, to congratulate you on your boy's safe return, you told her your boy's brother helped with the rescue."

Belle and Bud wore matching expressions of panic. Charley crouched low in the seat, and Adeline and Cassie gazed at Neva with wide, uncertain eyes. Neva pulled Adeline into her lap. Curling an arm around the little girl, she stretched her other arm across the back of the pew to gather Charley and Cassie close. Bud and Belle scooted in, too.

"That's right." On the opposite side of the church, Claude Garber jolted to his feet. He folded his arms over his chest. "I found that peculiar myself. There's only two ways I know for youngsters to be related. Being born to a set of parents or being adopted by them. I've never heard tell of any husband who'd adopt kids without his wife knowing about it. But I can sure name a few who've gone and —"

Reverend Savage slapped his hand down on the closest pew. Both men jerked their heads in his direction. "Mr. Muck, Mr. Garber, I want both of you to sit down and hold your tongues. Kindly remember this is a

430

house of God."

Mr. Muck plopped into his seat, but Mr. Garber remained standing and glared at the minister. "You're right, Preacher. This is a house of God. Folks who come through those doors shouldn't be carrying lies in with them. Isn't there some verse in the Bible that says the truth'll set a person free?"

Reverend Savage sighed. "Mr. Garber, you're missing the meaning of that Scripture. It references the truth of who Jesus is, God's Son. It isn't intended to be used as a battering ram to pummel confessions out of people."

"I still say lies don't have any place in here."

Several people murmured assent at the man's adamant statement.

Neva tried to put Adeline down so she could rise, but the little girl grabbed her around the neck and wouldn't let go. Cradling the child, she struggled to stand, and someone — someone strong — gripped her elbow and lifted her. She looked beyond Adeline's head full of soft blond curls to Jesse Caudel, who offered a slight nod in response to her weak smile of gratitude.

With Adeline's soft hair tickling her cheek, Neva moved up the aisle to Reverend Savage. "Mr. Muck and Mr. Garber have asked

431

me to tell the truth. So may I?"

The minister hesitated, his expression uncertain, but then he nodded and remained next to her, as if forming a united front.

Neva let her gaze rove slowly across the faces of the people with whom she had worshiped for the past fifteen years. Many averted their eyes. Others glowered at her, condemnation sizzling in their expressions. Both reactions stung. She took a deep breath.

"More than fourteen years ago, after the birth of my twins, Dr. Zielke told me I would never be a mother again. The news devastated me. You see, I was an orphan. I never had a family. So having my own family and raising several children was my dream. And then it was taken away. Until a month ago."

Mr. Caudel still stood in the aisle at the back of the church. He looked directly at her, approval glowing in his eyes.

Neva fixed her attention on him. "When Sheriff Caudel brought Charley, Cassie, and Adeline to me, I was so hurt. So humiliated. I considered sending them to an orphanage. But I couldn't bear the thought of them growing up without a family the way I had. So I decided to keep them. But in my embarrassment — in my shame — I kept secret about how they came to be with me."

Her arms were beginning to ache from the weight of the child she held, but inside she felt lighter and lighter as she confessed her wrong-doing. She shifted Adeline slightly, placed a quick kiss on the little girl's warm cheek, and went on. "But I'm not ashamed anymore. At least, not for the reason you might think. I'm ashamed of my cowardice, for purposely withholding the truth and in so doing forcing all five of Warren's children to live a lie."

She turned to Mr. Garber, who'd finally sat down but hadn't lost his stern pose. "You wanted the truth, Mr. Garber. Here it is. I'm grateful for Charley, Cassie, and Adeline because they are the fulfillment of a dream I thought was lost to me forever. They might not have come to me in a way I would choose, but they're here. I . . . I love them." She swung her gaze to the children. She smiled at each of them by turn. "All of them. They bring me joy."

Her knees began to quake. She stiffened her spine and the quaking stopped. She lifted her chin in triumph. "Raising them on my own won't be easy, but with God's strength I will do my best." She moved up the aisle, the heels of her pumps *clip-clipping* as loud as nails being pounded into a length of wood in the quiet room, and slipped back into the pew next to her children.

Reverend Savage stood for a moment with his hand curled over the back of the front pew, his expression thoughtful. Then he stepped behind the pulpit and began his sermon. Sheriff Caudel returned to his seat, but throughout the remainder of the service, Neva sensed his gaze aimed at her.

When the congregation rose for the closing hymn, Neva quirked her finger at the children. She'd been skewered by a half-dozen stony glowers as she'd returned to her seat, and she wouldn't allow the young ones to suffer the same treatment. She led them out the doors and down the porch stairs, moving as quickly as Bud's leg would allow.

When they were halfway across the churchyard, the pounding of footsteps sounded behind them. The sheriff darted into their pathway. "Mrs. Shilling, it's cold out here, and it's a lengthy walk for Bud. I noticed he's still limping. Let me give you a ride home. I brought my truck."

Neva sighed. "Mr. Caudel, I appreciate the offer, but there are six of us — seven including you — and your truck only has one seat."

"That's true, but I happen to know Charley and Cassie can fit behind the seat."

Neva ducked her head so he wouldn't see her smile.

"If Adeline sits on your lap, it'll be tight, but I think the rest of us can squeeze in."

Neva looked at Bud. He held his mouth in a thin line. His hip was likely paining him. She nodded. "All right. I would like a ride. Thank you, Sheriff."

"This way." He scooped up Adeline, then placed his hand in the center of Neva's back and guided her over the lawn. "And, Mrs. Shilling, when we get to your place, if you don't mind, I'd like to have a word with you."

Chapter 32

Arthur

Leon leaned forward and tapped Arthur on the shoulder. "Dad?"

Arthur grunted. "I'm driving, Leon."

"I know, but —"

"Don't bother me when I'm driving." From the corner of his eye, Arthur caught Leroy shooting a knowing look at his brother. He scowled toward the passenger seat where Leroy slouched in the corner. "What was that for?"

"Nothin'."

"Sit up and speak clearly."

Leroy straightened his spine and folded his hands in his lap. "Nothing, Father."

Leon snickered.

Arthur blew out a noisy breath. "I thought the two of you would enjoy a drive to Beloit, but if you're going to act like a couple of ninnies, we might as well turn around and go home."

"Aw, Dad." Leon draped his arms over the seat. "Don't turn around. I'm looking forward to eating lunch at a real restaurant."

"Then sit back and be quiet."

To Arthur's relief, both boys gazed out the window at the brown landscape and kept their mouths closed. Arthur knew he was being unnecessarily snappish. He would apologize. Later. When he'd had a chance to bring his irritation under control. The long drive should do it. If the drive didn't, a plate of pan-fried chicken with potatoes and gravy and buttered peas would help. At the very least, it wouldn't hurt.

He gave the steering wheel a light smack, shaking his head. What had Neva been thinking to stand up in front of all those people in church and announce she planned to raise her husband's ill-begotten children? Nobody would shop at her mercantile now. They wouldn't give their money to a woman who'd been so thoroughly scorned. She'd set herself up for disaster. And in church, no less. He snorted.

Leroy angled his gaze at Arthur. "Dad?"

"Didn't I ask you to be quiet?"

"Yeah."

"Then why can't you do it?"

"Because I'm pretty sure I know why you're so upset."

Arthur twisted his lips into a sneer. "Oh, you do, huh?"

"Uh-huh. It's because of Mrs. Shilling."

Leon bounced forward and slung his arms over the seat again. "That's what I was going to say."

Arthur slowed, downshifting when the car lurched in complaint. He pulled over and set the parking brake. The vehicle bounced in place, the engine occasionally coughing. He turned a frown on his busybody sons. But when he glimpsed the concern on their faces, his aggravation died.

He feigned innocence. "Why should I be upset about Mrs. Shilling?"

"Because she left with Sheriff Caudel," Leon said.

Leroy rolled his eyes. "That's not why. It's because she's keeping all those kids. Dad's gone sweet on her, but what does he want with a bunch of kids at his age? Jeepers, he's thirty-nine already."

Arthur spluttered, "Thirty-nine isn't exactly ancient, young man."

Leroy didn't seem to hear his father's outburst. "If it was only Bud and Belle, so what? They'll be grown and on their own about the same time we will be. But those littler ones'll be around for a long time." He shook his head, releasing a low whistle. "I don't blame you, Dad. I wouldn't want to be stuck with all of them either."

Arthur lowered his head and pressed his knuckles to his forehead, battling the urge to laugh. "Boys, you're both wrong." He raised his gaze. "And I'm sorry I got grouchy with you. I'm . . . worried about something. And I need to think it through. It would help if you would let me think in peace. Will you do that, please?"

They both nodded. Leroy said, "Sure, Dad. Go ahead and think."

Leon held up his hand like a witness in a courtroom. "We won't say a word. Not until we get to Beloit."

Arthur checked behind him — not a soul on the road today — and pulled out. The car bucked. He didn't drive often enough to shift smoothly. But once he hit second gear, the car stopped bouncing.

With the boys quiet again, he set his attention on the road and let his thoughts drift inward. Was he upset with Neva, or was he upset with himself? Not so long ago he would have celebrated her loss of revenue. No money coming in would force her to close the mercantile. To sell it. And he would have snatched it up in the space of one heartbeat. But now the thought of her being forced out — because of people's

439

ridiculous judgments — stirred an anger beyond any he'd experienced before.

When those men stood and challenged her this morning, he'd wanted to jump up and berate them. Even leap over the pews, grab them by their coat lapels, and smack their heads together the way he used to do to Leon and Leroy when they misbehaved. But he'd kept himself in his seat like a coward. Because if he defended Neva, the condemnation pouring down on her would spill over on him, and his business would suffer, too. He couldn't lose his income. Not even for the woman on whom, as Leroy had so aptly put it, he'd gone sweet.

"She deserves better." He growled the statement through his clenched teeth.

Leroy shot a quick look at him but didn't say anything.

Arthur bit down on the end of his tongue to keep any other words from escaping. He finished the drive in silence. And the succulent fried chicken, creamy gravy, and plump buttered peas served by a uniformed waiter in the Beaumont Hotel's dining room did him no good at all.

Beans with ham and a pan of cornbread might be considered a simple dinner, but no one seated at Neva's table complained. The sheriff, who accepted her invitation to eat with her family, ate three bowls of the flavorful beans, topping each with a crumbled chunk of moist cornbread. One bowl proved sufficient for everyone else, so they sat and visited while Mr. Caudel finished eating.

He spooned up his final bite, swallowed, then pushed the bowl aside with a satisfied sigh. "Thank you, Mrs. Shilling. That was real good."

"You don't want any more?" Belle asked.

He shook his head, patting his stomach. "Nope. I've had enough."

Belle reached for the tureen in the middle of the table. "Good. I hoped there'd be some left for the share-kettle."

Neva's face flamed, but the sheriff burst out laughing. She couldn't help but smile at his amusement. "Please excuse Belle's lack of tact. She worries about the homeless men."

He winked at the girl. "She's got a good heart. Like her momma. Nothing wrong with that."

Belle grinned, her cheeks blooming. "Cassie, bring the leftover cornbread." She scurried through the kitchen doorway.

Cassie picked up the half-empty cornbread platter and followed.

Adeline squealed, "Wait fo' me, Sissy!" She scampered after Cassie.

Mr. Caudel watched them go, a fond smile lighting his eyes.

Bud braced his palms on the table. "Ma, can I be excused?"

"May I . . ." Neva prompted.

He rolled his eyes, then grinned. "May I be excused, please?"

"Yes, you may."

"C'mon, Charley." With Charley close on Bud's heels, the two boys headed for the hallway.

The sheriff stacked his arms on the edge of the table. "When I asked if I could talk to you, I didn't intend to eat half your pot of beans. But I'm grateful you asked. That's the best Sunday dinner I've had since last week at the Savages' house."

The girls paraded through, Belle in the lead, carrying their oldest kettle, Cassie next, holding a wax paper–wrapped bundle of cornbread, and little Adeline bouncing along at the rear, her arms wrapped around the stack of battered tin bowls.

"Remember the spoons!"

"They're in my apron pocket, Momma," Belle called over her shoulder. She led the younger girls around the corner to the hallway, and soon the clatter of their feet on the stairs drifted to the dining room, followed by the slam of the back door.

Mr. Caudel jolted at the bang.

Neva grimaced. "That was Adeline. She never closes a door without slamming it."

He shook his head. "It's as busy as a three-ringed circus over here."

She laughed. "Five children provide even more entertainment than a three-ringed circus. You should see the commotion at bedtime."

A face-splitting grin creased his weathered cheeks. Then he pulled in a breath, cleared his throat, and assumed a serious expression. "I'm glad the kids are all out of the room. I wanted to talk to you alone."

Neva cupped her palms around her cool coffee mug. "Oh?"

"See, last week after I had lunch with the Savages, I talked to the preacher. About my folks. Then I talked to God." He bowed his head for a moment, chuckling. "I have to admit, I wasn't sure I wanted to talk to Him. Most of my prayers, well, I kind of felt like God ignored them."

Neva smiled gently, confused by his confession yet honored that he trusted her enough to share his thoughts with her. "I suppose we all feel that way from time to time."

He sighed. "Yeah, you're probably right." He looked at her again. "But Ernie — that is, Reverend Savage — told me not to give up on praying. He said praying isn't just for us to get things but for us to get closer to God. So this whole week I've been praying about something, and I didn't really expect an answer, but I prayed anyway. And this morning in church, when you went up front and said what you did, I got my answer."

She pressed her hand to her bodice. "What I said?"

He nodded. "Mrs. Shilling, I'm an orphan, too. A couple in Severlyn, Nebraska, chose me from a group of orphans who traveled on the train from New York, and they adopted me. They were real good to me. Raised me in the church, always treated me right, but somehow I never settled in. Never felt like theirs. Not deep in my heart. Do you know what I mean?"

Although she'd been raised by a loving couple, the orphans' asylum had never felt like home. "I think I do."

He nodded, the gesture rapid, almost eager. "I thought you would. Well, I left the

Caudels' farm when I was eighteen. That's seventeen years ago now. And I've never once gone back or written to my folks, or . . . or anything." Regret pursed his face. "They were nothing but kind to me, but I convinced myself they only wanted me for a hired hand. I wasn't really theirs. They couldn't love me the way they loved their daughters. The way I prayed they'd love me. Even after talking to the preacher and talking to God, I still had this doubt in the back of my mind that Pa and Ma really loved me like a son."

His forehead scrunched into a series of furrows, and he chewed the corner of his lip for a moment. "So this whole last week, every day I prayed God would show me somehow that I'd been wrong about them. That they could have wanted me for more than free farm labor."

Wonder broke across his features. "When you told everybody you loved the children born to your husband by another woman, it was as though God tapped me on the shoulder and said, 'See? A woman can love a child not of her womb. You are loved, Jesse. You are loved. By your ma and by Me.' "

Tears winked in his eyes, and Neva battled them herself. She bowed her head, humbled that God had used her difficult circumstance to bring healing to Mr. Caudel's fractured soul. She whispered, "Thank You, dear Father."

"Amen."

His heartfelt expression brought her head up.

He was gazing at her in admiration. "How did you do it, Mrs. Shilling? How did you open yourself to loving those kids?"

A Scripture her foster parents had encouraged her to memorize years ago formed easily in her mind and spilled from her lips. " 'He giveth power to the faint; and to them that have no might he increaseth strength.' "

"That's from the Bible?"

She nodded. "Isaiah chapter 40, verse 29. I couldn't love Warren and Violet's children on my own power. Without God's help I would be mired in my anger at Warren. I'd be allowing my anger at him to spill onto his children. But God has increased the strength of my heart. He let the seed of forgiveness take root and bloom, and with its blossom grew a love for Charley, Cassie, and Adeline. So you can cancel your plans to take them to an orphanage after Christmas." A grin teased the corner of her mouth. "I won't let them go."

"I think I've heard that before."

They both laughed. When the trickle of laughter faded, he rose. "Don't worry, Mrs. Shilling. That's one trip I'll gladly cancel." A thoughtful, faraway look crept into his eyes. "But I might be taking a different trip soon. I guess we'll wait and see if God answers that prayer, too." Then he gave a little jolt. "There's something else I need to talk to you about, something important, but I wanted to wait until Bud was better and you'd had a chance to, well, catch your breath."

Neva doubted she'd catch a breath until all five children were grown. "Go ahead."

He reached into his pocket and pulled out a folded sheet of paper. With slow movements he unfolded it and laid it flat on the table. "I'm not sure how much you know about law enforcement, but officials are able to communicate with each other pretty easily thanks to the telegraph. When there's a crime in one county — say a murder or a bank robbery or a burglary — the notice goes out through the wires. When the crimes are solved, the notice goes out, too, and sheriffs keep track of the closed and open cases."

The serious expression on his face, the waver in his tone, sent spiders of apprehension skittering up and down Neva's spine.

She wanted to tell him to stop talking. She wanted to get up and leave the room. But her muscles turned too stiff to move. Her tongue felt stuck to the roof of her mouth. She could only sit and listen as he went on in the same uneasy voice.

"Sheriff Abling in Beloit put together a list of thefts that have gone unsolved over the past sixteen years in Kansas. I wanted you to see the items." He slid the paper across the table to her.

With a trembling hand Neva turned the page and scanned the list. Rich & Baker furniture items. Mink coats. Radios and harpsichords and phonographs. Little boys' suits and little girls' dresses. Pearl necklaces and earbobs. Full sets of French Haviland china. A half dozen gemstone rings. A 1932 set of *Encyclopaedia Britannica.* Even Frigidaire iceboxes.

Her heart pounded so hard she feared it would leave her chest. The words on the page seemed to burn her retinas, but she didn't dare look up, or she'd see the encyclopedias on the shelves in the parlor, the china behind the intricately carved leaded-glass doors of the Rich & Baker cabinet. Nausea attacked. She clapped her hand over her mouth.

"Mrs. Shilling, are you all right?"

Of course she wasn't all right. She'd only just begun to accept that her husband was unfaithful. Now she feared he was a thief. A thief who had brought home his ill-gotten loot and bestowed it on her.

She sent a horrified look to the sheriff. "If I am in possession of some of these things, will I be arrested?"

He rose and eased around the table. He slowly seated himself next to her and touched the paper. "Is it possible you could be in possession of some of these things?"

She flung her hand toward the cabinet behind her, then pointed mutely to the harpsichord and the bookshelves. "That list is nearly an inventory of my belongings." She shook her head slowly, understanding dawning. "When I learned about Violet and the store in Beloit, I couldn't comprehend how Warren maintained two businesses, two households. I couldn't understand how he afforded to buy both of his w-wives such nice things. I know he had debt in Beloit, but none here, so I . . . Now . . ." She lowered her head and buried her face in her hands. "Oh, I'm such a fool."

Mr. Caudel folded the paper and put it back in his chest pocket. "Mrs. Shilling, you have no reason to feel foolish."

She gawked at him.

"If your husband was responsible for some of these thefts, he hid his dealings well. So well, trained law officers never suspected him. Two communities of people viewed him as an honest man and a good neighbor. None of those people knew. How could you have known?"

She'd lived with him. Worked side by side with him. Borne his children. "I should have known. I should have known."

He gazed at her for long seconds. Then he sighed. "I'm afraid I'll need to examine anything in your possession that resembles an item on this list. If we discover they are stolen goods, then —"

"Take them." She sat up straight and hugged herself, suddenly cold. "I don't want them if they were taken without pay."

He pulled in a breath as if gathering courage. He folded his hands on the table and lowered his gaze to his linked fingers. "There's something that's not on the list. In 1921 there was a robbery at a bank in Grand Rapids, Nebraska, by a single armed man. Almost twelve thousand dollars was taken. It's never been recovered."

Chills rolled over her, raising goose flesh from head to toe. Nineteen twenty-one . . . her golden year. The year she married Warren. The year they purchased this building with the earnings he claimed he'd saved over five years in the fur trade. But there was no fur trade. No earnings. Only a man who'd stolen other people's savings and used it to buy the building that gave Neva her security. Where was her security now?

CHAPTER 33

Arthur

Arthur rose Monday morning with a steely determination spurring him to action. As he dressed for work, he organized the thoughts that had kept him awake most of the night. He wouldn't let her do it. She'd dedicated her entire adult life to building the mercantile into a business that would support her family. He couldn't allow her to throw it away for three children spawned by a cheating cad of a husband. As painful as the parting would be for her — and for him, because he'd grown fond of the three little Shilling children, too — it had to be done.

He dressed in his best gray suit and pastel silk paisley tie — all soft, soothing colors he hoped would help lessen the verbal blows he had to deliver. With his stomach in knots and his heart aching, he headed for the kitchen. Halfway down the enclosed staircase, an unusual sound met him. It came from the kitchen. He paused, frowning, his head cocked to better identify the noise. Someone was . . . humming. His body gave an involuntary jolt, and he stared at the opening at the base of the stairs, uncertain whether he should proceed and intrude upon his housekeeper's cheerful tune.

The savory aroma of bacon drifted to him, enticing him to continue onward. He set his feet with force, giving the woman fair warning of his approach in case she wanted to bring an end to the tune. To his further surprise, she continued humming even when he stepped fully into the room. And she smiled at him. A quick flash of a smile, but it held welcome.

Arthur staggered to the little table, ready with three place settings, in the center of the warm room and plopped into his chair.

Mrs. Lafferty, still humming, retrieved a bowl of eggs from the refrigerator. She glanced at him over her shoulder, and her humming abruptly stopped. "Coffee's ready." Then she began singing softly, " 'Bringin' in the sheaves, bringin' in the sheaves, we shall come rejoyyyycin' . . .' "

Shaking his head, Arthur pushed away from the table, lifted his coffee mug, and crossed to the stove. As he poured the rich brew, feet thundered on the stairs. The boys burst into the room.

Mrs. Lafferty's song ended midline. She aimed a frown at the pair. "I thought for sure a herd of water buffalo were stampeding the kitchen. Slow down before you vibrate the plates off the shelves."

Both boys gawked at her with their mouths hanging open.

"And close your mouths, you goofy pair. You'll draw flies."

They snapped their mouths closed.

Arthur quickly took a sip from his mug to drown the laugh rising in his throat. He held his hand toward the table. "Get out from under Mrs. Lafferty's feet, boys."

They tiptoed to the table and sat, their wary gazes following the housekeeper's movements.

As she broke eggs into the sizzling skillet, she started humming again.

Arthur held his coffee cup beneath his chin and braved a comment. "You're in a good mood this morning, Mrs. Lafferty."

She stilled for a moment, then flicked a glance over her shoulder. "Some reason I shouldn't be?"

"You scolded us." Leon blasted the comment.

Leroy socked him on the arm, and he yelped.

Mrs. Lafferty shook her finger at the pair. "No horsin' around at the table."

"Yes, ma'am," they chorused, then turned their disbelieving faces toward Arthur.

He cleared his throat. "No. I can't think of any. It's just that you seem . . . especially cheerful."

She flipped the eggs with a spatula. A sizzle rose, and when it calmed, she spoke. "It's Monday."

Arthur frowned. "Yes?"

She transferred the eggs to a plate. "Monday comes after Saturday an' Sunday."

He still didn't understand.

She smacked plates of bacon, eggs, and biscuits on the table and released a little snort. "Mr. Randall, I don't see my girl on the weekend. It's Monday!"

Adeline. His desire for breakfast fled, chased away by the sweet memory of his time alone with Adeline and Cassie a week ago. Having grown up with one brother and raising two sons, he'd never been around little girls. At first he'd been stiff, uncertain. As had they. But then Adeline tugged at his pant leg and asked his name.

Remembering their title for Neva, he said, "Uncle Arthur." The little girl looked up at him with wide, innocent blue eyes and said, *"Klunka Auffer, I firsty."* She'd melted his heart with four words, three of which were badly pronounced.

The child had wormed her way into his affections, and she'd transformed Mrs. Lafferty. If he convinced Neva to send the children away, the older woman would be crushed. She was only his housekeeper, not a relative or even a friend. But he didn't want to see her revert to the silent, shuffling, never-smiling person she'd been before Adeline came along.

Arthur rose so quickly he bumped the table. The milk in the boys' glasses sloshed over the rims. He grimaced. "My apologies."

Mrs. Lafferty bustled over with a damp rag. "Accidents happen to everyone, Mr. Randall. I'm sure you'll be more careful next time." She probably used the same singsong, cheery voice when Adeline spilled her drink.

Arthur swallowed the bitter taste flooding his mouth. "No breakfast for me today. I have an errand to run."

His housekeeper squinted one eye at him. "I cooked up a pound of bacon, baked a dozen biscuits, and fried nine eggs. That's too much food to waste. Besides that, no man ought to start a day of work without a good breakfast. Sit back down, Mr. Randall."

Too startled to do otherwise, Arthur sat. His boys snickered. Mrs. Lafferty returned to the stove and gathered the dirty pots and pans. Although he had no appetite left at all, he'd eat. And then he'd run his errand.

He closed his eyes. It would hurt, but in time they'd all forget that two little blue-eyed girls and a sturdy little boy had been part of their lives.

Bud

After a full week away, Bud felt like a stranger when he stepped onto the school's play yard. Some kids stood in little groups, talking. Others darted around in wild games. It all looked the same as it had before, but something seemed different. Bud wasn't sure what to do.

"See you in class, Bud." Belle trotted over to a group of girls her age.

Cassie waved at the boys. "Bye, Charley. Bye, Bud." She ran to join a game of jump rope.

Bud glanced at Charley, who stood beside him with both sets of their schoolbooks stacked in his arms. "Lemme have those books now. You can go play some before the bell rings."

Charley shrugged. "Nah. I'll stay with you."

Bud grinned. Who would've thought he'd come to enjoy having a shadow? "Okay." They ambled across the yard in the direction of the school. The walk had brought out the ache in Bud's hip again, but he tried not to limp so nobody would call him a gimp. Kids were always eager to tease.

Martin pounded toward them. He held a battered football under his arm, and three of the boys from Bud's class chased after him. Bud kept going, expecting Martin to change course, but Martin didn't.

With a gasp Bud jerked backward, throwing out his arm to protect Charley. His elbow slammed into Charley's shoulder, and the stack of books went flying. Martin and the other boys trampled them as they ran by.

Heat exploded through Bud's middle. "Hey! Be careful, would ya?"

The throng skidded to a stop and whirled around. Seth pointed to his chest. "You talking to us?"

Bud balled his hands into fists. "Yeah. Look what you did." Charley had bent down and was gathering the books. A few pages stuck out at odd angles. Bud snatched up one of the books and held it toward the boys. "You're gonna have to pay for this if Miss Neff says it's ruined."

They sauntered over, Joey leading the pack. He took the book from Bud and pretended to study it. Then he shrugged and jammed it back at him. "Seems fine to me."

Bud huffed. "It's not fine, Joey. Some of the pages are torn."

Joey bent close, squinting and looking at the book again. Then he straightened. "Sorry. I don't see anything. Just like I didn't see you a minute ago. Or him." He jerked his head at Charley. The others sniggered.

Charley started to stand. With his arms full he had trouble getting his balance.

Seth took a step toward him. "Here. Lemme help you, kid." He brought his hand down on the stack, knocking the books to the ground again.

"Seth!" Bud punched the boy on the arm.

Seth spun on him, rubbing his arm. "What was that for? I was only trying to help."

Bud gawked at Seth. "Help? How'd that help?"

"The books were too heavy for him. He couldn't get up." Seth smirked. "He can get up now."

Joey, George, and Martin laughed.

Charley sat on his haunches with books all around him. He stared up at Bud, his eyes begging. Bud held out his hand to him. Before Charley took hold, George Garber leaped between them.

"Here, lemme get him up." He grabbed Charley's arm and jerked with such force Charley's feet left the ground. George let go, and Charley fell flat on the ground. The boys laughed so hard they doubled over, some of them slapping their knees.

"What's going on over here?" The sheriff's stern voice ended the laughter.

George backed up, holding his hands in the air. "We wasn't doing anything. Just playing."

"Is that right?" Sheriff Caudel helped Charley stand and brushed the dried grass from his knees. He frowned at George and the others. "It didn't look to me like Charley was enjoying the game."

"It wasn't a game." Bud pointed at his friends. Although right then he didn't want to claim them as friends. "Martin ran into us on purpose, knocked our books all over the place, even tore some of the pages. Then George knocked Charley down."

George's mouth dropped open. "How can you say that? I helped him up. He just tripped." He snickered. "He's kind of a clumsy kid." The others smirked and ducked their heads.

Sheriff Caudel put his hand on Charley's shoulder and sent a frown across the circle of boys. "Charley's a lot smaller than all of you. From now on, you leave him out of your . . . games. Is that clear?"

"Yes, sir," they mumbled.

The bell rang and the group shot off. Bud wished his hip worked right so he could chase them down, trip them, make them go facedown in the dirt the way they'd done to Charley.

Sheriff Caudel gathered up the books. He handed the early primers to Charley, but he held on to Bud's more advanced books. He walked with them to the porch, then handed Bud's books to him. "There you go."

Bud hugged the stack against his churning stomach. "Thanks."

The sheriff opened the door. "You boys have a good day now."

"Yes, sir." Charley scuffed up the hallway toward his classroom.

Bud remained rooted on the porch. He angled a glare at the sheriff. "Those boys weren't playing. They were out-and-out mean to Charley. They meant to hurt him."

"I know."

"Well, then, why didn't you do something?"

Sheriff Caudel folded his arms over his chest and tilted his head slightly. "I did. I told them to leave Charley alone."

Bud pinched his lips into a snide grimace. "That's nothin'."

"What would you have me do, Bud?"

He couldn't think of anything, which only made him madder.

The man leaned down slightly, putting him eye to eye with Bud. "I can't stay here all day and make sure bullies don't bother Charley. But you're here. You're his big brother. Will you look out for him?"

Bud stared into the sheriff's eyes for long seconds. The tardy bell blared. Bud jerked. "I gotta go. I'm late." Bud climbed the stairs to the second-level classrooms, slowed by his aching hip and the heavy books in his hands.

Sheriff Caudel called after him. "Charley was there for you when you needed him. I hope you'll be there for Charley when he needs you."

Bud didn't answer. He entered the classroom in the middle of roll call. Kids muttered to each other and pointed at him.

Miss Neff glanced up with a frown, but then she spotted Bud. She smiled and came

462

around her desk, her hand extended. "Bud, it's so good to have you back with us. Have you recovered from your dreadful experience?"

Even though his hip still bothered him a little bit, Bud nodded. "Yes, ma'am. And I finished most of the assignments that Belle brought home for me."

"Teacher's pet," someone whispered, and several people snickered.

Miss Neff shot a stern look at the class. "Children." The single word silenced them. She gave Bud's shoulder a pat. "You take your seat now. At recess time we'll review your assignments and get you caught up on anything you're lacking."

"Thank you, ma'am."

Miss Neff hurried back to her desk and returned to the roll call. "Fannie Latham."

"Here."

Bud eased his way between the rows to the double desk he shared with Belle. He sat and put his books away. Someone poked him on the back. He looked behind him. Martin Buckwelder was leaning into the aisle, bobbing a folded square of paper in his hand.

"Bud Shilling."

Bud yanked his gaze forward. "What?"

Titters erupted.

Miss Neff frowned.

Belle nudged him and whispered, "Say 'here.' "

Heat flooded Bud's face. "Here."

More titters.

Miss Neff snatched up her wide ruler and brought it down hard on the desk. The class went silent. The teacher used the ruler as a pointer and bounced it at the students. "I've had enough of your nonsense this morning." She dropped the length of wood into her desk drawer and closed it with a sharp snap. "I know we're all excited to have Bud with us again, but this is not a holiday. Every one of you needs to turn his or her attention to learning." She paused, searing each of them with her smoldering glare. "Now, let's rise for the Pledge of Allegiance. Wilber, will you kindly lead us?"

Wilber darted to the front of the room, and the students stood and lifted their right hands in a salute. Wilber began in a flat voice, "I pledge allegiance . . ."

When they finished, Miss Neff instructed them to take their seats and bring out their arithmetic books. Bud sat, and something poked him on the backside. He reached beneath him and found the paper Martin had tried to hand him.

Holding it flat against his lap so Miss Neff

wouldn't see, Bud unfolded it. A drawing of two stick men filled the center of the page, with "His Buddy" written above the taller one and a word Ma never allowed him to say scrawled above the other.

Bud crumpled the paper into a wad and jerked around to glare at Martin. Martin grinned and waggled his fingers at him. Joey and George covered their mouths, but Bud could tell they were laughing even without any sound coming out.

Bud faced forward again. His ears rang, and his face was so hot he wondered if people saw smoke rising from his hair. Why were his friends treating him this way? He hadn't done anything to them. And neither had Charley.

Sheriff Caudel's words sneaked through Bud's mind. *"You're his big brother. Will you look out for him?"* Bud fingered the wadded-up paper. If he stood up for Charley, would the boys call him that ugly name, too?

CHAPTER 34

Neva

Neva gave the front-door window shade a light tug and let it roll up. She gasped. A large man-shaped shadow lurked just outside the door.

He tapped his knuckles on the glass. "Mrs. Shilling, may I come in?"

Her knees went weak as relief flooded her. She unlocked the door and yanked it open. "Gracious, Mr. Caudel, you gave me a start. With the sun behind you, you were unrecognizable. I'm glad I'm not a cat. Otherwise I would have lost one of my nine lives."

He removed his hat as he stepped inside. "I'm sorry. I didn't mean to frighten you."

She managed a smile even though her pulse still raced. "Please don't apologize. I've been especially jumpy since our break-in." She pressed one palm to her heart and took a deep breath. She headed behind the counter to unlock the cash register. "Do you have information about . . ."

He followed her and popped open the jellybean jar. He fished out a half-dozen black beans and tossed the first one into his mouth. "Not yet. It might be a few days until Sheriff Abling gathers the appropriate information and responds."

She might go mad before she knew whether or not this mercantile was really hers. But what else could she do but go on as if nothing were wrong? She didn't want to worry the children.

"In the meantime I stopped by to see if there was anything I could do for you."

Could he bring Warren back to life? Insist he make restitution for the wrongs he'd perpetrated? She gave the key a sharp twist, and the drawer popped open with a tinny *ding.* "Such as?"

"Do you need me to drive to Beloit and pick up goods from the depot? With Thanksgiving coming I thought you might need to place a special order."

Last year she'd put a basket of sweet potatoes on the window ledge, bowls of unshelled pecans, walnuts, and hazelnuts next to the canned fruit, and a pyramid of orange pumpkins beside the door. By Thanksgiving Day not one potato, nut, or pumpkin remained. But thanks to the thief helping himself to her cashbox and now the lack of sales, she didn't have the funds to purchase treats for her customers.

Neva pushed the drawer shut and sighed. "In years past I have offered specialty items at the holidays. But . . ."

The sheriff put another jellybean in his mouth and bounced the last one in his cupped palm. "But not this year?"

"That's right. Not this year."

For long seconds he gazed at her with his eyes slightly narrowed, and she waited for him to question her reasons. When he spoke, he surprised her again. "Mrs. Shilling, I think it might be time for you to make a visit to school to talk to Charley's teacher."

"Why is that?"

"This morning at the school's play yard I broke up a skirmish between several older boys and Charley."

Neva drew back. "Charley was skirmishing?"

"No. He was a victim of the skirmish."

"Was he hurt?"

Mr. Caudel offered a weak shrug. "Not physically, I don't think. As for his feelings, they were pretty well battered." He pinched the jellybean between his fingers and rolled it back and forth, his brow furrowed. "I'd told him to talk to you about the way several of the pupils were treating him a while back."

"Yes. He mentioned it." She hung her head. She hadn't paid nearly enough attention.

"At that time Bud seemed to instigate a lot of the mistreatment." The tips of his fingers were turning black. He stuck the candy in his mouth and wiped his hand on his trouser leg. "But today Bud wasn't participating. He was downright indignant."

Neva rounded the counter and gaped at the sheriff. "Bud defended Charley?"

"He demanded I do something. But I think it'll take more than me telling those boys to leave Charley be. They've got it out for him. I think the teachers will have to get involved, or Charley may spend the entire year being the butt of jokes and the target of —"

The mercantile door opened, and Arthur strode in, bringing the heady scent of bay rum with him. The aroma was even sweeter when contrasted with the strong licorice on the sheriff's breath. "Neva, I —" He came to a stop, his startled gaze landing on the sheriff. "Oh. Excuse me. I didn't realize you had a customer."

"The sheriff came in to talk to me about

469

Charley."

"Is that so?" Arthur tucked his thumbs into his vest pockets.

"I've pretty much said all I intended to. Mrs. Shilling, you do what you think is best." Mr. Caudel dug in his trouser pocket and retrieved two pennies. He laid the coins on the counter. "Thanks for the jellybeans. I'll be in touch about —" He glanced at Arthur. "I'll be in touch." He ambled out, bobbing his head in farewell to Arthur as he went.

Arthur crossed to Neva in three wide strides. "You look upset. Is something wrong?"

She took her work apron from its peg, slipped it over her head, and tied the strings. "The sheriff said some boys were rough on Charley this morning in the play yard. He suggested I talk to Miss Franklin and ask her to intervene."

Arthur shook his head, pursing his lips into a scowl. "I was afraid something like this would happen since you made those children's origin so public."

Was he blaming her for the boys' behavior? "Charley got off to a rough start at school from the very beginning. Sometimes that happens. Children choose a . . . a . . ." She searched for the word Sheriff Caudel had used. "Target. Like chickens creating their pecking order. Charley's been pecked at for weeks already."

"That hardly seems like a favorable situation for him."

Neva broke out in chills. She moved to the mercantile windows and began raising the blinds to allow in the morning sun. Hopefully the wide-open windows would also invite in customers. She needed some sales.

Arthur trailed behind her. "I believe my concern about how people would react to the discovery of Warren's, er, indiscretion has been proved accurate."

What would everyone say if the sheriff's and her suppositions about Warren's other activities proved true? She shot a warning look at him. "I'm not changing my mind about being honest with the town about the children."

He chuckled. "Well, after your little speech in church yesterday, it wouldn't do much good to change your mind now. You can't take back the things you said."

"Nor do I want to."

"And by now your confession has probably been repeated and embellished dozens of times."

"I can't stop people from talking." Impatience sharpened her tone.

He held up his hands in surrender. "All right, I can see I'm stirring your ire, but I wouldn't be your friend if I let the topic lie."

She shot him a sharp look. Had he deliberately used the word *lie* to bait her? No hint of teasing or sarcasm showed in his expression. She willed her emotions to calm. Warren had misled her, disappointed her, betrayed her, but she wasn't talking with Warren right now.

She sighed and reached for the final shade. "I'd rather not discuss it."

His hand snaked out and caught her wrist as she raised the shade into place. "But we must. Please listen to me."

Moments ago she'd hoped for customers. Now, with the two of them standing in front of an uncovered window with her wrist trapped in his grasp, she hoped no one passed by.

"The people here have very strong convictions. You received a taste of their disapproval in church yesterday."

Neva extracted her wrist and hurried to the back of the store, away from the windows.

He followed. "You're an adult. You are capable of ignoring the slanderous comments or turning a blind eye to the reproachful stares. But what of the children? Is it fair to subject young children to such treatment?"

She spun to face him. "I am not subjecting them to anything except acceptance and affection."

He raised his eyebrows. "Aren't you? Neva, you set them up for rejection and condemnation by your very openness. Those children will always carry the stench of illegitimacy in this town. In a large community perhaps they could find a contingency of people who would be unaware and accept them. But Buffalo Creek is not a large community. Everyone knows everything."

She shifted her gaze to the side, grinding her teeth so tightly her jaw ached.

"The children will grow up without the pleasure of friends. When they get older, no family will want Charley to court their daughters or their sons to court Cassie or Adeline. The children will be forever lonely. Forever shunned, treated like lepers or pariahs." He gently chafed her upper arms with his open hands. He spoke kindly, as sweet as the essence of the bay rum, but even so his words flayed her. "And because of your involvement with them, you and your twins will be outcasts as well. Is that what you want?"

She crossed her arms over her apron bib and stepped away from his touch. "Of course it isn't what I want." Her heart ached, envisioning the existence he'd painted with his predictions. "But neither can I change it."

"Yes, you can." Arthur advanced toward her again. He took hold of her chin and turned her face to him. "You have the ability to save the children from an unhappy childhood. You can save yourself from becoming penniless and disregarded." His hand slipped from her chin and cupped her cheek. His fingertips eased into the hair at her temple, sending shivers across her scalp. "Send them away, Neva. If you send them away, your misery — and theirs — will come to an end."

Arthur

She jerked away from him so abruptly his hand remained suspended in the air between them, still tingling from its contact with her soft skin. She pointed to the door. "Go."

He closed his eyes and groaned. "Neva, please . . ."

"Go, Arthur."

He held his hands to her and beseeched her with his expression. "I only want —"

"You want me to abandon innocent children to save my mercantile."

Stated that way it did seem petty. How could something that made so much sense during the night seem ignoble and selfish under the glaring light of the overhead bulb? Arthur paused for a moment, organizing his thoughts, and tried again. "This isn't just a mercantile. It's your livelihood. It's Bud and Belle's only home."

He came close to laughing at himself. How quickly he'd changed his mind about this place and all because he'd come to know the woman. He admired her for wanting to care for the children — she possessed an amazingly giving heart — but she had to be realistic. "You've had this business for how many years now? Fifteen? Sixteen? Almost half of your life."

Her lips quivered. Her hand, still upraised and pointing to the door, trembled.

He gentled his voice to a soothing whisper. "Years, Neva. Years of toil and sweat and growing. You've known the children for what . . . mere weeks? Barely more than a month." But, oh, what a month of hearts expanding and affections growing.

He forced the inward reflection aside and

assumed a firm tone for her sake and for his. "Which carries the greater value? The years or the weeks?" He held out his hands, palms up like the trays in a balance scale, and raised one palm while lowering the other.

She stared at his hands. Her arm dropped to her side, and her entire frame wilted. She bowed her head, and one silvery tear rolled across her cheek and dripped onto her apron.

Her obvious despair pierced Arthur more deeply than he thought possible. He reached for her.

She shied away and hugged herself, almost seeming to shrink before his eyes. "No. Please . . . just go."

He'd wanted her to be reasonable, but he hadn't wanted to so thoroughly defeat her. Heaviness weighted his chest. He drew in a ragged breath. "I'm sorry, Neva."

"I am, too."

"For what?"

Her head still low, she peeked at him from the corner of her eyes. Her eyelashes were spiky and moist from tears, her hazel pupils almost luminescent. "For disappointing you."

He gazed at her in silence, perplexed by her anguished utterance.

"You've become a good friend, Arthur. I appreciate all you've done to help me since Warren's death. If we were to put the deeds of giving on a scale, your side would plunge downward compared to the paltry things I've done for you in return."

She had no idea what she'd done for him, awakening him to love again, inspiring him to look beyond his own needs to someone else's. He started to tell her so, but she went on.

"But I can't look at years and weeks. I have to look at souls and sales. What would God have me view as the most valued?" She imitated the gesture he'd made earlier, raising one hand as high as her chin and lowering the other to midthigh. "Souls, Arthur." She balled the hand beside her leg into a tight fist, lifted it, and pressed it to her heart. "Souls matter most. Even if it means I lose my mercantile — my home — I choose to love those children."

He bowed his head and forced his tight, aching throat to release a rasping confession. "I only meant to help, Neva."

Twin tears slipped past the curve of her smile. "I know. I appreciate that you care about the children and . . . and me."

He did care. How deeply he cared. But he'd failed in saving her. He'd failed her.

477

He'd failed himself. "What will you do if no one ever shops here again?"

Her gaze drifted to the side, as if some unseen being held her attention. "I will be strong. 'He giveth power to the faint . . .' "

Arthur shook his head, more confused than before.

She lifted her apron skirt and cleaned the tears from her face. Smoothing the skirt back into place over her pale-pink dress, she moved briskly past him and stepped behind the counter. "If you'll please excuse me, Arthur, I have work to do." She offered a wobbly grin. "Perhaps some signs in the window advertising specials on canned goods and broadcloth will entice a few people to set aside their prejudices and take advantage of saving a few pennies."

CHAPTER 35

Bud

Bud spent the noon break in the classroom with Miss Neff. He ate his sandwich and apple at his desk while completing a grammar assignment. But what did he care about when to use *then* as opposed to *than* when Joey and the other stupid boys might be bothering Charley on the play yard? His gaze drifted to the window. Was Sheriff Caudel out there keeping watch?

"Bud, turn your attention to your work, please."

He sighed. "Yes, ma'am." He aimed his pencil's point at the paper, but he didn't write. He couldn't focus. The voices of kids at play sneaked past the brick walls and tormented Bud. He sighed again and looked up. "Miss Neff?"

"Yes?"

"I need the outhouse."

"All right. Go ahead."

He bounded up and hurried toward the door.

"Come right back when you're finished. We need to get you all caught up on your work."

Bud paused long enough to nod. "Yes, ma'am." Then he clattered down the stairs, taking them two at a time. It jarred his hip, but he didn't care. He smacked the door with his palms, sending it flying, and he gave a leap off the porch. At the bottom he stopped and, shielding his eyes with his hand, scanned the play yard.

"Bud!" His sister's call pulled his attention to a slash of shade next to the building. Belle sat on the withered grass with Cassie and Charley.

Bud's knees went wobbly. He crossed to them and crouched down. He looked at Charley. "Hey. You okay?"

Belle made a face. "I had him come sit with me. Martin, George, and a couple of others tried to steal his lunch. Then I had to go get Cassie because Joey's sister pulled her hair and made her cry."

Bud turned to Cassie. One pigtail hung lower than the other. Her nose and eyes were still red. A strange feeling of protectiveness filled him. He chucked her under the chin. "Aw, you're tough, Cassie. Don't let some dumb ol' girl upset you, okay?"

The little girl gave him a sad smile. "Okay."

Belle threw her half-eaten apple in the lunch tin and slapped the lid closed. "What is wrong with everybody today? They're all being a bunch of . . . of nincompoops."

Bud shouldn't laugh but he couldn't help it. Belle was plenty upset to use that kind of language.

"They're always mean to me." Charley's quiet voice brought an end to Bud's laughter. The boy hung his head, his shoulders drooping. "They don't like me. I wish I knew why."

Bud knew why. He'd started it by shoving Charley away. Martin, Joey, and all the others were only following his lead. Only now he didn't want to act that way, but his buddies had gotten used to picking on Charley. Bud pushed upright, wincing when his hip stabbed.

He touched the top of Charley's short-cropped brown hair and waited until he looked at him. "Don't you worry. I'll take care of it." Bud grinned, purposely setting his lips crooked the way Pop used to do. "That's what big brothers are for."

The afternoon dragged, and Bud's anger built with each tick of the wall clock. The morning's encounter had lit a spark of indignation. Then little Cassie's forlorn face, Belle's confusion, and Charley's sad words at noon turned the spark into a flame. His buddies' snide smirks, the note Martin gave him, the kids' sniggers and whispers and pointing fingers — it all added fuel to the fire of fury.

When school let out at three, Bud shoved his books at Belle. "Take these and go on home without me."

She drew back, worry wrinkling her face. "What're you gonna do?"

"Settle things." Bud marched to Martin's desk, grabbed him by the arm, and growled, "Get Joey, George, and Seth, and meet me behind the outhouse." He stomped off before Martin had a chance to say anything.

He ducked behind the boys' outhouse. Many a fight had taken place on this patch of grass concealed from the school's windows. Bud had watched dozens of them, but he'd never participated. His whole body broke out in a cold sweat. He hoped he wouldn't have to fight today. But he would if the boys didn't listen to him.

Martin swaggered around the corner with at least a dozen boys clustered around him. Why had he brought so many? More chills attacked him, and his stomach threatened to give back his lunch.

The boys formed an uneven half circle, trapping Bud between them and the outhouse wall. Bud shifted so his back was to the wall. Nobody would sneak up behind him.

Martin walked straight to Bud and stopped inches in front of him. He set his feet wide and jammed his fists on the drooping waist of his baggy overalls. "All right. We're here. Now what?"

Martin was three inches taller and at least twenty pounds heavier, but Bud stood stock-still and refused to cower. "I'll tell you what. Now you listen. Charley's not gonna be your scapegoat anymore. You're gonna leave him alone."

"Or what?"

Bud didn't miss the challenge in Martin's voice. Part of him wanted to run away and hide. But he rose up as tall as he could make himself. "Or I'll make you."

Guffaws broke out from the crowd.

Joey left the circle and moved beside Martin. "Why should we? We don't want his kind in our school. Right?" He turned and looked at the other boys. A chorus of agreement rang out. Joey grinned at Bud. "See that? None of us want him. My dad said back in the old days when somebody came to town that nobody liked, they ran 'em out on a rail."

Seth hollered, "Then there's always tar and feathering, like we read in our history books. Betcha that'd make him leave."

Bud gawked at his friends. Belle's question came out of his mouth. "What is wrong with everybody?" He pushed Martin and Joey aside so he could talk to the whole bunch. "He's just a little boy. He can't hurt any of you."

Martin crossed his arms and sneered. "Seems to me not so long ago you were pickin' at him, too. What happened, Bud? Did falling down that well make you go soft . . . in the head?" Laughter rolled.

Heat exploded in Bud's face. "Maybe falling in the well did make me see Charley different than I had before. Maybe I figured out I was wrong to be mean to him. Maybe I —"

"Maybe you're what he is." Martin leaned close, his eyes sparking. "A —"

Bud wouldn't let him say the word printed on the paper. He brought back his fist and plowed it as hard as he could into Martin's face. Martin grunted and stumbled backward.

Everyone stood in shock, including Bud. Had he really just punched his best pal in the nose?

Martin wiped his nose with the back of his hand. It came away smeared with blood. Rage gleamed on his face. He pointed at Bud and hollered, "Get 'im!"

Jesse

Jesse sat on the edge of the merry-go-round's plank seat and observed the children leaving school. He chuckled. They ran out with a lot more eagerness than they exhibited trooping in. He returned waves, poked little boys in the tummies, and gave little girls' braids gentle tugs, earning smiles and giggles. A lot of the older kids sauntered up, too, to say hello. Funny how much he'd come to enjoy this school-day routine.

Shouts rose from somewhere behind him, and Jesse gave the ground a push with his heel, sending the merry-go-round into a slow spin. His gaze drifted across the play yard, and his senses went alert when he spotted two boys racing for the outhouse. Somehow he wasn't surprised when they ran behind it instead of going in.

He pushed off the seat and broke into a trot. The shouts and scuffling noises grew louder as he advanced, and before he rounded the corner, he already knew what he'd find. He collared the two closest boys participating in a wild melee and bellowed, "That's enough! Break it up!"

The kids who'd gathered to watch the fight scattered, leaving Jesse with a half-dozen boys tangled up on the ground. Bud Shilling lay at the bottom of the heap.

Jesse released the two he'd grabbed and reached for Bud. The others rolled out of the way, belligerence mottling their faces. He barked, "Don't any of you go anywhere," and they formed a little huddle on the trampled grass next to the outhouse wall.

Jesse set Bud on his feet and looked him up and down. His tattered shirttail drooped over his torn trousers. The boy's lip was puffy and bleeding. More blood dripped from his nose, and one eye was almost swollen shut. Jesse shook his head. "Lands, Bud, what happened here?"

Bud swung his arm to indicate the group lined up along the outhouse wall. "They jumped me!"

The Buckwelder boy charged forward. "He started it! Socked me right in the nose!" He pointed to his swollen snoot. "Probably broke it."

Jesse examined Martin's nose. Crusted blood rimmed one nostril, but it didn't look crooked. "You're all right." The boy skulked off. Jesse turned to Bud again. "Why'd you sock Martin?"

Bud quivered from head to toe. He clamped his jaw tight and turned aside.

Jesse shook his arm. "Come on, speak up. You must've had a reason. I can't imagine you'd take a poke at one of your friends without provocation."

Bud jerked his arm free. "I had a reason all right. He called Charley a . . . a . . ." He gulped, then quirked his finger. Jesse leaned down, and Bud whispered in his ear.

Jesse reared back. "That so?"

He squinted through his one good eye and nodded. "Tried to call me one, too. I wasn't gonna let him."

Martin bounded over again. "I didn't call nobody nothin'! He told me to meet him out here and then he punched me. Just punched me without prov . . . provo . . ." He spat out, "Provocation! Isn't that right, guys?" Most of the other boys voiced their agreement, and Martin aimed a triumphant grin at Jesse.

"You're a lowdown dirty liar." Bud started to jump at Martin.

Jesse caught him and pulled him back. "Here now, I said *that's enough.*" He put his hand on Bud's shoulder and held him in place. He sent his stern frown across the row of boys. "Did any of you hear Martin call Charley or Bud a vulgar name?"

"Huh-uh."

"Not me."

"I didn't hear nothin'."

Bud's muscles went tight beneath Jesse's hand. "They're all lyin'! Look here. I can show you." He dug in his pocket and pulled out a crumpled ball of paper. He shoved it at Jesse.

Jesse carefully unwadded the sheet.

"See what that says?" Bud nearly danced in place, fury pulsating from his slight frame. "Martin gave it to me in the classroom today. That's why I told him to meet me out here — to tell him he better quit pestering Charley. He brought a whole bunch of others with him —"

Martin pounded his palm with his fist. "You said to bring 'em!"

"— and said he wouldn't leave Charley alone, and then Joey said something about running Charley out of town on a rail. That's when Martin started to say I was . . . was that, too."

Jesse held the paper toward Martin. "This is what we call evidence, Martin, and it's pretty convicting. You go home. I'll be by later to talk to your pa."

Martin stomped off, muttering.

Jesse turned to the other boys. He shook

his head. "You all oughta be ashamed of yourselves, ganging up on one person that way. You could've done some real damage."

One boy separated himself from the others. Jesse recognized him — the younger of the Randall boys. "Sheriff, I wasn't fighting against Bud. I was trying to help him."

Bud fingered his swollen mouth. "That's true. Leon pulled Martin off me. Got a pretty good clop on the chin for doing it."

Jesse lifted the boy's face. A large purple knot was forming along his jaw. "All right, you go on home and put a cold rag on your face. Let your pa know what happened. If he has questions, he can find me."

"Yes, sir." Leon shuffled off, cradling his cheek with his hand.

Jesse balled his hands and rested them on his hips, glowering at the boys who stood in a sullen line. "You can tell your folks to count on a visit from me, too. Go on now. And behave yourselves."

Mumbling and flinging stormy glares over their shoulders, they trudged away.

Jesse blew out a breath and settled his gaze on Bud. "All right. As for you —"

Bud broke into sobs. He dove at Jesse and buried his face against Jesse's front. His hands grabbed handfuls of Jesse's shirt, and he clung, his entire body shaking. "Ain't right, Mr. Caudel. Ain't right what Martin said. 'Cause if Charley's a . . . one of them . . . that means it's true about my pop. It's not true. Is it?"

Jesse took Bud by the shoulders and pulled him loose. What a sorry mess he was with hair standing on end, blood and mucus smeared across his cheek, and one eye swollen completely shut and turning every color of the rainbow. His lip had puffed up until it looked like he had a wad of chewing tobacco jammed in his mouth. He also looked painfully, miserably, dejectedly young. Jesse sighed.

"C'mon, Bud. Let's get you home and cleaned up." He led the boy through the alley to the back door of the mercantile, then followed him inside.

Bud moved slowly up the hallway toward the store. "Ma?"

Mrs. Shilling whirled around the corner. "There you are! I was wondering when —" She stopped, her entire body jolting. Her eyes flew wide, and then she rushed at her son. "Bud! What happened to you? You look as if you were hit by a train."

Bud sagged against his mother, tears tracing a path through the dried blood and dirt on his face.

Jesse answered. "There was a fight after

school. Bud was a little outnumbered, so he got the worst of it." He curled his hand over Bud's shoulder. "I don't approve of fighting — I don't think it's a good solution to a problem — but he was standing up for right. And for that reason, I'm proud of him."

Mrs. Shilling gently ushered Bud to the stairs. "Go up and soak in the bathtub. Throw your clothes in the rag basket. They'll need lots of repair before you can wear them again."

Bud stood with one foot on the bottom riser. "Don't you need my help in the mercantile?"

Jesse stifled a laugh. The way the boy looked, he'd frighten away customers.

"I'm fine. You go." She remained at the base of the stairs, her concerned gaze following him until the bathroom door closed. Then she turned to Jesse. "Was the fight about Charley?"

Without a word Jesse handed her the rumpled sheet of paper Bud had given him.

Her face went white. "Oh, my . . ."

Jesse took it back. "I'm gonna need this. I intend to show it to Martin's father and tell him to have a talk with his boy about using inappropriate language."

Mrs. Shilling sighed. "You might discover

Martin learned the term from his father. They were quite obvious about their feelings in church Sunday morning."

He'd forgotten the Buckwelders were the family scrambling to separate themselves from the Shillings in the church pew. "Then I'll have a talk with Mr. Buckwelder about teaching his son inappropriate language."

She smiled. A weak smile, but a smile. It assured him.

He folded the paper and slipped it into his shirt pocket. "Before I brought Bud home, he asked me a question I didn't know how to answer. He knows the meaning of the name Martin called Charley. And he knows what that says about his father."

She cringed. "Oh."

The spatter of water running against a porcelain tub sounded overhead. Jesse wished hot water could wash away heartache as easily as it did dirt and blood. "He's one hurt, mixed-up boy."

"I'll take care of it."

"How?" He touched his bloodstained shirt where Bud had burrowed against him and sobbed. "There's no good way to tell a boy such things about the father he loves."

"I'll find a way."

She spoke with more strength than Jesse knew a woman could possess. No matter

492

what he found out from Abling, he suspected she'd survive. "All right then. I've got some visits to make. I'll leave you to your customers."

A sad sigh whisked from her lips.

"Unless you still need me for . . ." He didn't know what would help, but if she'd tell him something, he'd do it.

"Mr. Caudel, I haven't had but one customer all day." The strength departed, leaving a deep disappointment in its stead. "She bought a spool of thread, slapped her dime on the counter, and left without saying a word to me."

Jesse growled under his breath. "It's one thing for school kids to act like idiots, name-calling and striking out. But grownups should know better."

"They should, but . . ."

How could he encourage her? "People will settle down in time, forget."

"Maybe." She looked as defeated as Bud had.

He couldn't resist giving her shoulder a soft pat, the way he'd do to Bud or one of the other youngsters. "Give it some time."

She offered another weak smile. "I'll give it until I know whether this store is mine, legally paid for or not."

"And if it isn't?"

She pulled in a slow breath, appearing to gather courage. "Then I'll give it to the bank in Nebraska . . . and move."

He raised his eyebrows. "Move? Away?"

She tipped her head, fixing him with a weary-yet-determined look. "Arthur Randall bade me to consider the wisdom of letting Charley, Cassie, and Adeline remain in Buffalo Creek. Even if Warren did purchase this property legally, the folks in the community will still look askance at the children. I can't change my husband's indiscretions. The children will forever live beneath a cloud of condemnation. Arthur was right. It would be cruel to subject them to a lifetime of unhappiness."

Apparently she and Randall had a more personal relationship than he'd realized if she took his advice so seriously. "Where would you go?"

She smiled. "I read an article in a newspaper several months ago about California. Where it's always warm." Her smile quavered. "And where no one has ever heard of Warren Shilling."

CHAPTER 36

Neva

Neva leaned over and deposited a kiss on Cassie's warm cheek. "Good night, Cassie. Sleep well."

Cassie rubbed her eyes with her fist and yawned. "Night, Aunt Neva."

Neva tucked the cover beneath the little girl's chin and straightened. Pale lamplight flowed across the trundle next to Cassie's bed. Adeline's big eyes implored Neva to give her a kiss, too. Neva knelt beside the trundle and smoothed the child's hair from her eyes.

A lump grew in the back of her throat. How could she send this precious little girl away? No building — not even the one that had been her only real home — carried more importance than the well-being of this tender little soul.

She kissed Adeline, breathing in her sweet scent, and offered the same good-night wish she'd given Cassie. Adeline smiled, slipped her fingers into her mouth, and rolled over.

Neva extinguished the lamp and moved across the dark room to Belle's bed. She sat on the edge and picked up Belle's hand, which lay limply on top of her quilt. "Do you think you can sleep now?"

Belle had been more distraught about Bud's injuries than Neva. She sometimes thought what one twin suffered, the other automatically experienced as well. Belle had no external bruises, but her daughter's spirit had been sorely battered.

"Will you pray with me?" Belle still sounded hurt.

Neva closed her eyes and prayed aloud, asking God to kiss Belle's dreams with all things pleasant and awaken her in the morning with the reminder of His unwavering presence. Then she gave her daughter a hug and a kiss and tiptoed from the room.

Bud and Charley's door stood ajar, and she slipped through the opening. She went to Charley's bed first. He was asleep already, a book under one arm and a tin truck under the other. She gently extracted both items and laid them on the little table beside his bed next to the framed photo of Warren and Violet, which she'd retrieved from its hiding spot after the service on Sunday. She kissed the little boy's flushed cheek. He stirred but didn't wake.

Her chest pinched as she gazed at the image of her husband with Charley's mother, but she wouldn't hide it again.

She turned toward the other side of the room. Light from the hallway sconces painted a narrow path to Bud's bed. He half sat, half lay, supported by his pillows. Against the white pillowcase, his bruises looked even darker and more painful. Neva cringed as she eased onto the edge of his bed, careful not to jostle him.

"Not sleepy yet?" She whispered so she wouldn't bother Charley. "Dr. Zielke said the analgesic he gave you for pain might make you drowsy."

He shook his head.

"Is the pain easing?"

"On my outsides."

Her heart aching, Neva finger-combed his wavy russet hair back from his forehead. "I wish I had an analgesic for the hurt you feel on the inside." She'd take a dose of it, too.

"Do I hafta go to school tomorrow?"

"Yes, you do. Your injuries aren't severe enough for you to miss more school." She continued running her hand through his hair, as much for her comfort as his.

"But Martin and the guys —"

"Sheriff Caudel said he would visit each of their families. There won't be any more fighting." *Oh, please God, no more fighting or tormenting or mistreatment . . .*

"Ma, please, can't I stay here? I don't wanna go."

How could she make him understand hiding wasn't the answer? A memory flitted through her mind. She gave his hair one more sweep, then laid her hand in her lap. "Do you remember when you were little and someone gave us a jar of blackberry jam? You wanted some right away, but I told you we'd have it for our lunch. When I wasn't looking, you took the jar and went to your room and ate every last spoonful of the jam. Do you remember?"

He made a face. "Yeah. Gave me a bad stomachache."

She smiled. "Eating a pint of jam will do that. Do you remember what you did when you'd finished the jam?"

His tongue poked out at the corner of his mouth the way it always did when he was thinking. "I hid under the bed."

"Why?" She held her breath, hoping.

" 'Cause I'd done wrong. Didn't want you to know."

She released the air in a whoosh. "That's right. When folks do wrong, the first thing they want to do is hide." She placed her palm on Bud's chest, directly over his heart. "We haven't done anything wrong. Not me or you or Belle or Charley or Cassie or Adeline. We have no reason to hide."

He gazed at her in silence for several minutes, his uninjured eye blinking rapidly. Finally he sighed. "All right, Ma. I'll go."

"Good boy."

"But, Ma?"

"Yes, Bud?"

"Pop did wrong. Didn't he?"

She'd been praying since Sheriff Caudel showed her the ugly word written on the paper. She had an answer, and she could only hope it would help rather than heap more hurt on her son. "Yes, Bud, he did. It isn't legal for a man to take two wives at the same time. He was already married to me, so his union with Violet wasn't honored by God."

"So he sinned. He sinned really bad." A tear slid down his cheek. He covered his eyes with his forearm.

"Yes. But you know what, Bud? We all sin — we all do things we shouldn't. Every sin is 'really bad' because it disappoints God."

Bud lowered his arm. "Whaddaya mean?"

"What your father did was wrong, because the Bible says adultery is wrong. What I did

— not accepting Charley, Cassie, and Adeline — was wrong, because the Bible tells us to love the way Jesus loved, without reservation. What Martin did was wrong, because the Bible says to treat other people the way we want to be treated." She slipped her hand to his shoulder. "When God looks at sin, what He sees is the harm it brings. People want to define some sins as big and others as little, but the truth is, Bud, every sin is equally bad in God's eyes."

"So when Martin says bad things about Pop, he's just as wrong as Pop was?"

Neva nodded.

Bud lay still, gazing at her with one unblinking eye, for several quiet seconds. Then he sighed. "Wish there wasn't any sin at all. Wish everybody'd just do right and get along."

She gave his shoulder a gentle squeeze. "Instead of wishing, we can ask God to help us do the right things. And we can pray for those who are doing wrong to make better choices."

"So if the kids bother Charley some more, I'm s'posed to pray for them instead of fighting with them?"

She smiled. "It might save you another black eye."

He grinned, then winced.

500

Neva leaned in and brushed a light kiss on his temple. "Enough talking now. You get some sleep, hmm?"

"Okay." He eased downward and rolled to his side with the bruised side of his face away from the pillow.

Neva couldn't resist giving him one more kiss, this time in the tender spot on his neck below his ear where she used to nuzzle him when he was still a toddler. She smoothed his hair again, then tiptoed across the floor. She reached the door, and he whispered, "Ma?" She turned back.

"Today when all the guys jumped me, Leon Randall fought on my side."

"I know, Son. You told me earlier."

"I know, but . . . do you think maybe it means Leon wants to be my friend?" He sighed. "It'd be easier to go to school if I still had at least one friend. Besides Charley, I mean."

Neva's heart rolled over. "Sweetheart, sleep now. We'll talk more in the morning."

"All right. Night, Ma."

Neva closed the door and moved quietly up the hallway to the parlor. She sat in her rocking chair and pulled one of Charley's socks and her darning supplies from the basket beside her chair. As she put the needles to work repairing the dime-sized hole, Bud's sleepy comment, *"at least one friend,"* played through her mind.

Her hands stilled. What an unlikely ally Bud had discovered. Leroy and Leon had a reputation for creating havoc. People in town excused their misbehavior, shaking their heads in sympathy for the motherless boys. Why couldn't they extend the same sympathy to Charley, Cassie, and Adeline, who'd lost both mother and father? *Lord, I wish I could understand.*

She set her attention on the sock again. *"At least one friend."* A tiny spark of hope flickered to life. If Leon was willing to defend Bud after years of teasing him, then maybe Sheriff Caudel was right about the townsfolk eventually accepting the children. Maybe, if she ended up being able to keep the business she and Warren had built, she'd have the chance to raise all of Warren's children in the apartment that was her home.

She closed her eyes and lapsed into prayer. *God, I love this place, but I love the children more. Whatever is best for them is what I want to do. I told Bud we have no reason to hide. If I take the children away from here, I'll be hiding just the way he did under the bed. I don't want the children to be shuffled away in shame. So, my dear Father, work Your will. If we're to stay, change the hearts of the towns-people. If we're to go, guide me to Your chosen place for us. But please act swiftly so my children needn't suffer.*

Please act swiftly . . .

Neva repeated the prayer with such regularity it became a mantra. She prayed it after she talked with Charley and Cassie's teacher, who promised to keep an eye on the children and intervene if she witnessed maltreatment. The simple utterance left her heart when worries about how Warren had accumulated his money or questions about what she and the children would do in the future crept in. She offered the prayer with fervency at the close of each day when she counted the amount in her cash register and found it lacking. With every pause between tasks, sometimes with every heartbeat, the prayer rose from the depths of her soul. But nothing changed.

Customers failed to pour through the mercantile door. No one except Arthur Randall and his sons offered to share a church pew at Sunday morning service. She appreciated his kindness, but she sat else-where to keep the feelings for him that had sprung up in her heart from growing. A recent widow, one with so many uncertainties hanging over her, shouldn't encourage a man no matter how hard it was to shake her head in refusal.

Each afternoon when Neva asked Cassie with whom she played that day, she always answered, "Charley." Likewise, Charley said he played with Cassie. No one tormented them, but no one included them either. Bud and Belle received similar treatment, ignored by children they'd known their whole lives, which made the shunning even more painful for them.

"The kids look right past me, Momma, as if I wasn't even there," Belle reported with tears swimming in her eyes. Bud didn't shed tears. He wore a scowl as openly as Sheriff Caudel wore licorice stains on his fingertips. Even with no signs of the community softening, Neva continued to pray. *Please act swiftly.*

By the week of Thanksgiving, Bud's bruises had faded to yellowish smudges and all swelling had subsided. Unfortunately the wounds on his spirit hadn't faded, and Neva began to fear he would bear permanent scars on his insides.

Monday morning of Thanksgiving week, as Neva served oatmeal with dried apricots and a bit of honey, she approached the subject that had niggled in her mind since

Arthur Randall's last visit to the store. "Children, have you studied anything about the state of California?"

Charley and Cassie shook their heads, but Belle nodded. "We read about the gold rush of 1849. People rode in wagons across the United States with signs that said 'California or Bust' on the side. The people who left their homes to pan for gold were nicknamed the forty-niners." She tilted her head, curiosity lighting her face. "Why are you asking about California?"

Neva feigned nonchalance, pausing to take a sip of her coffee before answering. "Oh, I read an article about California a while back — about how people from Oklahoma and Arkansas were moving there for a better life than what the plains can offer."

Charley looked up. "Do we live in the plains, Aunt Neva?"

"Yes, we do." She took another sip, purposefully shivering. "This hot coffee tastes good this morning. There's such a bite in the air. The article I read said California is warm all the time. Is that what your teacher told you, Belle and Bud?"

The twins looked at each other and then at Neva, their faces wearing matching expressions of puzzlement. Bud put his spoon down. "Ma, are you thinking about going to California?"

Please act swiftly. "Would you think I was foolish if I said yes?"

The children, with the exception of Adeline, who was too interested in pinching chunks of apricot from her oatmeal to be disturbed, erupted with questions, all speaking at once.

Neva laughingly covered her ears with her hands. "Please, settle down!"

Their clamor stopped, but they sat as alert as a row of prairie dogs watching for hawks. Charley and Cassie wriggled with contained excitement. Belle's eyes danced. Even Bud replaced his glower with an expression of interest.

Knowing the children were excited rather than fretful relieved her mind, but at the same time it saddened her. They could leave their home so easily? She sighed. "It's time for school now."

"Aw, Ma . . ."

"But, Aunt Neva!"

"Momma."

She held up her hand to silence the outbursts. "Thanksgiving break is only two days away. We'll have time then to talk more. For now, concentrate on your studies."

Grumbling a bit, the older four left the table and headed to their rooms.

Adeline used her fingers to scoop out another bit of apricot and jam it into her mouth. Neva chortled. The child had more oatmeal smeared across her face than in her bowl. She tapped the end of the little girl's nose. "Adeline, you're a mess."

She hunched her shoulders and giggled.

"Would you like to stay here with Aunt Neva today?" With no customers to fill the day, why send Adeline elsewhere?

"Uh-huh. I stay Tant Neba."

Neva smiled. "Good. We'll have fun, yes?"

"Fun." Adeline grinned her adorable nose-crinkling grin.

Neva rested her chin in her hand and watched Adeline finish eating. Maybe at noon, when she put out the lunch sign, she'd bundle them both up against the chilly air and walk to the newspaper office. The editor, Marsh Bobart, also listed properties for sale and handled the legal paperwork. If she intended to sell the mercantile, she'd need Marsh's help.

CHAPTER 37

Arthur

"California?" The word exploded from Arthur.

Leon drew back. "Don't holler at me. I didn't tell 'em to move there."

His appetite gone, Arthur dropped his fork next to his plate. When he'd returned from work to Mrs. Lafferty's grumbles about missing Adeline, he thought the day couldn't get worse. But thinking about Neva packing up and moving so far away was much worse than listening to his housekeeper's bitter complaints.

Leroy stabbed a forkful of string beans. "What's in California?"

Leon shrugged. "Bud didn't say. Just said he and his ma were gonna talk about it more at Thanksgiving, decide if they wanna go."

Arthur leaned in. "If?"

Leon nodded. "Yeah. They haven't quite made up their minds yet. But I think Bud would go. He's fed up with the kids at school. And I don't blame him. Ever since I dove into that fight to defend him, the boys in our class have picked at me, too." He ducked his head, a sheepish look creeping over his features. "Not much fun being picked at. Kinda makes me not wanna pick at somebody else."

Leroy stared at his brother with his eyebrows high.

Arthur understood Leroy's surprise. His sons, bigger than most of the other children and with more energy than a dozen boys combined, had never hesitated at claiming status as leaders of the play yard. Even though worry still rolled in the back of his mind over the Shillings, Arthur experienced a rush of pride at his son's proclamation. Maybe the boy was growing up.

He clapped Leon on the shoulder. "The golden rule, Leon. That's what your mother practiced and wanted for you boys. I probably didn't enforce it as much as I should have" — he grimaced, realizing he hadn't enforced it at all — "but I'm glad you've stumbled upon it on your own." His throat went tight. "Your mother would be pleased."

Leon blushed red. "Aw, Dad . . ."

Leroy reached for another roll from the basket in the middle of the table. "If the

509

Shillings move, you could buy the mercantile. You've wanted it for a long time."

"Yes . . ." Arthur slumped back in his chair. "Yes, I have." He couldn't imagine anyone else in town buying it. Who had money these days? If he didn't buy it, it would sit empty. Go to rot. Ruin the appearance of the whole block, which would affect his business.

"Seems like a good opportunity for you." Leroy grinned and jammed the roll into his mouth.

A good opportunity, yes. But if he bought the building, he'd be single-handedly funding their move. He'd be helping the Shillings but devastating himself in the process. He groaned.

"Dad?" Both boys stared at him, their food forgotten.

He forced a smile and rose. "Go ahead and eat. I believe Mrs. Lafferty left a ginger cake on the counter for dessert. Help yourselves to it when you're done." He draped his napkin over his plate and strode toward the kitchen. "I have an errand to run."

Neva

Neva headed for the lean-to through the early evening shadows, a tray of sandwiches in her hands. The breeze whistling between the buildings stirred dry leaves into a miniature cyclone and tried to lift the towel she'd used to protect the sandwiches. Strands of hair, loosened from her bun, blew across her eyes. With her hands needed to hold tight to the towel, she couldn't push the wavy locks aside, so she turned her gaze to the breeze. The strands immediately lifted over her forehead and brought Arthur Randall into her line of vision.

She paused, watching him stride up the alley toward her with arms swinging and a look of determination on his face. She hadn't talked to him since the day of Bud's fight. As she stood as still as a statue, waiting for his approach, she realized she'd missed him. And she didn't know if it pleased her or perplexed her.

He stopped directly in front of her. The stern lines of his face softened. "Neva."

"Hello, Arthur."

He pointed to the tray. "For the hobos?"

She nodded.

"Let me take it. It looks heavy."

She transferred the tray to him, then moved alongside him to the lean-to.

He placed the tray on the cold stove, lifted one corner of the towel, and peeked at the stack. "Ham?"

"A few. Mostly cheese or peanut butter."

"Something for everyone." A grin lifted the corners of his mouth. "Some look as if a mouse did some nibbling."

She liked when he teased. She laughed lightly. "The bread had begun to mold. I cut off the bad spots, but I couldn't bring myself to throw away the entire slices. Too wasteful."

"Indeed." He tucked the edges of the towel under the tray and turned an approving smile on her. "I'm sure those passing through will enjoy them."

He'd never once berated her for feeding the down-and-out men. She appreciated his lack of censure. "I hope so. If I can't sell the loaves, at least I can give them away."

His brows pinched together, a gesture that spoke volumes.

She'd been too frank. Embarrassment brought a rush of heat to her cheeks. She adopted an overly cheery tone to override the touch of sarcasm in her last statement. "Thank you for carrying the sandwiches for me. And please thank Leon for coming to Bud's assistance at school. He might've been beaten worse if Leon hadn't joined the fight on his side."

Arthur slipped his hands into his jacket pockets and took a step that brought him close to her. "Leon said Bud took quite a pummeling. Something to do with the boys being unkind to Charley?"

"That's right." The sun's continued departure stole the remaining remnants of warmth. She shivered, eager to go inside. "The unkindness has stopped now, though."

"So why do you want to move?"

She gaped at him. Unexpectedly a laugh built in her chest. She let it roll.

He frowned. "Is something funny?"

She shook her head. "No. Not funny. Ironic. I only talked to Marsh Bobart this afternoon about possibly selling the mercantile. Less than six hours later here you are questioning me about it."

"I didn't hear it from Marsh Bobart."

"Then who?"

"Leon, who heard it from Bud."

Maybe she should have told the children to keep the possibility a secret. She didn't want to give Buffalo Creek residents more fuel for gossip. "Well, since you asked, I'm considering it for the reasons you mentioned — Charley and the little girls would have an opportunity to grow up without their father's choices haunting them."

"I didn't mean for you to go away."

His remorseful words touched her. "I know. But I won't separate the twins from their brother and sisters. If we can't all stay here, then we'll all go somewhere else. But we will stay together."

A train's mournful whistle carried from a distance.

Neva took a step toward the mercantile. "The men won't come for sandwiches if we're out here, and then the food will be wasted. I better go inside."

"May I escort you?"

She was capable of crossing her own backyard without accompaniment, but she nodded, and he gently cupped her elbow as they moved over the brittle grass together. He tempered his stride to match hers, and a spiral of loneliness rose from her center. Walking with Arthur, shielded from the wind by his larger frame, his hand warm and protective on her arm, made her long for a partner with whom to share her life.

Warren's schedule of coming and going had built within her an independent spirit, but it also left a part of her empty and wanting. Would she someday marry again, this time to a man who would walk beside her daily, bolster her, protect her, provide for her, and be honest with her?

Please, God. The prayer formed without effort and brought a desire to cry.

They reached the stoop, and she sniffed hard before turning her face to him. "Thank you. I appreciate your kindness despite our disagreements."

He nodded slowly, his eyes glimmering with an emotion Neva couldn't read. He smoothed his mustache with his finger and cleared his throat. "Neva, would you do a favor for me?"

Though she wasn't sure why, her heart began to pound. "What favor?"

"You didn't deliver Adeline to Mrs. Lafferty's care today. The woman was terribly lonely without the little girl's company, and" — he chuckled — "quite vocal about it when I arrived home from work. Would you allow her to continue watching Adeline until you've made your decision about leaving Buffalo Creek?"

Remorse struck. "I didn't set out to upset Mrs. Lafferty. I kept Adeline with me because I have the time to watch her."

Worry pinched his brow. "Yes. I've noticed the lack of activity at your place. They're still staying away."

A knot of hurt filled the back of her throat. She nodded.

He touched her arm. "But you know how

the town is — how a new wave of gossip sweeps away the old. In time they'll move on to some other perceived scandal, and things will return to normal."

"You might be right. Sheriff Caudel said the same thing, that in time people would forget." Neva gathered her courage and made a confession. "But I don't know if I can forget. I thought the people of this town were my friends. My twins have grown up alongside their children. We've worshiped together in church and rallied together in times of tragedy or need. They know me, yet they've turned on me over a situation that is completely out of my control."

Once the flow started, she couldn't stop. Her voice rose as the pain she'd tried to hide from the children found its way from her heart to Arthur's ears. "Even if they apologize and begin frequenting my mercantile again, how can I ever trust them?"

She'd said too much. His discomfort was palpable, evident in his stiff stance and red-streaked cheeks. She sighed. "If it means that much to Mrs. Lafferty, I'll send Adeline over again tomorrow. Of course, she'll be with me during the days the children are out of school for the upcoming holiday."

A thought trailed through her mind and spilled out of her mouth. "Would you, your

516

boys, and Mrs. Lafferty — she's been so kind to take care of Adeline — join us for Thanksgiving dinner?"

His eyes widened in obvious delight.

She hurried on in case he misinterpreted her invitation. Or maybe to assure herself she had no secret motives. "Every year the children and I invite the minister's family and anyone else who might not otherwise enjoy a big Thanksgiving dinner to sit at our table with us. I've already asked Sheriff Caudel and Betsy Ann Mullin. With Reverend Savage's family, it will be quite a crowd, but the table will accommodate four more."

The light in his expression faded. "Oh. Well . . ."

The train whistle blew again, much closer, and the *chug-chug* of the slowing engine created a soft background hum. She raised her voice to be heard over the train noise. "Leon and Bud have become friends. As have" — she swallowed — "as have we." She touched his coat sleeve. "Will you join us?"

He must have been holding his breath, because he exhaled a mighty whoosh of air. "All right. Yes, Neva, we accept the invitation. Thank you."

Arthur hurried up the alley, heading for home, but when he reached the backyard, he changed course. The air was cold, the hour late, but he presumed there were no closing hours for a minister's duties.

When he stepped onto the sidewalk, he spotted Sheriff Caudel approaching from the opposite direction. The sheriff raised his hand in greeting, and Arthur paused to allow the man to reach him.

"Sheriff."

Caudel nodded. "Good evening, Mr. Randall. Chilly out here, isn't it?"

Arthur buttoned his jacket. "Indeed. Good evening for a man to prop up his feet in front of a fireplace instead of wandering the streets."

"Can't argue with you there. Maybe I'll do that when I've finished making my rounds. I always like to check the businesses — make sure the doors are locked — before turning in for the evening."

Arthur wished he'd started the practice before Neva's store was robbed. "Any problems so far tonight?"

"Nope. Sure is a nice, quiet town you have here."

Arthur stifled a snort. "Except for Warren Shilling's shenanigans. He sure managed to make the hornets buzz."

The sheriff sighed, his breath forming a cloud that smelled strangely of licorice. "I know. I'll be glad when all that settles. Of course, the outcome might stir a whole new hornet's nest for Mrs. Shilling."

Arthur frowned. What did the man mean?

"I'm still hoping we'll find out Warren earned the money instead of stole it. That would take a great weight from Mrs. Shilling's shoulders."

Arthur jolted. "Stole what money?"

Caudel's face blazed, the color highlighted by the streetlamp. "I thought she'd — She said you gave her advice about —" He rolled his eyes heavenward and blew out a breath. "I thought you knew."

"You're babbling, Sheriff."

He yanked off his hat and whacked his thigh with it. "Listen, Randall, I made an assumption about your relationship with Mrs. Shilling."

Heat exploded in Arthur's face. He was probably glowing as bright as the bulbs on a Christmas tree right then.

"I thought she'd told you everything about her husband, but I must've been wrong. Let's just pretend we never had this conversation."

Despite being flustered — he found it

both gratifying and disquieting to realize the sheriff had recognized the feelings developing between him and Neva — he released a laugh. "Was that a conversation? It seemed more an exercise in frustrating one of your constituents."

Caudel laughed, too, but he sobered quickly. He slipped his hat back in place. "Right now you're likely Mrs. Shilling's only friend. I hope whatever happens in the next few weeks — whatever rumors start swirling around town — you'll stay friends with her and remember none of this was her fault. She's a victim, not a villain."

More riddles. Arthur started to question him, but the sheriff backed up two steps. "Enjoy your evening, Mr. Randall." He turned and trotted off as if the hornets they'd discussed had suddenly come swarming.

The chill evening air sent shivers through Arthur's frame. He considered going back to his house and sitting in front of the fireplace, but taking care of himself wouldn't do a thing for Neva. As the sheriff said, he was her only friend. No one else would see to her needs if he didn't. He took off once more, his arms swinging with his determined stride.

By the time he reached the little parsonage behind the chapel, his ears felt half frozen and his nose was dripping. He made use of his handkerchief before tapping on the door. Even before he got the square of white cloth tucked back in his pocket, the door opened, and the minister's young wife welcomed him with a big smile.

"Good evening, Mr. Randall."

He drew back in surprise. She knew who he was? When he and Mabel attended the chapel faithfully, a different preacher stood on the dais. Arthur had sat in on only a handful of Reverend Savage's sermons, and he'd never taken the time to introduce himself. He couldn't decide if he was more flattered or baffled.

She gestured him over the threshold, then snapped the door shut. "Are you here to see the reverend?"

Mrs. Savage didn't seem perturbed or even startled by his arrival. How often did people show up on the preacher's doorstep? "Yes, if he isn't too busy."

A dimpled grin rounded her cheeks. "He's reading the children their bedtime story. Since he usually isn't here during the day for their naptime story, he enjoys participating in the evening routine." She gestured toward the floral sofa in front of the window and moved toward an opening at the far side of the room. "Make yourself comfortable and I'll —"

Arthur reached for the doorknob. "No, I don't want to disrupt his time with your children. I'll come back another time."

She hurried across the floor and caught hold of his sleeve. "Now, Mr. Randall, you braved the cold to see him." She guided him to the sofa. "He'll only be a minute or two. I'll let him know you're here. Then I'll start a pot of water for tea. Or do you prefer coffee?"

Mabel used to fix him tea in the evenings. "Tea is fine." He sat.

Her bright smile returned. "Good. Now, please, take off your jacket and relax. Ernie will be right out." She bustled out of the room.

Arthur shrugged out of his coat and draped it over his knee. Despite the homey room and the friendliness of his hostess, an uneasy feeling sat heavily in his stomach. He hoped he hadn't made a mistake by coming here.

CHAPTER 38

Arthur

"I don't know if you can fix anything." Arthur held his cup of tepid tea between his palms and gazed down at a few flecks of tea leaves floating in the pale liquid. "But it just seems to me somebody needs to say something before Ne— Mrs. Shilling — has no choice but to sell her store and move away."

Reverend Savage had sat attentive and quiet the entire time Arthur shared his concerns for Neva and her children. Now he sighed and leaned back in his chair. "I'm so glad you came this evening, Mr. Randall. Of course, I'd observed people shifting aside when she entered church, but I hoped her openness about the situation had stirred feelings of empathy in the congregation. To know they've deliberately avoided shopping in the mercantile . . ." He shook his head. "That kind of judgmental attitude has no place within the Christian's heart."

"You're exactly right." A touch of anger entered Arthur's tone, stirred by a wave of protectiveness. "Mrs. Shilling is one of the most giving people I've ever met — taking in her husband's ill-begotten children, putting food in the barn's lean-to for hobos even after a drifter entered her store and robbed her, offering credit to local folks when most businesses in town have gone to a cash-only system."

He pictured Neva as she'd looked this evening, a strand of wavy nutmeg hair waving gently along her jaw and her hazel eyes shimmering with tears of frustration and pain. His throat tightened. "She deserves accolades, not acrimony."

Awareness dawned on the minister's face. "Mr. Randall, are you . . . smitten with Widow Shilling?"

If anyone else had asked, Arthur would have brusquely told him to mind his own business. But one couldn't be so blunt with a preacher. He choked out a harsh *ahem.* "She and I have become" — he borrowed the word she'd used earlier that evening — "friends, and it pains me to see her suffering. Wrong was perpetrated on her first by her philandering husband and now by the town she has faithfully served for many years." He set aside the teacup and banged his fist on his knee. "It's time for the nonsense to stop."

Reverend Savage nodded, his lips set in a somber line, but a hint of orneriness sparked in his eyes. "I commend you for defending her. It's never easy to take the path of right when so many others are moving in a different direction."

Arthur lowered his head. If Reverend Savage knew everything, he wouldn't praise Arthur. He smoothed his mustache with his fingertips, then looked the young preacher in the eyes. "Don't admire me too much. My initial reason for befriending her was to convince her to sell me her building so I could expand my emporium."

The minister gazed at him, attentive, without disparagement. "But now?"

"Now I think it would be a real disservice for me to shut her down. This town needs people like Neva Shilling, people with a giving spirit and a desire to serve. Especially in these times of hardship, Mrs. Shilling is a beacon of hope that things can be better if we're willing to give of ourselves."

"A beacon of hope . . ." Reverend Savage shifted his gaze to somewhere beyond Arthur and seemed to drift away in thought.

Arthur braced himself to rise.

The minister jerked his attention back to

Arthur and lifted his hand. "Mr. Randall, may I ask you a question?"

Arthur eased back into the seat.

"When I took over this ministry two years ago from Reverend Kempel, I visited you, as I did all the families whose names appeared on the membership roster, and you seemed quite adamant that you were no longer interested in attending. Seeing you and your sons in the service the past few weeks has been an answer to prayer."

Wonder ignited in Arthur's chest. This man had prayed for him to come to church?

"Would you mind sharing why you've chosen to return?"

If he told the truth, he might greatly disappoint this earnest young minister, but Arthur couldn't bring himself to prevaricate. "To be with Mrs. Shilling."

Reverend Savage nodded, apparently not surprised. "May I ask another question?"

What else would he have to confess? "I . . . I suppose."

"Do you have a relationship with God through belief in His Son, Jesus Christ?"

Arthur closed his eyes, the simple question carrying him backward so quickly that dizziness attacked. He'd knelt next to the dais with his dear Mabel on the Thursday night of a weeklong revival just one year into their marriage and pledged his life to the Lord. While Mabel lived, he'd been faithful in church attendance, faithful in prayer, faithful in seeking God's guidance. But with her death, his expressions of faith had died. He no longer had a relationship with Mabel. Did he have one with the Savior they'd accepted together?

He rubbed his eyes, then opened them. The minister gazed at him in silent expectation. Arthur blurted, "I'm a prodigal."

A soft, understanding smile crept over Reverend Savage's face. "And are you ready to come home?"

He jerked to his feet and jammed his arms into his jacket, the need to escape strong. "I've said all I came to say." And then some. "I don't know if you can do anything for Mrs. Shilling, but I'd appreciate your giving it some thought. If things don't change around here pretty quickly, we're going to lose a valuable community member."

Reverend Savage stood and extended his hand. "Mr. Randall, thank you for coming. I assure you, I will give these matters —"

These?

"— some serious prayer and ask God's guidance on how to best handle them." The impish glint returning, he squeezed Arthur's hand. "It seems to me having Mrs. Shilling as your friend is a very good influence for you. I'd hate to see a God-inspired friendship torn asunder."

Neva

Neva took advantage of the quiet days of no customers and no Adeline to prepare for the big dinner on Thanksgiving Day. On Tuesday she cleaned the parlor and dining room, laundered her good table linens and napkins, and extended the fine cherry table as far as it would go, adding all ten leaves. Eight chairs usually surrounded the table, but she gathered chairs and benches from various locations in the apartment until she had enough places for eighteen people.

From the cellar she collected potatoes, carrots, apples, onions, jars of green beans and pickles, and a quart of sour cherries. Everything else — bread and seasonings for the stuffing, flour, sugar, shortening, boxes of lime Jell-O, and cans of pineapple — she gleaned from the mercantile. As she loaded her arms, she experienced a sting of sadness mixed with anger. These goods shouldn't still be on the store shelves. But those who gathered around the table would appreciate the pies, salads, and cakes the items produced. She intended to make extra pies and leave them in the lean-to. Even hobos deserved a little something special on a holiday.

Wednesday she spent the morning baking pies — six apple, two cherry, and three custard. She didn't have pumpkin or sweet potatoes for the traditional pies, but she hoped the others would satisfy her guests. The stove's warmth and the pleasant aromas filling the kitchen put a bounce in her step. At noon she walked to the butcher's for a turkey. One twenty-four-pound bird remained in the display case. She purchased it despite its extravagant $4.56 price tag.

That afternoon she made two molded Jell-O salads, one with shredded raw carrots and one with pineapple and the few remaining walnuts from her pantry. The jewel-toned salads always looked so pretty on the table. They also looked tempting on the Frigidaire shelf. She hoped the children wouldn't stick their fingers in them before she could serve them.

On Wednesday evening after a simple supper of biscuits, boiled cabbage, and ham, Bud entertained the younger children with a game of pick-up sticks while Neva sliced the last of the stale bread for stuffing. Belle offered to help, and Neva asked her to set the table with their best china dishes and fine silver cutlery.

Belle left the kitchen but returned quickly, puzzlement pursing her face. "Momma, who all is coming tomorrow?"

Neva continued cubing the slices of bread. "I invited the Savages, the Randalls and their housekeeper, the sheriff, and the café owner."

Belle silently counted with her fingers. "With us and all of them, we only need sixteen chairs. Why do you have so many?"

"The table seemed to ask for eighteen place settings."

Belle giggled. "Oh, Momma, you're so silly."

This might be her last opportunity to use the beautiful china and the Rich & Baker table. Perhaps it was silly, but she wanted to enjoy the things before she had to give them back.

Neva gave her daughter's nose a light tap with her finger. "Well, we have enough dishes to serve eighteen, so go ahead and set them all out. Maybe we'll end up needing those extra seats."

With a grin Belle scampered off.

When Neva passed through the dining room later to tuck the children into bed, she paused and looked down the length of the table. Belle had done such a nice job, the silverware perfectly placed on the creamy napkins, each dinner plate topped with a salad plate and centered in front of the chairs, and their best crystal goblets standing sentry over the knives and spoons. She curled her hands over the chair at the head, where Warren would sit when he was home, and her eyes slipped closed.

Lord, grant us a time of sweet fellowship and gratitude tomorrow. So much is wrong in our small corner of the world and over the entire United States. But You are sovereign. You care. You bring hope and healing. Please flood us with Your presence tomorrow so we can carry away pleasant memories. Especially if this becomes our very last Thanksgiving in Buffalo Creek.

Bud

Ma kissed Charley good night, then did the same for Bud. Sometimes Bud thought about telling Ma he was too big to be tucked in and kissed like some little kid, but he'd missed it those weeks when she hadn't come in. And he could tell it made her happy to follow the nightly routine. So instead of ducking away, he reached up and pulled her into a hug. She rose up with a smile on her face, and Bud's chest went warm. It was good to see Ma smile.

She extinguished their lamp and then left, closing their door behind her. Bud lay listening to her footsteps leading away — probably to the parlor, where she'd sit and work on some mending or crocheting before she turned in. Ma always had busy hands. When the runners of the rocking chair began creaking against the floor, Bud closed his eyes and yawned, ready to sleep.

"Bud?" Charley whispered from the other side of the room.

Bud whispered, too, so they wouldn't bother the girls next door. "What?"

"Tomorrow's Thanksgiving."

Bud chuckled. He knew. The house smelled like pie, the table was all spruced up finer than a king's table, and Ma had come in with flour on her chin.

"Aunt Neva said we'd talk more about California on Thanksgiving."

Bud rolled to his side so he could look at Charley. Only a tiny bit of light entered their room from the window, and he had to stare hard to make out Charley's face. "She said we'd talk about it over Thanksgiving break. Not Thanksgiving."

"Oh." Disappointment colored Charley's tone and expression. "So we might not know by tomorrow?"

Bud leaned up on his elbow. "You sound

powerful eager to find out. Are you wanting to go or stay?"

Charley shrugged. "Dunno for sure. What about you?"

Bud chewed his lip. It still hurt a little bit from the mighty wallop he'd gotten from Martin. "Dunno either. Things here are kind of rough, but it's still my home. California sounds like a dandy place where a fellow could have a good time, but it's so far away. So . . ." He sighed. "I dunno."

Charley bit down on his lip, the same way Bud did. "Adeline's so little, she don't care, but Cassie wants to go. Belle told her oranges grow on trees all over the place in California, and Cassie loves oranges more than anything."

Bud would remember to tell Ma to put an orange in Cassie's Christmas stocking.

"Me? Oranges are all right, I guess. And it being warm all the time would be nice, too. Always have liked summer and running around without my shoes on. It'd be kind of like having summer year round."

Although Charley was singing California's praise, he still sounded uncertain. Bud prompted, "But . . ."

For a long time Charley lay there, looking across the room and blinking real slow, and Bud thought maybe he was going to drift off to sleep. Bud lay back down. And then Charley spoke again.

"Before me and the girls came here, Daddy said Aunt Neva would be waiting for us and we'd be all right." He paused for the length of two more blinks. "Who'll be waiting for us in California, Bud?"

CHAPTER 39

Jesse

At eleven thirty Jesse locked the door of his house behind him and set off for the mercantile. He rounded the corner of the sheriff's office and encountered Miss Mullin heading in the same direction. With a grin he stuck out his elbow.

She tittered but took hold, and the two moved together along the sidewalk. She sent him a sidelong glance. "You look right handsome today, Sheriff. Or should I just call you Mr. Caudel since you left your badge behind?"

Jesse chuckled self-consciously. He rarely wore a suit and tie, more comfortable in dungarees and a chambray shirt, but he figured he'd chosen correctly considering the fringed shawl, lace-decorated dress, cream-colored gloves, and flowered hat Miss Mullin sported. "You can call me whichever name you prefer as long as you don't call me late to dinner."

She laughed, covering her wide mouth with her fingers. "Oh, you are a card, Mr. Caudel."

He'd been called that before and plenty worse things, too. The ugliest titles — ungrateful, uncaring, self-serving — he'd heaped on himself lately. But he'd been praying to make restitution, and the retired sheriff's willingness to step in and substitute for Jesse for a week or so meant he could put his plan into action soon. He'd go as soon as he knew for sure whether Warren Shilling had been a thief as well as a philanderer. Eagerness sped his footsteps, and he nearly dragged Miss Mullin across the street to the mercantile's front door.

Bud was waiting inside, and he opened the door even before they knocked. "Hi, Sheriff, Miss Mullin. Happy Thanksgiving."

Jesse recalled his first meeting with Bud. The boy's welcome today was a lot friendlier. "Happy Thanksgiving to you, Bud."

Miss Mullin echoed, "Happy Thanksgiving."

Bud gestured toward the lit hallway at the back of the store. "Go on up. You can toss your shawl on the parlor sofa with the other coats, Miss Mullin."

"Oh, is everyone here already?" She

pursed her lips. "I wanted to arrive early enough to give your dear mother a hand."

"Just the Randalls so far. Mrs. Lafferty isn't coming after all. She woke up with a bad cold and didn't want to get out."

"Oh, poor Lela." Miss Mullin clicked her teeth on her tongue. "I'll make her some chicken soup tonight."

Bud shuddered, and Jesse could imagine what he was thinking — chicken soup from the café owner's stove would add to the older woman's malady rather than heal it. Bud said, "Soon as the Savages get here, Ma says we'll eat."

Jesse guided Miss Mullin through the hallway, then followed her up the stairs. Wonderful smells drifted to them, and Jesse's stomach rolled in anticipation. Miss Mullin licked her lips, too. Jesse stifled a chuckle. If she ate her own cooking, she'd likely see Mrs. Shilling's dinner as a real treat.

Charley and Cassie already sat at one end of the table, Arthur Randall and his two boys on the same end but the opposite side. Adeline was perched on Randall's knee like a little princess on a throne. Jesse tried not to stare at the incongruous sight.

Miss Mullin scurried past the table to the kitchen doorway, calling, "Toodle-oo, Neva!

537

May I be of help?" A flurry of female voices rose, and Jesse presumed Mrs. Shilling was putting Miss Mullin to work.

Jesse took the chair at the far end of the table on the same side as Charley and Cassie so Miss Mullin and the Savages could sit closer to their hostess.

Mr. Randall visited quietly with Charley and the little girls. Bumps and thumps and muffled voices carried from the kitchen. The good smells, the long table ready to accommodate a crowd, and the homey noises took him back to his childhood home, and the longing to revisit it — to revisit the people who'd filled the table — grew stronger than his hunger for food.

Feet clattered on the stairs, and Bud burst around the corner with Reverend and Mrs. Savage behind him. The adults each carried a toddler, and Bud took them to the four seats across the table from Jesse.

"Here you go. Ma put some catalogs on the chairs so Benji and Jenny can reach. She said to tell you she's sorry she doesn't have highchairs for them."

"We'll be just fine, Bud." Mrs. Savage pulled Jenny's knitted cap from her head, and the little girl's fine blond hair stood out like a nimbus.

Bud grinned and smoothed his hand over

the child's hair. "I'll tell Ma you're here."
He angled himself toward the kitchen
doorway and bellowed, "Ma! Everybody's
here!"

"Gracious, Bud," came his mother's voice,
"you needn't alert the entire town!"

Laughter erupted.

Grinning sheepishly, Bud slipped into a
chair two seats up from Charley.

The reverend gathered his family's outer-
wear and carried it to the parlor while Mrs.
Savage lifted the toddlers onto their stacks
of catalogs. She turned as if to enter the
kitchen, but Mrs. Shilling came out carrying a platter with the most beautifully
browned turkey Jesse had ever laid eyes on.
If it tasted half as good as it looked, he'd
have a very satisfied tongue.

She smiled at the minister's wife. "Please
join your family. I have plenty of help
already, and we'll have dinner on the table
in two shakes of a lamb's tail." She set the
turkey near the foot of the table and hurried back into the kitchen.

Saliva pooled in Jesse's mouth as the
bounty increased. The length of gold fabric
serving as a runner down the center of the
table nearly disappeared beneath the food.
Baskets of rolls. Rainbow-tinted glass sau-
cers of jam, butter, pickled beets, and sliced

cucumbers with onions. Crock bowls of green beans, stewed tomatoes, moist-looking stuffing, snowy mashed potatoes and gravy. It seemed the parade between the kitchen and dining room would never stop.

Finally Mrs. Shilling brought out two different Jell-O salads shaped like tires. She set one at each end of the table, and Adeline clapped her hands and crowed, "Yummy!" Little Jenny and Benji Savage imitated her. Everyone laughed.

Mr. Randall put Adeline on the floor and sent her to her chair with a pat on her bottom. Mrs. Shilling, Miss Mullin, and Belle took their seats, and Mrs. Shilling stood at the head of the table behind her chair. "Reverend, would you be kind enough to say grace?"

Jesse ducked his head to hide a smile. The minister would certainly offer a better prayer than the one he had at this table two months ago. Of course, if she asked him to pray today, he'd do better, too. He and God had talked a little more frequently of late.

Ernie folded his hands, and everyone around the table, including his two little ones, followed his example. "Our most gracious heavenly Father, we gather today to —"

A terrible clamor interrupted. Jesse looked up to a sea of startled faces.

Mrs. Savage caught her husband's arm. "I believe someone is fighting."

Mr. Randall bounded up. "They're behind the mercantile." Both of his sons jumped from their chairs as if ready to join the melee.

Jesse rose, holding up his hands. "Everyone, stay here. I'll take care of it." Rather than waiting for agreement, he darted through the parlor to the staircase. By taking the steps two at a time, he made it to the bottom in a few seconds.

He swung open the back door and trotted directly to three ragtag men, two of whom held tight to the third one, who struggled like a wildcat and yowled loud enough to wake the dead. "What's going on here?" Jesse roared over their shouts.

The pair wrestling the one into submission turned their angry glares on Jesse. The tallest one growled, "Who're you?"

"Jesse Caudel, the sheriff of Buffalo Creek. Now tell me what you're doing with this man."

With a nod to each other, the duo flung the man at Jesse's feet, then stood over him with triumphant grins creasing their dirty faces. The shorter one announced, "We're

541

bringing him to you, Sheriff."

"That's right," the tall one added. "We caught you a thief."

Neva

Neva stared out the kitchen window into the backyard, unable to believe what she saw. The hobos who'd so frightened her outside the cellar had returned, and they'd brought another unfortunate man with them. They must have been fighting over the few remaining crackers Belle had put in the lean-to the night before. Sympathy rolled through her. What kind of hunger drove men to scrabble over a handful of saltines?

She hurried into the dining room, where her guests jabbered in confusion. "Please excuse the delay. We'll eat soon, but first I need to —" She bustled off, determined to reach the sheriff before he ordered the men away.

She was calling his name before she reached the back door, and when she stepped outside, the two hobos, Herb and Ansel, dashed to her, both talking at once.

"Ma'am, ma'am, we caught him. We brought him back, ma'am. The sheriff here says he's gonna put him under arrest."

Their babble made no sense. She gaped at

542

one, then the other. "What?"

Sheriff Caudel crossed the yard, pulling the third hobo along by his collar. "According to these fellows, this is the man who took off with the contents of your cashbox."

"That's right." Herb threw his skinny shoulders back and glared at the accused thief. "He was bragging how the owner of Main Street Mercantile left the door open for him, easiest stealing he'd ever done."

Ansel bobbed his head. "As soon as we heard the name of the store, we knew we couldn't let him get by with it. So Herb and I jumped him. Took every dollar from him." He dug in his pocket and pulled out a wad of bills. He handed the mess to Neva with the dignity of a crown bearer bestowing jewels on a queen. "We can't say for sure it's all there, but what he had on him, we kept for you, ma'am."

Neva held the crumpled bills, tears distorting her vision. "I never thought I'd see this money again."

Ansel pulled his battered hat from his head and held it over his chest with chapped, dirt-rimmed fingers. "We're sorry it took us so long to bring it back. Sometimes the bulls threw us from the trains before we even took off. We ended up walking the last dozen miles, pretty much dragging him the whole way." He jabbed his thumb at the thief.

Neva glanced at the man with Sheriff Caudel. Dried grass and mud stains covered nearly every inch of his clothing. What a sorry sight he painted with his filthy clothes, downcast face, and thin, sunken cheeks.

Herb stepped near, wringing his dirty hands together. "After your kindness to us, we wanted to repay you." He stuck out his hand. "Are we square?"

Neva looked at the man's hand. Broken nails, dirt encrusted into every tiny crease. She pushed the bills into her apron pocket and then reached out. She held his cold, dry hand between hers and met his watery gaze. "No, sir, we aren't square."

The hobos sent startled glances at each other.

Neva smiled. "You're one up on me. But if you'll come inside and have dinner with my family, that should help even the score."

Jesse

Wasn't she something, inviting that pair of misfits to sit at her table? But he wasn't surprised by it. After all the other acts of compassion he'd seen her perform, he would've been more surprised if she hadn't asked them to come in and eat.

Jesse kept a firm grip on the thief's arm and eased close to Mrs. Shilling. "Ma'am, I'm going to take this one over to the sheriff's office and put him in a cell. You all go ahead and eat without me."

Still holding the hobo's hand, she turned a firm look on him. "Absolutely not. We will all eat together."

She sure could be stubborn when she set her mind to it, but so could he. "Your food will grow cold while you're waiting on me. Go ahead and eat, and I'll come by later for a plate of leftovers." She'd probably send a plate for this ne'er-do-well he had with him, too.

Mrs. Shilling sighed. "Mr. Caudel, when I said *all,* I meant all. There are three empty chairs around my table. Thanks to the arrival of Herb, Ansel, and —" She looked expectantly at the thief.

He mumbled, "Men ridin' the rails call me Rover. But my folks named me Rufus."

"Rufus," she went on, "the table will be complete. Now let's go." She aimed Herb for the back door and gestured for Ansel to follow. Jesse, too stunned to do otherwise, trailed behind them.

When they reached the top of the stairs, she paused and addressed the three men. "There's a washroom right here. Go in, clean your hands and faces, then" — she grinned at Jesse, and he automatically grinned back, knowing what she intended to say — "follow your nose to the dining room. We'll be waiting for you." She marched off without a backward glance.

No matter what she thought, he wouldn't leave the hobos unattended. He stood outside the washroom door while they went in one at a time and came out still whisker cheeked and attired in rags but with much cleaner hands and faces and carrying the essence of soap. A great improvement.

In spite of the enticing aromas, the men approached the dining room with trepidation. Pity struck. How out of place they must feel in Mrs. Shilling's neat, clean house. Did it remind them of the homes they'd lost, the families they'd left behind? "Don't worry. You're welcome here. Go ahead and sit."

Apparently Mrs. Shilling had already warned the other guests about the newcomers, because no one seemed shocked when the four of them entered the room. The hobos pulled off their hats and slid into the three empty chairs next to the Shilling children, leaving the only open chair at the head of the table. Jesse stood, uncertain.

From the other end of the table, Mrs. Shilling offered a smile. A genuine smile. A smile holding relief and a hint of accomplishment. "Mr. Caudel, as soon as you're seated, the reverend will say grace."

He sat. Once again they bowed their heads, the three hobos sniffling, and Ernie began to pray. "Our gracious, loving heavenly Father . . ."

CHAPTER 40

Neva

Snowflakes were dancing outside Neva's window when she awakened Sunday morning. She watched them land on the glass, one second resembling minute delicate doilies and the next teardrops as the inside warmth reached through the glass and melted them.

She rolled away from the sight and sighed. Should she awaken the children, bundle them, and take them to church service? They'd all stayed up past bedtime last night, with the exception of Adeline, who drowsed against Neva's arm while the rest of the family discussed the possibility of going to California. Of the four children old enough to participate in the discussion, only Cassie seemed ready to go. The others, although willing, lacked real enthusiasm. And Neva found herself battling the same uncertainty.

Bits and pieces of conversations with others and her own thoughts rolled through her mind, creating a jumbled maze of confusion.

"Those children will ever carry the stench of illegitimacy in this town. In a large community perhaps they could find a contingency of people who would be unaware and accept them. But Buffalo Creek is not a large community."

"People will settle down in time, forget."

"Send them away, Neva. If you send them away, your misery — and theirs — will come to an end."

"We haven't done anything wrong. Not me or you or Belle or Charley or Cassie or Adeline. We have no reason to hide."

The same question rose again. If she took the children and left, would she be hiding them or giving them the chance for a happier life?

"Momma?" Belle called from outside Neva's door.

"What is it, darlin'?"

"It's getting late. If you don't hurry, we'll be late for church."

She looked out the window again. "It's snowing."

"What difference does that make?"

Neva shook her head, releasing a soft huff of laughter. If her children wanted to go

549

after the way they'd been treated, how could she even think of keeping them home? She pushed the covers aside. "All right. I'm up. Go ahead and get dressed, and I'll —"

Giggles bubbled from the hallway. "Momma, we're all dressed and ready to go. We're waiting for you."

Neva turned her face to the ceiling, imagining God smiling down at her. *Wherever we end up — California or right here in Buffalo Creek — we'll be all right. You are with us.*

Arthur

Arthur ushered his sons into the church building. They stamped the snow from their feet and hung their coats on pegs in the small cloakroom, then moved into the sanctuary. Although they'd arrived only minutes before the service was due to begin, the room was mostly empty. Apparently the first snowfall of the season had kept the folks who lived far from town and those who walked to service at home. Except for Neva Shilling. His heart leaped.

"Come on, boys." He led them to the left-hand pew at the center of the rows. Neva sat on the end, her attention on Adeline, who was pointing to a picture in a story

Bible. He stood for a moment admiring the sweet turn of her jaw, the smooth line of her wavy reddish-brown hair twisted into a puffy bun dotted with melted snowflakes, and the neat fit of her navy-blue dress. Neva Shilling was a lady in the finest sense.

He touched her shoulder, and his heart gave a grander leap when she looked up and immediately smiled. "May we join you?" he asked.

He held his breath, waiting. Would she refuse him again? To his great relief she nodded and whispered to her children to scoot over. Arthur slid in next to her with Leon and Leroy crowded on his other side.

Leon grunted. "Can I sit in the pew behind you? With Bud?"

"You may sit in front of me where I can flick your ear if you don't behave."

A soft giggle sounded — Neva.

Arthur swallowed a smile. "And whether Bud joins you is up to his mother."

Neva gave her consent, and the two boys settled directly in front of Neva and Arthur. Their departure freed up inches of space, but Arthur felt no need to scoot away from her. And she didn't shift away either.

A smile pulled at his cheeks, and he ran his fingers over his mustache several times to bring it under control. He shouldn't sit here grinning like a besotted schoolboy in church, of all places.

Reverend Savage stepped onto the dais and invited the congregation to open their hymn books to "What a Friend We Have in Jesus." Three hymnals waited in the little holder on the back of the pew. Leroy grabbed one, Belle took another, and Neva reached for the third. She opened it and then held it so Arthur could look, too.

He tried to sing, but his voice refused to cooperate. A knot filled the back of his throat. There was something intimate, something special, about sharing a hymnal with her. Her soprano, however, came out clear and sweet, and he enjoyed listening.

" 'Do thy friends despise, forsake thee? Take it to the Lord in prayer!' " She glanced up at him as she sang, as though ascertaining if he was hearing the words. " 'In His arms He'll take and shield thee, thou wilt find a solace there.' "

The congregation went on to the fourth verse, and Arthur managed to join them. The final reference to the day believers joined the Father in heaven, where prayer was no longer needed, filled him with a sense of promise he hadn't experienced since Mabel was alive. When he'd told the preacher he was a prodigal, the man had asked if he was ready to come home, and Arthur hadn't answered. But he answered now.

Yes, Father, I'm ready to be Yours again.

The hymn ended, and Reverend Savage thanked the organist and then turned to those gathered in the pews. "We just sang one of my favorite hymns. Isn't it wonderful to think that we have such a friend in Jesus? He is a friend who never abandons us, never disappoints us, never discourages us. He's the kind of friend everyone needs, the kind of friend we should all aspire to be."

Neva lifted Adeline into her lap, and Cassie tried to climb up, too. Adeline squawked and slapped at her sister. Without thinking, Arthur lifted Adeline onto his knee, leaving Neva's lap open for Cassie. Adeline sat sideways and played with the buttons on his vest, content. Warmth flowed through his chest. How good it felt to help with the child, to have her trust him and accept his attention. In that moment if someone tried to take Adeline away, he would fight tooth and nail to keep her with him.

He glanced at Neva, and he answered her tender smile with one of his own before they both turned their attention to the front, where Reverend Savage paced back and forth as he continued his sermon.

"Unfortunately we often fail as friends. We allow petty grievances or disagreements to divide us. Sometimes we think we have good cause to be angry because those we call 'friends' do things that hurt us. But what was Jesus's advice in those situations?"

He returned to the pulpit and opened his Bible. "In the sixth chapter of Luke, Jesus stood in the presence of His disciples and a multitude of people, and He shared these words: 'Bless them that curse you, and pray for them which despitefully use you. And unto him that smiteth thee on the one cheek offer also the other; and him that taketh away thy cloak forbid not to take thy coat also. Give to every man that asketh of thee; and of him that taketh away thy goods ask them not again. And as ye would that men should do to you, do ye also to them likewise.' "

The impish glint Arthur had seen before flashed in the preacher's eyes. "Please take note that last verse does not say do to others as they have done to you, but rather do what you would like others to do to you."

Soft chuckles rolled through the room, and Leon and Bud exchanged quick grins, then turned their faces forward again.

"Turning the other cheek isn't easy. It's a lot easier to smite — or slap, for ease of understanding — than willingly offer your face to be slapped. And I don't believe Jesus really meant for us to invite someone who's physically slapped us to do it again. I believe it's a metaphorical reference. If someone hurts us, instead of striking back, we should be willing to forgive."

He stopped and gazed outward for several seconds as if he'd forgotten what he was doing. Just as the worshipers were beginning to squirm, he nodded, placed his Bible on the pulpit, and turned a smile on them. "Just this last Thursday on Thanksgiving Day, I had the privilege of witnessing an example of 'turning the other cheek.' My family and I enjoyed a wonderful dinner with one of our parishioners, Mrs. Neva Shilling, her children, and some other community members.

"I'm sure all of you heard about the robbery at the mercantile last month. The sheriff gave up the search for the thief, reasoning the person had hopped a passing train and was long gone. And he was right." The teasing grin returned. "Sort of."

Reverend Savage moved to the edge of the dais. "The thief had caught a train, but some other men encountered him farther along the line. These men had begged food at the Shillings' back door and had been fed. Because of that act of kindness, when the men encountered the one who'd stolen money from the mercantile, they brought him and the money back. It took them more than three weeks to make the journey, often traveling by foot and hindered by the thief's reluctance to return, but on Thanksgiving Day they again stepped into Neva Shilling's backyard. This time not to take but to give."

Arthur glanced at Neva. Her face glowed bright pink, and she seemed to hold her breath. He nudged her with his elbow and offered her an encouraging smile. She gave him a wobbly one in return.

"All three of these men were homeless beggars. The money the thief took could have bought them a warm hotel room, good meals, new clothes. But they didn't spend it. No, they returned it to the woman who had fed them." He wagged his finger, the way one might chide a naughty child. "Oh, I know what you're thinking. This isn't a case of repaying evil with good. It's a case of repaying good with good. But listen to the rest of the story."

With a smile he stepped onto the floor. "Mrs. Shilling invited the ones who'd brought back her money to sit at her dining room table and partake of Thanksgiving dinner. But do you know who else was welcomed to the table?" He paused, letting his gaze roam across each person in attendance. "The thief." He paused again. "The same thief who robbed her mercantile, who took money that should have been used to take care of her family's needs, who was dragged literally kicking and screaming back to Buffalo Creek to return the money, was invited to sit and dine like any other guest."

The minister shook his head in wonder, and Arthur did the same. Her kindness went beyond all reason, yet he didn't think her simpleminded or naive or even foolish. He deeply admired her.

Reverend Savage stepped back behind the pulpit and held up his Bible. "In that same chapter of Luke, verse 36, we find one of Jesus's admonitions to His believers. He says, 'Be ye therefore merciful, as your Father also is merciful.' " He carefully laid the Bible on the wooden support and then gripped the edges of the podium, his expression fervent. "We do wrong. We take things that don't belong to us. We say things that are hurtful or untrue. We hold grudges, and we nurse bitterness, and we refuse to reach out with compassion when opportunities for it arise. And regardless of the wrong, in every situation God extends His mercy to us. As His followers we are asked — no, commanded — to follow His example."

He once again moved his gaze from face to face as if trying to read their secret thoughts. "My dear friends, if you're here today and are holding on to a wrong, whether bitterness or vengeance or unforgiveness against your neighbor, now is the time for mercy. As you have been given mercy, extend it to those around you. Even if they haven't asked for it, even if you perceive they've done wrong, offer mercy.

" 'For with the same measure that ye mete withal it shall be measured to you . . .' " He quoted the scripture in a raspy whisper, not as a warning, but as a petition. "If you call Him 'Lord,' then do as He says. Mrs. Muck is going to play a closing song."

The organist slipped onto the bench and struck the opening chord.

Reverend Savage moved to the edge of the dais and held his arms open. "As the Spirit speaks to you, come. Respond. Receive mercy or extend mercy. Whatever you need to do, God is here, ready to listen."

The organist began to play an old, familiar hymn, and the words formed in Arthur's mind even after his lengthy time away. *All the way my Savior leads me . . .* " His hands were shaking, his entire body quivering with a desire he couldn't define or squelch. *"Can*

I doubt His tender mercy?" Others were leaving their seats, moving to the front and kneeling in prayer or reaching for the pastor's hand.

Arthur eased Adeline onto Leroy's lap, ignoring his son's startled expression. Then he rose, stepped past Leroy into the aisle, and made his way to the front. He knelt in the same place he'd knelt beside Mabel nearly twenty years ago, where a knothole formed a dark spot on the clear pine board.

He closed his eyes as a line from the song winged through his memory. *"Gushing from the Rock before me, Lo! A spring of joy I see."* A tear of joy slid from beneath Arthur's closed eyes and down his cheek in a warm rush. He'd rediscovered his joy.

CHAPTER 41

Neva

One by one, as church members left their pews or their spots at the dais, they approached Neva and offered handshakes, hushed words of apology, or promises to stop by the mercantile next week. After the hurt they'd caused her, she could have refused their gestures of reconciliation, but with the minister's words ringing in her heart — *"Be ye therefore merciful, as your Father also is merciful"* — she found the strength to offer mercy instead.

Arthur came last, and he dropped into the pew heavily, as if he'd just finished a long race. He turned his gaze to her, and the light shining in his molasses-colored eyes brought a rush of joyful tears. She touched his arm. "You've made peace with God, haven't you?"

"Thanks to you."

She shook her head firmly. "I don't have

the power to change anyone except myself, and even then I rely on God's strength."

He lifted her hand and delivered one gentle sweep of his lips across her knuckles — a feather-light brush of tenderness that sent Neva's heart a-pattering. He lowered it but held it loosely in his grasp. "You didn't change me. You simply showed me the way to be. So thank you, Neva Shilling, for living your faith in the face of hardship. You are a true inspiration."

Leroy, Leon, and Bud had ambled to the rear of the sanctuary, but now they returned. Leroy leaned down and whispered loudly enough for Neva to hear, "Um, Dad, I think the only time you're supposed to kiss a woman in church is on your wedding day." Leon and Bud snickered and Belle giggled.

Arthur's face flushed. He waved his hand in the direction of the cloakroom. "Go get your coats and hats on. Take the younger ones with you."

Leroy, with Belle's help, rounded up the children and herded them out of the sanctuary.

Arthur shifted sideways and took a firmer grip on Neva's hand. "I saw several people pause and speak to you on the way out. Were they . . ."

Neva smiled. "They were all kind. Reverend Savage's sermon seemed to move a few hearts."

He nodded. His fingers twitched. "So . . . do you think you'll . . . stay?"

Despite the numerous prayers she'd sent up, she didn't have an answer. At least, not one that would satisfy him. But she offered it anyway. "I don't know yet. Yes, a few people said they'd be in to shop this week. But I need more than a half-dozen customers in order to keep my business going." That is, if the mercantile truly was hers.

"I see."

Troubled by his disappointment, she sought to reassure him. "I believe today's turnaround is a start. Time will tell if I can make a living here and the children can enjoy a peaceful childhood. Maybe I won't have cause to leave."

He slipped his other hand beneath hers, sandwiching her small hand between his large, warm palms. Such a gentle gesture, one offering comfort and support. "I'll pray for God's mercy to overflow onto the hearts of the people of Buffalo Creek."

His protective hold on her hand and his words of promise were like a kiss from God. "Thank you."

"And, Neva, just as others asked your forgiveness, I must ask it, too."

She frowned, confused. "You've been nothing but kind. Even when I" — she ducked her head, remembering how she'd railed at him on several occasions — "was short-tempered."

"You were only short-tempered when I gave you reason to be. Please listen to me."

She met his gaze. Red streaked his clean-shaven cheeks, bright against the stark white of his crisp celluloid collar. Something glimmered in his rich brown eyes. Something that made her pulse speed and her mouth go dry. She swallowed. "Yes?"

"When I began performing small kindnesses for you, it was for very selfish motives. Warren was gone, and I saw his passing as my opportunity to purchase the building I'd wanted for a very long time. I thought if I buttered you up, I could" — his face pinched into a horrible grimace of regret — "hoodwink you into selling the mercantile to me."

She went hot, then cold. She jerked her hand free of his hold. "Oh." Twice she'd trusted and twice she'd been deceived. She wanted to be angry, but only consternation filled her. How could she have been so foolish?

His hands stretched briefly toward her, then he linked them in his lap. "I was wrong. Wrong to think building the emporium made me a better man than my poor but hardworking coal-mining father. Wrong to think an even bigger business would satisfy me deep inside. Wrong to try to take advantage of you. Wrong . . . so very, very wrong."

He paused and looked toward the front of the church. A soft smile turned up the tips of his mustache. "But I made things right with God again. I don't have a lot of years left with Leroy and Leon, but those I have will be spent showing them how to honor God and unselfishly serve others. Just as you have shown your children and me."

He faced her again. His lips trembled. "Will you please forgive me, Neva?"

She gazed at him for long minutes, torn between the desire to believe him and the desire to disdain his words. So many times Warren had professed his love for her, and she'd believed him, but he betrayed her in the worst way. Arthur by his own admission had betrayed her, too, pretending to care about her when all he wanted was the mercantile. But as she searched his face, she realized the difference between Warren and Arthur. Warren had never admitted wrongdoing, never apologized, never asked for forgiveness. She now witnessed true repentance in Arthur's moist eyes.

"Be ye therefore merciful, as your Father also is merciful." Reverend Savage's admonition, taken straight from God's Word, whispered to her heart. How could she deny forgiveness to Arthur when God, in His mercy, had forgiven her of her wrongs? A thread of peace wove itself through her.

She nodded slowly. "I forgive you."

His entire frame wilted, his breath easing out on a light, airy laugh. "Thank you."

Giggles, guffaws, and rustling noises carried from the cloakroom.

Arthur bobbed his head toward the sounds, a grin creeping up his cheek. "The children are restless."

She stifled a laugh. "Yes. The change in weather is likely affecting them. Adeline's never been so fidgety during a service." Heat filled her face as she remembered how happily Adeline sat on Arthur's knee, how happy he'd seemed to hold her. The little blond-haired girl and the burly dark-haired man made such a sweet pair. And now her thoughts were running amuck.

She rose. "Everyone else has gone. Even Reverend Savage. We'd better go, too."

He rose, but before they stepped into the aisle, he slipped his hands around her upper arms and turned her to face him. "Neva, I

565

know you've only been widowed a short time, but if you decide to stay in Buffalo Creek, and when a decent amount of time has passed, would you find it offensive for me to call on you?"

If only she could agree to his gallant request. She believed God had forged a friendship between them so he could learn the value of relationships over things and so she could learn to trust again. But until she knew whether or not she was in possession of stolen merchandise and an illegally purchased business, she couldn't guarantee she would be in Buffalo Creek long enough to enjoy a courtship. She'd be doing Arthur a great disservice by saying yes.

"Not offensive, Arthur. Flattering." She gently extricated herself from his hold. "But you're right that we'd need to wait for a decent amount of time to pass. The dear people of Buffalo Creek don't need further fuel for gossip where I'm concerned. But I can't say for sure I'll be in Buffalo Creek at the end of an appropriate time period. I . . . can't give you an answer. Not now."

"Understood and accepted." He smiled, a sweet smile that told her he wasn't one bit angry with her. He gave a little bow and moved aside.

She preceded him up the aisle and to the

cloakroom, where their children gathered in two circles — Leroy, Leon, Bud, and Charley on the left side, Belle and the little girls on the right. Adeline looked up, smiled as brightly as a ray of morning sunshine, and raced toward them.

Neva held out her arms in welcome, but Adeline dashed past Neva and reached for Arthur. Without a moment's pause, he scooped her up and settled her on his hip, a proud grin forming beneath his mustache.

The sight of Adeline tweaking the fringe of his mustache and the sounds of her little-girl giggle combined with Arthur's deep, throaty chuckle nearly melted Neva. *Oh, Lord, steel my heart . . .* But she'd offered the prayer too late. She already loved him.

He aimed his grin in her direction. "Mrs. Lafferty left a platter of sliced smoked ham in my icebox. I also have loaves of her homemade bread, cheese, canned peaches, and oatmeal cookies at the house — a veritable feast. Would you and your children like to join my boys and me?"

She shouldn't encourage him. Not with so much uncertainty. But he'd asked if she wanted to come, and she couldn't lie. Not on Sunday. "Thank you, Arthur. Yes."

Jesse

Jesse carefully replaced the telephone receiver on its hook. He stared at the notes he'd scrawled during his conversation with Sheriff Abling. He bowed his head and sent up a brief prayer for Mrs. Shilling. She'd need strength when he delivered Abling's findings.

With the folded notes held tightly in his hand, he walked the short distance to the mercantile. The snow continued to drift from the sky — fine, powdery snow that dusted the road and shifted away from his boots as he walked. He knocked on the front door with no response, so he walked around to the back of the building. But he paused when he reached the edge of the narrow backyard, glancing around. The snow here was undisturbed. Not a single footprint smudged the surface of white. Obviously she and the children hadn't returned from church.

He balled his hands into his pockets and hunkered into his jacket. Where would she have gone? It had to be somewhere in town since they didn't have a vehicle to carry them miles away. Then he snorted, inwardly berating himself. If she wasn't here, there was only one other place she could be — the Randalls'. And if she wasn't there, he wagered Randall would know where to find her.

The older of the Randall boys answered Jesse's knock and invited him in. Laughter and voices carried from elsewhere in the house, and Leroy led him directly to the source. As soon as Jesse entered the dining room, the happy chatter ended, though, pricking him with guilt for destroying their enjoyment. If he hadn't been so eager to get to Beloit and board a train for Nebraska, he would have waited until tomorrow.

Then he looked into Mrs. Shilling's face, and he was glad he'd come. She needed these answers as much as he needed to set things right with his folks.

Randall stood and approached. "Sheriff, is everything all right?"

Jesse kept his gaze fixed on Mrs. Shilling. "Not everything, but . . ." He held up the paper. "I have that information you've been waiting for." Curious gazes skewered him, but he kept his focus on the woman sitting between the pair of blond-pigtailed little girls.

She rose slowly, sending a half smile across the children. "I need to visit with Sheriff Caudel for a few minutes. You all stay here and enjoy your dessert." She moved toward Jesse, but then she paused and touched Randall's arm. "Will you come with me, Arthur?"

The man nodded, slipped his arm around her waist, and escorted her across the floor. "We'll go to the smoking room."

Jesse trailed the pair down a short hallway and into a small room tucked behind the staircase. Mr. Randall pushed a button and light from a six-arm brass chandelier flooded the space, illuminating a spindly two-person sofa and a huge overstuffed chair flanking a cold fireplace. The man closed the door behind him, muffling the sounds of the children's voices and sealing them in with the faint fragrance of cherry tobacco.

He guided Mrs. Shilling to the sofa and then gestured to the chair. "Please sit down, Sheriff."

Jesse would have preferred giving Mrs. Shilling the nicest seat, but he supposed then Randall wouldn't be able to sit beside her. As soon as they sat, Mrs. Shilling sent him a wary yet stalwart look.

"Are our fears about Warren confirmed?"

Randall placed his hand on Mrs. Shilling's shoulder in a protective gesture Jesse appreciated. She'd need his support after he told her everything Sheriff Abling had discovered.

Jesse met the woman's gaze and maintained an even, unruffled tone just as a good sheriff should. "Let me tell you first, we're pretty certain he didn't rob the bank in Grand Rapids."

Randall aimed an astounded look at Jesse and then at Mrs. Shilling. "Good heavens, Neva, you suspected him of bank robbery?"

Her spine lost its starch. She wilted in Randall's direction, but he held her upright with a firm arm around her shoulders. "I was afraid it could be true, yes." She covered her mouth with shaking fingers and whispered, "Praise God I was wrong."

Jesse had already thanked God for sparing her that hardship. "The owner of the trapping company confirmed Warren spent five years on his payroll. That whole time he lived in a tiny shack at the back of the man's property and hardly spent two nickels, always bragging that he was putting his money away so he could own a business someday. Because of the man's testimony, the state marshal isn't looking at Warren for the robbery."

Still leaning into Randall, she nodded. "But what of the other thefts?"

Randall's eyebrows rose. He gawked at the woman in obvious disbelief, but he kept quiet.

Jesse grimaced. "Unfortunately the marshal believes Warren was involved in stealing furniture and some of the other things I showed you. Officials can't be sure if he stole them outright or if he bought them from the thieves — we probably won't ever know for sure since we can't ask him. But we do know he had a whole lot of stolen goods being put to use in his houses. Some of them were sold in the auction in Beloit. The marshal will deal with that issue. As for the things Warren gave you . . ."

Mrs. Shilling sat up. "Take them. If they were stolen, I don't want them anymore."

Jesse ducked his head for a moment. She didn't quite understand, and he wished somebody else could explain it. As a lawman he wanted to make things better for people. But what he had to say would only hurt the woman sitting in front of him.

He leaned forward, resting his elbows on his knees, and looked her in the face. "Mrs. Shilling, the thing of it is, we can't just take those things back and call it even. You see, when they came to you, they were new. Now they aren't. So, with the exception of the jewelry, the businesses aren't interested in getting back their goods. They want what they would have received from the sale of the new item."

"Oh." She gulped. "Of course." She drew a slow breath. Released it. Pressed her palms flat against her throat. "H-how much do they want?"

Jesse wished he could turn away, examine the striped wallpaper or the brick fireplace or the view from the single window. But that would be cowardly, and a good lawman was never cowardly. He held her gaze and answered quietly, "To cover it all? A little over three thousand dollars."

A lesser woman would have swooned. Dissolved into tears. Screeched in fury. But Mrs. Shilling only lowered her hands to her lap, tipped her head back for a moment as if seeking assistance from above, and then settled her gaze on Jesse again. "Selling my belongings won't raise that much. But the mercantile is worth that much and more. If Mr. Bobart can find a buyer, it should bring in enough to cover the debt. Will the officials be patient and wait for it to sell?"

Jesse hadn't discussed that with Abling, but he'd seen debt collectors, with the assistance of law officers, come to a place and take it over, leaving the previous occupants homeless. But he wouldn't share that worry with her. Not on the Lord's day. Instead he'd pray for a fair buyer to step forward fast. "I hope so, ma'am."

She stood, extending her hand toward Jesse. "Thank you for letting me know. Now I can . . . move forward."

Jesse gripped her hand between his. "We both can."

Her brows pinched into a question.

He laughed softly. "Now that I've got your answers, I'm leaving — going home to Severlyn. Or at least I'm gonna try to go home. I've made things right between myself and God, so now it's time to make things right with my folks. You know, the prodigal heading back to say he's sorry and to ask forgiveness."

She smiled. "I'm happy for you."

"Me, too. I might not be able to find my ma and pa. A lot can change in seventeen years." Worry tried to take hold, but he pushed it aside. Hadn't he decided to trust God with this reunion? "But the preacher and I talked it all out, and we figure at least one of my sisters will still be living in the area. So I'll get to tell somebody I'm sorry for running off like I did."

"What if you can't find any of them?"

He'd thought that through already, and he had an answer. "Then I'll have to be satisfied that I tried my best and be thankful that I always have the heavenly Father my folks taught me to trust and serve.

That'll be enough."

"Yes. Yes, He's more than enough." Her words wheezed out on a breathy note of gratitude. She squeezed his hands. "I'll pray you safely there . . . and back?"

"Oh yeah, I'll be back in a couple of weeks or so." He stifled a chuckle. All those years with sisters tugging at him, expecting him to fix this or that, sure prepared him for sheriffing. "Not willing to give up my badge. I like being the sheriff of Buffalo Creek."

Randall's sharp *ahem* intruded — a warning Jesse couldn't miss. He released Mrs. Shilling's hand and took a backward step, grateful rather than resentful for the man's protectiveness. Arthur Randall and the Widow Shilling made a fine couple. "Dodds Schlacter will fill in while I'm gone. I'll make sure he knows what we talked about in case Sheriff Abling or the marshal calls."

He eased toward the door, glancing from Randall's stoic face to Mrs. Shilling's soft expression. "I'll go by the dining room, tell the kids about my trip so they won't look for me at the playground. You have a good week now, both of you."

Chapter 42

Neva

Sheriff Caudel disappeared around the corner. Arthur hurried after him, closed the door, then turned a serious look on Neva. "Let me buy it."

Neva gawked at him. "Wh-what?"

He crossed the room and took hold of her limp hands. "I have the money. I can give it to you tomorrow if need be. Let me buy the mercantile, Neva."

Her legs went weak, and she sank onto the sofa with him still holding her hands. Only an hour ago he'd told her that expanding his business wouldn't satisfy him. Had he changed his mind so quickly?

He slipped onto the sofa next to her, their arms forming a bridge across their knees. "I'll pay whatever you need to cover Warren's debt. Or more, if you have need of extra money for . . . other things." His forehead pinched as if a pain attacked.

"Such as a move to California."

She sucked in her lower lip and held it between her teeth, her thoughts tumbling. Marsh Bobart had said it could be months, years even, before a buyer stepped forward, given the tough economic conditions in the state. If Arthur had ready cash to clear the debt, she should leap at it. He was offering her a fresh slate, a fresh start where no censure or recrimination would touch her. So why didn't she accept?

"I'll give you the money, Neva, but I won't use the mercantile. Not even if you go to California. I'll maintain the building. I'll make sure it isn't broken into by mischief-makers or bums. But I'll keep it for you. For Bud and Charley, in case you want to give it to them someday."

Neva gazed at him in amazement. "You would do that? But why?"

A smile crept up his cheek, lifting the corners of his mustache and brightening his eyes. "Because I know how it feels to want to leave something of worth to your children. And because I want to prove to myself — and to you, too, I suppose — that I have changed. The moneygrubber has learned that souls are more important than sales, yes?"

"Oh, Arthur . . ." His image swam as tears

flooded her eyes. "That's a wonderful offer. May I have some time to pray about accepting it?"

"I wouldn't expect otherwise." He gave her hands a gentle squeeze and then lifted them to his lips. He pressed a lingering kiss on the back of one and then the other, then released her and stood. With his hands on his hips and one eyebrow angled high, he gazed down at her. "Of course, if you'd rather consider the money a loan, I'll let you pay me back over time. Say . . . half of one tenth of one percent of the amount monthly until it's paid in full?"

She laughed, and the tears dissolved, bringing him clearly into view again. She loved the hint of teasing that glinted in his eyes. "Paying an amount so insignificant, I'd be beholden to you for the rest of my life."

The teasing glint became a smoldering flame that warmed her from the inside out. He said quietly, "I wouldn't complain."

The arched clock on the mantel chimed three times, and Neva leaped up. "I had no idea the afternoon was slipping away so quickly. Adeline will be fussing for her nap. I'd better take the children home."

He opened the door and followed her up the hallway to the dining room. Except for the dirty dishes and a spattering of cookie crumbs, the room was empty. Shouts and laughter drifted from outside. Arthur guided her through the parlor, and they stepped out on the porch to witness a raucous, joy-filled scene better than any Norman Rockwell painting.

The snowfall had stopped, leaving behind a half inch of powdery fluff incapable of clumping, but it didn't seem to matter. On one side of the yard, a half-dozen boys — Leon, Leroy, Bud, Charley, and two more from the neighborhood — scooped up handfuls and flung it over the others' heads and then ducked behind trees, their chortles and blasting laughs more beautiful than the sound of sleigh bells. On the other side, Cassie and a neighbor girl lay on the ground, creating snow angels, while Belle led Adeline and two more little girls in stomping a weaving path around them.

Arthur chuckled. "I don't think Adeline is ready for a nap yet."

Neva waved at the three-year-old as the parade passed by. She giggled and waggled her fingers back, her smile bright.

Arthur leaned down and whispered, "You know, Neva, you can't have this kind of fun in California."

She shook her head, a soft laugh trickling

from her throat. "You're right about that."

He caught her chin and tipped her face to him. "Stay?" His breath created a little cloud of condensation that brushed Neva's cheek. His eyes glimmered with hope and something more — what Neva recognized as the greatest of these.

She gave him her own hope-filled look. "All of us?" She held her breath.

Arthur glanced across the yard, where their children continued to romp and play. His tender gaze fell on Adeline, then Cassie, and finally Charley. He smiled at her. "All of you."

Neva's chest expanded with joy. Her breath whooshed out on a note of happy laughter. She nodded. "Yes, Arthur. We'll stay."

A smile of pure hosanna broke across his face. He offered his hand and she took it. Then, together, they descended the steps to join their children.

READERS GUIDE

1. As the story opens, Neva learns her husband lied to her over the course of several years. In what ways does deception affect a person emotionally?

2. Why do you think Warren wanted Charley, Cassie, and Adeline to be sent to Neva? Was his request cruel or compassionate?

3. Jesse was raised by loving adoptive parents, but he never felt at home with them. Why do you think he struggled to believe his parents loved him? How did his early years prepare him for the challenges of law enforcement?

4. Arthur is determined to build a successful business that he can pass on to his sons. Why is this so important to him? How does his determination to succeed

have a negative effect on his family? Is it possible to be both a successful business-person and a solid family leader? If so, how?

5. Bud resented Charley's intrusion into his family. Why was he so opposed to Charley's presence? If you had the chance to advise Bud, what would you tell him?

6. Charley is bullied at school first because of Bud's mistreatment and then because of his status as an illegitimate child. Has your child ever been bullied? How did you handle the situation? How can we teach children that mistreating others is never appropriate?

7. Why did Neva hold herself responsible for Warren's infidelity? Have you ever felt accountable for someone else's choices? How do we know when to assume responsibility and when to release self-recrimination for something another person has done?

8. Jesse resented God for not answering his prayers. Ernie Savage advised him that "God knows what He's doing" when He

denies certain requests. How can we accept "no" answers without resentment?

9. Neva never outright lies about Charley, Cassie, and Adeline, but she withholds portions of the truth. Is withholding the truth the same as lying? Is it ever appropriate to hide part of the truth? Why or why not?

10. Bud and Neva have a discussion about sin during which Neva advises him that God views all sin as equal because all sin displeases God. Do you agree or disagree with Neva's statement? Later in the story Neva chooses mercy because God is merciful. Are we expected to forgive every hurt inflicted on us by others? Why or why not?

ACKNOWLEDGMENTS

My sincerest appreciation goes to the following people:

Mom and Daddy, for modeling faithfulness to each other and for teaching me to trust God.

Don, for standing by me in thick and thin. Marriage isn't always easy, but it's worth it.

Kristian, Kaitlyn, and Kamryn, for teaching me how much a heart can expand.

The Posse, for being the best group of prayer warriors ever.

Shannon, Julee, Carol, and the team at WaterBrook, for your expertise, encouragement, and efforts to make the stories shine.

Finally, and most importantly, God, for being my Strength when I am weak, my All when I am empty, and my Peace in the midst of every storm. May any praise or glory be reflected directly back to You.

The employees of Thorndike Press hope you have enjoyed this Large Print book. All our Thorndike, Wheeler, and Kennebec Large Print titles are designed for easy reading, and all our books are made to last. Other Thorndike Press Large Print books are available at your library, through selected bookstores, or directly from us.

For information about titles, please call:
  (800) 223-1244

or visit our Web site at:
  http://gale.cengage.com/thorndike

To share your comments, please write:
Publisher
Thorndike Press
10 Water St., Suite 310
Waterville, ME 04901